"They are here," he warned her. "I'm going to fight."

She nodded.

"Have you got Timon's pistol?"

She nodded again, groping for it in the waistband of her jeans.

"You do know how to use it?"

"Yes."

"Keep one bullet for the end."

She stared at him.

"Promise you won't hesitate."

"I promise," she whispered....

THE LEOPARD HUNTS IN DARKNESS

THE LEOPARD HUNTS IN DARKNESS

Wilbur Smith

FAWCETT CREST • NEW YORK

THE LEOPARD HUNTS IN DARKNESS was originally published in Great Britain by William Heinemann Ltd.

A Fawcett Crest Book
Published by Ballantine Books
Copyright © 1984 by Wilbur Smith

Library of Congress Catalog Card Number: 84-4078

ISBN 0-449-20725-0

This edition published by arrangement with Doubleday & Company, Inc.

Manufactured in the United States of America

First Ballantine Books Edition: June 1986

For Danielle,
with all my love

THIS SMALL WIND HAD TRAVELLED A THOUSAND MILES AND more, up from the great wastes of the Kalahari Desert which the little yellow Bushmen call the "Big Dry." Now when it reached the escarpment of the Zambezi valley, it broke up into eddies and backlashes among the hills and the broken ground of the rim.

The bull elephant stood just below the crest of one of the hills, much too canny to silhouette himself on the skyline. His bulk was screened by the new growth of leaves on the msasa trees, and he blended with the grey rock of the slope behind him.

He reached up twenty feet and sucked the air into his wide, hair-rimmed nostrils, and then he rolled his trunk down and delicately blew into his own gaping mouth. The two olfactory organs in the overhang of his upper lip flared open like pink rosebuds, and he tasted the air.

He tasted the fine peppery dust of the far deserts, the sweet pollens of a hundred wild plants, the warm bovine stench of the buffalo herd in the valley below, the cool tang of the water pool at which they were drinking and wallowing; these and other scents he identified, and accurately he judged the proximity of the source of each odour.

However, these were not the scents for which he was searching. What he sought was the other acrid offensive smell which overlaid all the others. The smell of native tobacco smoke mingled with the peculiar musk of the flesh-eater, rancid sweat in unwashed wool, of paraffin and carbolic soap and cured leather—the scent of man; it was there, as strong and close as it had been in all the long days since the chase had begun.

Once again the old bull felt the atavistic rage rising in him. Countless generations of his kind had been pursued by that odour. Since a calf, he had learned to hate and fear it, almost all his life he had been driven by it.

Only recently there had been a hiatus in the lifelong pursuit and flight. For eleven years there had been surcease, a time of quiet for the herds along the Zambezi. The bull could not know or understand the reason, that there had been bitter civil war among

1

his tormentors, war that had turned these vast areas along the south bank of the Zambezi into an undefended buffer zone, too dangerous for ivory-hunters or even for the game rangers whose duties included the culling of surplus elephant populations. The herds had prospered in those years, but now the persecution had begun again with all the old implacable ferocity.

With the rage and the terror still upon him, the old bull lifted his trunk again and sucked the dreaded scent into the sinuses of his bony skull. Then he turned and, moving silently, he crossed the rocky ridge, a mere greyish blur for an instant against the clear blue of the African sky. Still carrying the scent, he strode down to where his herd was spread along the back slope.

There were almost three hundred elephants scattered among the trees. Most of the breeding cows had calves with them, some so young that they looked like fat little piglets, small enough to fit under their mothers' bellies. They rolled up their tiny trunks onto their foreheads and craned upwards to the teats that hung on swollen dugs between the dams' front legs.

The older calves cavorted about, romping and playing noisy tag, until in exasperation one of their elders would tear a branch from one of the trees and, wielding it in his trunk, lay about him, scattering the importunate youngsters in squealing, mock consternation.

The cows and young bulls fed with unhurried deliberation, working a trunk deep into a dense, fiercely thorned thicket to pluck a handful of ripe berries and then place them well back in the throat like an old man swallowing aspirin; or using the point of a stained ivory tusk to loosen the bark of a msasa tree and then strip ten feet of it and stuff it happily beyond the drooping triangular lower lip; or raising their entire bulk on their back legs like a begging dog to reach up with outstretched trunk to the tender leaves at the top of a tall tree, or using a broad forehead and four tons of weight to shake another tree until it tossed and whipped and released a shower of ripe pods. Farther down the slope two young bulls had combined their strength to topple a sixty-footer whose top leaves were beyond even their long reach. As it fell with a crackle of tearing fibres, the herd bull crossed the ridge and immediately the happy uproar ceased, to be replaced by quiet that was startling in its contrast.

The calves pressed anxiously to their mothers' flanks, and the

2

grown beasts froze defensively, ears outstretched and only the tips of their trunks questing.

The bull came down to them with swinging stride, carrying his thick yellow ivories high, his alarm evident in the cock of his tattered ears. He was still carrying the man-smell in his head, and when he reached the nearest group of cows, he extended his trunk and blew it over them.

Instantly they spun away, instinctively turning downwind so that the pursuers' scent must always be carried to them. The rest of the herd saw the manoeuvre and fell into their running formation, closing up with the calves and nursing mothers in the centre, the old barren queens surrounding them, the young bulls pointing the herd and the older bulls and their attendant askaris on the flanks; and they went away in the ground-devouring stride that they could maintain for a day and a night and another day without check.

As he fled, the old bull was confused. No pursuit he had ever experienced was as persistent as this. It had lasted for eight days now, and yet the pursuers never closed in to make contact with the herd. They were in the south, giving him their scent, but almost always keeping beyond the limited range of his weak eyesight. There seemed to be many of them, more than he had ever encountered in all his wanderings, a line stretched like a net across the southern routes. Only once had he seen them. On the fifth day, having reached the limits of forbearance, he had turned the herd and tried to break back through their line, and they had been there to head him off, the tiny upright sticklike figures, so deceptively frail and yet so deadly, springing up from the yellow grass, barring his escape to the south, flapping blankets and beating on empty paraffin tins, until his courage failed and the old bull turned back, and led his herds once more down the rugged escarpment towards the great river.

The escarpment was threaded by elephant trails used for ten thousand years, trails that followed the easier gradients and found the passes and ports through the ironstone ramparts. The old bull worked his herd down one of these, and the herd strung out in single file through the narrow places and spread out again beyond.

He kept them going through the night. Though there was no moon, the fat white stars hung close against the earth, and the herd moved almost soundlessly through the dark forests. Once, after midnight, the old bull fell back and waited beside the trail, letting his herd go on. Within the hour he caught again the tainted man-smell on the wind, fainter and very much more distant—but there, always there, and he hurried forward to catch up with his cows.

In the dawn they entered the area which he had not visited in ten years. The narrow strip along the river had been the scene of intense human activity during the long-drawn-out war, and which for that reason he had avoided until now when he was reluctantly driven into it once again.

The herd moved with less urgency. They had left the pursuit far behind, and they slowed so that they could feed as they went. The forest was greener and more lush here on the bottom lands of the valley. The msasa forests had given way to mopani and giant swollen baobabs that flourished in the heat, and the old bull could sense the water ahead and he rumbled thirstily deep in his belly. Yet some instinct warned him of other danger ahead as well as behind. He paused often, swinging his great grey head slowly from side to side, his ears held out like sounding boards, his small weak eyes gleaming as he searched cautiously before moving on again.

Then abruptly he stopped once more. Something at the limit of his vision had caught his attention, something that glistened metallically in the slanted morning sunlight. He flared back with alarm, and behind him his herd backed up, his fear transmitted to them infectiously.

The bull stared at the speck of reflected light, and slowly his alarm receded, for there was no movement except the soft passage of the breeze through the forest, no sound but the whisper of it in the branches and the lulling chattering and hum of unconcerned bird and insect life around him. Still the old bull waited, staring ahead, and as the light altered he noticed there were other identical metal objects in a line across his front, and he shifted his weight from one forefoot to the other, making a little fluttering sound of indecision in his throat.

What had alarmed the old bull was a line of small square galvanized sheet-metal plaques. They were each affixed to the top of an iron dropper that had been hammered into the earth so many years ago that all man-smell had long ago dissipated. On each plaque was painted a laconic warning, which had faded in the brutal sunlight from crimson to pale pink, a stylized skull and

4

crossbones above the words, "DANGER. MINEFIELD."

The minefield had been laid years previously by the security forces of the now-defunct white Rhodesian government, at a *cordon sanitaire* along the Zambezi River, an attempt to prevent the guerrilla forces of ZIPRA and ZAPU from entering the territory from their bases across the river in Zambia. Millions of anti-personnel mines and heavier Claymores made up a continuous field so long and deep that it would never be cleared; the cost of doing so would be prohibitive to the country's new black government already in serious economic difficulties.

While the old bull still hesitated, the air became filled with a clattering roar, the wild sound of hurricane winds. The sound came from behind the herd, from the south again, and the old bull swung away from the minefield to face it.

Low over the forest tops rushed a grotesque dark shape, suspended on a whistling silver disc. Filling the sky with noise, it bore down upon the bunched herd, so low that the down-draught from its spinning rotor churned the branches of the tree-tops into thrashing confusion and flung up a fog of red dust from the earth's dry surface.

Driven by this new menace, the old bull turned and rushed forward beyond the sparse line of metal discs and his terror-stricken herd charged after him into the minefield.

He was fifty metres into the field before the first mine exploded under him. It burst upwards into the thick leather pad of his right hind foot, cutting half of it away like an axe-stroke. Raw red meat hung in tatters from it and white bone gleamed deep in the wound as the bull lurched forward on three legs. The next mine hit him squarely in the right fore, and smashed his foot into bloody mince to the ankle. The bull squealed in agony and panic and fell back on his haunches pinned by his shattered limbs, while all around him his breeding herd ran on into the minefield.

The thump, thump of detonations was intermittent at first, strung out along the edge of the field, but soon they took on a broken staccato beat like that of a maniac drummer. Occasionally four or five mines exploded simultaneously, an intense blurt of sound that struck the hills of the escarpment and shattered into a hundred echoes.

Underlying it all, like the string section of some hellish orchestra, was the whistling clatter of the helicopter rotor as the machine dipped and swung and dropped and rose along the periphery of the minefield, worrying the milling herd like a sheepdog its flock, darting here to head off a bunch of animals that had broken back, racing there to catch a fine young bull who had miraculously run unscathed through the field and reached the clear ground of the river-bank, settling in his path, forcing him to stop and turn, then chasing him back into the minefield until a mine tore his foot away and he went down trumpeting and screaming.

Now the thunder of bursting mines was as continuous as a naval bombardment, and each explosion threw a column of dust high into the still air of the valley, so that the red fog cloaked some of the horror of it. The dust twisted and eddied as high as the tree-tops and transformed the frenzied animals to tormented wraiths lit by the flashes of the bursting mines.

One old cow with all four feet blown away lay upon her side and flogged her head against the hard earth in her attempts to rise. Another dragged herself forward on her belly, back legs trailing, her trunk flung protectively over the tiny calf beside her until a Claymore went off under her chest and burst her ribs outwards like the staves of a barrel, at the same instant tearing away the hindquarters of the calf at her side.

Other calves, separated from their dams, rushed squealing through the dust fog, ears flattened against their heads in terror, until a clap of sound and a flash of brief fire bowled them over in a tangle of shattered limbs.

It went on for a long time, and then the barrage of explosions slowed, became intermittent once more, and gradually ceased. The helicopter settled to earth, beyond the line of warning markers. The beat of its engine died, and the spinning rotor stilled. The only sound now was the screaming of the maimed and dying beasts lying in the churned earth below the dust-coated trees. The hatch of the helicopter was open and a man dropped lightly from it to the earth.

He was dressed in a faded denim jacket from which the sleeves had been carefully removed, and tight-fitting tie-dyed jeans. In the days of the Rhodesian war, denim had been the unofficial uniform of the guerrilla fighters. On his feet he wore fancy, tooled, western boots, and pushed up on the top of his head gold-rimmed Polaroid aviator's sunglasses. These and the row of ball-point pens clipped into the breast-pocket of his jacket were badges of rank among the veteran guerrillas. Under his right arm he carried an AK 47 assault rifle, as he walked to the edge of the minefield and

6

stood for a full five minutes impassively watching the carnage lying out there in the forest. Then the black man walked back towards the helicopter.

Behind the canopy, the pilot's face was turned attentively towards him, with his earphones still in place over his elaborate Afro-style hairdo, but the officer ignored him and concentrated instead on the machine's fuselage.

All the insignia and identification numbers had been carefully covered with masking tape, and oversprayed with black enamel from a hand-held aerosol can. In one place the tape had come loose, exposing a corner of the identification lettering. The officer pressed it back into place with the heel of his hand, inspected his work briefly but critically, and turned away to the shade of the nearest mopani.

He propped his AK 47 against the trunk, spread a handkerchief upon the earth to protect his jeans and sat down with his back to the rough bark. He lit a cigarette with a gold Dunhill lighter and inhaled deeply, before letting the smoke trickle gently over his lips.

Then he smiled for the first time, a cool reflective smile, as he considered how many men, and how much time and ammunition it would take to kill three hundred elephant in the conventional manner.

"The comrade commissar has lost none of his cunning from the old days of the bush war—who else would have thought of this?" He shook his head in admiration and respect.

When he had finished the cigarette, he crushed the butt to powder between his thumb and forefinger, a little habit from those far-off days, and closed his eyes.

The terrible chorus of groans and screams from the minefield could not keep him from sleep. Later, it was the sound of men's voices that woke him. He stood up quickly, instantly alert, and glanced at the sun. Past noon.

He went to the helicopter and woke the pilot.

"They are coming."

He took the loud hailer from its clamp on the bulkhead and waited in the open hatchway until the first of them came out from among the trees, and he looked at them with amused contempt.

"Baboons!" he murmured, with the contempt of the educated man for the peasant, of one African for another of a different tribe.

They came in a long file, following the elephant trail. Two or

7

three hundred, dressed in animal-skin cloaks and ragged western cast-offs, the men leading and the women bringing up the rear. Many of the women were bare-breasted, and some of them were young with a saucy tilt to the head and a lyrical swing of round buttocks under brief animal-tail kilts. As the denim-clad officer watched them, his contempt changed to appreciation: perhaps he would find time for one of them later, he thought, and put his hand into the pocket of his jeans at the thought. They lined the edge of the minefield, jabbering and screeching with delight, some of them capering and giggling and pointing out to each other the masses of stricken beasts.

The officer let them vent their glee. They had earned this pause for self-congratulation. They had been eight days on the trail, almost without rest, acting in shifts as beaters to drive the elephant herd down the escarpment. While he waited for them to quieten, he considered again the personal magnetism and force of character that could weld this mob of primitive illiterate peasants into a cohesive and effective whole. One man had engineered the entire operation.

"He is a man!" the officer nodded, then roused himself from the indulgence of hero-worship and lifted the trumpet of the loud hailer to his lips.

"Be quiet! Silence!" He stilled them, and began to allocate the work that must be done.

He picked the butcher gangs from those who were armed with axe and panga. He set the women to building the smoking racks and plaiting baskets of mopani bark, others he ordered to gather wood for the fires. Then he turned his attention back to the butchers.

None of the tribesmen had ever ridden in an aircraft and the officer had to use the pointed toe of his western boot to persuade the first of them to climb into the hatch for the short hop over the mine-sown strip to the nearest carcass.

Leaning out of the hatchway, the officer peered down at the old bull. He appraised the thick curved ivory, and then saw that the beast had bled to death during the waiting hours, and he signalled the pilot lower.

He placed his lips close to the eldest tribesman's ear.

"Let not your feet touch the earth, on your life!" he shouted, and the man nodded jerkily. "The tusks first, then the meat."

The man nodded again.

8

The officer slapped his shoulder and the elder jumped down onto the bull's belly that was already swelling with fermenting gases. He balanced agilely upon it. The rest of his gang, clutching their axes, followed him down.

At the officer's hand signal the helicopter rose and darted like a dragonfly to the next animal that showed good ivory from the lip. This one was still alive, and heaved itself into a sitting position, reaching up with bloody dust-smeared trunk to try and pluck the hovering helicopter from the air.

Braced in the hatch, the officer sighted down the AK 47 and fired a single shot into the back of the neck where it joined the skull, and the cow collapsed and lay as still as the body of her calf beside her. The officer nodded at the leader of the next gang of butchers.

Balanced on the gigantic grey heads, careful not to let a foot touch the earth, the axemen chipped the tusks loose from their castles of white bone. It was delicate work, for a careless stroke could drastically diminish the value of the ivory. They had seen the officer in tie-dyed jeans, with a short, well-timed swing of the rifle-butt, break the jaw of a man who merely queried an order. What would he do with one who ruined a tusk? They worked with care. As the tusks were freed, the helicopter winched them up and then carried the gang to the next carcass.

By nightfall most of the elephant had died of their massive wounds or had been shot to death, but the screams of those who had not yet received the *coup de grâce* mingled with the hubbub of the gathering jackal and hyena packs to make the night hideous. The axemen worked on by the light of grass torches, and by the first light of dawn all the ivory had been gathered in.

Now the axemen could turn their attention to butchering and dismembering the carcasses. The rising heat worked more swiftly than they could. The stench of putrefying flesh mingled with the gases from ruptured entrails and drove the skulking scavengers to fresh paroxysms of gluttonous anticipation. The helicopter carried each haunch or shoulder as it was hacked free to the safe ground beyond the minefield. The women cut the meat into strips and festooned it on the smoking racks above the smouldering fires of green wood.

While he supervised the work, the officer was calculating the spoils. It was a pity they could not save the hides, for each was worth a thousand dollars, but they were too bulky and could not

9

be sufficiently preserved. Putrefaction would render them worthless. On the other hand, mild putrefaction would give the meat more zest on the African palate—in the same way that an Englishman enjoys his game high.

Five hundred tons of wet meat would lose half its weight in the drying process, but the copper mines of neighbouring Zambia, with tens of thousands of labourers to feed, were eager markets for proteins. Two dollars a pound for the crudely smoked meat was the price that had already been agreed. That was a million U.S. dollars—and then of course there was the ivory.

The ivory had been ferried by the helicopter half a mile beyond the sprawling camp to a secluded place in the hills. There it had been laid out in rows, and a selected gang set to work removing the fat white cone-shaped nerve mass from the hollow end of each tusk and cleansing the ivory of any blood and muck that might betray it to the sensitive nose of an oriental customs officer.

There were four hundred tusks. Some of those taken from immature animals weighed only a few pounds, but the old bull's tusks would go well over eighty pounds apiece. A good average was twenty pounds over the lot. The going price in Hong Kong was a hundred dollars a pound, or a total of eight hundred thousand dollars. The profit on the day's work would be over one million dollars, in a land where the average annual income of each adult male was less than six hundred dollars.

Of course, there had been the other small costs of the operation. One of the axemen had overbalanced and tumbled from his perch on an elephant carcass. He had landed flat on his buttocks, directly on top of an anti-personnel mine.

"Son of a demented baboon." The officer was still irritated by the man's stupidity. It had held work up for almost an hour while the body was retrieved and prepared for burial.

Another man had lost a foot from an overzealous axe-stroke, and a dozen others had lesser cuts from swinging pangas. One other man had died during the night with an AK 47 bullet through the belly when he objected to what the officer was doing to his junior wife in the bushes beyond the smoking racks—but when the profit was considered, the costs were small indeed. The comrade commissar would be pleased, and with good reason.

It was the morning of the third day before the team working on the ivory had completed their task to the officer's satisfaction.

Then they were sent down the valley to assist at the smoking racks, leaving the ivory camp deserted. There must be no eyes to discover the identity of the important visitor who would come now to inspect the spoils.

He arrived in the helicopter. The officer was standing to attention in the clearing beside the long rows of gleaming ivory. The down-draught of the rotor tore at his jacket, and fluttered the legs of his jeans, but he maintained his rigid stance.

The machine settled to earth and a commanding figure stepped down, a handsome man, straight and strong, with very white square teeth against the dark mahogany of his face, crisp kinky African hair cropped closely to the finely shaped skull. He wore an expensive pearl-grey suit of Italian cut over a white shirt and dark blue tie. His black shoes were handmade of soft calf.

He held out his hand towards the officer. Immediately the younger man abandoned his respectful pose and ran to him, like a child to its father.

"Comrade Commissar!"

"No! No!" he chided the officer gently, still smiling. "Not Comrade Commissar any longer, but Comrade Minister now. No longer leader of a bunch of unwashed bush fighters, but Minister of State of a sovereign government." The minister permitted himself a smile as he surveyed the rows of fresh tusks. "And the most successful ivory-poacher of all time—is that not true?"

•   •   •

Craig Mellow winced as the cab hit another pothole in the surface of Fifth Avenue just outside the entrance to Bergdorf Goodman. Like most New York cabs, its suspension would have better suited a Sherman tank.

"I've had a softer ride through the Mbabwe depression in a Land-Rover," Craig thought, and had a sudden nostalgic twinge as he remembered that rutted, tortuous track through the bad lands below the Chobe River, that wide green tributary of the great Zambezi.

That was all so far away and long ago, and he pushed the memory aside and returned to brooding over the sense of slight that he felt at having to ride in a yellow cab to a luncheon meeting with his publisher, and having to pick up the tab for the ride himself. There had been a time when they would have sent a

11

chauffeur-driven limousine for him, and the destination would have been the Four Seasons or La Grenouille, not some pasta joint in the Village. Publishers made these subtle little protests when a writer had not delivered a manuscript for three years and spent more time romancing his stockbroker and living it up at Studio 54 than at his typewriter.

"Well, I guess I've got it coming." Craig made a face, reached for a cigarette, and then arrested the movement as he remembered that he had given them up. Instead he pushed the thick lock of hair off his forehead and watched the faces of the crowds on the sidewalk. There had been a time when he found the bustle exciting and stimulating after the silences of the African bush; even the sleazy façades and neon frontings onto the littered streets had been different and intriguing. Now he felt suffocated and claustrophobic, and he longed for a glimpse of open sky, rather than that narrow ribbon that showed between the high tops of the buildings.

The cab braked sharply, interrupting his thoughts, and the driver muttered "Sixteenth Street" without looking round.

Craig pushed a ten-dollar bill through the slot in the armoured Perspex screen that protected the driver from his passengers. "Keep it," he said, and stepped out onto the sidewalk. He saw the restaurant immediately, all cutesy ethnic awnings and straw-covered Chianti bottles in the window.

When Craig crossed the sidewalk he moved easily, without trace of a limp, so that nobody watching him would have guessed at his disability. Despite his misgivings, it was cool and clean inside the restaurant and the smell of food was appetizing.

Ashe Levy stood up from a booth at the back of the room and beckoned to him.

"Craig, baby!" He put one arm around Craig's shoulders and patted his cheek paternally. "You're looking good, you old hound dog, you!"

Ashe cultivated his own eclectic style. His hair was brush-cut and he wore gold-rimmed spectacles. His shirt was striped with a contrasting white collar, platinum cuff-links and tie-pin, and brown brogues with a pattern of little holes punched in the toe-caps. His jacket was cashmere with narrow lapels. His eyes were very pale, and always focused just a little to one side of Craig's own. Craig knew that he smoked only the very best Tijuana gold.

"Nice place, Ashe. How did you find it?"

"A change from the boring old 'Seasons.'" Ashe grinned slyly, pleased that the gesture of disapproval had been noted. "Craig, I want you to meet a very talented lady."

She had been sitting well back in the gloom at the back of the booth, but now she leaned forward and held out her hand. The spotlamp caught the hand, and so it was the first impression that Craig had of her.

The hand was narrow with artistic fingers, the nails were scrubbed clean, although they were clipped short and unpainted, the skin was tanned to gold with prominent aristocratic veins showing bluish beneath it. The bones were fine, but there were callouses at the base of those long straight fingers—a hand that was accustomed to hard work.

Craig took the hand and felt the strength of it, the softness of the dry cool skin on the back and the rough places on the palm, and he looked into her face.

She had thick eyebrows that stretched in an unbroken curve from the outer corner of one eye to the other. Her eyes, even in the poor light, were green with honey-coloured specks surrounding the pupil. Their gaze was direct and candid.

"Sally-Anne Jay," Ashe said. "This is Craig Mellow."

The nose was straight but slightly too large, and the mouth too wide to be beautiful. Her thick dark hair was pulled back severely from the broad forehead, her face was as honey-tanned as her hands and there was a fine peppering of freckles across her cheeks.

"I read your book," she said. Her voice was level and clear, her accent mid-Atlantic, but only when he heard its timbre did he realize how young she was. "I thought it deserved everything that happened to it."

"Compliment or slap?" He tried to make it sound light and unconcerned, but he found himself hoping fervently that she was not one of those who attempted to demonstrate their own exalted literary standards by denigrating a popular writer's work to his face.

"Very good things happened to it," she pointed out, and Craig felt absurdly pleased, even though that seemed to be the end of that topic as far as she was concerned. To show his pleasure he held her hand a little longer than was necessary, and she took it back from him and replaced it firmly in her lap.

So she wasn't a scalp-hunter, and she wasn't going to gush.

Anyway, he told himself, he was bored with literary groupies trying to storm his bed, and gushers were as bad as knockers—almost.

"Let's see if we can get Ashe to buy us a drink," he suggested, and slipped into the booth facing her across the table.

Ashe made his usual fuss over the wine list, but they ended up with a ten-dollar Frascati after all.

"Nice smooth fruit." Ashe rolled it on his tongue.

"It's cold and wet," Craig said, and Ashe smiled again as they both remembered the '70 Corton-Charlemagne they had drunk the last time.

"We are expecting another guest later," Ashe told the waiter. "We'll order then." And turning to Craig, "I wanted an opportunity for Sally-Anne to show you her stuff."

"Show me," Craig invited, immediately defensive once again. The woods were full of them, the ones who wanted to ride on his strike—with unpublished manuscripts for him to endorse, investment advisers who would look after all those lovely royalties for him, others who would allow him to write their life stories and generously split the profits with him or sell him insurance or a South Sea Island paradise, commission him to write movie scripts for a small advance and an even smaller slice of any profits, all kinds gathering like hyenas to the lion's kill.

Sally-Anne lifted a portfolio from the floor beside her and placed it on the table in front of Craig. While Ashe adjusted the spotlight, she untied the ribbons that secured the folder and sat back.

Craig opened the cover and went very still. He felt the goose bumps rise along his forearms, and the hair at the nape of his neck prickle—this was his reaction to greatness, to anything perfectly beautiful. There was a Gauguin in the Metropolitan Museum on Central Park—a Polynesian madonna carrying the Christ child on her shoulder. She had made his hair prickle. There were passages of T. S. Eliot's poetry and of Lawrence Durrell's prose that made his hair prickle every time he read them.

The opening bar of Beethoven's Fifth Symphony, those incredible *jeté* leaps of Rudolf Nureyev, and the way Nicklaus and Borg struck the ball on their good days—those things had made him prickle, and now this girl was doing it to him also.

It was a photograph. The finish was eggshell grain so every detail was crisp, the colours clear and perfectly true.

14

The photograph was of an elephant, an old bull. He faced the camera in the characteristic attitude of alarm, ears spread like dark flags. Somehow he portrayed the whole vastness and timelessness of a continent, and yet he was at bay, and one sensed that all his great strength was unavailing, that he was confused by things that were beyond his experience and the trace memories of his ancestors, that he was about to be overwhelmed by change—like Africa itself.

Shown, too, in the photograph was the land, the rich red earth riven by wind, baked by sun, ruined by drought. Craig could almost taste the dust on his tongue. Then, over it all, the limitless sky, containing the promise of succour, the silver cumulus nimbus piled like a snow-clad mountain range, bruised with purple and royal blue, pierced by a single beam of light from a hidden sun that fell on the old bull like a benediction.

She had captured the meaning and the mystery of his native land in the five hundredth of a second that it took the lens shutter to open and close again, while he had laboured for long agonizing months and not come anywhere near it, and, secretly recognizing his failure, was afraid to try again. He took a sip of the insipid wine that had been offered to him as a rebuke for this crisis of confidence, and now the wine had a quinine after-taste that he had not noticed before.

"Where are you from?" he asked the girl, without looking at her.

"Denver, Colorado," she said. "But my father has been with the Embassy in London for years. I did most of my schooling in England." That accounted for the accent. "I went to Africa when I was eighteen, and fell in love with it," she said, completing her life story simply.

It took a physical effort for Craig to touch the photograph and gently turn it face down. Beneath it was another of a young woman seated on a black lava rock beside a desert water-hole. She wore the distinctive leather bunny-ears headdress of the Ovahimba tribe. Her child stood beside her and nursed from her naked breast. The woman's skin was polished with fat and ochre. Her eyes were those from a fresco in a Pharaoh's tomb, and she was beautiful.

"Denver, Colorado, forsooth!" Craig thought and was surprised at his own bitterness, at the depths of his sudden resentment. How dare a damned foreign girl-child encapsulate so unerringly the complex spirit of a people in this portrait of a young woman. He

15

had lived all his life with them and yet never seen an African so clearly as at this moment in an Italian restaurant in Greenwich Village.

He turned the photograph with a suppressed violence. Beneath it was a view into the trumpet-shaped throat of the magnificent maroon and gold bloom of *Kigelia africana*, Craig's favourite wild flower. In the lustrous depths of the flower nestled a tiny beetle like a precious emerald, shiny iridescent green. It was a perfect arrangement of shape and colour, and he found he hated her for it.

There were many others. One of a grinning lout of a militiaman with an AK 47 rifle on his shoulder and necklace of cured human ears around his neck, a caricature of savagery and arrogance; another of a wrinkled witch-doctor hung with horns and beads and skulls and all the grisly accoutrements of his trade, his patient stretched out on the bare, dusty earth before him in the process of being crudely cupped, her blood making shiny serpents across her skin. The patient was a woman in her prime with patterns of tattoos on her breasts and cheeks and forehead. Her teeth were filed to points like those of a shark, a relic of the days of cannibalism, and her eyes, like those of a suffering animal, seemed filled with all the stoicism and patience of Africa.

Then there was another contrasting photograph of African children in a schoolroom of poles and rude thatch. They shared a single book between three of them, but all their hands were raised eagerly to the young black teacher's questions and all their faces lit by the burning desire for knowledge—it was all there, a complete record of hope and despair, of abject poverty and great riches, of savagery and tenderness, of unrelenting elements and bursting fruitfulness, of pain and gentle humour. Craig could not bring himself to look at the photographer again and he turned the stiff glossy sheets slowly, savouring each image and delaying the moment when he must face her.

Craig stopped suddenly, struck by a particularly poignant composition, an orchard of bleached bones. She had used black and white to heighten the dramatic effect, and the bones shone in the brilliant African sunlight, acres of bones, great femur and tibia bleached like driftwood, huge rib cages like the frames of stranded ocean clippers, and skulls the size of beer barrels with darkened caves for eye sockets. Craig thought of the legendary elephants'

16

graveyard, the old hunters' myth of the secret place where the elephants go to die.

"Poachers," she said. "Two hundred and eighty-six carcasses," and now Craig looked up at her at last, startled by the number.

"At one time?" he asked, and she nodded.

"They drove them into one of the old minefields."

Involuntarily, Craig shuddered and looked down at the photograph again. Under the table-top his right hand ran down his thigh until he felt the neat strap that held his leg, and he experienced a choking empathy for the fate of those great pachyderms. He remembered his own minefield, and felt again the slamming impact of the explosion into his foot, as though he had been hit by the full swing of a sledgehammer.

"I'm sorry," she said softly. "I know about your leg."

"She does her homework," Ashe said.

"Shut up," Craig thought furiously. "Why don't you both shut up." He hated anyone to mention the leg. If she had truly done her homework, she would have known that—but it was not only mention of the leg, it was the elephants also. Once Craig had worked as a ranger in the game department. He knew them, had come to love them, and the evidence of this slaughter sickened and appalled him. It increased his resentment of the girl; she had inflicted this upon him and he wanted to revenge himself, a childish urge to retaliate. But before he could do it, the late guest arrived, diverting them into a round of Ashe's introductions.

"Craig, I want you to meet a special sort of guy." All of Ashe's introductions came with a built-in commercial. "This is Henry Pickering. Henry is a senior vice-president of the World Bank—listen and you'll hear all those billions of dollars clashing around in his head. Henry, this is Craig Mellow, our boy genius. Not even excluding Karen Blixen, Craig is just one of the most important writers ever to come out of Africa, that's all he is!"

Henry nodded. "I read the book." He was very tall and thin and prematurely bald. He wore a grey banker's suit and stark white shirt, with a little individual touch of colour in his necktie and twinkly blue eyes. "For once you are probably not exaggerating, Ashe."

He kissed Sally-Anne's cheek platonically, sat down, tasted the wine that Ashe poured for him and pushed the glass back an inch. Craig found himself admiring his style.

"What do you think?" Henry Pickering asked Craig, glancing down at the open portfolio of photographs.

"He loves them, Henry," Ashe Levy cut in swiftly. "He's ape over them—I wish you could have seen his face when he got his first look—loves them, man, loves them!"

"Good," Henry said softly, watching Craig's face. "Have you explained the concept?"

Ashe Levy shook his head. "I wanted to serve it up hot. I wanted to hit him with it."

He turned to Craig.

"A book," he said. "It's about a book. The title of the book is 'Craig Mellow's Africa.' What happens is you write about the Africa of your ancestors, about what it was and what it has become. You go back and you do an in-depth assessment. You speak to the people—"

"Excuse me," Henry interrupted him, "I understand that you speak one of the two major languages—Sindebele, isn't it—of Zimbabwe?"

"Fluently," Ashe answered for Craig. "Like one of them."

Henry nodded. "Good. Is it true that you have many friends—some highly placed in government?"

Ashe fielded the question again. "Some of his old buddies are cabinet ministers in the Zimbabwe government. You can't go much higher."

Craig dropped his eyes to the photograph of the elephant grave-yard. "Zimbabwe." He was not yet comfortable with the new name that the black victors had chosen. He still thought of it as Rhodesia. That was the country his ancestors had hacked out of the wilderness with pick and axe and Maxim machine-gun. Their land, once his land—by any name still his home.

"It's going to be top quality, Craig, no expense spared. You can go where you want to, speak to anybody, the World Bank will see to that, and pay for it." Ashe Levy was running on enthusiastically, and Craig looked up at Henry Pickering.

"The World Bank—publishing?" Craig asked sardonically, and when Ashe would have replied again, Henry Pickering laid a restraining hand on his forearm.

"I'll take the ball awhile, Ashe," he said. He had sensed Craig's mood; his tone was gentle and placatory. "The main part of our business is loans to underdeveloped countries. We have almost a billion invested in Zimbabwe. We want to protect our investment.

18

Think of it as a prospectus; we want the world to know about the little African state that we would like to turn into a showpiece, an example of how a black government can succeed. We think your book could help do that for us."

"And these?" Craig touched the pile of photographs.

"We want the book to have visual as well as intellectual impact. We think Sally-Anne can provide that."

Craig was quiet for many seconds while he felt the terror slither around deep inside him, like some loathsome reptile. The terror of failure. Then he thought about having to compete with these photographs, of having to provide a text that would not be swamped by the awesome view through this girl's lens. He had a reputation at stake, and she had nothing to lose. The odds were all with her. She would be not an ally but an adversary, and his resentment came back in full force, so strong that it was a kind of hatred.

She was leaning towards him across the table, the spotlight catching her long eyelashes and framing those green-flecked eyes. Her mouth was quivering with eagerness, and a tiny bubble of saliva like a seed pearl sparkled on her lower lip. Even in his anger and fear, Craig wondered what it would be like to kiss that mouth.

"Craig," she said, "I can do better than those if I have the chance. I can go all the way, if you give me the chance. Please!"

"You like elephants?" Craig asked her. "I'll tell you an elephant story. The big old bull elephant had a flea that lived in his left ear. One day the elephant crossed a rickety bridge, and when he got to the other side, the flea said in his ear, 'Hoo boy! We sure rocked that bridge!'"

Sally-Anne's lips closed slowly and then paled. Her eyelids fluttered, the dark lashes beating like butterflies' wings, and as the tears began to sparkle behind them she leaned back out of the light.

There was a silence, and in it Craig felt a rush of remorse. He felt sickened by his own cruelty and pettiness. He had expected her to be tough and resilient, to come back with a barbed retort. He had not expected the tears. He wanted to comfort her, to tell her that he didn't mean it the way it sounded. He wanted to explain his own fear and insecurity, but she was rising and picking up the folio of photographs.

"Parts of your book were so understanding, so compassionate, I wanted so badly to work with you," she said softly. "I guess it was dumb to expect you to be like your book." She looked at Ashe. "I'm sorry, Ashe, I'm just not hungry any more."

Ashe Levy stood quickly. "We'll share a cab," he said. Then softly to Craig, "Well done, hero, call me when you've got the new typescript finished," and he hurried after Sally-Anne. As she went through the door the sunlight back-lit her and Craig saw the shape of her legs through her skirt. They were long and lovely, and then she was gone.

Henry Pickering was fiddling with his glass, studying the wine thoughtfully.

"It's pasteurized Roman goat urine," Craig said. He found his voice was uneven. He signalled the wine waiter and ordered a Meursault.

"That's better," Henry understated it. "Well, perhaps the book wasn't such a great idea after all, was it?" He glanced at his wristwatch. "We'd better order."

They talked of other things—the Mexican loan default, Reagan's mid-term assessment, the gold price—Henry preferred silver for a quick appreciation and thought diamonds would soon be looking good again. "I'd buy De Beers to hold," he advised.

A svelte young blonde from one of the other tables came across while they were taking coffee.

"You're Craig Mellow," she accused him. "I saw you on TV. I loved your book. Please, please, sign this for me."

While he signed her menu, she leaned over him and pressed one hard hot little breast against his shoulder.

"I work at the cosmetics counter in Saks Fifth Ave," she breathed. "You can find me there any time." The odour of expensive, pilfered perfumes lingered after she had left.

"Do you always turn them away?" Henry asked a little wistfully.

Craig laughed. "Man is only flesh and blood."

Henry insisted on paying the tab. "I have a limo," he offered. "I could drop you."

"I'll walk off the pasta," Craig said.

"Do you know, Craig, I think you'll go back to Africa. I saw the way you looked at those photographs. Like a hungry man."

"It's possible."

"The book. Our interest in it. There was more to it than Ashe understood. You know the top blacks there. That interests me. The ideas you expressed in the book fit into our thinking. If you

20

do decide to go back, call me before you do. You and I could do each other a favour."

Henry climbed into the back seat of the black Cadillac, and then with the door still open he said, "I thought her pictures were rather good, actually." He closed the door and nodded to the chauffeur.

• • •

Bawu was moored between two new commercially built yachts, a forty-five-foot Camper and Nicholson and a Hatteras convertible, and she stood the comparison well enough, although she was almost five years old. Craig had put in every screw with his own hands. He paused at the gates of the marina to look at her, but somehow today he did not derive as much pleasure as usual from her lines.

"Been a couple of calls for you, Craig," the girl behind the reception desk in the marina office called out to him and he went in. "You can use this phone."

He checked the slips she handed him, one from his broker marked "urgent," another from the literary editor of a midwestern daily. There hadn't been too many of those recently.

He phoned the broker first. They had sold the Mocatta gold certificates that he had bought for three hundred and twenty dollars an ounce at five hundred and two dollars. He instructed them to put the money on call deposit.

Then he dialled the second number. While he waited to be connected, the girl behind the desk moved around more than was really necessary, bending over the lowest drawers of the filing cabinet to give Craig a good look at what she had in her white Bermudas and pink halter-top.

When Craig connected with the literary editor, she wanted to know when they were publishing his new book.

"What book?" Craig thought bitterly, but he answered, "We haven't got a firm date yet—but it's in the pipeline. Do you want to do an interview in the meantime?"

"Thanks, but we will wait until publication, Mr. Mellow."

"Long wait, my darling," Craig thought, and when he hung up the girl looked up brightly.

"The party is on *Firewater* tonight." There was a party on one of the yachts every single night of the year. "Are you coming across?"

She had a flat tight belly between the shorts and top. Without the glasses, she might be quite pretty—and what the hell, he had just made a quarter of a million dollars on the gold certificates and a fool of himself at the lunch table.

"I'm having a private party on *Bawu*," he said, "for two." She had been a good patient girl and her time had come.

Her face lit up so he saw he had been right. She really was quite pretty. "I finish in here at five."

"I know," he said. "Come straight down."

Wipe one out and make another happy, he thought. It should even out, but of course it didn't.

• • •

Craig lay on his back under a single sheet in the wide bunk with both hands behind his head and listened to the small sounds in the night, the creak of the rudder in its restrainer, the tap of a halyard against the mast and the slap of wavelets under the hull. Across the basin the party on *Firewater* was still in full swing, there was a faint splash and a distant burst of drunken laughter as they threw somebody overboard, and beside him the girl made regular little wet fluttering sounds through her lips as she slept.

She had been eager and very practised, but nevertheless Craig felt unrequited and restless. He wanted to go up on deck, but that would have disturbed the girl and he knew she would still be eager and he could not be bothered further. So he lay and let the images from Sally-Anne's portfolio run through his head like a magic-lantern show, and they triggered others that had long lain dormant but now came back to him fresh and vivid, accompanied by the smells and tastes and sounds of Africa, so that instead of the revels of drunken yachties, he heard again the beat of native drums along the Chobe River in the night; instead of the sour waters of the East River he smelled tropical raindrops on baked earth, and he began to ache with the bitter-sweet melancholy of nostalgia and he did not sleep again that night.

The girl insisted on making breakfast for him. She did so with not nearly the same expertise as she had made love, and after she had gone ashore it took him nearly an hour to clean up the galley. Then he went up to the saloon.

22

He drew the curtain across the porthole above his navigation and writing desk, so as not to be distracted by the activities of the marina, and settled down to work. He reread the last batch of ten pages, and realized he would be lucky if he could salvage two of them. He set to it grimly and the characters balked and said trite asinine things. After an hour he reached up for his thesaurus from the shelf beside his desk to find an alternative word.

"Good Lord, even I know that people don't say 'pusillanimous' in real conversation," he muttered as he brought down the volume, and then paused as a slim sheath of folded writing-paper fluttered out from between the pages.

Secretly welcoming the excuse to break off the struggle, he unfolded it, and with a little jolt discovered it was a letter from a girl called Janine—a girl who had shared with him the agonies of their war wounds, who had travelled with him the long slow road to recovery, had been at his side when he walked again for the first time after losing the leg, had spelled him at the helm when they sailed *Bawu* through her first Atlantic gale. A girl whom he had loved and almost married, and whose face he now had the greatest difficulty recalling.

Janine had written the letter from her home in Yorkshire, three days before she married the veterinary surgeon who was a junior partner in her father's practice. He reread the letter slowly, all ten pages of it, and realized why he had hidden it away from himself. Janine was only bitter in patches, but some of the other things she wrote cut deeply.

". . . You had been a failure so often and for so long that your sudden success clean bowled you . . ."

He checked at that. What else had he ever done besides the book—that one single book? And she had given him the answer.

". . . You were so innocent and gentle, Craig, so lovable in a gawky boyish way. I wanted to live with that, but after we left Africa it dried up slowly, you started becoming hard and cynical . . ."

". . . Do you remember the very first day we met, or almost the very first, I said to you, 'You are a spoilt little boy, and you just give up on everything worthwhile'? Well, it's true, Craig. You gave up on our relationship. I don't just mean the other little dolly-birds, the literary scalp-hunters with no elastic in their drawers, I mean you gave up on the caring. Let me give you a little advice for free, don't give up on the only thing that you've ever done well, don't give up on the writing, Craig. That would be truly sinful . . ."

He remembered how haughtily he had scoffed at that notion when he had first read it. He didn't scoff now—he was too afraid. It was happening to him, just as she had predicted.

"I truly came to love you, Craig, not all at once, but little by little. You had to work very hard to destroy that. I don't love you any more, Craig, I doubt I'll ever love another man, not even the one I'll marry on Saturday—but I like you, and I always will. I wish you well, but beware of your most implacable enemy—yourself."

Craig refolded the letter, and he wanted a drink. He went down to the galley and poured a Bacardi—a large one, easy on the lime. While he drank it he reread the letter and this time a single phrase struck him.

"After we left Africa it dried up slowly . . . the understanding, the genius."

"Yes," he whispered. "It dried up. It all dried up."

Suddenly his nostalgia became the unbearable ache of homesickness. He had lost his way, the fountain in him *had* dried up, and he wanted to go back to the source.

He tore the letter to tiny pieces and dropped them into the scummy waters of the basin, left the empty glass on the coaming of the hatch and crossed the gang-plank to the jetty.

He didn't want to have to talk to the girl, so he used the pay phone at the gate of the marina.

It was easier than he expected. The switchboard operator put him through to Henry Pickering's secretary.

"I'm not sure that Mr. Pickering is available. Who is calling, please?"

"Craig Mellow." Pickering came on almost immediately.

"There is an old Matabele saying, 'The man who drinks Zambezi waters must always return to drink again,'" Craig told him.

"So you're thirsty," Pickering said. "I guessed that."

"You said to call you."

"Come and see me."

"Today?" Craig asked.

"Hey, man, you're hot to trot! Hold on, let me check my calendar—what about six o'clock this evening? That's the soonest I can work it in."

Henry's office was on the twenty-sixth floor and the tall windows faced up the deep sheer crevasses of the avenues to the expansive green swathe of Central Park in the distance.

Henry poured Craig a whisky and soda and brought it to him at the window. They stood looking down into the guts of the city and drinking in silence, while the big red ball of the sun threw weird shadows through the purpling dusk.

"I think it's time to stop being cute, Henry," Craig said at last. "Tell me what you really want from me."

"Perhaps you're right," Henry agreed. "The book was a little bit of a cover-up. Not really fair—although, speaking personally, I'd like to have seen your words with her pictures—"

Craig made an impatient little gesture, and Henry went on.

"I am vice-president in charge of the Africa division."

Craig nodded. "I saw your title on the door."

"Despite what a lot of our critics say, we aren't a charitable institution, we are one of the bulwarks of capitalism. Africa is a continent of economically fragile states. With the obvious exceptions of South Africa and the oil producers farther north, they are mostly subsistence agricultural societies, with no industrial backbone and very few mineral resources."

Craig nodded again.

"Some of those who have recently achieved their independence from the old colonial system are still benefitting from the infrastructure built up by the white settlers, while most of the others—Zambia and Tanzania and Maputo, for instance—have had long enough to let it run down into a chaos of lethargy and ideological fantasy. They are going to be hard to save." Henry shook his head mournfully and looked even more like an undertaker stork. "But with others, like Zimbabwe, Kenya and Malawi, we have got a fighting chance. The system is still working; as yet the farms haven't been totally decimated and handed over to hordes of peasant squatters, the railroads work, there are some foreign exchange earnings from copper and chrome and tourism. We can keep them going, with a little luck."

"Why bother?" Craig asked. "I mean, you said you are not in the charity game, so why bother?"

"Because if we don't feed them, then sooner or later we are going to have to fight them, it's as simple as that. If they begin to starve, guess into whose big red paws they are going to fall."

"Yes. You're making sense." Craig sipped his whisky.

"Returning to earth for a moment," Henry went on, "the countries on our shortlist have one exploitable asset, nothing tangible like gold, but many times more valuable. They are attractive to tourists from the west. If we are ever going to see any interest on the billions that we have got tied up in them, then we are going to have to make good and sure that they stay attractive."

"How do you do that?"

"Let's take Kenya as an example," Henry suggested. "Sure, it's got sunshine and beaches, but then so have Greece and Sardinia, and they are a hell of a lot closer to Paris and Berlin. What the Mediterranean hasn't got is African wildlife, and that's what the tourists will fly those extra hours to see, and that's the collateral on our loan. Tourist dollars are keeping us in business."

Craig frowned. "Okay, but I don't see how I come in."

"Wait for it, we'll get there in time," Henry told him. "Let me lay it out a little first. It's like this—unfortunately, the very first thing that the newly independent black African sees when he looks around after the white man flies out is ivory and rhinoceros horn and meat on the hoof. One rhinoceros or bull elephant represents more wealth than he could earn in ten years of honest labour. For fifty years a white-run game department has protected all these marvellous riches, but now the whites have run to Australia or Johannesburg, an Arab sheikh will pay twenty-five thousand dollars for a dagger with a genuine rhinoceros-horn handle and the victorious guerrilla fighter has an AK 47 rifle in his hands. It's all very logical."

Craig nodded. "Yes, I've seen it."

"We had the same thing in Kenya. Poaching was big business and it was run from the top. I mean the very top. It took us fifteen years and the death of a president to break it up. Now Kenya has the strictest game laws in Africa—and, more important, they are being enforced. We had to use all our influence. We even had to threaten to pull the plug, but now our investment is protected." Henry looked smug for a moment, then his melancholia overwhelmed him again. "Now we have to travel exactly the same road again in Zimbabwe. You saw those photographs of the kill in the minefield. It's being organized again, and once again we suspect it's somebody in a very high place. We have to stop it."

"I'm still waiting to hear how it affects me."

"I need an agent in the field. Somebody with experience—perhaps even somebody who once worked in the game and wildlife

26

department, somebody who speaks the local language, who has a legitimate excuse for moving around and asking questions—perhaps an author researching a new book, who has contacts high up in government. Of course, if my agent has an international reputation, it would open even more doors, and if he were a dedicated proponent of the capitalist system and truly believed in what we are doing, he would be totally effective."

"James Bond, me?"

"Field investigator for the World Bank. The pay is forty thousand dollars a year, plus expenses and a lot of job satisfaction, and if there isn't a book in it at the end, I'll stand you to lunch at La Grenouille with the wine of your choice."

"Like I said at the beginning, Henry, isn't it time to stop being cute and level with me completely?"

It was the first time Craig had heard Henry laugh, and it was infectious, a warm, throaty chuckle.

"Your perception confirms the wisdom of my choice. All right, Craig, there is a little more to it. I didn't want to make it too complicated—not until you had got your feet wet first. Let me freshen your drink."

He went to the cocktail cabinet in the shape of an antique globe of the world, and while he clinked ice on glass he went on.

"It is vitally important for us to have a complete picture of what's going on below the surface in all of the countries in which we have an involvement. In other words, a functioning intelligence system. Our set-up in Zimbabwe isn't nearly as effective as I'd like it to be. We have lost a key man lately—motor car accident—or that's what it looked like. Before he went, he gave us a hint—he had picked up the rumours of a *coup d'état* backed by the Ruskies."

Craig sighed. "We Africans don't really put much store in the ballot box any more. The only things that count are tribal loyalties and a strong arm. *Coup d'état* makes better sense than votes."

"Are you on the team?" Henry wanted to know.

"I take it that 'expenses' include first-class air tickets?" Craig demanded wickedly.

"Every man has his price," Henry darted back, "is that yours?"

Craig shook his head. "I don't come that cheap, but I'd hate like hell to have a Soviet stooge running the land where my leg is buried. I'll take the job."

"Thought you might." Henry offered his hand. It was cool and

27

startlingly powerful. "I'll send a messenger down to your yacht with a file and a survival kit. Read the file while the messenger waits and send it back. Keep the kit."

Henry Pickering's survival kit contained an assortment of press cards, a membership of the TWA Ambassadors Club, an unlimited World Bank Visa credit card, and an ornate metal and enamel star in a leather case embossed "Field Assessor—World Bank."

Craig weighed it in his palm. "You could beat a man-eating lion to death with it," he muttered. "I don't know what else it will be good for."

The file was a great deal more rewarding. When he finished reading it, he realized that the alteration of name from Rhodesia to Zimbabwe was probably one of the least drastic changes that had swept over the land of his birth since he had left it just a few short years before.

•   •   •

Craig nursed the hired Volkswagen over the undulating golden grass-clad hills, using an educated foot on the throttle. The Matabele girl at the Avis desk in the Bulawayo airport had cautioned him.

"The tank is full, sir, but I don't know when you will get another tankful. There is very little gasoline in Matabeleland."

In the town itself he had seen the vehicles parked in long lines at the filling stations, and the proprietor of the motel had briefed Craig as he signed the register and picked up the keys to one of the bungalows.

"The Maputo rebels keep hitting the pipeline from the east coast. The hell of it is that just across the border the South Africans have got it all and they are happy to deal, but our bright laddies don't want politically tainted gas, so the whole country grinds to a halt. A plague on political dreams—to exist we have to deal with all kinds of people and it's about time they accepted that."

So now Craig drove with care, and the gentle pace suited him. It gave him time to examine the familiar countryside, and to assess the changes that the years had wrought.

He turned off the main macadamized road fifteen miles out of town, and took the yellow dirt road to the north. Within a mile he reached the boundary, and saw immediately that the gate hung at a drunken angle and was wide open—the first time he had ever seen it that way. He parked and tried to close it behind him, but the frame was buckled and the hinges had rusted. He abandoned the effort and left the road to examine the sign that lay in the grass.

The sign had been pulled down, the retaining bolts ripped clear out. It lay face up, and, though sun-faded, was still legible:

KING'S LYNN AFRIKANDER STUD
HOME OF "BALLANTYNE'S ILLUSTRIOUS IV"
GRAND CHAMPION OF CHAMPIONS
PROPRIETOR: JONATHAN BALLANTYNE

Craig had a vivid mental image of the huge red beast with its humped back and swinging dewlap waddling under its own weight of beef around the show-ring with the blue rosette of the champion on its cheek, and Jonathan "Bawu" Ballantyne, Craig's maternal grandfather, leading it proudly by the brass ring through its shiny wet nostrils.

Craig walked back to the VW and drove on through grassland that had once been thick and gold and sweet, but through which the bare dusty earth now showed like the balding scalp of a middle-aged man. He was distressed by the condition of the grazing. Never, not even in the four-year drought of the fifties, had King's Lynn grass been allowed to deteriorate like this, and Craig could find no reason for it until he stopped again beside a clump of camel-thorn trees that threw their shade over the road.

When he switched off the engine, he heard the bleating among the camel thorns and now he was truly shocked.

"Goats!" he spoke aloud. "They are running goats on King's Lynn." Bawu Ballantyne's ghost must be without rest or peace. Goats on his beloved grassland. Craig went to look for them. There were two hundred or more in one herd. Some of the agile multicoloured animals had climbed high into the trees and were eating bark and seedpods, while others were cropping the grass down to the roots so that it would die and the soil would sour. Craig had seen the devastation that these animals had created in the tribal trustlands.

There were two naked Matabele boys with the herd. They were delighted when Craig spoke to them in their own language. They stuffed the cheap candy that he had brought with him for just such a meeting into their cheeks, and chattered without inhibition.

Yes, there were thirty families living on King's Lynn now, and each family had its herd—the finest goats in Matabeleland, they boasted through sticky lips, and under the trees a horned old billy mounted a young nanny with a vigorous humping of his neck. "See!" cried the herdboys, "they breed with a will. Soon we will have more goats than any of the other families."

"What happened to the white farmers that lived here?" Craig asked.

"Gone!" they told him proudly. "Our warriors drove them back to where they came from and now the land belongs to the children of the revolution."

They were six years old, but still they had the revolutionary cant word-perfect.

Each of the children had a slingshot made from old rubber tubing hanging from his neck, and around his naked waist a string of birds that he had killed with the slingshot: larks and warblers and jewelled sunbirds. Craig knew that for their noon meal they would cook them whole on a bed of coals, simply letting the feathers sizzle off and devouring the tiny blackened carcasses with relish. Old Bawu Ballantyne would have strapped any herdboy that he caught with a slingshot.

The herdboys followed Craig back to the road, begged another piece of candy from him and waved him away like an old dear friend. Despite the goats and songbirds, Craig felt again the overwhelming affection for these people. They were, after all, his people and it was good to be home again.

He stopped again on the crest of the hills and looked down on the homestead of King's Lynn. The lawns had died from lack of attention, and the goats had been in the flower-beds. Even at this distance, Craig could see that the main house was deserted. Windows were broken, leaving unsightly gaps like missing teeth, and most of the asbestos sheets had been stolen from the roof and the roof-timbers were forlorn and skeletal against the sky. The roofing sheets had been used to build ramshackle squatters' shacks down near the old cattle-pens.

Craig drove down and parked beside the dip tank. The tank was dry, and half-filled with dirt and rubbish. He went past it to the squatters' encampment. There were half a dozen families living here. Craig scattered the yapping cur dogs that rushed out at him with a few well-aimed stones, then greeted the old man who sat at one of the fires.

"I see you, old father." Again there was delight at his command of the language. He sat at the fire for an hour, chatting with the old Matabele, the words coming more and more readily to his tongue and his ear turning to the rhythm and nuances of Sindebele. He learned more than he had in the four days since he had been back in Matabeleland.

"They told us that after the revolution every man would have a fine motor car, and five hundred head of the best white man's cattle." The old man spat into the fire. "The only ones with motor cars are the government ministers. They told us we would always have full bellies, but food costs five times what it did before Smith and the white men ran away. Everything costs five times more— sugar and salt and soap—everything."

During the white regime a ferocious foreign exchange control system and a rigid internal price control structure had isolated the country from the worst effects of inflation, but now they were experiencing all the joys of re-entering the international community, and the local currency had already been devalued twenty per cent.

"We cannot afford cattle," the old man explained, "so we run goats. Goats!" He spat again into the fire and watched his phlegm sizzle. "Goats! Like dirt-eating Shona." His tribal hatred boiled like his spittle.

Craig left him muttering and frowning over the smoky fire and walked up to the house. As he climbed the steps to the wide front veranda, he had a weird premonition that his grandfather would suddenly come out to meet him with some tart remark. In his mind's eye he saw again the old man, dapper and straight, with thick silver hair, skin like tanned leather and impossibly green Ballantyne eyes, standing before him.

"Home again, Craig, dragging your tail behind you!"

However, the veranda was littered with rubble and bird-droppings from the wild pigeons that roosted undisturbed in the rafters.

He picked his way along the veranda to the double doors that led into the old library. There had been two huge elephant tusks framing this doorway, the bull which Craig's great-great-grandfather had shot back in the 1860s. Those tusks were family heirlooms, and had always guarded the entrance to King's Lynn. Old grandpa Bawu had touched them each time he passed, so that there had been a polished spot on the yellow ivory. Now there were

31

only the holes in the masonry from which the bolts holding the ivory had been torn. The only family relics he had inherited and still owned were the collection of leatherbound family journals, the laboriously hand-written records of his ancestors from the arrival of his great-great-grandfather in Africa over a hundred years before. The tusks would complement the old books. He would search for them, he promised himself. Surely such rare treasures must be traceable.

He went into the derelict house. The shelving and built-in cupboards and floor-boards had been stripped out by the squatters in the valley for firewood, the window-panes used as targets by small black boys with slingshots. The books, the portrait photographs from the walls, the carpets and heavy furniture of Rhodesian teak were all gone. The homestead was a shell, but a sturdy shell. With an open palm Craig slapped the walls that great-great-grandfather Zouga Ballantyne had built of hand-hewn stone and mortar that had had almost a hundred years to cure to adamantine hardness. His palm made a solid ringing tone. It would take only a little imagination and a great deal of money to transform the shell into a magnificent home once again.

Craig left the house and climbed the kopje behind it to the walled family cemetery that lay under the msasa trees beneath the rocky crest. There was grass growing up between the headstones. The cemetery had been neglected but not vandalized, as had many of the other monuments left from the colonial era.

Craig sat on the edge of his grandfather's grave and said, "Hello, Bawu. I'm back," and started as he almost heard the old man's voice, full of mock scorn speaking in his mind.

"Yes, every time you burn your arse you come running back here. What happened this time?"

"I dried up, Bawu," he answered the accusation aloud and then was silent. He sat for a long time and very slowly he felt the tumult within him begin to subside.

"The place is in a hell of a mess, Bawu," he spoke again, and the little blue-headed lizard on the old man's headstone scuttled away at the sound of his voice. "The tusks are gone from the veranda, and they are running goats on your best grass."

Again he was silent, but now he was beginning to calculate and scheme. He sat for nearly an hour, and then stood up.

"Bawu, how would you like it if I could move the goats off

32

your pasture?" he asked, and walked back down the hill to where he had left the Volkswagen.

•   •   •

It was a little before five o'clock when he drove back into town. The estate agency and auctioneering floor opposite the Standard Bank was still open for business. The sign had even been repainted in scarlet, and as soon as Craig entered, he recognized the burly red-faced auctioneer in khaki shorts and short-sleeved, open-necked shirt.

"So you didn't take the gap, like the rest of us did, Jock," Craig said, greeting Jock Daniels.

"Taking the gap" was the derogatory expression for emigrating. Out of 250,000 white Rhodesians, almost 150,000 had taken the gap since the beginning of hostilities, and most of those had left since the war had been lost and the black government of Robert Mugabe had taken control.

Jock stared at him. "Craig!" he exploded. "Craig Mellow!" He took Craig's hand in a horny brown paw. "No, I stayed, but sometimes it gets hellish lonely. But you've done well, by God you have. They say in the papers that you have made a million out of that book. People here could hardly believe it. Old Craig Mellow, they said, fancy Craig Mellow of all people."

"Is that what they said?" Craig's smile stiffened, and he took his hand back.

"Can't say I liked the book myself." Jock shook his head. "You made all the blacks look like bloody heroes—but that's what they like overseas, isn't it? Black is beautiful—that's what sells books, hey?"

"Some of my reviewers called me a racist," Craig murmured. "You can't keep all the people happy all of the time."

Jock wasn't listening. "Another thing, Craig, why did you have to make out that Mr. Rhodes was a queer?"

Cecil Rhodes, the father of the white settlers, had been dead for eighty years, but the old-timers still called him Mr. Rhodes.

"I gave the reasons in the book." Craig tried to placate him.

"He was a great man, Craig, but nowadays it's the fashion for you young people to tear down greatness—like mongrels snapping at the heels of a lion." Craig could see that Jock was warming to his subject, and he had to divert him.

33

"How about a drink, Jock?" he asked, and Jock paused. His rosy cheeks and swollen purple nose were not solely the products of the African sun.

"Now, you're making sense." Jock licked his lips. "It's been a long thirsty day. Just let me lock up the shop."

"If I fetched a bottle, we could drink it here and talk privately."

The last of Jock's antagonism evaporated. "Damn good idea. The bottle store has a few bottles of Dimple Haig left—and get a bucket of ice while you are about it."

They sat in Jock's tiny cubicle of an office and drank the good whisky out of cheap thick tumblers. Jock's mood mellowed perceptively.

"I didn't leave, Craig, because there was nowhere to go. England? I haven't been back there since the war. Trade unions and bloody weather—no thanks. South Africa? They are going to go the same way that we did—at least we've got it over and done with." He poured again from the pinch bottle. "If you do go, they let you take two hundred dollars with you. Two hundred dollars to start again when you are sixty-five years old—no bloody thanks."

"So what's life like, Jock?"

"You know what they call an optimist here?" Jock asked. "It's somebody who believes that things can't get any worse." He bellowed with laughter and slapped his bare hairy thigh. "No. I'm kidding. It's not too bad. As long as you don't expect the old standards, if you keep your mouth shut and stay away from politics, you can still live a good life—probably as good as anywhere in the world."

"The big farmers and ranchers—how are they doing?"

"They are the elite. The government has come to its senses. They've dropped all that crap about nationalizing the land. They've come to face the fact that if they are going to feed the black masses, then they need the white farmers. They are becoming quite proud of them: when they get a state visitor—a communist Chinese or a Libyan minister—they give him a tour of white farms to show him how good things are looking."

"What about the price of land?"

"At the end of the war, when the blacks first took over and were shouting about taking the farms and handing them over to the masses, you couldn't give the land away." Jock gargled with his whisky. "Take your family company for instance, Rholands

34

Ranching Company—that includes all three spreads: King's Lynn, Queen's Lynn and that big piece of country up in the north bordering the Chizarira Game Reserve—your uncle Douglas sold the whole damned shooting match for quarter of a million dollars. Before the war he could have asked ten million."

"Quarter of a million." Craig was shocked. "He gave it away!"

"That included all the stock—prize Afrikander bulls and breeding cows, the lot," Jock related with relish. "You see, he had to get out. He had been a member of Smith's cabinet from the beginning and he knew that he was a marked man once the black government took over. He sold out to a Swiss-German consortium, and they paid him in Zürich. Old Dougie took his family and went to Aussie. Of course, he already had a few million outside the country, so he could buy himself a nice little cattle station up in Queensland. It's us poor buggers with everything we have tied up here that had to stay."

"Have another drink," Craig offered, and then steered Jock back to Rholands Ranching. "What did the consortium do with Rholands?"

"Cunning bloody Krauts!" Jock was slurring a little by now. "They took all the stock, bribed somebody in government to give them an export permit, and shipped them over the border to South Africa. I hear they sold for almost a million and a half down there. Remember, they were the very top breeding-stock, champions of champions. So they cleared over a million, and then they repatriated their profit in gold shares and made another couple of million."

"They stripped the ranches and now they have abandoned them?" Craig asked, and Jock nodded weightily.

"They're trying to sell the company, of course. I've got it on my books—but it would take a pile of capital to restock the ranches and get them going again. Nobody is interested. Who wants to bring money into a country which is tottering on the brink? Answer me that!"

"What is the asking price for the company?" Craig inquired airily, and Jock Daniels sobered miraculously, and fastened Craig with a beady auctioneer's eye.

"You wouldn't be interested?" And his eye became beadier. "Did you really make a million dollars out of that book?"

"What are they asking?" Craig repeated.

"Two million. That's why I haven't found a buyer. Lots of the local boys would love to get their paws on that grazing—but two million. Who the hell has that kind of money in this country—"

"Supposing they could be paid in Zürich, would that make a difference to the price?" Craig asked.

"Do a Shona's armpits stink!"

"How much difference?"

"They might take a million—in Zürich."

"A quarter of a million?"

"No ways, never—not in ten thousand years," Jock shook his head emphatically.

"Telephone them. Tell them the ranches are overrun with squatters, and it would cause a political hoo-ha to try and move them now. Tell them they are running goats on the grazing, and in a year's time it will be a desert. Point out they will be getting their original investment out intact. Tell them the government has threatened to seize all land owned by absentee landlords. They could lose the lot."

"All that is true," Jock grumped. "But a quarter of a million! You are wasting my time."

"Phone them."

"Who pays for the call?"

"I do. You can't lose, Jock."

Jock sighed with resignation. "All right, I'll call."

"When?"

"Friday today—no point in calling until Monday."

"All right, in the meantime can you get me a few cans of gas?" Craig asked.

"What do you want gas for?"

"I'm going up to the Chizarira. I haven't been up there for ten years. If I'm going to buy it, I'd like to look at it again."

"I wouldn't do that, Craig. That's bandit country."

"The polite term is political dissidents."

"They are Matabele bandits," Jock said heavily, "and they'll either shoot your arse full of more holes than you can use, or they will kidnap you for ransom—or both."

"You get me some gas and I'll take the chance. I'll be back early next week to hear what your pals in Zürich have to say about the offer."

•   •   •

It was marvellous country, still wild and untouched—no fences, no cultivated lands, no buildings—protected from the influx of cattle and peasant farmers by the tsetse-fly belt which ran up from the Zambezi valley into the forests along the escarpment.

On the one side it was bounded by the Chizarira Game Reserve and on the other by the Mzolo Forest Reserve, both of which areas were vast reservoirs of wildlife. During the depression of the 1930s, old Bawu had chosen the country with care and paid six-pence an acre for it. One hundred thousand acres for two thousand five hundred pounds. "Of course, it will never be cattle country," he told Craig once, as they camped under the wild fig trees beside a deep green pool of the Chizarira River and watched the sand-grouse come slanting down on quick wings across the setting sun to land on the sugar-white sandbank beneath the far shore. "The grazing is sour, and the tsetse will kill anything you try to rear here—but for that reason it will always be an unspoiled piece of old Africa."

The old man had used it as a shooting lodge and a retreat. He had never strung barbed-wire or built even a shack on the ground, preferring to sleep on the bare earth under the spreading branches of the wild fig.

Very selectively Bawu had hunted here—elephant and lion and rhinoceros and buffalo—only the dangerous game, but he had jealously protected them from other rifles. Even his own sons and grandsons had been denied hunting rights.

"It's my own little private paradise," he told Craig, "and I'm selfish enough to keep it like that."

Craig doubted that the track through to the pools had been used since he and the old man had last been here together ten years before. It was totally overgrown, elephant had pushed mopani trees down like primitive road-blocks, and heavy rains had washed it out.

"Eat your heart out, Mr. Avis," said Craig, and put the sturdy little Volkswagen to it.

However, the front-wheel-drive vehicle was light enough and nippy enough to negotiate even the most unfriendly dry river-beds, although Craig had to corduroy the bottoms with branches to give it purchase in the fine sand. He lost the track half a dozen times, and only found it after laboriously casting ahead on foot.

He hit one ant-bear hole and had to jack up the front end to get out, and half the time he was finding ways round the elephant road-blocks. In the end he had to leave the Volkswagen and cover the last few miles on foot. He reached the pools in the final glimmering of daylight.

He curled up in the single blanket that he had filched from the motel, and slept through without dreaming or stirring, to wake in the ruddy magic of an African dawn. He ate cold baked beans out of the can and brewed coffee, then he left his pack and blanket under the wild figs and went down along the bank of the river.

On foot he could cover only a tiny portion of the wide wedge of wild country that spread over a hundred thousand acres, but the Chizarira River was the heart and artery of it. What he found here would allow him to judge what changes there had been since his last visit.

Almost immediately he realized that there were still plenty of the more common varieties of wildlife in the forest: the big, spooky, spiral-horned kudu went bounding away, flicking their fluffy white tails, and graceful little impala drifted like roseate smoke among the trees. Then he found signs of the rarer animals. First, the fresh pug-marks of a leopard in the clay at the water's edge where the cat had drunk during the night, and then, the elongated teardrop-shaped spoor and grapelike droppings of the magnificent sable antelope.

For his lunch he ate slices of dried sausage which he cut with his clasp-knife and sucked lumps of tart white cream of tartar from the pods of the baobab tree. When he moved on he came to an extensive stand of dense wild ebony bush, and followed one of the narrow twisting game trails into it. He had gone only a hundred paces when he came on a small clearing in the midst of the thicket of interwoven branches, and he experienced a surge of elation.

The clearing stank like a cattle-pen, but even ranker and gamier. He recognized it as an animal midden, a dunghill to which an animal returns habitually to defecate. From the character of the faeces, composed of digested twigs and bark, and from the fact that these had been churned and scattered, Craig knew immediately that it was a midden of the black rhinoceros, one of Africa's rarest and most endangered species.

Unlike its cousin the white rhinoceros, who is a grazer on grassland and a lethargic and placid animal, the black rhinoceros is a browser on the lower branches of the thick bush which it frequents. By nature it is a cantankerous, inquisitive, stupid and nervously irritable animal. It will charge anything that annoys it, including men, horses, trucks and even locomotives.

Before the war, one notorious beast had lived on the escarpment of the Zambezi valley where both road and railway began the plunge down towards the Victoria Falls. It had piled up a score of eighteen trucks and buses, catching them on a steep section of road where they were reduced to a walking pace, and taking them head-on so that its horn crunched through the radiator in a burst of steam. Then, perfectly satisfied, it would trot back into the thick bush with squeals of triumph.

Puffed up with success, it finally overreached itself when it took on the Victoria Falls express, lumbering down the tracks like a medieval knight in the jousting lists. The locomotive was doing twenty miles per hour and the rhinoceros weighed two tons and was making about the same speed in the opposite direction, so the meeting was monumental. The express came to a grinding halt with wheels spinning helplessly, but the rhinoceros had reached the end of his career as a wrecker of radiators.

The latest deposit of dung on the midden had been within the preceding twelve hours, Craig estimated with delight, and the spoor indicated a family group of bull and cow with calf at heel. Smiling, Craig recalled the old Matabele myth which accounted for the rhino's habit of scattering its dung, and for its fear of the porcupine—the only animal in all the bush from which it would fly in snorting panic.

The Matabele related that once upon a time a rhino had borrowed a quill from the porcupine to sew up a tear caused by a thorn in his thick hide. The rhino promised to return the quill at their next meeting. After repairing the rent with bark twine, the rhino placed the quill between his lips while he admired his handiwork, and inadvertently swallowed it. Now he is still searching for the quill, and assiduously avoiding the porcupine's recriminations.

The total world-wide population of the black rhinoceros probably did not exceed a few thousand and to have them still surviving here delighted Craig and made his tentative plans for the area much more viable.

Still grinning, he followed the freshest tracks away from the midden, hoping for a sighting, and had gone only half a mile when, just beyond the wall of impenetrable bush that flanked the narrow trail, there was a sudden hissing, churring outcry of alarm calls and a cloud of brown oxpeckers rose above the scrub. These

39

noisy birds lived in a symbiotic relationship with the larger African game animals, feeding exclusively on the ticks and bloodsucking flies that infested them, and in return acting as wary sentinels to warn of danger.

Swiftly following the alarm, there was a deafening chuffing and snorting like that of a steam engine: with a crash, the bush parted and Craig got his longed-for sighting as an enormous grey beast burst out onto the path not thirty paces ahead of him and, still uttering blasts of affronted indignation, peered short-sightedly over its long polished double horns for something to charge.

Aware that the beast's weak eyes could not distinguish a motionless man at more than fifteen paces, and that the light breeze was blowing directly into his face, Craig stood frozen but poised to hurl himself to one side if the charge came his way. The rhino was switching his bulk from side to side with startling agility, the din of his ire unabated, and in Craig's fevered imagination his horn seemed to grow longer and sharper every second. Stealthily he reached for the clasp-knife in his pocket. The beast sensed the movement and trotted a half dozen paces closer, so that Craig was on the periphery of his effective vision and in serious danger at last.

Using a short underhanded flick, he tossed the knife high over the beast's head into the ebony thicket behind it, and there was a loud clatter as it struck a branch.

Instantly the rhino spun around and launched its huge body in a full and furious charge at the sound. The bush opened as though before a centurion tank, and the clattering, crashing charge dwindled swiftly as the rhinoceros kept going up the side of the hill and over the crest in search of an adversary. Craig sat down heavily in the middle of the path and doubled over with breathless laughter in which were echoes of mild hysteria.

Within the next few hours, Craig had found three of the pans of stinking, stagnant water that these strange beasts prefer to the clean running water of the river, and he had decided where to site the hides from which his tourists could view them at close range. Of course, he would furnish salt-licks beside the water-holes to make them even more attractive to the beasts, and bring them in to be photographed and gawked at.

Sitting on a log, beside one of the water-holes, he reviewed the factors that favoured his plans. It was under an hour's flight from here to the Victoria Falls, one of the seven natural wonders of the world, that already attracted thousands of tourists each month. It would be only a short detour to his camp here, so that added little to the tourists' original airfare. He had an animal that very few other reserves or camps could offer, together with most of the other varieties of game, concentrated in a relatively small area. He had undeveloped reservations on both boundaries to ensure a permanent source of interesting animal life.

What he had in mind was a champagne and caviar type of camp, on the lines of those private estates bordering the Kruger National Park in South Africa. He would put up small camps, sufficiently isolated from each other so as to give the occupants the illusion of having the wilderness to themselves. He would provide charismatic and knowledgeable guides to take his tourists by Land-Rover and on foot close to rare and potentially dangerous animals and make an adventure of it, and luxurious surroundings when they returned to camp in the evening—air-conditioning and fine food and wines, pretty young hostesses to pamper them, wildlife movies and lectures by experts to instruct and entertain them. And he would charge them outrageously for it all, aiming at the very upper level of the tourist trade.

It was after sunset when Craig limped back into his rudimentary camp under the wild figs, his face and arms reddened by the sun, tsetse-fly bites itching and swollen on the back of his neck, and the stump of his leg tender and aching from the unaccustomed exertions. He was too tired to eat. He unstrapped his leg, drank a single whisky from the plastic mug, rolled into his blanket and was almost immediately asleep. He woke for a few minutes during the night, and while he urinated he listened with sleepy pleasure to the distant roaring of a pride of hunting lions, and then returned to his blanket.

He was awakened by the whistling cries of the green pigeons feasting on the wild figs above his head, and found he was ravenously hungry and happy as he could not remember being for years.

After he had eaten, he hopped down to the water's edge, carrying a rolled copy of the *Farmers' Weekly* magazine, the African farmers' bible. Then, seated in the shallows with the coarse-sugar sand pleasantly rough under his naked backside and the cool green waters soothing his still aching stump, he studied the prices of stock offered for sale in the magazine and did mental arithmetic. His ambitious plans were swiftly moderated when he realized what it would cost to restock King's Lynn and Queen's Lynn with thoroughbred bloodstock. The consortium had sold the original stud for a million and a half, and prices had gone up since then.

He would have to begin with good bulls, and grade cows— slowly build up his blood-lines. Still, that would cost plenty, the ranches would have to be re-equipped, and the development of the tourist camp here on the Chizarira River was going to cost another bundle. Then he would have to move the squatter families and their goats off his grazing—the only way to do that was to offer them financial compensation. Old grandfather Bawu had always told him, "Work out what you think it will cost, then double it. That way you will come close."

Craig threw the magazine up onto the bank and lay back with only his head above water while he did his sums.

On the credit side, he had lived frugally aboard the yacht, unlike a lot of other suddenly successful authors. The book had been on the best-seller lists on both sides of the Atlantic for almost a year, main choice of three major book clubs, Reader's Digest Condensed books, the TV series, paperback contracts, translations into a number of foreign languages, including Hindi—even though, at the end, the taxman had got in among his earnings.

Then again he had been lucky with what was left to him after these depredations. He had speculated in gold and silver, had made three good coups on the stock exchange, and finally had transferred most of his winnings into Swiss francs at the right time. Added to that, he could sell the yacht. A month earlier he had been offered a hundred and fifty thousand dollars for *Bawu*, but he would hate to part with it. Apart from that, he could try hitting Ashe Levy for a substantial advance on the undelivered novel and hock his soul in the process.

He reached the bottom line of his calculations and decided that if he pulled out all the stops, and used up all his lines of credit, he might be able to raise a million and a half, which would leave him short by at least as much again.

"Henry Pickering, my very favourite banker, are you ever in for a surprise!" He grinned recklessly as he thought of how he was planning to break the first and cardinal rule of the prudent investor and put it all in one basket. "Dear Henry, you have been selected by our computer to be the lucky lender of one and a half big Ms to a one-legged dried-up sometime scribbler." That was the best he could come up with at the moment, and it wasn't really worth worrying seriously until he had an answer from Jock Daniels' consortium. He switched to more mundane considerations.

He ducked down and sucked a mouthful of the sweet clear water. The Chizarira was a lesser tributary of the great Zambezi, so he was drinking Zambezi waters again, as he had told Henry Pickering he must. "Chizarira" was a hell of a mouthful for a tourist to pronounce, let alone remember. He needed a name under which to sell his little African paradise.

"Zambezi Waters," he said aloud. "I'll call it Zambezi Waters," and then almost choked as very close to where he lay a voice said clearly, "He must be a mad man."

It was a deep melodious Matabele voice. "First, he comes here alone and unarmed, and then he sits among the crocodiles and talks to the trees!"

Craig rolled over swiftly onto his belly, and stared at the three men who had come silently out of the forest and now stood on the bank, ten paces away, watching him with closed, expressionless faces.

They were, all three of them, dressed in faded denims—the uniform of the bush fighters—and the weapons they carried with casual familiarity were the ubiquitous AK 47s with the distinctive curved black magazine and laminated woodwork.

Denim, AK 47s and Matabele—no doubt in Craig's mind who these were. Regular Zimbabwean troops now wore jungle fatigues or battle-jackets, most were armed with Nato weapons and spoke the Shona language. These were former members of the disbanded Zimbabwe People's Revolutionary Army, now turned political rebels, men subject to no laws, nor higher authority, forged by a long murderous and bloody bush war into hard, ruthless men with death in their hands and death in their eyes. Although Craig had been warned of the possibility, and had indeed been half-expecting this meeting, still the shock made him feel dry-mouthed and nauseated.

"We don't have to take him," said the youngest of the three guerrillas. "We can shoot him and bury him secretly—that is good as a hostage." He was under twenty-five years of age, Craig guessed, and had probably killed a man for every year of his life.

"The six hostages we took on the Victoria Falls Road gave us weeks of trouble, and in the end we had to shoot them anyway," agreed the second guerrilla, and they both looked to the third man. He was only a few years older than they were, but there was no doubt that he was the leader. A thin scar ran from the corner of

43

his mouth up his cheek into the hairline at the temple. It puckered his mouth into a lopsided, sardonic grin.

Now Craig remembered the incident that they were discussing. Guerrillas had stopped a tourist bus on the main Victoria Falls Road and abducted six men, Canadian, Americans and a Briton, and taken them into the bush as hostages for the release of political detainees. Despite an intensive search by police and regular army units, none of the hostages had been recovered.

The scarred leader stared at Craig with smoky dark eyes for long seconds, and then, with his thumb, slid the rate-of-fire selector on his rifle to automatic.

"A true Matabele does not kill a blood brother of the tribe." It took Craig an enormous effort to keep his voice steady, devoid of any trace of terror. His Sindebele was so flawless and easy that it was the leader of the guerrillas who blinked.

"Hau!" he said, which is an expression of amazement. "You speak like a man—but who is this blood brother you boast of?"

"Comrade Minister Tungata Zebiwe," Craig answered, and saw the instant shift in the man's gaze, and the sudden discomfiture of his two companions. He had hit a chord that had unbalanced them, and had delayed his own execution for the moment, but the leader's rifle was still cocked and on fully automatic, still pointed at his belly.

It was the youngster who broke the silence, speaking too loudly, to cover his own uncertainty. "It is easy for a baboon to shout the name of the black-maned lion from the hilltop, and claim his protection, but does the lion recognize the baboon? Kill him, I say, and have done with it."

"Yet he speaks like a brother," murmured the leader, "and Comrade Tungata is a hard man—"

Craig realized that his life was still at desperate risk. A little push either way was all that was needed.

"I will show you," he said, still without the slightest quaver in his voice. "Let me go to my pack."

The leader hesitated.

"I am naked," Craig told him. "No weapons—not even a knife—and you are three, with guns."

"Go!" the Matabele agreed. "But go with care. I have not killed a man for many moons—and I feel the lack."

Craig stood up carefully from the water and saw the interest in their eyes as they studied his leg foreshortened halfway between

44

knee and ankle, and the compensating muscular development of the other leg and the rest of his body. The interest changed to wary respect as they saw how quickly and easily Craig moved on one leg. He reached his pack with water running down the hard flat muscles of chest and belly. He had come prepared for this meeting, and from the front pocket of his pack he pulled out his wallet and handed a coloured snapshot to the guerrilla leader.

In the photograph two men sat on the hood of an ancient Land-Rover. They had their arms around each other's shoulders, and both of them were laughing. Each of them held a beer can in his free hand and with it was saluting the photographer. The accord and camaraderie between them was evident.

The scarred guerrilla studied it for a long time and then slipped the selector on his rifle to lock. "It is Comrade Tungata," he said, and handed the photograph to the others.

"Perhaps," conceded the youngster reluctantly, "but a long time ago. I still think we should shoot him." However, this opinion was now more wistful than determined.

"Comrade Tungata would swallow you without chewing," his companion told him flatly, and slung his rifle over his shoulder.

Craig picked up his leg and in a moment had fitted it to the stump—and instantly all three guerrillas were intrigued, their murderous intentions set aside as they crowded around Craig to examine this marvellous appendage.

Fully aware of the African love of a good joke, Craig clowned for them. He danced a jig, pirouetted on the leg, cracked himself across the shin without flinching, and finally took the hat of the youngest, most murderous guerrilla from his head, screwed it into a ball and with a cry of "Pele!" drop-kicked it into the lower branches of the wild fig with the artificial leg. The other two hooted with glee, and laughed until tears ran down their cheeks at the youngster's loss of dignity as he scrambled up into the wild fig to retrieve his hat.

Judging the mood finely, Craig opened his pack and brought out mug and whisky bottle. He poured a generous dram and handed the mug to the scar-faced leader.

"Between brothers," he said.

The guerrilla leaned his rifle against the trunk of the tree and accepted the mug. He drained it at one swallow, and blew the fumes ecstatically out of his nose and mouth. The other two took their turn at the mug with as much gusto.

When Craig pulled on his trousers and sat down on his pack, placing the bottle in front of him, they all laid their weapons aside and squatted in a half circle facing him.

"My name is Craig Mellow," he said.

"We will call you Kuphela," the leader told him, "for the leg walks on its own." The others clapped their hands in approbation, and Craig poured each of them a whisky to celebrate his christening.

"My name is Comrade Lookout," the leader told him. Most of the guerrillas had adopted *noms-de-guerre*. "This is Comrade Peking." A tribute to his Chinese instructors, Craig guessed. "And this," the leader indicated the youngest, "is Comrade Dollar." Craig had difficulty remaining straight-faced at this unlikely juxtaposition of ideologies.

"Comrade Lookout," Craig said, "the *kanka* marked you."

The *kanka* were the jackals, the security forces, and Craig guessed the leader would be proud of his battle scars.

Comrade Lookout caressed his cheek. "A bayonet. They thought I was dead and they left me for the hyena."

"Your leg?" Dollar asked in return. "From the war also?"

An affirmative would tell them that he had fought against them. Their reaction was unpredictable, but Craig paused only a second before he nodded. "I trod on one of our own mines."

"Your own mine!" Lookout crowed with delight at the joke. "He stood on his own mine!" And the others thought it as funny, but Craig detected no residual resentment.

"Where?" Peking wanted to know.

"On the river, between Kazungula and Victoria Falls."

"Ah, yes." They nodded at each other. "That was a bad place. We crossed there often," Lookout remembered. "That is where we fought the Scouts."

The Ballantyne Scouts had been one of the elite units of the security forces, and Craig had been attached to them as an armourer.

"The day I trod on the mine was the day the Scouts followed your people across the river. There was a terrible fight on the Zambian side, and all the Scouts were wiped out."

"Hau! Hau!" they exclaimed with amazement. "That was the day! We were there—we fought with Comrade Tungata on that day."

"What a fight—what a fine and beautiful killing when we

46

trapped them," Dollar remembered with the killing light in his eyes again.

"They fought! Mother of Nkulu kulu—how they fought! Those were real men!"

Craig's stomach churned queasily with the memory. His own cousin, Roland Ballantyne, had led the Scouts across the river that fateful day. While Craig lay shattered and bleeding on the edge of the minefield, Roland and all his men had fought to the death a few miles farther on. Their bodies had been abused and desecrated by these men, and now they were discussing it like a memorable football match.

Craig poured more whisky for them. How he had loathed them and their fellows—"terrs," they called them, terrorists—loathed them with the special hatred reserved for something that threatens your very existence and all that you hold dear. But now, in his turn, he saluted them with the mug, and drank. He had heard of R.A.F. and Luftwaffe pilots meeting after the war and reminiscing as they were doing, more like comrades than deadly enemies.

"Where were you when we rocketed the storage tanks in Harare and burned the fuel?" they asked.

"Do you remember when the Scouts jumped from the sky onto our camp at Molingushi? They killed eight hundred of us that day—and I was there!" Peking recalled with pride. "But they did not catch me!"

Yet now Craig found that he could not sustain that hatred any longer. Under the veneer of cruelty and savagery imposed upon them by war, they were the true Matabele that he had always loved, with that irrepressible sense of fun, that deep pride in themselves and their tribe, that abounding sense of personal honour, of loyalty and their own peculiar code of morals. As they chatted, Craig warmed to them, and they sensed it and responded to him in turn.

"So what makes you come here, Kuphela? A sensible man like you, walking without even a stick into the leopard's cave? You must have heard about us—and yet you came here?"

"Yes, I have heard about you. I heard that you were hard men, like old Mzilikazi's warriors."

They preened a little at the compliment.

"But I came here to meet you and talk with you," Craig went on.

"Why?" demanded Lookout.

"I will write a book, and in the book I will write truly the way you are and the things for which you are still fighting."

"A book?" Peking was suspicious immediately.

"What kind of book?" Dollar backed him.

"Who are you to write a book?" Lookout's voice was openly scornful. "You are too young. Book-writers are great and learned people." Like all barely literate Africans, he had an almost superstitious awe of the printed word, and reverence for the grey hairs of age.

"A one-legged book-writer," Dollar scoffed, and Peking giggled and picked up his rifle. He placed it across his lap and giggled again. The mood had changed once more. "If he lies about this book, then perhaps he lies about his friendship with Comrade Tungata," Dollar suggested with relish.

Craig had prepared for this also. He took a large manila envelope from the flap of his pack and shook from it a thick sheath of newspaper cuttings. He shuffled through them slowly, letting their disbelieving mockery change to interest, then he selected one and handed it to Lookout. The serial of the book had been shown on Zimbabwe television two years previously, before these guerrillas had returned to the bush, and it had enjoyed an avid following throughout its run.

"Hau!" Lookout exclaimed. "It is the old king, Mzilikazi!"

The photograph at the head of the article showed Craig on the set with members of the cast of the production. The guerrillas immediately recognized the black American actor who had taken the part of the old Matabele king. He was in costume of leopardskin and heron-feathers.

"And that is you—with the king." They had not been as impressed, even by the photograph of Tungata.

There was another cutting, a photo taken in the big Doubleday Book Shop on Fifth Avenue, of Craig standing beside a huge pyramid of the book, with a blow-up of his portrait from the back cover riding atop it.

"That is you!" They were truly stunned now. "Did you write that book?"

"Now do you believe?" Craig demanded, but Lookout studied the evidence carefully before committing himself.

His lips moved as he read slowly through the text of the articles, and when he handed them back to Craig, he said seriously,

48

"Kuphela, despite your youth, you are indeed an important book-writer."

Now they were almost pathetically eager to pour out their grievances to him, like petitioners at a tribal *indaba* where cases were heard and judgement handed down by the elders of the tribe. While they talked, the sun rose up across a sky as blue and unblemished as a heron's egg, and reached its noon and started its stately descent towards its bloody death in the sunset.

What they related was the tragedy of Africa, the barriers that divided this mighty continent and which contained all the seeds of violence and disaster, the single incurable disease that inflicted them all—tribalism.

Here it was Matabele against Mashona.

"The dirt-eaters," Lookout called them, "the lurkers in caves, the fugitives on the fortified hilltops, the jackals who will only bite when your back is turned to them."

It was the scorn of the warrior for the merchant, of the man of direct action for the wily negotiator and politician.

"Since great Mzilikazi first crossed the river Limpopo, the Mashona have been our dogs—*amaholi*, slaves and sons of slaves."

This history of displacement and domination of one group by another was not confined to Zimbabwe, but over the centuries had taken place across the entire continent. Farther north, the lordly Masai had raided and terrorized the Kikuyu who lacked their warlike culture; the giant Watutsi, who considered any man under six feet six to be a dwarf, had taken the gentle Hutu as slaves— and in every case, the slaves had made up for their lack of ferocity with political astuteness, and as soon as the white colonialists' protection was withdrawn, had either massacred their tormentors, as the Hutu had the Watutsi, or had bastardized the doctrine of Westminster government by discarding the checks and balances that make the system equitable, and had used their superior numbers to place their erstwhile masters into a position of political subjugation, as the Kikuyu had the Masai.

Exactly the same process was at work here in Zimbabwe. The white settlers had been rendered inconsequential by the bush war, and the concepts of fair play and integrity that the white administrators and civil servants had imposed upon all the tribes had been swept away with them.

"There are five dirt-eating Mashona for every one Matabele *indoda*," Lookout told Craig bitterly, "but why should that give them any right to lord it over us? Should five slaves dictate to a king? If five baboons bark, must the black-maned lion tremble?"

"That is the way it is done in England and America," Craig said mildly. "The will of the majority must prevail—"

"I piss with great force on the will of the majority," Lookout dismissed the doctrine of democracy airily. "Such things might work in England and America—but this is Africa. They do not work here—I will not bow down to the will of five dirt-eaters. No, not to the will of a hundred, nor a thousand of them. I am Matabele, and only one man dictates to me—a Matabele king."

Yes, Craig thought, this *is* Africa. The old Africa awakening from the trance induced in it by a hundred years of colonialism, and reverting immediately to the old ways.

He thought of the tens of thousands of fresh-faced young Englishmen who for very little financial reward had come out to spend their lives in the Colonial Service, labouring to instil into their reluctant charges their respect for the Protestant work-ethic, the ideal of fair-play and Westminster government—young men who had returned to England prematurely aged and broken in health, to eke out their days on a pittance of a pension and the belief that they had given their lives to something that was valuable and lasting. Did they, Craig wondered, ever suspect that it might all have been in vain?

The borders that the colonial system had set up had been neat and orderly. They followed a river, or the shore of a lake, the spine of a mountain range, and where these did not exist, a white surveyor with a theodolite had shot a line across the wilderness. "This side is German East Africa, this side is British." But they took no cognizance of the tribes that they were splitting in half as they drove in their pegs.

"Many of our people live across the river in South Africa," Peking complained. "If they were with us, then things would be different. There would be more of us, but now we are divided."

"And the Shona is cunning, as cunning as the baboons that come down to raid the maize fields in the night. He knows that one Matabele warrior would eat a hundred of his, so when first we rose against them, he used the white soldiers of Smith's government who had stayed on—"

Craig remembered the delight of the embittered white soldiers who considered they had not been defeated but had been betrayed, when the Mugabe government had turned them loose on the dissenting Matabele faction.

"The white pilots came in their aeroplanes, and the white troops of the Rhodesian Regiment—"

After the fighting the shunting-yards at Bulawayo station had been crowded with refrigerated trucks each packed from floor to roof with the bodies of the Matabele dead.

"The white soldiers did their work for them, while Mugabe and his boys ran back to Harare and climbed shaking and snivelling under their women's skirts. Then, after the white soldiers had taken our weapons, they crawled out again, shook off the dust of their retreat, and came strutting back like conquerors."

"They have dishonoured our leaders—"

Nkomo, the Matabele leader, had been accused of harbouring rebels and accumulating caches of weapons, and driven in disgrace by Mashona-dominated government into enforced retirement.

"They have secret prisons in the bush where they take our leaders," Peking went on. "There they do things to our men that do not bear talking of.

"Now that we are deprived of weapons, their special units move through the villages. They beat our old men and women, they rape our young women, they take our young men away, never to be seen or heard of again."

Craig had seen a photograph of men in the blue and khaki of the former British South Africa police, so long the uniform of honour and fair play, carrying out interrogations in the villages. In the photograph they had a naked Matabele spread-eagled on the earth, an armed and uniformed constable standing with both booted feet and his full weight on each ankle and wrist to pin him, while two other constables wielded clubs as heavy as baseball bats. They were using full strokes from high above the head, and raining blows on the man's back and shoulders and buttocks. The photograph had been captioned "Zimbabwe Police interrogate suspect in attempt to learn whereabouts of American and British tourists abducted as hostages by Matabele dissidents." There had been no photographs of what they did to the Matabele girls.

"Perhaps the government troops were looking for the hostages which you admit you seized," Craig pointed out tartly. "A little while ago you would have been quite happy to kill me or take me hostage as well."

51

"The Shona began this business long before we took our first hostage," Lookout shot back at him.

"But you *are* taking innocent hostages," Craig insisted. "Shooting white farmers—"

"What else can we do to make people understand what is happening to our people? We have very few leaders who have not been imprisoned or silenced, and even they are powerless. We have no weapons except these few we have managed to hide, we have no powerful friends, while the Shona have Chinese and British and American allies. We have no money to continue the struggle—and they have all the wealth of the land and millions of dollars of aid from these powerful friends. What else can we do to make the world understand what is happening to us?"

Craig decided prudently that this was neither the time nor the place to offer a lecture on political morality—and then he thought wryly, "Perhaps my morality is old-fashioned, anyway." There was a new political expediency in international affairs that had become acceptable: the right of impotent and voiceless minorities to draw violent attention to their own plight. From the Palestinians and the Basque separatists to the bombers of Northern Ireland blowing young British guardsmen and horses to bloody tatters in a London street, there was an odd, new morality abroad. With these examples before them, and from their own experience of successfully bringing about political change by violence, these young men were children of the new morality.

Though Craig could never bring himself to condone these methods, not if he lived a hundred years, yet he found himself in grudging sympathy with their plight and their aspirations. There had always been a strange and sometimes bloody bond between Craig's family and the Matabele. A tradition of respect and understanding for a people who were fine friends and enemies to be wary of, an aristocratic, proud and warlike race that deserved better than they were now receiving.

There was an elitist streak in Craig's make-up that hated to see a Gulliver rendered impotent by Lilliputians. He loathed the politics of envy and the viciousness of socialism which, he felt, sought to strike down the heroes and reduce every exceptional man to the common greyness of the pack, to replace true leadership with the oafish mumblings of trade-union louts, to emasculate all initiative by punitive tax schemes and then gradually to shepherd a

52

numbed and compliant populace into the barbed-wire enclosure of Marxist totalitarianism.

These men were terrorists—certainly. Craig grinned. Robin Hood was also a terrorist—but at least he had some style and a little class.

"Will you see Comrade Tungata?" they demanded with almost pitiful eagerness.

"Yes. I will see him soon."

"Tell him we are here. Tell him we are ready and waiting."

Craig nodded. "I will tell him."

They walked back with him to where he had left the Volkswagen, and Comrade Dollar insisted on carrying Craig's pack. When they reached the dusty and slightly battered VW, they piled into it with AK 47 barrels protruding from three windows.

"We will go with you," Lookout explained, "as far as the main Victoria Falls Road, for if you should meet another of our patrols when you are alone, it might go hard for you."

They reached the macadamized Great North Road well after night had fallen. Craig stripped his pack and gave them what remained of his rations and the dregs of the whisky. He had two hundred dollars in his wallet and he added that to the booty. Then they shook hands.

"Tell Comrade Tungata we need weapons," said Dollar.

"Tell him that, more than weapons, we need a leader." Comrade Lookout gave Craig the special grip of thumb and palm reserved for trusted friends. "Go in peace, Kuphela," he said. "May the leg that walks alone carry you far and swiftly."

"Stay in peace, my friend," Craig told him.

"No, Kuphela, rather wish me bloody war!" Lookout's scarred visage twisted into a dreadful grin in the reflected headlights.

When Craig looked back, they had disappeared into the darkness as silently as hunting leopards.

•   •   •

"I wouldn't have taken any bets on seeing you again," Jock Daniels greeted Craig when he walked into the auctioneer's office the next morning. "Did you make it up to the Chizarira—or did good sense get the better of you?"

"I'm still alive, aren't I?" Craig evaded the direct question.

53

Jock nodded. "Good boy. No sense messing with those Matabele *shufta*—bandits the lot of them."

"Did you hear from Zürich?"

Jock shook his head. "Only sent the telex at nine o'clock local time. They are an hour behind us."

"Can I use your telephone? A few private calls?"

"Local? I don't want you chatting up your birds in New York at my expense."

"Of course."

"Right—as long as you mind the shop for me, while I'm out."

Craig installed himself at Jock's desk and consulted the cryptic notes that he had made from Henry Pickering's file.

His first call was to the American Embassy in Harare, the capital three hundred miles north-east of Bulawayo.

"Mr. Morgan Oxford, your cultural attaché, please," he asked the operator.

"Oxford." The accent was crisp Boston and Ivy League.

"Craig Mellow. A mutual friend asked me to call you and give you his regards."

"Yes, I was expecting you. Won't you come in here any time and say hello?"

"I'd enjoy that," Craig told him, and hung up.

Henry Pickering was as good as his word. Any message handed to Oxford would go out in the diplomatic bag and be on Pickering's desk within twelve hours.

His next call was to the office of the minister of tourism and information, and he finally got through to the minister's secretary. Her attitude changed to warm co-operation when he spoke to her in Sindebele.

"The comrade minister is in Harare for the sitting of Parliament," she told him, and gave Craig his private number at the House.

Craig got through to a parliamentary secretary on his fourth attempt. The telephone system had slowly begun deteriorating, he noticed. The blight of all developing countries was lack of skilled artisans; prior to independence all linesmen had been white, and since then most of them had taken the gap.

This secretary was Mashona and insisted on speaking English as proof of her sophistication.

"Kindly state the nature of the business to be discussed." She was obviously reading from a printed form.

"Personal. I am acquainted with the comrade minister."

"Ah yes. P-e-r-s-o-n-n-e-l." The secretary spelled it out laboriously as she wrote it.

"No—that's p-e-r-s-o-n-a-l," Craig corrected her patiently. He was beginning to adjust to the pace of Africa again.

"I will consult the comrade minister's schedule. You will be obliged to telephone again."

Craig consulted his list. Next was the government registrar of companies, and this time he was lucky. He was put through to an efficient and helpful clerk who made a note of his requirements.

"The Share Register, Articles and Memorandum of Association of the company trading as Rholands Ltd., formerly known as Rhodesian Lands and Mining Ltd." He heard the disapproval in the clerk's tone of voice. "Rhodesian" was a dirty word nowadays, and Craig made a mental resolution to change the company's name, if ever he had the power to do so. "Zimlands" would sound a lot better to an African ear.

"I will have roneoed copies ready for you to collect by four o'clock," the clerk assured him. "The search fee will be fifteen dollars."

Craig's next call was to the surveyor general's office, and again he arranged for copies of documents—this time the titles to the company properties—the ranches King's Lynn, Queen's Lynn and the Chizarira estates.

Then there were fourteen other names on his list, all of whom ranching in Matabeleland when he left, close neighbours and friends of his family, those that grandpa Bawu had trusted and liked.

Of the fourteen he could contact only four, the others had all sold up and taken the long road southward. The remaining families sounded genuinely pleased to hear from him. "Welcome back, Craig. We have all read the book and watched it on TV." But they clammed up immediately he started asking questions. "Damned telephone leaks like a sieve," said one of them. "Come out to the ranch for dinner. Stay the night. Always a bed for you, Craig. Lord knows, there aren't so many of the old faces around any more."

Jock Daniels returned in the middle of the afternoon, red-faced and sweating. "Still burning up my telephone?" he growled. "Wonder if the bottle store has another bottle of that Haig."

Craig responded to this subtlety by crossing the road and bringing back a pinch bottle in a brown paper bag.

55

"I forgot that you have to have a cast-iron liver to live in this country." He unscrewed the cap and dropped it into the waste-paper basket.

At ten minutes to five o'clock he telephoned the minister's parliamentary office again.

"The Comrade Minister Tungata Zebiwe has graciously consented to meet you at ten o'clock on Friday morning. He can allow you twenty minutes."

"Please convey my sincere thanks to the minister."

That gave Craig three days to kill and meant he would have to drive the three hundred miles to Harare.

"No reply from Zürich?" He sweetened Jock's glass.

"If you made me an offer like that, I wouldn't bother to answer either," Jock grumped, as he took the bottle from Craig's hand and added a little more to the glass.

Over the next few days Craig availed himself of the invitations to visit Bawu's old friends and was smothered with traditional old Rhodesian hospitality.

"Of course, you can't get all the luxuries—Crosse and Black-well jams, or Bronnley soap—any more," one of his hostesses explained as she piled his plate with rich fare, "but somehow it's fun making do." And she signalled the white-robed table servant to refill the silver dish with baked sweet potatoes.

He spent the days with tanned, slow-speaking men in wide-brimmed felt hats and short khaki trousers, examining their sleek fat cattle from the passenger seat of an open Land-Rover.

"You still can't beat Matabeleland beef," one told him proudly. "Sweetest grass in the whole world. Of course, we have to send it all out through South Africa, but the prices are damned good. Glad I didn't run for it. Heard from old Derek Sanders in New Zealand, working as a hired hand on a sheep station now—and a bloody tough life, too. No Matabele to do the dirty work over there."

He looked at his black herders with paternal affection. "They are just the same, under all the political claptrap. Salt of the bloody earth, my boy. My people, I feel that they are all family, glad I didn't desert them."

"Of course, there are problems," another of his hosts told him. "Foreign exchange is murder—difficult to get tractor spares, and medicine for the stock—but Mugabe's government is starting to wake up. As food-producers we are getting priority on import permits for essentials. Of course, the telephones only work when they do and the trains don't run on time any longer. There is rampant inflation, but the beef prices keep in step with it. They have opened the schools, but we send the kids down south across the border so they can get a decent education."

"And the politics?"

"That's between black and black. Matabele and Mashona. The white man's out of it, thank God. Let the bastards tear each other to pieces if they want to. I keep my nose clean, and it's not a bad life—not like the old days, of course, but then it never is, is it?"

"Would you buy more land?"

"Haven't got the money, old boy."

"But if you did have?"

The rancher rubbed his nose thoughtfully. "Perhaps a man could make an absolute mint one day if the country comes right, land prices what they are at the moment—or he could lose the lot if it goes the other way."

"You could say the same of the stock exchange, but in the meantime it's a good life?"

"It's a good life—and, hell, I was weaned on Zambezi waters. I don't reckon I would be happy breathing London smog or swatting flies in the Australian outback."

On Thursday morning Craig drove back to the motel, picked up his laundry, repacked his single canvas hold-all, paid his bill and checked out.

He called at Jock's office. "Still no news from Zürich?"

"Telex came in an hour ago." Jock handed him the flimsy, and Craig scanned it swiftly.

"Will grant your client thirty-day option to purchase all Rholands Company paid-up shares for one half million U.S. dollars payable Zürich in full on signature. No further offers countenanced." They did not come more final than that. Bawu had said double your estimate, and so far he had it right.

Jock was watching his face. "Double your original offer," he pointed out. "Can you swing half a million?"

"I'll have to talk to my rich uncle," Craig teased him. "And anyway I've got thirty days. I'll be back before then."

"Where can I reach you?" Jock asked.

"Don't call me. I'll call you."

He begged another tankful from Jock's private stock and took the Volkswagen out on the road to the north-east, towards Mashonaland and Harare and ran into the first road-block ten miles out of town.

"Almost like the old days," he thought, as he climbed down onto the verge. Two black troopers in camouflage battle-jackets searched the Volkswagen for weapons with painstaking deliberation, while a lieutenant with the cap-badge of the Korean-trained Third Brigade examined his passport.

Once again Craig rejoiced in the family tradition whereby all the expectant mothers in his family, on both the Mellow and the Ballantyne side, had been sent home to England for the event. That little blue booklet with the gold lion and unicorn and *Honi soit qui mal y pense* printed on the cover still demanded a certain deference even at a Third Brigade road-block.

It was late afternoon when he crossed the line of low hills and looked down on the little huddle of skyscrapers that rose so incongruously out of the African veld, headstones to the belief in the immortality of the British Empire.

The city that had once borne the name of Lord Salisbury, the foreign secretary who had negotiated the Royal Charter of the British South Africa Company, had reverted to the name Harare after the original Shona chieftain whose cluster of mud and thatch huts the white pioneers had found on the site in September 1890 when they finally completed the long trek up from the south. The streets also had changed their names from those commemorating the white pioneers and Victoria's empire to those of the sons of the black revolution and its allies—"a street by any other name"—Craig resigned himself.

Once he entered the city he found there was a boom-town atmosphere. The pavements were thronged with noisy black crowds, and the foyer of the modern sixteen-storied Monomatapa Hotel resounded to twenty different languages and accents, as tourists jostled visiting bankers and businessmen, foreign dignitaries, civil servants and military advisers.

There was no vacancy for Craig until he spoke to an assistant manager who had seen the TV production and read the book. Then Craig was ushered up to a room on the fifteenth floor with a view over the park. While he was in his bath, a procession of waiters arrived bearing flowers and baskets of fruit and a complimentary bottle of South African champagne. He worked until after midnight on his report to Henry Pickering and was at the parliament buildings in Causeway by nine-thirty the next morning.

The minister's secretary kept him waiting for forty-five minutes before leading him through into the panelled office beyond, and Comrade Minister Tungata Zebiwe stood up from his desk.

Craig had forgotten how powerful was this man's presence, or perhaps he had grown in stature since their last meeting. When he remembered that once Tungata had been his servant, his gunboy, when Craig was a ranger in the Department of Game Conservation, it seemed that it had been a different existence. In those days he had been Samson Kumalo, for Kumalo was the royal blood-line of the Matabele kings, and he was their direct descendant. Bazo, his great-grandfather, had been the leader of the Matabele rebellion of 1896 and had been hanged by the settlers for his part in it. His great-great-grandfather, Gandang, had been half-brother to Lobengula, the last king of the Matabele whom Rhodes' troopers had ridden to an ignoble death and unmarked grave in the northern wilderness after destroying his capital at GuBulawayo, the place of the killing.

Royal were his blood-lines, and kingly still his bearing. Taller than Craig, well over six feet and lean, not yet running to flesh, which was often the Matabele trait, his physique was set off to perfection by the cut of his Italian silk suit, shoulders wide as a gallows tree and a flat greyhound's belly. He had been one of the most successful bush fighters during the war, and he was warrior still, of that there was no doubt. Craig experienced a powerful and totally unexpected pleasure in seeing him once more.

"I see you, Comrade Minister," Craig greeted him, speaking in Sindebele, avoiding having to choose between the old familiar "Sam" and the *nom de guerre* that he now used, Tungata Zebiwe, "the Seeker after Justice."

"I sent you away once," Tungata answered in the same language. "I discharged all debts between us—and sent you away." There was no return light of pleasure in his smoky dark eyes, the heavily boned jaw set hard.

"I am grateful for what you did," Craig was unsmiling also, covering his pleasure. It was Tungata who had signed a special ministerial order allowing Craig to export his self-built yacht *Bawu* from the territory in the face of the rigid exchange-control laws which forbade the removal of even a refrigerator or an iron bedstead. At that time the yacht had been Craig's only possession, and he had still been crippled by the mine blast and confined to a wheelchair.

"I do not want your gratitude," said Tungata, yet there was something behind the burnt-honey-coloured eyes that Craig could not fathom.

"Nor the friendship I still offer you?" Craig asked gently.

"All that died on the battlefield," Tungata said. "It was washed away in blood. You chose to go. Now why have you returned?"

"Because this is my land."

"Your land—" He saw the reddish glaze of anger suffuse the whites of Tungata's eyes. "Your land. You speak like a white settler. Like one of Cecil Rhodes' murdering troopers."

"I did not mean it that way."

"Your people took the land at rifle-point, and at the point of a rifle they surrendered it. Do not speak to me of your land."

"You hate almost as well as you fought," Craig told him, feeling his own anger begin to prickle at the back of his eyes, "but I did not come back to hate. I came back because my heart drew me back. I came back because I felt I could help to rebuild what was destroyed."

Tungata sat down behind his desk and placed his hands upon the white blotter. They were very powerful. He stared at them in a silence that stretched out for many seconds.

"You were at King's Lynn," Tungata broke the silence at last, and Craig started. "Then you went north to the Chizarira."

Craig nodded. "Your eyes are bright. They see all."

"You have asked for copies of the titles to that land." Again Craig was startled, but he remained silent. "But even you must know that you must have government approval to purchase land in Zimbabwe. You must state the use to which you intend to put that land and the capital available to work it."

"Yes, even I know that," Craig agreed.

Tungata looked up at him. "So you come to me to assure me of your friendship. Then, as an old friend, you will ask another favour, is that not so?"

Craig spread his hands, palm upward in a gesture of resignation.

"One white rancher on land that could support five hundred Matabele families. One white rancher growing fat and rich while his servants wear rags and eat the scraps he throws them," Tungata sneered, and Craig shot back at him.

"One white rancher bringing millions of capital into a country starving for it, one white rancher employing dozens of Matabele and feeding and clothing them and educating their children, one white rancher raising enough food to feed ten thousand Matabele, not a mere five hundred. One white rancher cherishing the land, guarding it against goats and droughts, so it will produce for five hundred years, not five—" Craig let his anger boil over and returned Tungata's glare, standing stiff-legged over the desk.

"You are finished here," Tungata growled at him. "The kraal is closed against you. Go back to your boat, your fame and your fawning women, be content that we took only one of your legs— go before you lose your head as well."

Tungata rolled his hand over and glanced at the gold wrist-watch.

"I have nothing more for you," he said, and stood up. Yet, behind his flat, hostile stare, Craig sensed that undefinable thing still there. He tried to fathom it—not fear, he was certain, not guile. A hopelessness, a deep regret, perhaps, even a sense of guilt—or perhaps a blend of many of these things.

"Then, before I go, I have something else for you," Craig stepped closer to the desk and lowered his voice. "You know I was on the Chizarira. I met three men there. Their names were Lookout, Peking and Dollar and they asked me to bring you a message—"

Craig got no further, for Tungata's anger turned to red fury. He was shaking with it, it clouded his gaze and knotted the muscles at the points of his heavy lantern jaw.

"Be silent," he hissed, his voice held low by an iron effort in control. "You meddle in matters that you do not understand, and that do not concern you. Leave this land before they overwhelm you."

Craig returned his gaze defiantly. "I will go, but only after my application to purchase land has been officially denied."

"Then you will leave soon," Tungata replied. "That is my promise to you."

In the parliamentary parking lot the Volkswagen was baking in the morning sun. Craig opened the doors and while he waited for the interior to cool, he found he was trembling with the after-effects of his confrontation with Tungata Zebiwe. He held up one hand before his eyes and watched the tremor of his fingertips. In the Game Department after having hunted down a man-eating lion or a crop-raiding bull elephant, he would have the same adrenalin come-down.

He slipped into the driver's seat, and while he waited to regain control of himself, he tried to arrange his impressions of the meeting and to review what he had learned from it.

Craig had been under surveillance by one of the state intelligence agencies from the moment of his arrival in Matabeleland. Perhaps he had been singled out for attention as a prominent writer—he would probably never know—but his every move had been reported to Tungata.

Yet he could not fathom the true reasons for Tungata's violent opposition to his plans. The reasons he had given were petty and spiteful, and Samson Kumalo had never been either petty or spiteful. Craig was sure that he had sensed correctly that strange mitigating counter-emotion beneath the forbidding reception. There were currents and undercurrents in the deep waters upon which Craig had set sail.

He thought back to Tungata's reaction to his mention of the three dissidents he had met in the wilderness of Chizarira. Obviously Tungata had recognized their names, and his rebuke had been too vicious to have come from a clear conscience. There was much that Craig still wanted to know, and much that Henry Pickering would find interesting.

Craig started the VW and drove slowly back to the Monomatapa down the avenues that had originally been laid out wide enough to enable a thirty-six-ox span to make a U-turn across them.

It was almost noon when he got back to the hotel room. He opened the liquor cabinet and reached for the gin bottle. Then he put it back unopened and rang room service for coffee instead. His daylight drinking habits had followed him from New York, and he knew they had contributed to his lack of purpose. They would change, he decided.

He sat down at the desk at the picture window and gazed down on the billowing blue jacaranda trees in the park while he assembled his thoughts, and then picked up his pen and brought his report to Henry Pickering up to date—including his impressions of Tungata's involvement with the Matabeleland dissidents and his almost guilty opposition to Craig's land-purchase application.

This led logically to his request for financing, and he set out his figures, his assessment of Rholands' potential, and his plans for King's Lynn and Chizarira as favourably as he could. Trading on Henry Pickering's avowed interest in Zimbabwe tourism, he dwelt at length on the development of "Zambezi Waters" as a tourist attraction.

He placed the two sets of papers in separate manila envelopes, sealed them and drove down to the American Embassy. He survived the scrutiny of the marine guard in his armoured cubicle, and waited while Morgan Oxford came through to identify him.

The cultural attaché was a surprise to Craig. He was in his early thirties, as Craig was, but he was built like a college athlete, his hair was cropped short, his eyes were a penetrating blue and his handshake firm, suggesting a great deal more strength than he exerted in his grip.

He led Craig through to a small back office and accepted the two unaddressed manila envelopes without comment.

"I've been asked to introduce you around," he said. "There is a reception and cocktail hour at the French ambassador's residence this evening. A good place to begin. Six to seven—does that sound okay?"

"Fine."

"You staying at the Mono or Meikles?"

"Monomatapa."

"I'll pick you up at 1745 hours."

Craig noted the military expression of time and thought wryly, "Cultural attaché?"

•   •   •

Even under the socialist Mitterrand regime, the French managed a characteristic display of *élan*. The reception was on the lawns of the ambassador's residence, with the tricolour undulating gaily in the light evening breeze and the perfume of frangipani blossom creating an illusion of coolness after the crackling heat of the day. The servants were in white ankle-length *kanza* with crimsom fez and sash, the champagne, although non-vintage, was Bollinger, and the *foie gras* on the biscuits was from the Périgord. The police band under the spathodea trees at the end of the lawn played light Italian operetta with an exuberant African beat, and only the motley selection of guests distinguished the gathering from a Rhodesian governor-general's garden party that Craig had attended six years previously.

The Chinese and the Koreans were the most numerous and noticeable, basking in their position of special favour with the government. It was they who had been most constant in aid and material support to the Shona forces during the long bush war, while the Soviets had made a rare error of judgement by courting

63

the Matabele faction, for which the Mugabe government was now making them atone in full measure.

Every group on the lawn seemed to include the squat figures in the rumpled pyjama suits, grinning and bobbing their long lank locks like mandarin dolls, while the Russians formed a small group on their own. Those in uniform were junior officers—there was not even a colonel among them, Craig noted. The Russians could only move upstream from where they were now.

Morgan Oxford introduced Craig to the host and hostess. The ambassadoress was at least thirty years younger than her husband. She wore a bright Pucci print with Parisian chic. Craig said, "*Enchanté, madame,*" and touched the back of her hand with his lips; when he straightened, she gave him a slow speculative appraisal before turning to the next guest in the reception line.

"Pickering warned me you were some kind of cocksman," Morgan chided him gently, "but let's not have a diplomatic incident."

"All right, I'll settle for a glass of bubbly."

Each armed with a champagne flute, they surveyed the lawn. The ladies from the Central African republics were in national dress, a marvellous cacophony of colour like a hatching of forest butterflies, and their men carried elaborately carved walking-sticks or fly-whisks made from animal tails, and the Muslims among them wore embroidered pillbox fezes with the tassel denoting that they were *hadji* who had made the pilgrimage to Mecca.

Craig thought of his grandfather, the arch-colonist. "Sleep well, Bawu. It is best that you never lived to see this."

"We had better check you in with the Brits, seeing that's your home base," Morgan suggested, and introduced him to the British High Commissioner's wife, an iron-jawed lady with a lacquered hair-style modelled on Margaret Thatcher's.

"I can't say I enjoyed all that detailed violence in your book," she told him severely. "Do you think it was really necessary?"

Craig kept any trace of irony out of his voice. "Africa is a violent land. He who would hide that fact from you is no true story-teller." He wasn't really in the mood for amateur literary critics, and he looked past her and rove the lawn, seeking distraction.

What he found made his heart jump against his ribs like a caged animal. From across the lawn she was watching him with green eyes from under that unbroken line of dark thick brows. She wore a cotton skirt with patch-pockets that left her calves bare, open sandals that laced around her ankles and a simple T-shirt. Her thick dark hair was tied with a leather thong at the back of her neck; it was freshly washed and shiny. Although she wore no make-up, her tanned skin had the lustre of abounding health and her lips were rouged with the bright young blood beneath. Over one shoulder was slung a Nikon FM with motor drive and both her hands were thrust into the pockets of her skirt.

She had been watching him, but the moment Craig looked directly at her, she lifted her chin in a gesture of mild disdain, held his eye for just long enough and then turned her head unhurriedly to the man who stood beside her, listening intently to what he was saying and then showing white teeth in a small controlled laugh. The man was an African, almost certainly Mashona, for he wore the crisply starched uniform of the regular Zimbabwean army and the red staff tabs and stars of a brigadier-general. He was as handsome as the young Harry Belafonte.

"Some guys have a good eye for horseflesh," Morgan said softly, mocking again. "Come along, then, I'll introduce you."

Before Craig could protest, he had started across the lawn and Craig had to follow.

"General Peter Fungabera, may I introduce Mr. Craig Mellow. Mr. Mellow is the celebrated novelist."

"How do you do, Mr. Mellow. I apologize for not having read your books. I have so little time for pleasure." His English was excellent, his choice of words precise but strongly accented.

"General Fungabera is Minister of Internal Security, Craig," Morgan explained.

"A difficult portfolio, General." Craig shook his hand, and saw that though his eyes were penetrating and cruel as a falcon's, there was a humorous twist to his smile, and Craig was instantly attracted to him. A hard man, but a good one, he judged.

The general nodded. "But then nothing worth doing is ever easy, not even writing books. Don't you agree, Mr. Mellow?"

He was quick and Craig liked him more, but his heart was still pumping and his mouth was dry so he could concentrate only a small part of his attention on the general.

"And this," said Morgan, "is Miss Sally-Anne Jay." Craig turned to face her. How long ago since he had last done so, a month perhaps? But he found that he remembered clearly every golden fleck in her eyes and every freckle on her cheeks.

"Mr. Mellow and I have met—though I doubt he would remember." She turned back to Morgan and took his arm in a friendly, familiar gesture. "I am so sorry I haven't seen you since I got back from the States, Morgan. Can't thank you enough for arranging the exhibition for me. I have received so many letters—"

"Oh, we've had feedback also," Morgan told her. "All of it excellent. Can we have lunch next week? I'll show you." He turned to explain. "We sent an exhibition of Sally-Anne's photographs on a tour of all our African consular offices. Marvellous stuff, Craig, you really must see her work."

"Oh, he has." Sally-Anne smiled without warmth. "But unfortunately Mr. Mellow does not have your enthusiasm for my humble efforts." And then without giving Craig a chance to protest, she turned back to Morgan. "It's wonderful, General Fungabera has promised to accompany me on a visit to one of the rehabilitation centres, and he will allow me to do a photographic series—" With a subtle inclination of her body she effectively excluded Craig from the conversation, and left him feeling gawky and wordless on the fringe.

A light touch on his upper arm rescued him from embarrassment and General Fungabera drew him aside just far enough to ensure privacy.

"You seem to have a way of making enemies, Mr. Mellow."

"We had a misunderstanding in New York." Craig glanced sideways at Sally-Anne.

"Although I did detect a certain arctic wind blowing there, I was not referring to the charming young photographer, but to others more highly placed and in a better position to render you disservice." Now all Craig's attention focused upon Peter Fungabera as he went on softly, "Your meeting this morning with a cabinet colleague of mine was," he paused, "shall we say, unfruitful?"

"Unfruitful will do very nicely," Craig agreed.

"A great pity, Mr. Mellow. If we are to become self-sufficient in our food supplies and not dependent on our racist neighbours in the south, then we need farmers with capital and determination on land that is now being abused."

"You are well informed, General, and far-seeing." Did everyone in the country already know exactly what he intended? Craig wondered.

"Thank you, Mr. Mellow. Perhaps when you are ready to make

66

your application for land purchase, you will do me the honour of speaking to me again. A friend at court, isn't that the term? My brother-in-law is the Minister for Agriculture."

When he smiled, Peter Fungabera was irresistible. "And now, Mr. Mellow, as you heard, I am going to accompany Miss Jay on a visit to certain closed areas. The international press have been making a lot of play regarding them. Buchenwald, I think one of them wrote, or was it Belsen? It occurs to me that a man of your reputation might be able to set the record straight, a favour for a favour, perhaps—and if you travelled in the same company as Miss Jay, then it might give you an opportunity to sort out your misunderstanding, might it not?"

• • •

It was still dark and chilly when Craig parked the Volkswagen in the lot behind one of the hangars at New Sarum air force base and, lugging his hold-all, ducked through the low side-entrance into the cavernous interior.

Peter Fungabera was there ahead of him, talking to two air force non-commissioned officers, but the moment he saw Craig he dismissed them with a casual salute and came towards Craig smiling.

He wore a camouflage battle-jacket and the burgundy-red beret and silver leopard's-head cap-badge of the Third Brigade. Apart from a holstered side-arm, he carried only a leather-covered swagger-stick.

"Good morning, Mr. Mellow. I admire punctuality." He glanced down at Craig's hold-all. "And the ability to travel lightly."

He fell in beside Craig and they went out through the tall rolling doors onto the hardstand.

There were two elderly Canberra bombers parked before the hangar. Now the pride of the Zimbabwe air force, they had once mercilessly blasted the guerrilla camps beyond the Zambezi. Beyond them stood a sleek little silver and blue Cessna 210, and Peter Fungabera headed towards it just as Sally-Anne appeared from under the wing. She was engrossed in her walkaround checks and Craig realized she was to be their pilot. He had expected a helicopter and a military pilot.

She was dressed in a Patagonia wind-breaker, blue jeans and soft leather mosquito boots. Her hair was covered by a silk scarf. She looked professional and competent as she made a visual check of the fuel level in the wing-tanks and then jumped down to the tarmac.

"Good morning, General. Would you like to take the right-hand seat?"

"Shall we put Mr. Mellow up front? I have seen it all before."

"As you wish." She nodded coolly at Craig, "Mr. Mellow," and climbed up into the cockpit. She cleared with the tower and taxied to the holding point, pulled on the hand-brake and murmured, "Too much pork for good Hebrew education causes trouble."

As a conversational starter it took some following. Craig was dumbfounded, but she ignored him and only when her hands began to dart over the controls setting the trim, checking masters, mags and mixture, pushing the pitch fully fine, did he understand that the phrase was her personal acronym for the pre-take-off check-list, and the mild misgivings that he had had about female pilots began to recede.

After take-off, she turned out of the circuit on a north-westerly heading and engaged the automatic pilot, opened a large-scale map on her lap and concentrated on the route. Good flying technique, Craig admitted, but not much for social intercourse.

"A beautiful machine," Craig tried. "Is it your own?"

"Permanent loan from the World Wildlife Trust," she answered, still intent on the sky directly ahead.

"What does she cruise at?"

"There is an air-speed indicator directly in front of you, Mr. Mellow." She crushed him effortlessly.

It was Peter Fungabera who leaned over the back of Craig's seat and ended the silence.

"That's the Great Dyke," he pointed out the abrupt geological formation below them. "A highly mineralized intrusion—chrome, platinum, gold—" Beyond the dyke, the farming lands petered out swiftly and they were over a vast area of rugged hills and sickly green forests that stretched endlessly to a milky horizon.

"We will be landing at a secondary airstrip, just this side of the Pongola Hills. There is a mission station there and a small settlement, but the area is very remote. Transport will meet us there but it's another two hours' drive to the camp," the general explained.

"Do you mind if we go down lower, General?" Sally-Anne asked, and Peter Fungabera chuckled.

"No need to ask the reason. Sally-Anne is educating me in the importance of wild animals, and their conservation."

Sally-Anne eased back the throttle and went down. The heat was building up and the light aircraft began to bounce and wobble as it met the thermals coming up from the rocky hills. The area below them was devoid of human habitation and cultivation.

"God-forsaken hills," the general growled. "No permanent water, sour grazing and fly."

However, Sally-Anne picked out a herd of big beige hump-backed eland in one of the open vleis beside a dry river-bed, and then, twenty miles farther on, a solitary bull elephant.

She dropped to tree-top level, pulled on the flaps and did a series of steep slow turns around the elephant, cutting him off from the forest and holding him in the open, so he was forced to face the circling machine with ears and trunk extended.

"He's magnificent!" she cried, the wind from the open window buffeting them and whipping her words away. "A hundred pounds of ivory each side," and she was shooting single-handed through the open window, the motor drive on her Nikon whirring as it pumped film through the camera.

They were so low that it seemed the bull might grab a wing-tip with his reaching trunk, and Craig could clearly make out the wet exudation from the glands behind his eyes. He found himself gripping the sides of his seat.

At last Sally-Anne left him, levelled her wings and climbed away. Craig slumped with relief.

"Cold feet, Mr. Mellow? Or should that be singular, foot?"

"Bitch," Craig thought. "That was a low hit." But she now was talking to Peter Fungabera over her shoulder.

"Dead, that animal is worth ten thousand dollars, tops. Alive, he's worth ten times that, and he'll sire a hundred bulls to replace him."

"Sally-Anne is convinced that there is a large-scale poaching ring at work in this country. She has shown me some remarkable photographs—and I must say, I am beginning to share her concern."

"We have to find them and smash them, General," she insisted.

"Find them for me, Sally-Anne, and I will smash them. You already have my word."

Listening to them talking, Craig felt again an old-fashioned emotion that he had been aware of the first time he had seen these

69

two together. There was no missing the accord between them, and Fungabera was a dashingly handsome fellow. Now he darted a glance over his shoulder and found the general watching him closely and speculatively, a look he covered instantly with his smile.

"How do you feel about the issue, Mr. Mellow?" he said, and suddenly Craig was telling him about his plans for Zambezi Waters on the Chizarira. He told them about the black rhinoceros and the protected wilderness areas surrounding it, and he told them how accessible it was to Victoria Falls, and now Sally-Anne was listening as intently as the general. When he finished, they were both silent for a while, and then the general said, "Now, Mr. Mellow, you are making good sense. That is the kind of planning that this country desperately needs, and its profit potential will be understood by even the most backward and unsophisticated of my people."

"Wouldn't Craig be easier, General?"

"Thank you, Craig—my friends call me Peter."

Half an hour later Craig saw a galvanized iron roof flash in the sunlight dead ahead, and Sally-Anne said, "Tuti Mission Station," and began letting down for a landing. She banked steeply over the church and Craig saw tiny figures around the cluster of huts waving up at them.

The strip was short and narrow and rough, and the wind was across, but Sally-Anne crabbed in and kicked her straight at the moment before touchdown, then held the port wing down with a twist of the wheel. She was really very good indeed, Craig realized.

There was a sand-coloured army Land-Rover waiting under a huge marula tree off to one side of the strip, and three troopers saluted Peter Fungabera with a stamping of boots that raised dust and a slapping of rifle-butts. Then while Craig helped Sally-Anne tie down the aircraft, they loaded the meagre baggage into the Land-Rover.

As the Land-Rover drew level with the mission schoolhouse beside the church, Sally-Anne asked, "Do you think they have a women's room here?" and Peter tapped the driver on the shoulder with his swagger-stick and the vehicle stopped.

Wide-eyed black children crowded the veranda and the schoolmistress came out to greet Sally-Anne, as she climbed the steps and gave her a little curtsey of welcome. The teacher was about

70

the same age as Sally-Anne, with long slim legs under her simple cotton skirt. Her dress was surgically clean and crisply ironed, and her white gym shoes were spotless. Her skin was glossy as velvet, and she had the typical moon face, shining teeth and gazelle eyes of the Nguni maiden, but there was a grace in her carriage, an alert and intelligent expression and a sculpturing of her features that was truly beautiful.

She and Sally-Anne talked for a few moments and then she led the white woman through the door.

"I think you and I should understand each other, Craig." Peter watched them disappear. "I have seen you looking at Sally-Anne and me. Let me just say, I admire Sally-Anne's accomplishments, her intelligence and her initiative—however, unlike many of my peers, miscegenation has no attraction for me whatsoever. I find most European women mannish and overbearing, and white flesh insipid. If you will pardon my plain-speaking."

Craig smiled. "I am relieved to hear it, Peter."

"On the other hand, the little schoolteacher there strikes me as—you are the wordmaster, give me a word for her, please."

"Toothsome."

"Good."

"Nubile."

Peter chuckled. "Even better. I really must find time to read your book." And then he was serious again as he went on, "Her name is Sarah. She has four A-levels and a high-school teacher's diploma; she has qualifications in nursing, she is beautiful and yet modest, respectful and dutiful with traditional good manners— did you see how she did not look directly at us men?—that would have been forward." Peter nodded approval. "A modern woman with old-fashioned virtues. Yet her father is a witch-doctor who dresses in skins, divines by throwing the bones, and does not wash from one year to the next. Africa," he said. "My wonderful, endlessly fascinating ever-changing never-changing Africa."

The two young women returned from the outhouses behind the school and were chatting animatedly with each other, while Sally-Anne clicked away with her camera, capturing images of the children with their teacher who seemed not much older than they. The two men watched them from the Land-Rover.

"You strike me as a man of action, Peter—and I cannot believe you lack the bride-price?" Craig asked. "What are you waiting for?"

"She is Matabele, and I am Mashona. Capulet and Montague," Peter explained simply. "And that is an end of it."

The children, led by Sarah, sang them a song of welcome from the veranda and then at Sally-Anne's request recited the alphabet and the multiplication tables, while she photographed their intent expressions. When she climbed back into the Land-Rover, they trilled their farewells and waved until the billowing dust hid them.

The track was rough and the Land-Rover bounced over the deep ruts formed in the rainy season in black glutinous mud and dried now to the consistency of concrete. Through gaps in the forest they glimpsed blue hills on the northern horizon, sheer and riven and uninviting.

"The Pongola Hills," Peter told them. "Bad country." And then as they neared their destination, he began telling them what they might expect when at last they arrived.

"These rehabilitation centres are not concentration camps—but are, as the name implies, centres of re-education and adaptation to the ordinary world."

He glanced at Craig. "You, as well as any of us, know that we have lived through a dreadful civil war, eleven years of hell that have brutalized an entire generation of young people. Since their early teens, they have known no life without an automatic rifle in their hands, they have been taught nothing but destruction and learned nothing except that a man's desires can be achieved simply by killing anybody who stands in his way."

Peter Fungabera was silent for a few moments, and Craig could see that he was reliving his own part in those terrible years. Now he sighed softly.

"They, poor fellows, were misled by some of their leaders. To sustain them in the hardships and privations of the bush war they were made promises that could never be kept. They were promised rich farming land and hundreds of head of prime cattle, money and motor cars and many wives of their choice." Peter made an angry gesture. "They were built up to great expectations, and when these could not be met, they turned against those who made the promises. Every one of them was armed, every one a trained soldier who had killed and would not hesitate to kill again. What were we to do?" Peter broke off and glanced at his wrist-watch. "Time for lunch and a stretch of the legs," he suggested.

The driver parked where the track crossed a high earthen causeway, and a timber bridge over a river-bed in which cool green waters swirled over the rippled sandbanks and tall reeds nodded their heads from either bank. The escort built a fire, roasted maize cobs over it and brewed Malawi tea, while Peter walked his guests in leisurely fashion along the causeway and went on with his lecture.

"We Africans once had a tradition. If one of our young people became intractable and flouted the tribal laws, then he was sent into bush camp where the elders licked him back into shape. This rehabilitation centre is a modernized version of the traditional bush camp. I will not attempt to hide anything from you. It is no Club Med holiday home that we are going to visit. The men in it are tough, and only hard treatment will have any effect on them. On the other hand, they are not extermination camps—let us rather say that they are equivalent to the detection barracks of the British Army." Craig could not help but be impressed by Peter Fungabera's honesty. "You are free to speak to any of the detainees, but I must ask you not to go wandering off into the bush on your own. That applies to you especially, Sally-Anne," Peter smiled at her. "This is a very isolated and wild spot. Animals like hyenas and leopards are attracted by offal and sewage, and become fearless and bold. Ask me if you want to leave the camp, and I will provide you with an escort."

They ate the frugal lunch, husking the scorched maize with their fingers and washing it down with the strong, black, over-sweetened tea.

"If you are ready, we will go on." Peter led them back to the Land-Rover, and an hour later they reached Tuti Rehabilitation Centre.

During the bush war it had been one of the "protected villages" set up by the Smith government in an attempt to shield the black peasants from intimidation by the guerrillas. There was a central rocky kopje that had been cleared of all vegetation, a pile of large grey granite boulders on top of which had been built a small, sandbagged fort with machine-gun embrasures, firing platforms, communication trenches and dugouts. Below this was the encampment, orderly rows of mud-and-thatched huts, many with half walls to allow air circulation, built around a dusty open space which could have been parade-ground or football field, for there were rudimentary goal-posts set up at each end, and, incongruously, a sturdy whitewashed wall at the side nearest the fort.

A double fence of barbed-wire, sandwiching a deep ditch, surrounded the camp. The wire was ten feet high and tightly woven. The floor of the ditch was armed with closely planted, sharpened wooden stakes, and there were high guard-towers on bush poles at each corner of the stockade. The guards at the only gate saluted the Land-Rover, and they drove slowly down the track that skirted the parade-ground.

In the sun, two or three hundred young black men, dressed only in khaki shorts, were performing vigorous calisthenics to the shout of uniformed black instructors. In the thatched open-walled huts hundreds more were sitting in orderly rows on the bare earth, reciting in chanted unison the lesson on the blackboard.

"We'll do a tour later," Peter told them. "First we will get you settled."

Craig was allocated a dugout in the fort. The earthen floor had been freshly swept and sprinkled with water to cool it and lay the dust. The only furnishings were a plaited-reed sleeping-mat on the floor and a sacking screen covering the doorway. On the reed mat were a box of matches and a packet of candles. Craig guessed that these were a luxury reserved for important guests.

Sally-Anne was allocated the dugout across the trench from his. She showed no dismay at the primitive conditions, and when Craig glanced around the screen, he saw her sitting on her reed mat in the lotus position, cleaning the lens of her camera and reloading film.

Peter Fungabera excused himself and went up the trench to the command post at the hilltop. A few minutes later an electric generator started running and Craig could hear Peter on the radio talking in rapid Shona which he could not follow. He came down again half an hour later.

"It will be dark in an hour. We will go down and watch the detainees being given the evening meal."

The detainees lined up in utter silence, shuffling forward to be fed. There were no smiles or horseplay. They did not show even the slightest curiosity in the white visitors and the general.

"Simple fare," Peter pointed out. "Maize-meal porridge and greens."

Each man had a dollop of the fluffy stiff cake spooned into his bowl, and topped by another of stewed vegetable.

74

"Meat once a week. Tobacco once a week. Both can be withheld for bad behaviour." Peter was telling it exactly as it was. The men were lean, ribs racked out from under hard-worked muscle, no trace of fat on any one of them. They wolfed the food immediately, still standing, using their fingers to wipe the bowl clean. Lean, but not emaciated, finely drawn but not starved, Craig judged, and then his eyes narrowed.

"That man is injured." The purple bruising showed even over his sun-darkened skin.

"You may speak to him," Peter invited, and when Craig questioned him in Sindebele, the man responded immediately.

"Your back—what happened?"

"I was beaten."

"Why?"

"Fighting with another man."

Peter called over one of the guards and spoke quietly to him in Shona, then explained, "He stabbed another prisoner with a weapon made of sharpened fencing wire. Deprived of meat and tobacco for two months and fifteen strokes with a heavy cane. This is precisely the type of antisocial behaviour we are trying to prevent."

As they walked back across the parade-ground past the whitewashed wall, Peter went on, "Tomorrow you have the run of the camp. We will leave the following morning early."

They ate with the Shona officers in the mess, and the fare was the same as that served to the detainees with the addition of a stew of stringy meat of indeterminate origin and dubious freshness. As soon as they finished eating, Peter Fungabera excused himself and led his officers out of the dugout, leaving Craig and Sally-Anne alone together.

Before Craig could think of anything to say, Sally-Anne stood without a word and left the dugout. Craig had reached the limit of his forbearance and was suddenly angry with her. He jumped up and followed her out. He found her on the firing platform of the main trench, perched up on the sandbag parapet, hugging her knees and staring down on the encampment. The moon was just past full and already well clear of the hills on the horizon. She did not look round as Craig stepped up beside her, and Craig's anger evaporated as suddenly as it had arisen.

"I acted like a pig," he said.

She hugged her knees a little tighter and said nothing.

"When we first met I was going through a bad time," he went on doggedly. "I won't bore you with the details, but the book I was trying to write was blocked and I had lost my way. I took it out on you."

Still she showed no sign of having heard him. Down in the forest beyond the double fence there was a sudden hideous outcry, shrieks of mirthless laughter rising and falling, sobbing and wailing, taken up and repeated at a dozen points around the camp perimeter, dying away at last in a descending series of chuckles and grunts and agonized moans.

"Hyena," said Craig, and Sally-Anne shivered slightly and straightened up as if to rise.

"Please." Craig heard the desperate note in his own voice. "Just a minute more. I have been searching for a chance to apologize."

"That isn't necessary," she said. "It was presumptuous of me to expect you to like my work." Her tone was not in the least conciliatory. "I guess I asked for it—and did you ever let me have it!"

"Your work—your photographs"—his voice dropped—"they frightened me. That was why my reaction was so spiteful, so childish."

Now she turned to look at him for the first time and the moon silvered the planes of her face. "Frightened you?" she asked.

"Terrified me. You see, I wasn't able to work. I was beginning to believe that it had been only a one-time thing, that the book was a fluke, and there was no real talent left in me. I kept going back to the cupboard and each time it was bare"—she was staring at him now, her lips slightly parted and her eyes mysterious cups of darkness—"and then you hit me with those damned photographs, and dared me to match them."

She shook her head slowly.

"You might not have meant that, but that's what it was—a challenge. A challenge I didn't have the courage to accept. I was afraid, I lashed out at you, and I have been regretting it ever since."

"You liked them?" she asked.

"They shook my little world. They showed me Africa again, and filled me with longing. When I saw them, I knew what was missing in me. I was struck with homesickness like a little boy on his first lonely night at boarding-school." He felt a choking in his throat and was unashamed of it. "It was those photographs of yours that made me come back here."

"I didn't understand," she said, and they were both silent. Craig knew that if he spoke again, it might come out as a sob, for the tears of self-pity were prickling the rims of his eyelids.

Down in the encampment below them someone began to sing. It was a fine African tenor voice that carried faint but clear to the hilltop, so that Craig could recognize the words. He knew it as an ancient Matabele regimental fighting chant, but now it was sung as a lament, seeming to capture all the suffering and tragedy of a continent; and not even the hyena cried while the voice sang:

"The Moles are beneath the earth,
 'Are they dead?' asked the daughters of Mashobane.
 Listen, pretty maids, do you not hear
 Something stirring, in the darkness?"

The singer's voice died away at last, and Craig imagined all the hundreds of other young men lying in wakeful silence on their sleeping-mats, haunted and saddened by the song as he was.

Then Sally-Anne spoke again. "Thank you for telling me," she said. "I know what it must have cost you." She touched his bare upper arm, a light brush of her fingertips which thrilled along his nerve ends and made his heart trip.

Then she uncurled her legs and dropped lightly off the parapet and slipped away down the communication trench. He heard the sacking flap fall over the entrance to her dugout and the flare of a match as she lit a candle.

He knew he would be unable to sleep, so he stayed on alone, listening to the African night and watching the moon.

Slowly he felt the words rising up in him, like water in a well that has been pumped down to the mud. His sadness fell away, and was replaced by excitement.

He went down to his own dugout and lit one of the candles, stuck it in a niche of the wall and from his bag took his notebook and ball-point pen. The words were bubbling and frothing in his brain, like boiling milk. He put the point of the pen to the lined white paper—and it sped away across the page like a living thing. Words came spurting out of him in a joyous, long-pent-up orgasm and spilled untidily over the paper. He stopped only to relight fresh candles from the guttering stump.

In the morning his eyes were red and burning from the strain.

He felt weak and shaky as though he had run too far and too fast, but the notebook was three-quarters filled and he was strangely elated.

His elation lasted well into the hot brilliant morning, enhanced by Sally-Anne's change of attitude. She was still reserved and quiet, but at least she listened when he spoke and replied seriously and thoughtfully. Once or twice she even smiled, and then her too-large mouth and nose were at last in harmony with the rest of her face. Craig found it difficult to concentrate on the plight of the men that they had come to study, until he realized Sally-Anne's compassion and listened to her speaking freely for the first time.

"It would be so easy to dismiss them as brutish criminals," she said softly, watching their expressionless faces and guarded eyes, "until you realize how they have been deprived of all humanizing influences. Most of them were abducted from their schoolrooms in their early teens and taken into the guerrilla training camps. They have nothing, have never had any possession of their own except an AK 47 rifle. How can we expect them to respect the persons and properties of others? Craig, please ask that one how old he is."

"He does not know," Craig translated for her. "He does not know when he was born, or where his parents are."

"He does not even have a simple birthright," Sally-Anne pointed out, and suddenly Craig remembered how churlishly he could reject a wine that was not exactly to his taste, or how thoughtlessly he could order a new suit of clothing, or enter the first-class cabin of an airliner—while these men wore only a ragged pair of shorts, without even a pair of shoes or a blanket to protect them.

"The abyss between the haves and the have-nots of this world will suck us all into destruction," Sally-Anne said as she recorded through her Nikon lens that dumb-animal resignation that lies beyond despair. "Ask that one how he is treated here," she insisted, and when Craig spoke to him the man stared at him without comprehension, as though the question was meaningless, and slowly Craig's sense of well-being burned off like mist in the morning.

In the open huts the lessons were political orientation and the role of the responsible citizen in the socialist state. On the blackboards, diagrams showed the relationship of parliament to the judiciary and the executive branches of the state. They had been copied onto the boards in a laboured, semi-literate hand by bored instructors and were recited parrot-fashion by the rows of squatting detainees. Their obvious lack of comprehension depressed Craig even more.

As they trudged back up the hill to their quarters, a thought struck Craig and he turned to Peter Fungabera.

"All the men here are Matabele, aren't they?"

Peter nodded. "That is true. We keep the tribes segregated— it reduces friction."

"Are there any Shona detainees?" Craig insisted.

"Oh, yes," Peter assured him. "The camps for them are up in the eastern highlands—exactly the same conditions—"

At sunset the generator powering the radio was started and twenty minutes later Peter Fungabera came down to the dugout where Craig was rereading and correcting his writing of the previous night.

"There is a message for you, Craig, relayed by Morgan Oxford at the American Embassy."

Craig jumped to his feet eagerly. He had arranged for Henry Pickering's reply to be passed on to him as soon as it was received. He took the sheet of notepaper on which Peter had jotted the radio transmission, and read: "For Mellow. Stop. My personal enthusiasm for your project not shared by others. Stop. Ashe Levy unwilling to advance or guarantee. Stop. Loans Committee here requires substantial additional collateral before funding. Stop. Regrets and best wishes. Henry."

Craig read the message once fast and then again very slowly.

"None of my business," Peter Fungabera murmured, "but I presume this concerns your plans for the place you call Zambezi Waters?"

"That's right—and it puts the kibosh on those, I'm afraid," Craig told him bitterly.

"Henry?"

"A friend, a banker—perhaps I relied on him too much."

"Yes," Peter Fungabera said thoughtfully, "it looks that way, doesn't it?"

Even though he had missed the previous night, Craig had difficulty sleeping. His mat was iron-hard and the hellish chorus of the hyena pack in the forest echoed his sombre mood.

On the long drive back to the airstrip at Tuti Mission, he sat beside the driver and took no part in the conversation of Peter and Sally-Anne in the seat behind him. Only now did he realize how much store he had set on buying Rholands, and he was bitterly

79

angry with Ashe Levy who had refused his support and with Henry Pickering who had not tried hard enough, and his damned Loans Committee who could not see the ends of their own noses.

Sally-Anne insisted on stopping once again at the mission schoolhouse to renew her acquaintance with Sarah, the Matabele teacher. This time Sarah was prepared and offered her visitors tea. In no mood for pleasantries, Craig found a seat on the low veranda wall well separated from the others, and began scheming without real optimism how he might circumvent Henry Pickering's refusal.

Sarah came to him demurely with an enamel mug of tea on a carved wooden tray. As she offered it, her back was turned to Peter Fungabera.

"When the man-eating crocodile knows the hunter is searching for him, he buries himself in the mud at the bottom of the deepest pool," she spoke softly in Sindebele, "and when the leopard hunts, he hunts in darkness."

Stunned, Craig looked into her face. Her eyes were no longer downcast, and there was a fierce and angry glow in their dark depths.

"Fungabera's puppies must have been noisy," she went on just as softly, "they could not feed while you were there. They would have been hungry. Did you hear them, Kuphela?" she asked, and this time Craig flinched with surprise. Sarah had used the name that Comrade Lookout had given him. How had she known that? What did she mean by Fungabera's puppies?

Before Craig could reply, Peter Fungabera looked up and saw Craig's face. He rose to his feet easily but swiftly and crossed the veranda to Sarah's side. Immediately the black girl dropped her gaze from Craig's face, bobbed a little curtsey and retired with the empty tray.

"Do not let your disappointment depress you too much, Craig. Do come and join us." Peter placed a friendly hand on Craig's shoulder.

On the short drive from the mission station to the airstrip Sally-Anne suddenly leaned forward and touched Craig's shoulder.

"I have been thinking, Craig. This place you call Zambezi Waters can only be about half an hour's flying time from here. I found the Chizarira River on the map. We could make a small detour and fly over it on the way home."

Craig shook his head. "No point."

"Why not?" she asked, and he passed her the sheet of notepaper with Pickering's message.

"Oh, I am so sorry." It was genuine, Craig realized, and her concern comforted him a little.

"I would like to see the area," Peter Fungabera cut in suddenly, and when Craig shook his head again, his voice hardened. "We will go there," he said with finality, and Craig shrugged his indifference.

Craig and Sally-Anne pored over her map. "The pools should be here, where this stream joins the main river-course." And she worked swiftly with callipers and her wind-deflection computer.

"Okay," she said. "Twenty-two minutes' flying time with this wind."

While they flew, and Sally-Anne studied the terrain and compared it to her map, Craig brooded over the Matabele girl's words. "Fungabera's puppies." Somehow it sounded menacing, and her use of the name "Kuphela" troubled him even more. There was only one explanation: she was in touch with and was probably a member of the group of dissident guerrillas. What had she meant by the leopard and crocodile allegory, and Fungabera's puppies? And whatever it was, just how unbiased and reliable would she be if she were a guerrilla sympathizer?

"There is the river," said Sally-Anne as she eased the throttle closed and began a shallow descending turn towards the glint of waters through the forest-tops.

She flew very low along the river-bank and, despite the thick cloak of vegetation, picked out herds of game animals, even once, with a squeal of glee, the great rocklike hulk of a black rhinoceros in the ebony thickets.

Then suddenly she pointed ahead. "Look at that!"

In a loop of the river, there was a strip of open land hedged in with tall riverine trees, where the grass had been grazed like a lawn by the zebra herds who were already raising dust as they galloped away in panic from the approaching aircraft.

"I bet I could get down there," Sally-Anne said and pulled on the flaps, slowing the Cessna and lowering the nose to give herself better forward vision. Then she let down the landing-gear.

She made a series of slow passes over the open ground, each lower than the previous one, until at the fourth pass her wheels were only two or three feet above the ground and they could see

81

each individual hoofprint of the zebra in the dusty earth.

"Firm and clear," she said, and on the next pass touched down, and immediately applied maximum safe braking that pulled the aircraft to a dead stop in less than a hundred and fifty paces.

"Bird lady," Craig grinned at her and she smiled at the compliment.

They left the aircraft and set off across the plain towards the forest wall, passed through it along a game trail and came out on a rocky bluff above the river.

The scene was a perfect African cameo. White sandbanks and water-polished rock glittering like reptiles' scales, trailing branches decked with weaver birds' nests over deep green water, tall trees with white serpentine roots crawling over the rocks—and beyond that, open forest.

"It's beautiful," said Sally-Anne, and wandered off with her camera.

"This would be a good site for one of your camps." Peter Fungabera pointed at the great lumpy heaps of elephant dung on the white sandbank below them.

"Grandstand view."

"Yes, it would have been," Peter agreed. "If—if only—"

"It seems too good to pass up—at that price. There must be millions of profit in it."

"For a good African socialist, you talk like a filthy capitalist," Craig told him morosely. Peter chuckled and said, "They do say that socialism is the ideal philosophy—just as long as you have capitalists to pay for it."

Craig looked up sharply, and for the first time saw the glitter of good old western European avarice in Peter Fungabera's eyes. Both of them were silent, watching Sally-Anne in the river-bed as she made compositions of tree and rock and sky and photographed them.

"Craig." Peter had obviously reached a decision. "If I could arrange the collateral that the World Bank requires, I would expect a commission in Rholands shares."

"I guess you would be entitled to it." Craig felt the embers of his dead hopes flicker, and at that moment Sally-Anne called, "It's getting late and we have two and a half hours' flying to Harare."

Back at New Sarum air force base Peter Fungabera shook hands with both of them.

"I hope your pictures turn out fine," he said to Sally-Anne, and to Craig, "You will be at the Monomatapa? I will contact you there within the next three days."

He climbed into the army jeep that was waiting for them, nodded to his driver, and saluted them with his swagger-stick as he drove away.

"Have you got a car?" Craig asked Sally-Anne, and when she shook her head, "I can't promise to drive as well as you fly— will you take a chance?"

She had an apartment in an old block in the avenues opposite Government House. He dropped her at the entrance.

"How about dinner?" he asked.

"I've got a lot of work to do, Craig."

"Quick dinner, promise—peace offering. I'll have you home by ten." He crossed his heart theatrically, and she relented.

"Okay, seven o'clock here," she agreed, and he watched the way she climbed the steps before he started the Volkswagen. Her stride was businesslike and brisk, but her backside in the blue jeans was totally frivolous.

Sally-Anne suggested a steak-house where she was greeted like royalty by the huge, bearded proprietor, and where the beef was simply the best Craig had ever tasted, thick and juicy and tender. They drank a Cabernet from the Cape of Good Hope and from a stilted beginning their conversation eased as Craig drew her out.

"It was fine just as long as I was a mere technical assistant at Kodak, but when I started being invited on expeditions as official photographer and then giving my own exhibitions, he just couldn't take it," she told him. "First man ever to be jealous of a Nikon."

"How long were you married?"

"Two years."

"No children?"

"Thank God, no."

She ate like she walked, quickly, neatly and efficiently, yet with a sensuous streak of pleasure, and when she was finished she looked at her gold Rolex.

"You promised ten o'clock," she said and, despite his protests, scrupulously divided the bill in half and paid her share.

When he parked outside the apartment, she looked at him seriously for a moment before she asked, "Coffee?"

"With the greatest of pleasure." He started to open the door, but she stopped him.

"Right from the start, let's get it straight," she said. "The coffee

83

is instant Nescafé—and that's all. No gymnastics—nothing else, okay?"

"Okay," he agreed.

"Let's go."

Her apartment was furnished with a portable tape-recorder, canvas-covered cushions and a single camp-bed on which her sleeping-bag was neatly rolled. Apart from the cushions, the floor was bare but polished, and the walls were papered with her photographs. He wandered around studying them while she made the coffee in the kitchenette.

"If you want the bathroom, it's through there," she called. "Just be careful."

It was more dark-room than ablution, with a light-proof black nylon zip-up tent over the shower stall and jars of chemical and packets of photographic paper where in any other feminine bathroom there would have been scents and soaps.

They lolled on the cushions, drank the coffee, played Beethoven's Fifth on the tape, and talked of Africa. Once or twice she made passing reference to his book, showing that she had read it with attention.

"I've got an early start tomorrow—" At last she reached across and took the empty mug out of his hand. "Good night, Craig."

"When can I see you again?"

"I'm not sure, I'm flying up into the highlands early tomorrow. I don't know how long." Then she saw his expression and relented. "I'll call you at the Mono when I get back, if you like?"

"I like."

"Craig, I'm beginning to like you—as a friend, perhaps, but I'm not looking for romance. I'm still hurting—just as long as we understand that," she told him as they shook hands at the door of the apartment.

Despite her denial, Craig felt absurdly pleased with himself as he drove back to the Monomatapa. At this stage he did not care to analyse too deeply his feelings for her, or to define his intentions towards her. It was merely a pleasant change not to have another celebrity buff trying to add his name to her personal score-board. Her powerful physical attraction for him was made more poignant by her reluctance, and he respected her talents and accomplishments and was in total sympathy with her love of Africa and her compassion for its peoples.

"That's enough for now," he told himself as he parked the Volkswagen.

The assistant manager met him in the hotel lobby, wringing his hands with anguish, and led him through to his office.

"Mr. Mellow, I have had a visit from the police special branch while you were out. I had to open your deposit box for them and let them into your room."

"God damn it, they are not allowed to do that!" Craig was outraged.

"You don't understand, here they can do whatever they like," the assistant manager hurried on. "They removed nothing from the box, Mr. Mellow—I can assure you of that."

"Nevertheless, I'd like to check it," Craig demanded grimly.

He thumbed through his traveller's checks and they tallied. His return air-ticket was intact, as was his passport—but they had been through the "survival kit" that Henry Pickering had provided. The gilt field assessor's identification badge was loose in its leather cover.

"Who could order a search like this?" he asked the assistant manager as they relocked the box.

"Only someone pretty high up."

"Tungata Zebiwe," he thought bitterly. "You vicious, nosy bastard—how you must have changed."

•   •   •

Craig took the report of his visit to Tuti Rehabilitation Centre for Henry Pickering up to the embassy, and Morgan Oxford accepted it and offered him coffee.

"I might be here a longer time than I thought," Craig told him, "and I just can't work in an hotel room."

Morgan shrugged. "Apartments are hell to find. I'll see what I can do."

He phoned him the next day. "Craig, one of our girls is going home on a month's vacation. She is a fan of yours, and she will sublet her flat for six hundred dollars. She leaves tomorrow."

The apartment was a bed-sitter, but it was comfortable and airy. There was a broad table that would do as a writing-desk. Craig set a pile of blank Typex bond paper in the centre of it with a brick as a paperweight, his Concise Oxford Dictionary beside that and said aloud: "Back in business."

He had almost forgotten how quickly the hours could pass in never-never land, and in the deep pure joy of watching the finished sheets of paper pile up at the far end of the table.

Morgan Oxford phoned him twice during the next few days, each time to invite him to diplomatic parties, and each time Craig refused, and finally unplugged the telephone. When he relented on the fourth day and plugged the extension in again, the telephone rang almost immediately.

"Mr. Mellow"—it was an African voice—"we have had great difficulty finding you. Hold on, please, for General Fungabera."

"Craig, it's Peter." The familiar heavy accent and charm. "Can we meet this afternoon? Three o'clock? I will send a driver."

Peter Fungabera's private residence was fifteen miles out of town on the hills overlooking Lake Macillwane. The house had originally been built in the 1920s by a rich remittance man, black-sheep younger son of an English aircraft manufacturer. It was surrounded firstly by a wide veranda and white fretwork eaves and then by five acres of lawns and flowering trees.

A bodyguard of Third Brigade troopers in full battle-dress checked Craig and his driver carefully at the gate before allowing them up to the main house. When Craig climbed the front steps, Peter Fungabera was waiting for him at the top. He was dressed in white cotton slacks and a crimson short-sleeved silk shirt, which looked magnificent against his velvety black skin. With a friendly arm around Craig's shoulders, he led him down the veranda to where a small group was seated.

"Craig, may I introduce Mr. Musharewa, governor of the Land Bank of Zimbabwe. This is Mr. Kapwepwe, his assistant, and this is Mr. Cohen, my attorney. Gentlemen, this is Mr. Craig Mellow, the famous author."

They shook hands. "A drink, Craig? We are drinking Bloody Marys."

"That will do very well, Peter."

A servant in a flowing white *kanza*, reminiscent of colonial days, brought Craig his drink and, when he left, Peter Fungabera said simply, "The Land Bank of Zimbabwe has agreed to stand as your personal surety for a loan of five million dollars from the World Bank or its associate bank in New York."

Craig gaped at him.

"Your connection with the World Bank is not a particularly closely guarded secret, you know. Henry Pickering is well known to us too," Peter smiled, and went on quietly. "Of course, there are certain conditions and stipulations, but I don't think they will be prohibitive." He turned to his white attorney. "You have the documents, Izzy? Good. Will you give Mr. Mellow a copy and then read through it for us, please."

Isadore Cohen adjusted his spectacles, squared up the thick pile of documents on the table in front of him and began.

"Firstly, this is a land purchase approval," he said. "Authority for Craig Mellow, a British subject and a citizen of Zimbabwe, to purchase a controlling interest in the land-owning private company known as Rholands (Pty) Ltd. The approval is signed by the state president and countersigned by the minister of agriculture."

Craig thought of Tungata Zebiwe's promise to quash that approval and then he remembered that the minister of agriculture was Peter Fungabera's brother-in-law. He glanced across at the general, but he was listening intently to his lawyer's recitation.

As he came to each document in the pile, Isadore Cohen read through it carefully, not omitting even the preamble, and pausing at the end of each paragraph for questions and explanations.

Craig was so excited that he had difficulty sitting still and keeping his expression and voice level and businesslike. The momentary panic he had felt at Peter's sudden mention of the World Bank was forgotten and he felt like whooping and dancing up and down the veranda: Rholands was his, King's Lynn was his, Queen's Lynn was his, and Zambezi Waters would be his.

Even in his excitement there was one paragraph that rang with a hollow note when Isadore Cohen read it out.

"What the hell does that mean—*'enemy of the state and the people of Zimbabwe'*?" he demanded.

"It's a standard clause in all our documentation," Isadore Cohen placated him, "merely an expression of patriotic sentiment. The Land Bank is a government institution. If the borrower were to engage in treasonable activity and was declared an enemy of the state and people, the Land Bank would be obliged to repudiate all its obligations to the guilty party."

"Is that legal?" Craig was dubious, and when the lawyer reassured him, he went on, "Do you think the lending bank will accept that?"

"They have done so already on other contracts of surety," the bank governor told him. "As Mr. Cohen says, it's a standard clause."

Peter Fungabera smiled. "After all, Craig, you aren't intending to lead an armed revolution to overthrow our government, are you?"

Craig returned his smile weakly. "Well, okay, if the American lending bank will accept that, then I suppose it must be kosher."

The reading took almost an hour, and then Governor Musharewa signed all the copies, and both his assistant and Peter Fungabera witnessed his signature. Then it was Craig's turn to sign and again the witnesses followed him, and finally Isadore Cohen impressed his seal of Commissioner of Oaths on each document.

"That's it, gentlemen. Signed, sealed and delivered."

"It only remains to see if Henry Pickering will be satisfied."

"Oh, did I forget to mention it?" Peter Fungabera grinned wickedly. "Governor Musharewa spoke to Pickering yesterday afternoon, ten a.m. New York time. The money will be available to you just as soon as the surety is in his hands." He nodded to the hovering house servant. "Now you can bring the champagne."

They toasted each other, the Land Bank, the World Bank, and Rholands Company, and only when the second bottle was empty did the two black bankers take reluctant leave.

As their limousine went down the drive, Peter Fungabera took Craig's arm. "And now we can discuss my raising fee. Mr. Cohen has the papers."

Craig read them, and felt the blood drain from his face. "Ten per cent," he gasped. "Ten per cent of the paid-up shares of Rholands."

Peter Fungabera frowned. "We really must change that name. As you see, Mr. Cohen will hold the shares as my nominee. It might save embarrassment later."

Craig pretended to reread the contract while he tried to muster a protest. The two men watched him in silence. Ten per cent was robbery, but where else could Craig go?

Isadore Cohen slowly unscrewed the cap of his pen and handed it to Craig.

"I think you will find a cabinet minister and an army commander a most useful sleeping partner in this enterprise," he said, and Craig accepted the pen.

"There is only one copy." Craig still hesitated.

"We only need one copy"—Peter was still smiling—"and I will keep it."

Craig nodded.

There would be no proof of the transaction, shares held by a nominee, no documentation except in Peter Fungabera's hands. In a dispute it would be Craig's word against that of a senior minister—but he wanted Rholands. More than anything in his life, Craig wanted Rholands.

He dashed his signature across the foot of the contract and on the other side of the table the two men relaxed visibly and Peter Fungabera called for a third bottle of champagne.

• • •

Up to now, Craig had needed only a pen and a pile of paper, and time had been his to squander or use as the fancy led him.

Suddenly he was faced with the enormous responsibility of ownership, and time telescoped in upon him. There was so much to do and so little time to do it that he felt crippled with indecision, appalled by his own audacity, and despairing of his own organizational skills.

He wanted comfort and encouragement, and he thought immediately of Sally-Anne. He drove round to her apartment, but the windows were closed, the mail overflowed her box, and there was no answer to his knock.

He returned to the bed-sitter, sat at his table and pulled a blank sheet from the pile and headed it, "Work to be done," and stared at it.

He remembered what a girl had once said of him: "You have only done one thing well in your life." And writing a book was a far cry from getting a multimillion-dollar ranching company back on its feet. He felt panic rising within him and crushed it back. His was a ranching family—he had been raised with the ammoniacal smell of cow dung in his nostrils, and had learned to judge beef on the hoof when he was small enough to perch up on Bawu's saddle-pommel like a sparrow on a fence pole.

"I can do it," he told himself fiercely, and began to work on his list. He wrote:

1) Ring Jock Daniels. Accept offer to purchase Rholands.
2) Fly to New York.
   a) World Bank meeting.
   b) Open checking account and deposit funds.
   c) Sell *Bawu*.
3) Fly Zürich.
   a) Sign share purchase.
   b) Arrange payment to sellers.

His panic began to subside. He picked up the telephone and dialled British Airways. They could get him out on the Friday flight to London, and then Concorde to New York.

He caught Jock Daniels in his office. "Where the hell you been?" He could hear Jock had made a good start on the evening's drinking.

"Jock, congratulations—you have just made yourself twenty-five grand commission," Craig told him and enjoyed the silence.

Craig's list began to stretch out, ran into a dozen pages:

39) Find out if Okky van Rensburg is still in the country.

Okky had been the mechanic on King's Lynn for twenty years. Craig's grandfather had boasted that Okky could strip down a John Deere tractor and build up a Cadillac and two Rolls-Royce Silver Clouds from the spare parts. Craig needed him.

Craig laid down his pen and smiled at his memory of the old man. "We are coming home, Bawu," he said aloud. He looked at his watch and it was ten o'clock, but he knew he would not be able to sleep.

He put on a light sweater and went out to walk the night streets, and an hour later he was standing outside Sally-Anne's apartment. His feet had made their own way, it seemed.

He felt a little tingle of excitement. Her window was open and her light burning.

"Who is it?" Her voice was muffled.

"It's me, Craig." There was a long silence.

"It's nearly midnight."

"It's only just eleven—and I have something to tell you."

"Oh, okay—door is unlocked."

She was in her dark-room. He could hear the splash of chemicals.

"I'll be five minutes," she called. "Do you know how to make coffee?"

When she came out, she was dressed in a sloppy cable-knit jersey that hung to her knees and her hair was loose on her shoulders. He had never seen it like that, and he stared.

"This had better be good," she warned him, fists on her hips.

"I've got Rholands," he said, and it was her turn to stare.

"Who or what is Rholands?"

"The company that owns Zambezi Waters. I own it. It's mine. Zambezi Waters is mine. Is that good enough?"

She started to come to him, her arms rising to embrace him, and he mirrored the movement, and instantly she caught herself and stopped, forcing him to do the same. They were two paces apart.

"That's marvellous news, Craig. I am so happy for you. How did it happen? I thought it was all off."

"Peter Fungabera arranged a surety for a loan of five million dollars."

"My God. Five million. You're borrowing five million? How much is the interest on five million?"

He had not wanted to think about that. It showed on his face, and she was immediately contrite.

"I'm sorry. That was insolent. I'm truly happy for you. We must celebrate—" Quickly she moved away from him.

In the cabinet in the kitchenette, she found a bottle of Glenlivet whisky with a few inches left in the bottom and added it to the steaming coffee.

She saluted him with the mug. "Here's success to Zambezi Waters. Now, first tell me all about it—and then I've got news for you also."

Until after midnight he elaborated his plans for her: the development of the twin ranches in the south, the rebuilding of the homestead and the restocking with blood cattle, but mostly he dwelt upon his plans for Zambezi Waters and its wildlife, knowing that this was where her interest would centre.

"I was thinking—I'd need a woman's touch in planning and laying out the camps, not just any woman, but one with an artistic flair and a knowledge and love of the African bush."

"Craig, if that is meant to describe me, I'm on a grant from the World Wildlife Trust, and I owe them all my time."

"It wouldn't take up much time," he protested, "just a consultancy. You could fly up for a day whenever you could fit it in." He saw her weaken. "And then, of course, once the camps were running, I'd want you to give a series of lectures and slide-shows of your photographs for the guests—" and he saw that he had touched the right key. Like any artist, she relished an opportunity to exhibit her work.

"I'm not making any promises," she told him sternly, but they both knew she would do it, and Craig felt his new burden of responsibility lighten appreciably.

"You said you had news for me," he reminded her at last, grateful for the chance to draw the evening out further. But he was not prepared for her sudden change to deadly seriousness.

"Yes, I've got news." She paused, seemed to gather herself, and then went on, "I have picked up the spoor of the master poacher."

"My God! The bastard who wiped out those herds of jumbo? That is real news. Where? How?"

"You know that I've been up in the eastern highlands for the last ten days. What I didn't tell you is that I am running a leopard study in the mountains for the Wildlife Trust. I have people working for me in most of the leopardy areas of the forest. We are counting and mapping the territories of the cats, recording their litters and kills, trying to estimate the effect of the new human influx on them—all that sort of thing—which brings me to one of my men. He is a marvellously smelly old Shangane poacher, he must be eighty years old and his youngest wife is seventeen and presented him with twins last week. He is a complete rogue, with a tremendous sense of humour, and a taste for Scotch whisky— two tots and he gets talkative. We were up in the Vumba mountains, just the two of us in camp, and after the second tot he let it slip that he had been offered two hundred dollars a leopard-skin. They would take as many as he could catch, and they would supply the steel spring traps. I gave him another tot and learned that the offer had come from a very well-dressed young black, driving a government Land-Rover. My old Shangane told the man he was afraid that he would be arrested and sent to jail, but he was assured that he would be safe—that he would be under the protection of one of the great chiefs in Harare, a comrade minister who had been a famous warrior in the bush war and who still commanded his own private army."

There was a hard cardboard folder on the camp-bed. Sally-Anne fetched it and placed it in Craig's lap. Craig opened it. The top sheet was a full list of the Zimbabwe cabinet. Twenty-six names, each with the portfolio set out beside it.

"We can narrow that down immediately—very few of the cabinet did any actual fighting," Sally-Anne pointed out. "Most of them spent the war in a suite at the Ritz in London or in a guest dacha on the Caspian Sea."

She sat down on the cushion beside Craig, reached across and turned to the second sheet.

"Six names." She pointed. "Six field commanders."

"Still too many," Craig murmured, and saw that Peter Fungabera's name headed the six.

"We can do better," Sally-Anne agreed. "A private army. That must mean dissidents. The dissidents are all Matabele. Their leader would have to be of the same tribe."

She turned to the third sheet. On it was a single name.

"One of the most successful field commanders. Matabele. Minister of tourism, and the Wildlife Department comes under him. It's an old chestnut, but those set to guard a treasure are too often those who loot it. It all fits."

Craig read the name aloud softly, "Tungata Zebiwe," and found that he didn't want it to be true. "But he was with me in the Game Department, he was my ranger—"

"As I said, the keepers have more opportunity to despoil than any other."

"But what would Sam do with the money? The master poacher must be coining millions of dollars. Sam lives a very frugal life, everybody knows that, no big house, no expensive cars, no gifts for women nor privately owned land—no other expensive indulgences."

"Except, perhaps, the most expensive of all," Sally-Anne demurred quietly. "Power."

Craig's further protestation died unuttered, and she nodded. "Power. Don't you see it, Craig? Running a private army of dissidents takes money, big, big money."

Slowly the pattern was shaking itself into place, Craig admitted. Henry Pickering had warned him of an approaching Soviet-backed coup. The Russians had supported the Matabele ZIPRA faction during the war, so their candidate would almost certainly be Matabele.

Still Craig resisted it, clinging to his memories of the man who had been his friend, probably the finest friend of his entire lifetime. He remembered the essential decency of the man he had then known as Samson Kumalo, the mission-educated Christian of integrity and high principles, who had resigned with Craig from the Game Department when they suspected their immediate superior of being involved in a poaching ring. Was he now the master poacher himself? The man of fine compassion who had helped

93

Craig when he was crippled and broken to take his single possession, his yacht, with him when he left Africa. Was he now the power-hungry plotter?

"He is my friend," Craig said.

"He was. But he has changed. When last you saw him, he declared himself your enemy," Sally-Anne pointed out. "You told me that yourself."

Craig suddenly remembered the search of his deposit box at the hotel by the police on high orders. Tungata must have suspected that Craig was an agent of the World Bank, would have guessed that he had been detailed to gather information on poaching and power-plotting—all that could have accounted for his unaccountably violent opposition to Craig's plans.

"I hate it," Craig muttered. "I hate the idea like hell, but I think that you just may be right."

"I am sure of it."

"What are you going to do?"

"I'm going to Peter Fungabera with what evidence I have."

"He will smash Sam," Craig said, and she came back quickly, "Tungata is evil, Craig, a despoiler!"

"He is my friend."

"He *was* your friend," Sally-Anne contradicted him again. "You don't know what he has become—you don't know what happened to him in the bush. War can change any human being. Power can change him even more radically."

"Oh God, I hate it."

"Come with me to Peter Fungabera. Be there when I put the case against Tungata Zebiwe." Sally-Anne took his hand, a small gesture of comfort.

Craig did not make the mistake of returning her grip.

"I'm sorry, Craig." She squeezed his fingers. "I truly am," she said, and then she took her hand away.

* * *

Peter Fungabera made time for them in the early morning, and they drove out together to his home in the hills.

A servant showed them through to the general's office, a huge, sparsely furnished room that overlooked the lake and had once been the billiard room. One wall was covered with a blown-up map of the entire territory. It was flagged with multicoloured markers. There was a long table under the windows, covered with reports and dispatches and parliamentary papers, and a desk of red African teak in the centre of the uncarpeted stone floor.

Peter Fungabera rose from the desk to greet them. He was barefooted, and dressed in a simple white loincloth tied at the hip. The bare skin of his chest and arms glowed as though it had been freshly oiled, and the muscles moved beneath it like a sackful of living cobras. Clearly Peter Fungabera kept himself in a warrior's peak of fighting condition.

He smiled as he came to greet them. "Excuse my undress, but I really am more at ease when I can be completely African."

There were low stools of intricate carved ebony set in front of the desk.

"I will have chairs brought," Peter offered. "I have few white visitors here."

"No, no." Sally-Anne settled easily on one of the stools.

"You know I am always pleased to see you, but I am due in the House at ten hundred hours."

"I'll come to it without wasting time," Sally-Anne agreed. "We think we know who the master poacher is."

Peter had been about to seat himself at the desk, but now he leaned forward with his fists on the desk-top, and his gaze was sharp and demanding.

"You said I had only to give you the name and you would smash him," Sally-Anne reminded him, and Peter nodded.

"Give it to me," he ordered, but Sally-Anne related her sources and her deductions, just as she had to Craig. Peter Fungabera heard her out in silence, frowning or nodding thoughtfully as he followed her reasoning. Then she gave her conclusion, the last name left on her list.

"Comrade Minister Tungata Zebiwe," Peter Fungabera repeated softly after her, and at last he sank back onto his own chair and picked up his leather-covered swagger-stick from the desk. He stared over Sally-Anne's head at the map-covered wall, slapping the baton into the rosy pink palm of his left hand.

The silence drew out until Sally-Anne had to ask, "Well?"

Peter Fungabera dropped his gaze to her face again.

"You have chosen the hottest coal in the fire for me to pick up in my bare hands," he said. "Are you sure that you have not been influenced by Comrade Zebiwe's treatment of Mr. Mellow?"

95

"That is unworthy," Sally-Anne told him softly.

"Yes, I suppose it is." Peter Fungabera looked at Craig.

"What do you think?"

"He was my friend, and he has done me great kindness."

"That was once upon a time," Peter pointed out. "Now he has declared himself your enemy."

"Still I like and admire him."

"And yet—?" Peter prodded gently.

"And yet, I believe Sally-Anne may be on the right spoor," Craig conceded unhappily.

Peter Fungabera stood up and crossed the floor silently to stand before the vast wall-map.

"The whole country is a tinder-box," he said, staring at the coloured flags. "The Matabele are on the point of a rebellion. Here! Here! Here! Their guerrillas are gathering in the bush." He tapped the map. "We have been forced to nip the plotting of their more irresponsible leaders who were moving towards armed revolt. Nkomo is in forced retirement, two of the Matabele cabinet members have been arrested and charged with high treason. Tungata Zebiwe is the only Matabele still in the cabinet. He commands enormous respect, even outside his own tribe, while the Matabele look upon him as their only remaining leader. If we were to touch him—"

"You are going to let him go!" Sally-Anne said hopelessly. "He will get away with it. So much for your socialist paradise. One law for the people, another for the—"

"Be silent, woman," Peter Fungabera ordered, and she obeyed.

He returned to his desk. "I was explaining to you the consequences of hasty action. Arresting Tungata Zebiwe could plunge the entire country into bloody civil war. I didn't say that I would not take action, but I certainly would do nothing without proof positive, and the testimony of independent witnesses of impeccable impartiality to support my actions." He was still staring at the map across the room. "Already the world accuses us of planning tribal genocide against the Matabele, while all we are doing is maintaining the rule of law, and searching for a formula of accommodation with that warlike, intractable tribe. At the moment Tungata Zebiwe is our only reasonable and conciliatory contact with the Matabele. We cannot afford to destroy him lightly." He paused, and Sally-Anne broke her silence.

"One thing I have not mentioned, but which Craig and I have discussed. If Tungata Zebiwe is the poacher, then he is using the profits to some special end. He gives no visible evidence of extravagance, but we know there is a connection between him and dissidents."

Peter Fungabera's expression had set hard, and his eyes were terrible. "If it's Zebiwe, I'll have him," he promised himself more than her. "But when I do, I'll have proof for the world to see—and he will not escape me."

"Then you had best move pretty damned quickly," Sally-Anne advised.

•   •   •

"Well, you've picked a good time to sell." The yacht broker stood in *Bawu*'s cockpit and looked nautical in his double-breasted blazer and marine cap with golden anchor device—seven hundred dollars from Bergdorf Goodman. His tan was even and perfect—sun-lamp at the New York Athletic Club. There was a fine web of wrinkles around his piercing blue eyes—not from squinting through a sextant or from tropical suns on far oceans and coral beaches, Craig was certain, but from perusing price-tags and check figures.

"Interest rates are down—people are buying yachts again."

For Craig, it was like discussing the terms of a divorce with a lawyer, or the arrangements with a funeral director. *Bawu* had been part of his life for too long.

"She is in good nick, all tight and shipshape, and your price is sensible. I'll bring some people to see her tomorrow."

"Just make sure I'm not here," Craig warned him.

"I understand, Mr. Mellow." The man could even sound like an undertaker.

•   •   •

Ashe Levy also sounded like an undertaker when Craig telephoned. However, he sent an office messenger down to the marina to collect the first three chapters Craig had completed in Africa. Then Craig went to lunch with Henry Pickering.

"It really is good to see you." Craig had forgotten how much he had grown to like this man in just two short meetings.

"Let's order first," Henry suggested, and decided on a bottle of the Grands-Echézeaux.

Craig smiled. "Courageous fellow. I am always too afraid to pronounce it in case they think I am having a sneezing fit."

"Most people have the same reluctance. Must be why it is the least known of the world's truly great wines. Keeps the price down, thank God."

Appreciatively they nosed the wine and gave it the attention it deserved. Then Henry set his glass down.

"Now tell me what you think of General Peter Fungabera," he invited.

"It's all in my reports. Didn't you read them?"

"I read them, but tell me just the same. Sometimes a little thing may come out in conversation that just didn't get into a report."

"Peter Fungabera is a cultivated man. His English is remarkable—his choice of words, his powers of expression—but it all has a strong African accent. In uniform he looks like a general officer in the British Army. In casual clothes he looks like the star of a TV series, but in a loincloth he looks what he really is, an African. That's what we tend to forget with all of them. We all know about Chinese inscrutability, and British phlegm, but we seldom consider that the black African has a special nature—"

"There!" Henry Pickering murmured smugly. "That wasn't in your reports. Go on, Craig."

"We think them slow-moving by our own bustling standards, and we do not realize that it is not indolence but the deep consideration they bring to any subject before acting. We consider them simple and direct—when really they are the most secretive and convoluted people, more tribally clannish than any Scot. They can maintain a blood fued over a hundred years, like any Sicilian—"

Henry Pickering listened intently, prodding him with a leading question only when he slowed. Once he asked, "Something that I still find a little confusing, Craig—the subtle difference between the terms Matabele, Ndebele and Sindebele. Can you explain?"

"A Frenchman calls himself a Français, but we call him a Frenchman. A Matabele calls himself an Ndebele, but we call him a Matabele."

"Ah." Henry nodded. "And the language he speaks is Sindebele, isn't it?"

"That's right. Actually the word Matabele seems to have acquired colonial connotations since independence—"

Their talk ranged on easily, relaxed and free-flowing, so that it was with surprise that Craig realized that they were almost the last party left in the restaurant and that the waiter was hovering with the bill.

"What I was trying to say," Craig concluded, "is that colonialism has left Africa with a set of superimposed values. Africa will reject them and go back to its own—"

"And probably be the happier for it," Henry Pickering finished for him. "Well, Craig, you have certainly earned your wage. I'm truly pleased that you are going back. I can see that you will soon be our most productive field agent in that theatre. When do you return?"

"I only came to New York to pick up a check."

Henry Pickering laughed that delightful purring laugh of his. "You hint with a sledge-hammer—I shudder at the prospect of a direct demand from you." He paid the bill and stood up. "Our house lawyer is waiting. First you sign away your body and soul and then I give you drawing rights up to the total of five million dollars."

The interior of the limousine was silent and cool, and the suspension ironed out most of the trauma of the New York street surfaces.

"Now enlarge on Sally-Anne Jay's conclusions regarding the head of the poaching ring," Henry invited.

"At this stage, I don't see any alternative candidate for the master poacher, perhaps even the leader of the dissidents."

Henry was silent for a moment. Then he said, "What do you make of General Fungabera's reluctance to act?"

"He is a prudent man, and an African. He will not rush in. He will think it out deeply, lay his net with care, but when he does act, I think we will all be surprised at how devastatingly swift and decisive it will be."

"I would like you to give General Fungabera all the assistance you can. Full co-operation, please, Craig."

"You know Tungata was my friend."

"Divided loyalty?"

"I don't think so, not if he is guilty."

"Good! My board is very happy with your achievements so far. I am authorized to increase your remuneration to sixty thousand dollars per annum."

Craig grinned at him. "Lovely. That will be a big help on the interest payment on five million dollars."

•   •   •

It was still light when the cab dropped Craig at the gates of the marina. The smog of Manhattan was transformed by the low angle of the sun to a lovely purple mist which softened the grim silhouettes of the great towers of concrete.

As Craig stepped on the gangplank, the yacht dipped slightly under his weight, and alerted the figure in the cockpit.

"Ashe!" Craig was taken by surprise. "Ashe Levy, the fairy princess of struggling authors."

"Baby." Ashe came down the deck to him with a landlubber's uncertain steps. "I couldn't wait, I had to come to you right away."

"I am touched." Craig's tone was acid yellow. "Always when I don't need help you come at a gallop."

Ashe Levy ignored it and put a hand on each of Craig's shoulders. "I read it. I read it again—and then I locked it in my safe." His voice sank. "It's beautiful."

Craig checked his next jibe and searched Ashe Levy's face for signs of insincerity. Instead he realized that, behind the gold-rimmed spectacles, Ashe Levy's eyes were steely with tears of emotion.

"It's the best stuff that you have ever done, Craig."

"It's only three chapters."

"It hit me right in my gut."

"It needs a lot of polishing."

"I doubted you, Craig. I'll admit that. I was beginning to believe that you didn't have another book in you, but this—it was just too much to take in. I've been sitting here for the last few hours going over it in my mind, and I find I can recite parts of it by heart."

Craig studied him carefully. The tears might be a reflection of the sunset off the water. Ashe removed his spectacles and blew his nose loudly. The tears were genuine, yet Craig could still scarcely believe them. There was only one positive test.

"Can you advance on it, Ashe?"

Now he didn't need money, but he needed the ultimate reassurance.

"How much do you need, Craig? Two hundred grand?"

"You really like it, then?" Craig let go a small sigh, as the writer's eternal doubts were dispelled for a brief blessed period. "Let's have a drink, Ashe."

"Let's do better than that," said Ashe. "Let's get drunk."

Craig sat in the stern with his feet up on the rudder-post, watching the dew form little diamonds on the glass in his hand, and no longer really listening to Ashe Levy's enthusiasms about the book. Instead he let his mind out to roam, and thought that it would be best not to have all one's good fortunes at the same time. But to spread them out and savour each more fully.

He was inundated with delights. He thought about King's Lynn and in his nostrils lingered the odour of the loams of the Matabele grassland. He thought about Zambezi Waters and heard again the rush of a great body in the thorn brush. He thought about the twenty chapters which would follow the first three, and his trigger finger itched with anticipation. Was it possible, he wondered, that he might be the happiest man in the world at that moment?

Then abruptly he realized that the full appreciation of happiness can only be achieved by sharing it with another—and he found a small empty space down deep inside him, and a shadow of melancholy as he remembered strangely flecked eyes and a firm young mouth. He wanted to tell her about it, he wanted her to read those three chapters, and suddenly he longed with all his soul to be back in Africa where Sally-Anne Jay was.

•　•　•

Craig found a second-hand Land-Rover in Jock Daniels' used car lot. He closed his ears to Jock's impassioned sales *spiel* and listened instead to the motor. The timing was off, but there was no knocking or slapping. The front-wheel transmission engaged smoothly, the clutch held against the brakes. When he gave it a run in an area of erosion and steep dongas on the outskirts of town, the silencer box fell off, but the rest held together. At one time he had been able to take his other old Land-Rover down into its separate parts and reassemble it over a weekend. He knew he could save this one. He beat Jock down a thousand dollars and still grossly overpaid, but he was in a hurry.

Into the Land-Rover he loaded everything he had saved from the sale of the yacht: a suitcase full of clothing, a dozen of his favourite books and a leather trunk with brass bindings, his heaviest piece of luggage, which contained the family journals.

These journals were his entire inheritance, all that Bawu had left him. The rest of the old man's multimillion-dollar estate, including the Rholands shares, had gone to his eldest son, Douglas, Craig's uncle, who had sold out and cut for Australia. Yet those battered old leatherbound, handwritten texts had been the greater treasure. Reading them had given Craig a sense of history and a pride in his ancestral line, which had armed him with sufficient confidence and understanding of period to sit down and write the book, which had in turn brought him all this: achievement, fame and fortune. Even Rholands itself had come back to him through that box of old papers.

He wondered how many thousands of times he had driven the road out to King's Lynn—but never like this, never as the *patron*. He stopped just short of the main gate so that his feet could touch his own earth for the first time.

He stood upon it and looked around him at the golden grassland and the open groves of flat-topped acacia trees, at the lines of blue-grey hills in the distance and the unblemished blue bowl of sky over it all, then he knelt like a religious supplicant. It was the only movement in which the leg still hampered him a little. He scooped up the earth in his cupped hands. It was almost as rich and as red as the beef that it would grow. By eye he divided the handful into two parts and let a tenth part spill back to earth.

"That's your ten per cent, Peter Fungabera," he whispered to himself, "but this is mine—and I swear to hold it for all my lifetime and to protect and cherish it, so help me God."

Feeling only a little foolish at his own theatrics, he let the earth fall, dusted his hands on the seat of his pants and went back to the Land-Rover.

On the foothills before the homestead he met a tall lanky figure coming down the road. The man wore an oily unwashed blanket over his back and a brief loincloth; over his shoulder he carried his fighting-sticks. His feet were thrust into sandals cut from old car tyres, and his earrings were plastic stoppers from acid jars embellished with coloured beads that expanded his earlobes to three times normal size. He drove before him a small herd of multicoloured goats.

"I see you, elder brother," Craig greeted him, and the old man exposed the gap in his yellow teeth as he grinned at the courtesy of the greeting and his recognition of Craig.

"I see you, Nkosi." He was the same old man whom Craig had found squatting in the outbuildings of King's Lynn.

"When will it rain?" Craig asked him and handed him a packet of cigarettes that he had brought for precisely such a meeting.

They fell into the leisurely question-and-answer routine that in Africa must precede any serious discussions.

"What is your name, old man?"—a term of respect rather than an accusation of senility.

"I am called Shadrach."

"Tell me, Shadrach, are your goats for sale?" Craig could at last ask without being thought callow, and immediately a craftiness came into Shadrach's eyes.

"They are beautiful goats," he said. "To part with them would be like parting with my own children."

Shadrach was the acknowledged spokesman and leader of the little community of squatters who had taken up residence on King's Lynn. Through him, Craig found he could negotiate with all of them, and he was relieved. It would save days and a great deal of emotional wear and tear.

He would not, however, deprive Shadrach of an opportunity to show off his bargaining skill, nor insult him by trying to hasten the proceedings, so these were extended over the next two days while Craig reroofed the old guest cottage with a sheet of heavy canvas, replaced the looted pump with a Lister diesel to raise water from the borehole and set up his new camp-bed in the bare bedroom of the cottage.

On the third day the sale price was agreed and Craig found himself the owner of almost two thousand goats. He paid off the sellers in cash, counting each note and coin into their hands to forestall argument, and then loaded his bleating acquisitions into four hired trucks and sent them into the Bulawayo abattoirs, flooding the market in the process and dropping the going price by fifty percent for a net loss on the entire transaction of a little over ten thousand dollars.

"Great start in business," he grinned, and sent for Shadrach.

"Tell me, old man, what do you know about cattle?"—which was rather like asking a Polynesian what he knew about fish, or a Swiss if he had ever seen snow.

Shadrach drew himself up in indignation. "When I was this high," he said stiffly, indicating an area below his right knee, "I squirted milk hot from the cow's teat into my own mouth. At this height," he moved up to the kneecap, "I had two hundred head in my sole charge. I freed the calves with these hands when they

103

stuck in their mothers' wombs; I carried them on these shoulders when the ford was flooded. At this height"—two inches above the knee—"I killed a lioness, stabbing her with my assegai when she attacked my herd—"

Patiently Craig heard out the tale as it rose in small increments to shoulder height and Shadrach ended, "And you dare to ask me what I know about cattle!"

"Soon on this grass I will graze cows so sleek and beautiful that to look upon them will dim your eyes with tears. I will have bulls whose coats shine like water in the sun, whose humps rise like great mountains on their backs and whose dewlaps, heavy with fat, sweep the earth when they walk as the rain-winds sweep the dust from the drought-stricken land."

"Hau!" said Shadrach, an expletive of utter astonishment, impressed as much by Craig's lyricism as by his declaration of intention.

"I need a man who understands cattle—and men," Craig told him.

Shadrach found him the men. From the squatter families he chose twenty, all of them strong and willing, not too young to be silly and flighty, not too old to be frail.

"The others," said Shadrach contemptuously, "are the products of the unions of baboons and thieving Mashona cattle-rustlers. I have ordered them off our land."

Craig smiled at the possessive plural, but he was impressed with the fact that when Shadrach ordered, men obeyed.

Shadrach assembled his recruits in front of the rudely refurbished cottage and gave them a traditional *giya*, the blood-rousing speech and mime with which the old Matabele indunas primed their warriors on the eve of battle.

"You know me!" he shouted. "You know that my great-great-grandmother was the daughter of the old king, Lobengula, 'the one who drives like the wind.'"

"Eh—he!" They began to enter into the spirit of the occasion.

"You know that I am a prince of the royal blood, and in a proper world I would rightfully be an induna of one thousand, with widow-bird feathers in my hair and oxtails on my war shield." He stabbed at the air with his fighting-sticks.

"Eh—he!" Watching their expressions, Craig saw the real respect in which they held the old man, and he was delighted with his choice.

"Now!" Shadrach chanted. "Because of the wisdom and far-sightedness of the young Nkosi here, I am indeed become an induna. I am the induna of King's Lynn," he pronounced it "Kingi Lingi," "and you are my *amadoda*, my chosen warriors."

"Eh—he!" they agreed and stamped their bare feet on the earth with a cannon-fire clap.

"Now, look upon this white man. You might think him young and unbearded—but know you, that he is the grandson of Bawu and the great-grandson of Taka-Taka."

"Hau!" gasped Shadrach's warriors, for those were names to conjure with. Bawu they had known in the flesh, Sir Ralph Ballantyne only as a legend. Taka-Taka was the onomatopoeic name the Matabele had given Sir Ralph from the sound of the Maxim machine-gun which the old freebooter had wielded to such effect during the Matabele war and the rebellion.

They looked upon Craig with new eyes.

"Yes," Shadrach urged them, "look at him. He is a warrior who carried terrible scars from the bush war. He killed hundreds of the cowardly, women-raping Mashona"—Craig blinked at the poetic licence Shadrach had taken unto himself—"he even killed a few of the brave lion-hearted Matabele ZIPRA fighters. So you know him now as a man—not a boy."

"Eh—he!" They showed no rancour at Craig's purported bag of their brethren.

"Know also that he comes to turn you from goat-keeping women, sitting in the sun scratching your fleas, into proud cattle-men once more, for"—Shadrach paused for dramatic effect—"soon on this grass will graze cows so sleek and beautiful that to look upon them—"

Craig noted that Shadrach could repeat his own words perfectly, displaying the remarkable memory of the illiterate. When he ended with a high storklike leap in the air and a clatter of his fighting-sticks, they applauded him wildly and then looked to Craig expectantly.

"One hell of an act to follow," Craig told himself as he stood before them. He spoke quietly, in low, musical Sindebele.

"The cattle will be here soon, and there is much work to be done before they arrive. You know about the wage that the government has decreed for farm-workers. That I will pay, and food rations for each of you and your families." This was received without any great show of enthusiasm. "And in addition," Craig paused, "for each year of service completed, you will be given a fine young cow and the right to graze her upon the grass of Kingi-Lingi, the right also to put her to my great bulls so that she might bear you beautiful calves—"

"Eh—he!" they shouted, and stamped with joy, and at last Craig held up both hands.

"There might be some among you who will be tempted to lift that which belongs to me, or who will find a shady tree under which to spend the day instead of stringing fencing-wire or herding the cattle." He glared at them, so they quailed a little. "Now this wise government forbids a man to kick another with his foot—but be warned, I can kick you without using my own foot."

He stooped and in one deft movement plucked off his leg and stood before them with it in his hand. They gaped in amazement.

"See, this is not my own foot!" Their expressions began to turn sickly, as though they were in the presence of terrible witchcraft. They began to shuffle nervously and look around for escape.

"So," Craig shouted, "without breaking the law, I can kick whom I wish." Making two swift hops, he used the momentum to swing the toe of the boot of his disembodied leg into the backside of the nearest warrior.

For a moment longer the stunned silence persisted, and then they were overwhelmed by their own sense of the ridiculous. They laughed until their cheeks were streaked with tears. They staggered in circles beating their own heads, they hugged each other, heaving and gasping with laughter. They surrounded the unfortunate whose backside had been the butt of Craig's joke, and abused him further, prodding him and shrieking with laughter. Shadrach, all princely dignity discarded, collapsed in the dust and wriggled helplessly as wave after wave of mirth overcame him.

Craig watched them fondly. Already they were his people, his special charges. Certainly, there would be rotters among them. He would have to weed them out. Certainly, even the good ones would at times deliberately test his vigilance and his forbearance, as was the African way, but in time also they would become a close-knit family and he knew that he would come to love them.

•   •   •

The fences were the first priority. They had fallen into a state of total disrepair. There were miles of barbed-wire missing, almost certainly stolen. When Craig tried to replace it, he realized why.

106

There was none for sale in Matabeleland. No import permits had been issued that quarter for barbed-wire.

"Welcome to the special joy of farming in black Zimbabwe," the manager of the Farmers Co-operative Society in Bulawayo told him. "Somebody wangled an import permit for a million dollars' worth of candy and milk chocolate, but there was none for barbed-wire."

"For God's sake"—Craig was desperate—"I've got to have fencing. I can't run stock without it. When will you receive a consignment?"

"That rests with some little clerk in the Department of Commerce in Harare." The manager shrugged, and Craig turned sadly back to the Land-Rover, when suddenly an idea came to him.

"May I use your telephone?" he asked the manager.

He dialled the private number that Peter Fungabera had given him, and after he had identified himself, a secretary put him straight through.

"Peter, we've got a big problem."

"How can I help you?"

Craig told him, and Peter murmured to himself as he made notes. "How much do you need?"

"At least twelve hundred bales."

"Is there anything else?"

"Not at the moment—oh yes, sorry to bother you, Peter, but I've been trying to find Sally-Anne. She doesn't answer the telephone or reply to telegrams."

"Phone me back in ten minutes," Peter Fungabera ordered, and when Craig did so, he told him, "Sally-Anne is out of the country. Apparently she flew up to Kenya in the Cessna. She is at a place called Kitchwa Tembu on the Masai Mara."

"Do you know when she will be back?"

"No, but as soon as she re-enters the country again I'll let you know."

Craig was impressed at the reach of Peter Fungabera's arm, that he could follow a person's movements even outside Zimbabwe. Obviously, Sally-Anne was on some list for special attention, and the thought struck him that he himself was probably on that very same list.

Of course, he knew why Sally-Anne was at Kitchwa Tembu. Two years previously Craig had visited that marvelous safari camp on the Mara plains at the invitation of the owners, Geoff and Jorie

107

Kent. This was the season when the vast herds of buffalo around the camp would start dropping their calves, and the battles between the protective cows and the lurking packs of predators intent on devouring the new-born calves provided one of the great spectacles of the African veld. Sally-Anne would be there with her Nikon.

On his way back to King's Lynn, he stopped at the post office and sent her a telegram through Abercrombie and Kent's office in Nairobi: "Bring me back some tips for Zambezi Waters. Stop. Is the hunt still on. Query. Best, Craig."

Three days later a convoy of trucks ground up the hills of King's Lynn and a platoon of Third Brigade troopers off-loaded twelve hundred bales of barbed-wire into the roofless tractor sheds.

"Is there an invoice to pay?" Craig asked the sergeant in charge of the detail. "Or any papers to sign?"

"I do not know," he answered. "I know only I was ordered to bring these things—and I have done so."

Craig watched the empty trucks roar away down the hill, and there was an indigestible lump in his stomach. He suspected that there would never be an invoice. He knew also that this was Africa, and he did not like to contemplate the consequences of alienating Peter Fungabera.

For five days he worked with his Matabele fencing gangs, bared to the waist, with heavy leather gloves protecting his hands. He flung his weight on the wire-strainers and sang the work chants with his men, but all that time the lump of conscience was heavy in his belly, and he could not suffer it longer.

There was still no telephone on the estate, so he drove into Bulawayo. He reached Peter at the Houses of Parliament.

"My dear Craig, you really are making a fuss about nothing. The quartermaster general has not yet invoiced the wire to me. But if it makes you feel better, then send me a check and I will see that the business is settled immediately. Oh, Craig, make the check payable 'Cash,' will you?"

• • •

Over the next few weeks, Craig discovered in himself the capacity to live on much less sleep than he had ever believed possible. He was up each morning at four-thirty and chivvied his Matabele gangs from their huts. They emerged sleepily, still blanket-wrapped and shivering at the chill, coughing from the wood-smoke of the watch-fire, and grumbling without any real malice.

At noon Craig found the shade of an acacia and slept through the siesta as they all did. Then, refreshed, he worked through the afternoon until the ringing tone of the railway-line gong suspended from the branch of a jacaranda tree below the homestead sounded the hour and the cry of *"Shayile!* It has struck!" was flung from the gang and they trooped back up the hills.

Then Craig washed off the sweat and dust in the concrete reservoir behind the cottage and ate a hasty meal. By the time night fell, he was sitting at the cheap deal table in the cottage in the hissing white light of the gas lantern with a sheet of paper in front of him and a ball-point pen in his hand, transported into the other world of his imagination. Some nights he wrote through until long after midnight, and then at four-thirty was out in the dewy not-yet dawn again, feeling alert and vigorous.

The sun darkened his skin and bleached the cow-lick of hair over his eyes, the hard physical work toned up his muscles and toughened his stump so he could walk the fences all day without discomfort. There was so little time to spare, that his cooking was perfunctory and the bottle of whisky remained in his bag with the seal unbroken—so that he grew lean and hawk-faced.

Then one evening as he parked the Land-Rover under the jacaranda trees and started up towards the cottage, he was forced to stop. The aroma of roasting beef and potatoes was like running into a brick wall. The saliva spurted from under his tongue and he started forward again, suddenly ravenous.

In the tiny makeshift kitchen a gaunt figure stood over the wood fire. His hair was soft and white as cotton wool, and he looked up accusingly as Craig stood in the doorway.

"Why did you not send for me?" he demanded in Sindebele. "Nobody else cooks on Kingi-Lingi."

"Joseph!" Craig cried, and embraced him impetuously. The old man had been Bawu's cook for thirty years. He could lay a formal banquet for fifty guests, or whip up a hunters' pot on a bush fire. Already there was bread baking in the tin trunk he had improvised as an oven and he had gleaned a bowl of salad from the neglected garden.

Joseph extricated himself from Craig's embrace, a little ruffled by this breach of etiquette. "Nkosana"—Joseph still used the diminutive address—"your clothes were filthy and your bed was unmade," he lectured Craig sternly. "We have worked all day to tidy the mess you have made."

Only then did Craig notice the other man in the kitchen.

"Kapa-lala." He laughed delightedly, and the houseboy grinned and bobbed with pleasure. He was at work with the heavy black smoothing-iron filled with glowing coals. All Craig's clothes and bed-linen had been washed and were being ironed to crisp perfection. The walls of the cottage had been washed down and the floor polished to a gloss. Even the brass taps on the sink shone like the buttons on a marine's dress uniform.

"I have made a list of the things we need," Joseph told Craig. "They will do for the time being, but it is unfitting that you should live like this in a hovel. Nkosi Bawu, your grandfather, would have disapproved." Joseph the cook had a definite sense of style. "Thus, I have sent a message to my senior wife's uncle who is a master thatcher and told him to bring his eldest son, who is a bricklayer, and his nephew, who is a fine carpenter. They will be here tomorrow to begin repairing the damage that these dogs have done to the big house. As for the gardens, I know a man—" and he ticked off on his fingers what he considered necessary to restore King's Lynn to some sort of order. "Thus we will be ready to invite thirty important guests to Christmas dinner, like we used to in the old days. Now, Nkosana, go and wash. Dinner will be ready in fifteen minutes."

•   •   •

With the home paddocks securely fenced and the work on the restoration of the outbuildings and main homestead well in hand, Craig could at last begin the vital step of restocking. He summoned Shadrach and Joseph and gave King's Lynn into their joint care during his absence. They accepted the responsibility gravely. Then Craig drove to the airport, left the Land-Rover in the car park and boarded the commercial flight southwards.

For the next three weeks he toured the great cattle stud ranches of Northern Transvaal, the province of South Africa whose climate and conditions most closely resembled those of Matabeleland. The purchases of blood cattle were not transactions that could be hurried. Each was preceded by days of discussion with the seller, and study of the beasts themselves, while Craig enjoyed the traditional hospitality of the Afrikaner country folk. His hosts were men whose ancestors had trekked northwards from the Cape of Good Hope, drawn by their oxen, and had lived all their lives close to their animals. So while Craig purchased their stock, he drew upon their accumulated wisdom and experience and came from each transaction with his own knowledge and understanding of cattle immensely enriched. All he learned reinforced his desire to follow Bawu's successful experiments with cross-breeding the indigenous Afrikander strain, known for its hardiness and disease- and drought-resistance, with the quicker-yielding Santa Gertrudis strain.

He bought young cows that had been artificially inseminated and were well in calf. He bought bulls of fine pedigree from famous bloodlines, and laboured through the documentation and inspection and inoculation and quarantine and insurance that were necessary before they could be permitted to cross an international border. In the meantime he arranged for road transportation northwards to King's Lynn by contractors who specialized in carrying precious livestock.

He spent almost two million of his borrowed dollars before flying back to King's Lynn to make the final preparations for the arrival of his cattle. The deliveries of the blood-stock were to be staggered over a period of months, so that each consignment could be properly received and allowed to settle down before the arrival of the next batch.

The first to arrive were four young bulls, just ready to take up their stud duties. Craig had paid fifteen thousand dollars for each of them. Peter Fungabera was determined to make an important occasion out of their arrival. He persuaded two of his brother ministers to attend the welcoming ceremony, though neither the prime minister nor the minister of tourism, Comrade Tungata Zebiwe, was available on that day.

Craig rented a marquee tent, while Joseph happily and importantly prepared one of his legendary *alfresco* banquets. Craig was still smarting from having paid out two million dollars, so he went cheap on the champagne, ordering the imitation from the Cape of Good Hope rather than the genuine article.

The ministerial party arrived in a fleet of black Mercedes, accompanied by their heavily armed bodyguards, all sporting aviator-type sunglasses. Their ladies were dressed in full-length safari pants, of the wildest and most improbable colours. The cheap sweet champagne went down as though a plug had been pulled out of a bath, and they were all soon twittering and giggling like a flock of glossy starlings. The minister of education's senior wife unbuttoned her blouse, produced a succulent black breast, and gave the infant on her hip an early lunch while herself taking

111

on copious quantities of champagne. "Refuelling in flight," one of Craig's white neighbours, who had been an R.A.F. bomber-pilot, remarked with a grin.

Peter Fungabera was the last to arrive, wearing full dress, and driven by a young aide, a captain in the Third Brigade whom Craig had noticed on several other occasions. This time Peter introduced him.

"Captain Timon Nbebi."

He was so thin as to appear almost frail. His eyes behind the steel-rimmed spectacles were too vulnerable for a soldier, and his grip was quick and nervous. Craig would have liked to have spoken to him, but by this time the transporter carrying the bulls was already grinding up the hills.

It arrived in a cloud of fine red dust before the enclosure of split poles that Craig had built to receive the bulls. The gangplank was lowered, but before the tail-gate was raised Peter Fungabera climbed up onto the dais and addressed the assembly.

"Mr. Craig Mellow is a man who could have chosen any country in the world to live in and, as an internationally best-selling writer, would have been welcomed there. He chose to return to Zimbabwe and, in doing so, has declared to all the world that here is a land where men of any colour, of any tribe—black or white, Mashona or Matabele—are free to live and work, unafraid and unmolested, safe in the rule of just laws."

After the political commercial, Peter Fungabera allowed himself a little joke. "We will now welcome to our midst these other new immigrants, in the sure knowledge that they will be the fathers of many fine sons and daughters, and contribute to the prosperity of our own Zimbabwe."

Peter Fungabera led the applause as Craig lowered the gate and the first new immigrant emerged to stand blinking in the sunlight. He was an enormous beast, over a ton of bulging muscles under the glistening red-brown hide. He had just endured sixteen hours penned up in a noisy, lurching machine. The tranquillizers he had been given had worn off, leaving him with a drug hangover and a grudge against the entire world. Now he looked down on the clapping throng, on the swirling colours of the women's national costumes, and he found at last a focus for his irritation and frustration. He let out a long ferocious bellow, and, dragging his handlers behind him, launched himself like an avalanche down the gangplank.

The handlers released their hold on the restrainers, and the split-pole barrier exploded before his charge, as did the ministerial party. They scattered like sardines at the rush of a hungry barracuda. High officials overtook their wives, in a race for the sanctuary of the jacaranda trees; infants strapped on the women's backs howled as loudly as their dams.

The bull went into one side of the luncheon marquee, still at a dead run, gathering up the guy ropes on his massive shoulders, so the tent came down in graceful billows of canvas, trapping beneath it a horde of panic-stricken revellers. He emerged from the farther side of the collapsing marquee just as one of the younger ministerial wives sprinted, shrilling with terror, across his path. He hooked at her with one long forward-raked horn, and the point caught in the fluttering hem of her dress. The bull jerked his head up and the brightly coloured material unwrapped from the girl's body like the string from a child's top. She spun into an involuntary pirouette, caught her balance, and then, stark naked, went bounding up the hill with long legs flashing and abundant breasts bouncing elastically.

"Two to one, the filly to win by a tit," howled the R.A.F. bomber-pilot ecstatically. He had also fuelled up on the cheap champagne.

The gaudy dress had wrapped itself around the bull's head. It served to goad him beyond mere anger into the deadly passion of the corrida bull facing the matador's cape. He swung his great armed head from side to side, the dress swirling rakishly like a battle ensign in a high wind, and exposing one of his wicked little eyes—which lighted on the honourable minister of education, the least fleet-footed of the runners, who was making heavy weather of the slope.

The minister was carrying the burden of flesh that behoves a man of such importance. His belly wobbled mountainously beneath his waistcoat. His face was grey as last night's ashes, and he screamed in a girlish falsetto of terror and exhaustion, "Shoot it! Shoot the devil!"

His bodyguards ignored the instruction. They were leading him by fifty paces and rapidly widening the gap.

Craig watched helplessly from his grandstand position on the transporter, as the bull lowered his head and drove up the slope after the fleeing minister. Dust spurted from under his hooves, and he bellowed again. The blast of sound, only inches from the ministerial backside, seemed physically to lift and propel the honourable minister the last few paces, and he turned out to be a much better climber than sprinter. He went up the trunk of the first jacaranda like a squirrel and hung precariously in the lower branches with the bull directly beneath him.

The bull bellowed again in murderous frustration, glaring up at the cowering figure, tore at the earth with his front hooves, and gored the air with full-blooded swings of his vicious, white-tipped horns.

"Do something!" shrieked the minister. "Make it go away!"

His bodyguards looked back over their shoulders and, seeing the impasse, regained their courage. They halted, unslung their weapons and began cautiously closing in on the bull and his victim.

"No!" Craig yelled over the rattle of loading automatic weapons. "Don't shoot!" He was certain that his insurance did not cover "death by deliberate rifle-fire," and, quite apart from the fifteen thousand dollars, a volley would sweep the area behind the bull, which included the marquee and it occupants, a scattering of fleeing women and children and Craig himself.

One of the uniformed bodyguards raised his rifle and took aim. His recent exertions and terror did nothing for the steadiness of his hand. The muzzle of his weapon described widening circles in the air.

"No!" Craig bellowed again and flung himself face down on the floor of the trailer. At that moment a tall, skinny figure stepped between the wavering rifle-muzzle and the great bull.

"Shadrach!" whispered Craig thankfully, as the old man imperiously pushed up the rifle-barrel and then turned to face the bull.

"I see you, Nkunzi Kakhulu! Great bull!" he greeted him courteously.

The bull swung its head to the sound of his voice, and very clearly he saw Shadrach also. He snorted and nodded threateningly.

"Hau! Prince of cattle! How beautiful you are!" Shadrach advanced a pace towards those vicious pike-sharp horns.

The bull pawed at the earth and then made a warning rush at him. Shadrach stood him down and the bull stopped.

"How noble your head!" he crooned. "Your eyes are like dark moons!"

The bull hooked his horns towards him, but the swing was less vicious and Shadrach answered with another step forward. The shrieks of terror-stricken women and children died away. Even the most faint-hearted stopped running and looked back at the old man and the red beast.

"Your horns are sharp as the stabbing assegai of great Mzilikazi."

Shadrach kept moving forward and the bull blinked uncertainly and squinted at him with red-rimmed eyes.

"How glorious are your testicles," Shadrach murmured soothing, "like huge round boulders of granite. Ten thousand cows will feel their weight and majesty."

The bull backed up a pace and gave another half-hearted toss of his head.

"Your breath is hot as the north wind, my peerless king of bulls." Shadrach stretched out his hand slowly, and they watched in breathless silence.

"My darling." Shadrach touched the glossy, wet, chocolate-coloured muzzle and the bull jerked away nervously and then came back cautiously to snuffle at Shadrach's fingers. "My sweet darling, father of great bulls—" Gently Shadrach slipped his forefinger into the heavy bronze nosering and held the bull's head. He stooped and placed his mouth over the gaping, pink-lined nostrils and blew his own breath loudly into them. The bull shuddered, and Craig could clearly see the bunched muscle in his shoulders relaxing. Shadrach straightened and, with his finger still through the nosering, walked away—and placidly the bull waddled after him with his dewlap swinging.

A weak little cheer of relief and disbelief went up from his audience, and subsided as Shadrach cast a withering, contemptuous eye around him.

"Nkosi!" he called to Craig. "Get these chattering Mashona monkeys off our land. They are upsetting my darling," he ordered, and Craig hoped fervently that none of his highly placed guests understood Sindebele.

Craig marvelled once again at the almost mystical bond that existed between the Nguni peoples and their cattle. From that age, long obscured by the mists of time, when the first herds had been driven out of Egypt to begin the centuries-long migrations southwards, the destinies of black man and beast had been inexorably linked. This humpbacked strain of cattle had originated in India, its genus *Bos indicus* distinct from the European *Bos taurus*, but over the ages the cattle had become as African as the tribes that cherished and shared their lives with them. It was strange, Craig pondered, that the cattle-herding tribes seemed always to have been the most dominant and warlike. People such as the Masai and Bechuana and Zulu had always lorded it over the mere tillers of the earth. Perhaps it was their constant need to search for grazing, to defend it against others and to protect their herds from predators, both human and animal, that made them so bellicose.

He watched Shadrach lead the huge bull away. There was no mistaking that lordly arrogance now—master and beast were noble in their alliance. Not so the minister of education, still clinging, catlike, to his perch in the jacaranda. Craig went to add his entreaties to those of his bodyguards, who were encouraging him to descend to earth once more.

• • •

Peter Fungabera was the last of the official party to leave. He accompanied Craig on a tour of the homestead, sniffing appreciatively the sweet odour of the golden thatching grass that already covered half the roof area.

"My grandfather replaced the original thatch with asbestos during the war," Craig explained. "Your RPG-7 rocket shells were hot little darlings."

"Yes," Peter agreed evenly. "We started many a good bonfire with them."

"To tell the truth, I am grateful for the chance to restore the building. Thatch is cooler and more picturesque, and both the wiring and plumbing needed replacing—"

"I must congratulate you on what you have accomplished in such a short time. You will soon be living in the grand manner that your ancestors have always enjoyed since they first seized this land."

Craig looked at him sharply, searching for malice, but Peter's smile was as charming and easy as always.

"All these improvements add vastly to the value of the property," Craig pointed out. "And you own a goodly share of them."

"Of course." Peter laid a hand placatingly on Craig's forearm. "And you still have much work ahead of you. The development of Zambezi Waters, when will you begin on that?"

"I am almost ready to do so—as soon as the rest of the stock arrives, and I have Sally-Anne to assist with the details."

"Ah," said Peter. "Then you can begin immediately. Sally-

116

Anne Jay flew into Harare airport yesterday morning." Craig felt a tingle of rising pleasure and anticipation.

"I'll go into town this evening to phone her."

Peter Fungabera clucked with annoyance. "Have they not installed your telephone yet? I'll see you have it tomorrow. In the meantime you can patch through on my radio."

The telephone linesman arrived before noon the following day, and Sally-Anne's Cessna buzzed in from the east an hour later. Craig had a smudge-pot of old engine oil and rags burning to mark the disused airstrip and give her the wind direction, and she touched down and taxied to where he had parked the Land-Rover.

When she jumped down from the cabin, Craig found he had forgotten the alert, quick way she moved, and the shape of her legs in tight-fitting blue denim. Her smile was of genuine pleasure and her handshake firm and warm. She was wearing nothing beneath the cotton shirt. She noticed his eyes flicker down and then guiltily up again, but she showed no resentment.

"What a lovely ranch, from the air," she said.

"Let me show you," he offered, and she dropped her bag on the back seat of the Land-Rover and swung her leg over the door like a boy.

It was late afternoon when they got back to the homestead.

"Kapa-lala has prepared a room for you, and Joseph has cooked his number-one dinner. We have the generator running at last, so there are lights and the hot-water donkey has been boiling all day, so there is a hot bath—or I could drive you in to a motel in town?"

"Let's save gas." She accepted with a smile.

She came out on the veranda with a towel wrapped like a turban round her damp hair, flopped down in the chair beside him and put her feet up on the half-wall.

"God, that was glorious." She smelled of soap and she was still pink and glowing from the bath.

"How do you like your whisky?"

"Right up and lots of ice."

She sipped and sighed, and they watched the sunset. It was one of those raging-red African skies that placed them and the world in thrall; to speak during it would have been blasphemous. They watched the sun go in silence, and then Craig leaned across and handed her a thin sheaf of papers.

"What is this?" She was curious.

"Part-payment for your services as consultant and visiting lecturer at Zambezi Waters." Craig switched on the light above her chair.

She read slowly, going over each sheet three or four times, and then she sat with the sheaf of papers clutched protectively in her lap and stared out into the night.

"It's only a rough idea, just the first few pages. I have suggested the photographs that should face each text," Craig broke the silence awkwardly. "Of course, I've only seen a few. I am certain you have hundreds of others. I thought we would aim at two hundred and fifty pages, with the same number of your photographs—all colour, of course."

She turned her head slowly towards him. "*You* were afraid?" she asked. "Damn you, Craig Mellow—now *I* am scared silly."

He saw that there were tears in her eyes again. "This is so—" She searched for a word and gave up. "If I put my photographs next to this, they will seem—I don't know—puny, I guess, unworthy of the deep love you express so eloquently for this land."

He shook his head, denying it. She dropped her eyes to the writing and read it again.

"Are you sure, Craig, are you sure you want to do this book with me?"

"Yes—very much."

"Thank you," she said simply, and in that moment Craig knew at last, for sure, that they would be lovers. Not now, not tonight, it was still too soon—but one day they would take each other. He sensed that she knew that too, for though after that they spoke very little, her cheeks darkened under her tan with shy young blood whenever he looked across at her, and she could not meet his eyes.

After dinner Joseph served coffee on the veranda, and when he left Craig switched out the lights and in darkness they watched the moon rise over the tops of the msasa trees that lined the hills across the valley.

When at last she rose to go to her bed, she moved slowly and lingered unnecessarily. She stood in front of him, the top of her head reaching to his chin, and once again said softly, "Thank you," tilted her head back, and went up on tiptoe to brush his cheek with soft lips. But he knew she was not yet ready, and he made no effort to hold her.

• • •

By the time the last shipment of cattle arrived, the second homestead at Queen's Lynn five miles away was ready for occupation and Craig's newly hired white overseer moved in with his family. He was a burly, slow-speaking man who, despite his Afrikaner blood, had been born and had lived in the country all his life. He spoke Sindebele as well as Craig did, understood and respected the blacks and in turn was liked and respected by them. But best of all, he knew and loved cattle, like the true African he was.

With Hans Groenewald on the estate, Craig was able to concentrate on developing Zambezi Waters for tourism. He chose a young architect who had designed the lodges on some of the most luxurious private game ranches in southern Africa, and had him fly up from Johannesburg.

The three of them, Craig, Sally-Anne and the architect, camped for a week on Zambezi Waters, and walked both banks of the Chizarira River, examining every inch of the terrain, choosing the sites of five guest-lodges and the service complex which would support them. At Peter Fungabera's orders they were guarded by a squad of Third Brigade troopers under the command of Captain Timon Nbebi.

Craig's first impressions of this officer were confirmed as he came to know him better. He was a serious, scholarly young man who spent all his leisure time studying a correspondence course in political economics from the University of London. He spoke English and Sindebele, together with his native Shona, and he and Craig and Sally-Anne held long conversations at night over the camp-fire, trying to arrive at some solution to the tribal enmities that were racking the country. Timon Nbebi's views were surprisingly moderate for an officer in the elite Shona brigade, and he seemed genuinely to desire a working accommodation between the tribes.

"Mr. Mellow," he said, "can we afford to live in a land divided by hatred? When I look at Northern Ireland or the Lebanon and see the fruits of tribal strife, I become afraid."

"But you are a Shona, Timon," Craig pointed out gently. "Your allegiance surely lies with your own tribe."

"Yes," Timon agreed. "But first I am a patriot. I cannot ensure peace for my children with an AK 47 rifle. I cannot become a proud Shona by murdering all the Matabele."

These discussions could have no conclusion, but were made more poignant by the very necessity of an armed bodyguard even in this remote and seemingly peaceful area. The constant presence of armed men began to irk both Craig and Sally-Anne, and one evening towards the end of their stay at Zambezi Waters, they slipped their guards.

They were truly at ease with each other at last, able to share a friendly silence, or to talk for an hour without pause. They had begun to touch each other, still brief, seemingly casual contacts of which they were both, however, intensely aware. She might reach out and cover the back of his hand with hers to emphasize a point, or brush against him as they pored over the architect's rough sketches of the lodges. Though she was certainly more agile than he was, Craig would take her elbow to help her jump across a rock-pool in the river or lean over her to point out a woodpecker's nest or a wild beehive in the tree-top.

This day, alone at last, they found a clay anthill which rose above the level of the surrounding ebony and overlooked a rhino midden. It was a good stand from which to observe and photograph. Seated on it, they waited for a visit from one of the grotesque prehistoric monsters. They talked in whispers, heads close together, but this time not quite touching.

Suddenly Craig glanced down into the thick bush below them and froze. "Don't move," he whispered urgently. "Sit very still!"

Slowly she turned her head to follow his gaze, and he heard her little gasp of shock.

"Who are they?" she husked, but Craig did not reply.

There were two that he could see, for only their eyes were visible. They had come as silently as leopards, blending into the undergrowth with the skill of men who had lived all their lives in hiding.

"So, Kuphela," one of them spoke at last, his voice low but deadly. "You bring the Mashona killer dogs to this place to hunt us."

"That is not so, Comrade Lookout," Craig answered him in a hoarse whisper. "They were sent by the government to protect me."

"You are our friend—you did not need protection from us."

"The government does not know that." Craig tried to put a world of persuasion into his whisper. "Nobody knows that we

120

have met. Nobody knows that you are here. That I swear on my life."

"Your life it may well be," Comrade Lookout agreed. "Tell me quickly why you are here, if not to betray us."

"I have bought this land. That other white man in our party is a builder of homes. I wish to make a reserve here for tourists to visit. Like Wankie Park."

They understood that. The famous Wankie National Park was also in Matabeleland, and for minutes the two guerrillas whispered together and then looked up at Craig again.

"What will become of us," Comrade Lookout demanded, "when you have built your houses?"

"We are friends," Craig reminded him. "There is room for you here. I will help you with food and money, and in return you will protect my animals and my buildings. You will secretly watch over the visitors who come here, and there will be no more talk of hostages. Is that an agreement between friends?"

"How much is our friendship worth to you, Kuphela?"

"Five hundred dollars every month."

"A thousand," Comrade Lookout counter-offered.

"Good friends should not argue over mere money," Craig agreed. "I have only six hundred dollars now, but the rest I will leave buried beneath the wild fig-tree where we are camped."

"We will find it," Comrade Lookout assured him, "and every month we will meet either here or there." Lookout pointed out two rendezvous, both prominent hillocks well distanced from the river, their peaks only bluish silhouettes on the horizon. "The signal of a meeting will be a small fire of green leaves, or three rifle-shots evenly spaced."

"It is agreed."

"Now, Kuphela, leave the money in that ant-bear hole at your feet and take your woman back to camp."

Sally-Anne stayed very close beside him on the return, even taking his arm for reassurance every few hundred yards and looking back fearfully over her shoulder.

"My God, Craig, those were real *shufta*, proper dyed-in-the-wool guerrillas. Why did they let us go?"

"The best reason in the world—money." Craig's chuckle was a little hoarse and breathless even in his own ears, and the adrenalin still buzzed in his blood. "For a miserly thousand dollars a month, I have just hired myself the toughest bunch of bodyguards and

121

gamekeepers on the market. Pretty good bargain."

"You're doing a deal with them?" Sally-Anne demanded. "Isn't that dangerous? It's treason or something, surely?"

"Probably. We just have to make sure that nobody finds out about it, won't we?"

• • •

The architect turned out to be another bargain. His designs were superb; the lodges would be built of natural stone, indigenous timber and thatch. They would blend unobtrusively into the chosen sites along the river. Sally-Anne worked with him on the interior layouts and the furnishings, and introduced charming little touches of her own.

During the next few months, Sally-Anne's work with the World Wildlife Trust took her away for long periods at a time, but on her travels she recruited the staff that they would need for Zambezi Waters.

First, she seduced a Swiss-trained chef away from one of the big hotel chains. Then she chose five young safari guides, all of them African-born, with a deep knowledge and love of the land and its wildlife and, most importantly, with the ability to convey that knowledge and love to others.

Then she turned her attention to the design of the advertising brochures, using her own photographs and Craig's text. "A kind of dress rehearsal for our book," she pointed out when she telephoned him from Johannesburg, and Craig realized for the first time just what he had taken on in agreeing to work with her. She was a perfectionist. It was either right or it wasn't, and to get it right she would go to any lengths, and force him and the printers to do the same.

The result was a miniature masterpiece in which colour was carefully co-ordinated and even the layout of blocks of print balanced her illustrations. She sent out copies to all the African travel specialists around the world, from Tokyo to Copenhagen.

"We have to set an opening date," she told Craig, "and make sure that our first guests are newsworthy. You'll have to offer them a freebie, I'm afraid."

"You aren't thinking of a pop star?" Craig grinned, and she shuddered.

"I telephoned Daddy at the Embassy in London. He may be

able to get Prince Andrew—but I'll admit it's a big 'may be.' Henry Pickering knows Jane Fonda—"

"My God, I never realized what an up-market broad you are."

"And while we are on the subject of celebrities, I think I can get a best-selling novelist who makes bad jokes and will probably drink more whisky than he is worth!"

When Craig was ready to commence actual construction on Zambezi Waters, he complained to Peter Fungabera about the difficulty of finding labourers in the deep bush. Peter replied, "Don't worry, I'll fix that." And five days later, a convoy of army trucks arrived carrying two hundred detainees from the rehabilitation centres.

"Slave labour," Sally-Anne told Craig with distaste.

However, the access road to the Chizarira River was completed in just ten days, and Craig could telephone Sally-Anne in Harare and tell her, "I think we can confidently set the opening date for July first."

"That's marvellous, Craig."

"When can you come up again? I haven't seen you for almost a month."

"It's only three weeks," she denied.

He offered a bait. "I have done another twenty pages on our book. We must go over it together soon."

"Send them to me."

"Come and get them."

"Okay," she capitulated. "Next week, Wednesday. Where will you be, King's Lynn or Zambezi Waters?"

"Zambezi Waters. The electricians and plumbers are finishing up. I want to check it out."

"I'll fly up."

She landed on the open ground beside the river where Craig's labour gangs had surfaced a strip with gravel to make an all-weather landing-ground and had even rigged a proper wind-sock for her arrival.

The instant she jumped down from the cockpit Craig could see that she was furiously angry.

"What is it?"

"You've lost two of your rhino." She strode towards him. "I spotted the carcasses from the air."

"Where?" Craig was suddenly as angry as she was.

"In the thick bush beyond the gorge. It's poachers for certain. The carcasses are lying within fifty paces of each other. I made a few low passes, and the horns have been taken."

"Do you think they are Charlie and Lady Di?" he demanded.

Earlier, from the air, Craig and Sally-Anne had done a rhino count and had identified twenty-seven individual animals on the estate, including four calves and nine breeding pairs of mature animals to whom they had given names. Charlie and Lady Di were a pair of young rhinoceros who had probably just come together. On foot Craig and Sally-Anne had been able to get close to them in the thick jesse bush that the pair had taken as their territory. Both of the animals carried fine horns, the male's much thicker and heavier. The front horn, twenty inches long and weighing twenty pounds, would be worth at least ten thousand dollars to a poacher. The female, Lady Di, was a smaller animal with a thinner, finely curved pair of horns, and she had been heavily pregnant when last they saw her.

"Yes. It's them. I'm sure of it."

"There is some rough going this side of the gorge," Craig muttered. "We won't get there before dark."

"Not with the Land-Rover," Sally-Anne agreed, "but I think I have found a place where I can get down. It's only a mile or so from the kill."

Craig unslung his rifle from the clips behind the driver's seat of the Land-Rover and checked the load.

"Okay. Let's go," he said.

The poachers' kill was in the remotest corner of the estate, almost on the rim of the rugged valley wall that fell away to the great river in the depths. The landing-ground that Sally-Anne had spotted was a narrow natural clearing at the head of the river gorge, and she had to abort her first approach and go round again. At the second attempt, she sneaked in over the tree-tops and hit it just right.

They left the Cessna in the clearing and started down into the mouth of the gorge. Craig led, with the rifle cocked and ready. The poachers might still be at the kill.

The vultures guided them the last mile. They were roosting in every tree around the kill, like grotesque black fruit. The area around the carcasses was beaten flat and open by the scavengers, and strewn with loose vulture feathers. As they walked up, half a dozen hyena went loping away with their peculiar high-shouldered gait. Even their fearsomely toothed jaws had not been able completely to devour the thick rhinoceros hide, though the poachers had hacked open the belly cavities of their victims to give them easy access.

The carcasses were at least a week old. The stench of putrefaction was aggravated by that of the vulture dung which whitewashed the remains. The eyes had been picked from the sockets of the male's head, and the ears and cheeks had been gnawed away. As Sally-Anne had seen from the air, the horns were gone, the hack marks of an axe still clearly visible on the exposed bone of the animal's nose.

Looking down upon that ruined and rotting head, Craig found that he was shaking with anger and that the saliva had dried out in his mouth.

"If I could find them, I would kill them," he said, and beside him Sally-Anne was pale and grim.

"The bastards," she whispered, "the bloody, bloody bastards."

They walked across to the female. Here also the horns had been hacked off and her belly cavity slit open. The hyena had dragged the calf out of her womb and devoured most of it.

Sally-Anne squatted down beside the pathetic remains. "Prince Billy," she whispered. "Poor little devil."

"There's nothing more we can do here." Craig took her arm and lifted her to her feet. "Let's go."

She dragged a little in his grip as he led her away.

•   •   •

From the peak of the hill that Craig had arranged as the rendezvous with Comrade Lookout, they looked out across the brown land to where the river showed as a lush serpentine sprawl of denser forest almost at the extreme range of their vision.

Craig had lit the signal fire of smoking green leaves a little after noon, and had fed it regularly since then. Now the sky was turning purple and blue and the hush and chill of evening fell over them, so that Sally-Anne shivered.

"Cold?" Craig asked.

"And sad." Sally-Anne tensed but did not pull away when he put his arm around her shoulders. Then slowly she relaxed and pressed against him for the warmth of his body. Darkness blotted out their horizon and crept in upon them.

"I see you, Kuphela." The voice was so close as to startle them both, and Sally-Anne jerked away from Craig almost guiltily. "You summoned me." Comrade Lookout stayed outside the feeble glow of the fire.

"Where were you when somebody killed two of my *bejane* and stole their horns?" Craig accused him roughly. "Where were you who promised to stand guard for me?"

There was a long silence out in the darkness.

"Where did this thing happen?"

Craig told him.

"That is far from here, far also from our camp. We did not know." His tone was apologetic—obviously Comrade Lookout felt he had failed in a bargain. "But we will find the ones who did this. We will follow them and find them."

"When you do, it is important that we know the name of the person who buys the horns from them," Craig ordered.

"I will bring the name of that person to you," Comrade Lookout promised. "Watch for our signal fire on this hill."

Twelve days later, through his binoculars, Craig picked up the little grey feather of smoke on the distant whale-back of the hill. He drove alone to the assignation, for Sally-Anne had left three days previously. She had wanted desperately to stay, but one of the directors of the Wildlife Trust was arriving in Harare and she had to be there to greet him.

"I guess my grant for next year depends on it," she told Craig ruefully as she climbed into the Cessna, "but you phone me the minute you hear from your tame bandits."

Craig climbed the hill eagerly and on the crest he was breathing evenly and his leg felt strong and easy. He had grown truly hard and fit in these last months, and his anger was still strong upon him as he stood beside the smouldering remains of the signal fire.

Twenty minutes passed before Comrade Lookout moved silently at the edge of the forest, still keeping in cover and with the automatic rifle in the crook of his arm.

"You were not followed?" Craig shook his head reassuringly. "We must always be careful, Kuphela."

"Did you find the men?"

"Did you bring our money?"

"Yes." Craig drew the thick envelope from the patch-pocket of his bush-jacket. "Did you find the men?"

"Cigarettes," Comrade Lookout teased him. "Did you bring cigarettes?"

Craig tossed a pack to him, and Comrade Lookout lit one and inhaled deeply. "Hau!" he said. "That is good."

"Tell me," Craig insisted.

"There were three men. We followed their spoor from the kill—though it was almost ten days old, and they had tried to cover it." Comrade Lookout drew on his cigarette until sparks flew from the glowing tip. "Their village is on the escarpment of the valley three days' march from here. They were Batonka apes." The Batonka—one of the primitive hunter-gatherer tribes—live along the valley of the Zambezi. "And they had the horns of your rhinoceros with them still. We took the three of them into the bush and we spoke to them for a long time." Craig felt his skin crawl as he imagined that extended conversation. He felt his anger subside to be replaced with a hollow feeling of guilt. He should have cautioned Comrade Lookout on his methods.

"What did they tell you?"

"They told me that there is a man, a city man who drives a motor car and dresses like a white man. He buys the horns of rhinoceros, the skins of leopards and the teeth of ivory, and he pays more money than they have ever seen in their lives."

"Where and when do they meet him?"

"He comes in each full moon, driving the road from Tuti Mission to the Shangani River. They wait on the road in the night for his coming."

Craig squatted beside the fire and thought for a few minutes, then looked up at Comrade Lookout. "You will tell these men that they will wait beside the road next full moon with the rhinoceros horns until this man comes in his motor car—"

"That is not possible," Comrade Lookout interrupted him.

"Why?" Craig asked.

"The men are dead."

Craig stared at him in utter dismay. "All three of them?"

Comrade Lookout nodded. "All three." His eyes were cold and flat and merciless.

"But—" Craig couldn't bring himself to ask the question. He had set the guerrillas onto the poachers. It must have been like setting a pack of fox-terriers onto a domesticated hamster. Even though he had not meant it to happen, he was surely responsible. He felt sickened and ashamed.

"Do not worry, Kuphela," Comrade Lookout reassured him kindly. "We have brought you the horns of your *bejane*, and the men were only dirty Batonka apes anyway."

Carrying the bark string bag of rhinoceros horns over his shoulder, Craig went down to the Land-Rover. He felt sick and weary and his leg hurt, but the draw-string of the bag cutting into his flesh did not gall him as sorely as his own conscience.

•　•　•

The rhinoceros horns stood in a row on Peter Fungabera's desk. Four of them—the tall front horns and the shorter rear horns.

"Aphrodisiac," Peter murmured, touching one of them with his long, tapering fingers.

"That's a fallacy," Craig said. "Chemical analysis shows they contain no substance that could possibly be aphrodisiac in effect."

"They are nothing more than a type of agglutinated hair mass," Sally-Anne explained. "The effects that the failing Chinese roué seeks when he crushes it to powder and takes it with a draught of rose-water is merely sympathetic medicine—the horn is long and hard, *voilà!*"

"Anyway, the Arab oilmen will pay more for their knife-handles than the cunning old Chinese will pay for their personal daggers," Craig pointed out.

"Whatever the final market, the fact is that there are two less rhino on Zambezi Waters than there were a month ago, and in another month how many more will have gone?"

Peter Fungabera stood up and came round the desk on bare feet. His loincloth was freshly laundered and crisply ironed. He stood in front of them.

"I have been pursuing my own lines of investigation," he said quietly, "and all of it seems to point in the same direction as Sally-Anne's own reasoning led her. It seems absolutely certain that there is a highly organized poaching ring operating across the country. The tribesmen in the game-rich areas are being enticed into poaching and gathering the valuable animal products. They are collected by middlemen, many of whom are junior civil servants, such as district officers and Game Department rangers. The booty is accumulated in various remote and safe caches until the value is sufficient to warrant a large single consignment being sent out of the country."

Peter Fungabera began to pace slowly up and down the room.

"The consignment is usually exported on a commercial Air Zimbabwe flight to Dar-es-Salaam on the Tanzania coast. We are not sure what happens at that end, but it probably goes out on a Soviet or Chinese freighter."

Sally-Anne nodded. "The Soviets have no qualms about wild-life conservation. Sable-fur production and whaling are big foreign-exchange-earners for them."

"What portfolio do Air Zimbabwe operations fall under?" Craig asked suddenly.

"The portfolio of the minister of tourism, the honourable Tungata Zebiwe," Peter replied smoothly, and they were all silent for a few moments before he went on. "When a consignment is due, the products are brought into Harare, all on the same day or night. They are not stored but go directly onto the aircraft under tight security conditions and are flown out almost immediately."

"How often does this happen?" Craig asked and Peter Fungabera glanced inquiringly at his aide, who was standing unobtrusively at the back of the room.

"That varies," Captain Timon Nbebi replied. "In the rainy season the grass is long and the conditions in the bush are bad. There is little hunting activity, but during the dry months the poachers can work more efficiently. However, we have learned through our informant that a consignment is almost due and will in fact go out within the next two weeks—"

"Thank you, Captain," Peter Fungabera interrupted him with a small frown of annoyance; obviously he had wanted to deliver that information himself. "What we have also learned is that the head of the organization often takes an active part in the operation. For instance, that massacre of elephant in the abandoned mine-field"—Peter looked across at Sally-Anne—"the one that you photographed so vividly—well, we have learned that a government minister, we do not know for certain which one, went to the site in an army helicopter. We know that on two further occasions a high government official, reputedly of ministerial rank, was present when consignments were brought in to the airport for shipment."

"He probably does not trust his own men not to cheat him," Craig murmured.

"With the bunch of cutthroats he's got working for him, who can blame him?" Sally-Anne's voice was hoarse with her outrage, but Peter Fungabera seemed unaffected.

"We believe that we will be forewarned of the next consignment. As I have intimated, we have infiltrated a man into their organization. We will watch the movements of our suspect as the date approaches and, with luck, catch him red-handed. If not, we will seize the consignment at the airport and arrest all those handling it. I am certain we will be able to convince one of them to turn state's evidence."

Watching his face, Craig recognized that same cold, flat, merciless expression that he had last seen when Comrade Lookout reported the death of the three poachers. It was only a fleeting glimpse behind the urbane manner and then Peter Fungabera had turned back to his desk.

"For reasons that I have already explained to you, I require independent and reliable witnesses to any arrest that we might be fortunate enough to make. I want both of you to be there. So I would be obliged if you could hold yourselves ready to move at very short notice, and if you could inform Captain Nbebi where you may be contacted at all times over the next two or three weeks."

As they rose to leave, Craig asked suddenly, "What is the maximum penalty for poaching?" and Peter Fungabera looked up from the papers he was rearranging on his desk.

"As the law stands now, it is a maximum of eighteen months' hard labour for any one of a dozen or so offences under the act—"

"That's not enough." Craig had a vivid mental image of the violated and rotting carcasses of his animals.

"No," Peter agreed. "It's not enough. Two days ago in the House I introduced an amendment to the bill, as a private member's motion. It will be read for the third time on Thursday, and I assure you it has the full support of the party. It will become law on that day."

"And," Sally-Anne asked, "what are the new penalties to be?"

"For unauthorized dealing in the trophies of certain scheduled wild game, as opposed to mere poaching or hunting, for buying and reselling and exporting, the maximum penalty will be twelve years at hard labour and a fine not exceeding one hundred thousand dollars."

They thought about that for a moment, and then Craig nodded. "Twelve years—yes, that is enough."

• • • •

Peter Fungabera's summons came in the early morning, when Craig and Hans Groenewald, his overseer, had just returned to the homestead from the dawn patrol of the pastures. Craig was in the middle of one of Joseph's gargantuan breakfasts when the telephone rang, and he was still savouring the homemade beef sausage as he answered it.

"Mr. Mellow, this is Captain Nbebi. The general wants you to meet him as soon as possible at his operational headquarters, the house at Macillwane. We are expecting our man to move tonight. How soon can you be here?"

"It's a six-hour drive," Craig pointed out.

"Miss Jay is already on her way to the airport. She should be at King's Lynn within the next two hours to pick you up."

Sally-Anne arrived within the two hours, and Craig was waiting on the airstrip. They flew directly to Harare airport and Sally-Anne drove them out to the house in the Macillwane hills.

As they drove through the gates, they were immediately aware of the unusual activity in the grounds. On the front lawn stood a Super Frelon helicopter. The pilot and his engineer were leaning against the fuselage, smoking and chatting. They looked up expectantly as Sally-Anne and Craig came up the driveway and then dismissed them as unimportant. There were four sand-coloured army trucks drawn up in a line behind the house, with Third Brigade troopers in full battle-kit grouped around them. Craig could sense their excitement.

Peter Fungabera's office had been turned into operational headquarters. Two camp tables had been set up facing the huge relief map on the wall. At the first table were seated three junior officers. There was a radio apparatus on the second table, and Timon Nbebi was leaning over the operator's shoulder, speaking into the microphone in low rippling Shona that Craig could not follow, breaking off abruptly to give an order to the black sergeant at the map, who immediately moved one of the coloured markers to a new position.

Peter Fungabera greeted Craig and Sally-Anne perfunctorily and waved them to stools, then went on speaking into the telephone. When he hung up he explained quickly, "We know the location of three of the dumps—one is at a *shamba* in the Chi-

131

manimani mountains, it's mostly leopard-skins and some ivory. The second is at a trading-post near Chiredzi in the south—that's mostly ivory. And the third is coming from the north. We think that it's being held at Tuti Mission Station. It's the biggest and most valuable shipment—ivory and rhino horn."

He broke off as Captain Nbebi handed him a note, read it swiftly and said, "Good. Move two platoons up the north road as far as Karoi," and then turned back to Craig.

"The operation is code-named 'Bada'—that is Shona for 'leopard.' Our suspect will be referred to as Bada during the entire operation." Craig nodded. "We have just heard that Bada has left Harare. He is in his official Mercedes with a driver and two bodyguards—all three of them Matabele, of course."

"Which way?" Sally-Anne asked quickly.

"At this stage, he seems to be heading north, but it's still too early to be sure."

"To meet the big shipment—" There was the light of battle in Sally-Anne's eyes, and Craig could feel his own excitement tickling the hairs at the back of his neck.

"We must believe that is so," Peter agreed. "Now let me explain our disposition if Bada moves north. The shipments from Chimanimani and Chiredzi will be allowed through unhindered as far as the airport. They will be seized as soon as they arrive, and the drivers, together with the reception committee, arrested, to be used as witnesses later. Of course, their progress will be under surveillance at all times from the moment the trucks are loaded. The owners of the two warehouses will be arrested as soon as the trucks leave and are clear of the area."

Both Craig and Sally-Anne were listening intently, as Peter went on, "If Bada moves either east or south, we will switch the focus of the operation to that sector. However, we had anticipated that as the most valuable shipment is in the north, that's where he will go—if, of course, he goes at all. It looks as though we were right. As soon as we are certain, then we can move ourselves."

"How are you planning to catch him?" Sally-Anne demanded.

"It will be very much a matter of opportunity, and what we will do depends necessarily on Bada's actions. We have to try and make a physical connection between him and the consignment. We will watch both the vehicle carrying the contraband and his Mercedes, and as soon as they come together, we will pounce—"

Peter Fungabera emphasized this act of pouncing by slapping his leather-covered swagger-stick into the palm of his hand with a crack like a pistol-shot, and Craig found that he was already so keyed up that he started nervously and then grinned sheepishly at Sally-Anne.

The radio set crackled and the side-band hummed, then a disembodied voice spoke in Shona. Captain Nbebi acknowledged curtly, and glanced across at Peter.

"It's confirmed, sir. Bada is moving north on the Karoi road at speed."

"All right, Captain, we can go up to condition three," Peter ordered, and strapped on the webbing belt with his holstered side-arm. "Do you have anything from the surveillance teams on the Tuti road?"

Captain Nbebi called three times into the microphone and was answered almost immediately. The reply to his question was brief.

"Negative at this time, General," he reported to Peter.

"It's still too early." Peter adjusted his burgundy-red beret to a rakish angle, and the silver leopard's head glinted over his right eye. "But we can begin moving into our forward postions now." He led the way through the french doors onto the veranda.

The helicopter crew saw him, quickly dropped their cigarettes, ground them out and vaulted up into the hatch. Peter Fungabera climbed up into the fuselage and the starter-motor whined and the rotor began to spin overhead.

As they settled down on the bench seats and clinched their waistbelts, Craig asked impulsively the question that had been troubling him, but he asked it in a voice low enough not to be heard by the others in the rising bellow of the main engine.

"Peter, this is a full-scale military operation, almost a crusade. Why not merely hand it over to the police?"

"Since they fired their white officers, the police have become a bunch of heavy-handed bunglers"—then Peter gave him a rake-hell smile—"and after all, old boy, they are my rhino also."

The helicopter lifted off with a gut-sliding swoop, and its nose rotated onto a northerly heading. Keeping low, hugging the contours, it bore away, and the rush of air through the open hatch made further conversation impossible.

They kept well to the west of the main northern road, not risking a sighting by the occupants of the Mercedes. An hour later, as the helicopter hovered and then began its descent to the small military

133

fort at Karoi, Craig glanced at his wrist-watch. It was after four o'clock.

Peter Fungabera saw the gesture and nodded. "It looks as though it's going to be a night operation," he agreed.

The village of Karoi had once been a centre for the white-owned ranches in the area, but now it was a single street of shabby trading-stores, a service station, a post office and a small police station. The military base was a little beyond the town, still heavily fortified from the days of the bush war with a barbed-wire surround and sloped walls of sandbags twenty feet thick.

The local commandant, a young black second lieutenant, was clearly overawed by the importance of his visitor and saluted theatrically every time Peter Fungabera spoke.

"Get this idiot out of my sight," Peter snarled at Captain Nbebi, as he took over the command post. "And get me the latest report on Bada's position."

Captain Nbebi looked up from the radio set. "Bada passed through Sinoia twenty-three minutes ago."

"Right. Do we have an accurate description of the vehicle?"

"It's a dark-blue Mercedes 280 SE with a ministerial pennant on the hood. Registration PL 674. No motor-cycle outriders or other escort vehicle. Four occupants."

"Make sure that all units have that description—and repeat once more that there is to be no shooting. Bada is to be taken unharmed. Harm him and we could well have another Matabele rebellion on our hands. Nobody is to fire at him or his vehicle, even to save their own lives. Make that clear. Any man who disobeys will have to face me personally."

Nbebi called each unit individually, repeated Peter's orders and waited while they were acknowledged. Then they waited impatiently, drinking tea from chipped enamel mugs and watching the radio set.

It crackled abruptly to life and Timon Nbebi sprang to it.

"We have located the truck," he translated triumphantly. "It's a green five-ton Ford with a canvas canopy. A driver and a passenger in the cab. Heavily laden, well down on the suspension and using extra-low gear on the inclines. It crossed the drift on the Sanyati River ten minutes ago, heading from the direction of Tuti Mission towards the road junction twenty-five miles north of here."

"So, Bada and the truck are on a course to intercept each other," said Peter Fungabera softly, and there was the hunter's gleam in his eyes.

• • •

Now the radio set was the focus of all their attention. Each time it came alive all their eyes instantly swivelled to it.

The reports came in regularly, tracing the swift progress of the Mercedes northwards towards them and that of the lumbering truck, grinding slowly down the dusty, rutted secondary road from the opposite direction. In the periods between each report, they sat in silence, sipping the strong over-sweetened tea and munching sandwiches of coarse brown bread and canned bully beef.

Peter Fungabera ate little. He had tilted back his chair and placed his feet on the commandant's desk. He tapped the swagger-stick against the lacings of his rubber-soled jungle boots with a monotonous rhythm that began to irritate Craig. Suddenly Craig found himself craving a cigarette again, the first time in months, and he stood up and began to pace the small office restlessly.

Timon Nbebi acknowledged another report and, when he replaced the microphone, translated from the Shona, "The Mercedes has reached the village. They have stopped at the service station to refill with gasoline."

Tungata Zebiwe was only a few hundred yards from where they sat. Craig found the knowledge disconcerting. Up to now, it had been more an intellectual exercise than an actual life-and-death chase. He had ceased to think of Tungata as a man, he was merely "Bada," the quarry, to be outguessed and hunted into the trap. Now suddenly he remembered him as a man, a friend, an extraordinary human being, and he was once more torn between his residual loyalty of friendship and his desire to see a criminal brought to justice.

The command post was suddenly claustrophobic, and he went out into the tiny yard enclosed by high thick walls of sandbags. The sun had set, and the brief African twilight purpled the sky overhead. He stood staring up at it. There was a light footstep behind him and he glanced down.

"Don't be too unhappy," Sally-Anne pleaded softly. He was touched by her concern.

"You don't have to go," she went on. "You could stay here."

He shook his head. "I want to be sure—I want to see it for myself," he said. "But I'll not hate it any less."

135

"I know," she said. "I respect you for that."

He looked down at her upturned face and knew that she wanted him to kiss her. The moment for which he had waited so long and so patiently had arrived. She was ready for him at last, her need as great as his.

Gently he touched her cheek with his fingertips, and her eyelids fluttered half-closed. She swayed towards him, and he realized that he loved her. The knowledge took his breath away for a moment. He felt an almost religious awe.

"Sally-Anne," he whispered, and the door of the command post crashed open and Peter Fungabera strode out into the yard.

"We are moving out," he snapped, and they drew apart. Craig saw her shake herself lightly as though waking from sleep and her eyes came back into focus.

Side by side, they followed Peter and Timon to the open Land-Rover at the gate of the fort.

•　　•　　•

The evening was chill after the heat of the day, and the wind clawed at them, for the windscreen had been strapped down on the Land-Rover's hood.

Timon Nbebi drove with Peter Fungabera in the passenger seat. Craig and Sally-Anne were crowded into the back seat with the radio operator. Timon drove cautiously with parking lights only burning, and the two open army trucks packed with Third Brigade troopers in full battle-gear kept close behind them.

The Mercedes was less than half a mile ahead. Occasionally they could see the glow of its tail-lights as it climbed the road up one of the heavily wooded hills.

Peter Fungabera checked the odometer. "We've come twenty-three miles. The turn-off to the Sanyati and Tuti is only two miles ahead." He tapped Timon on the shoulder with the swagger-stick. "Pull over. Call the unit at the junction."

Craig found himself shivering as much from excitement as the cold. With the engine still running, Timon called ahead to the road junction where the forward observation team was concealed.

"Ah! That's it!" Timon could not keep the elation from his voice. "Bada has turned off the main road, General. The target truck has stopped and is parked two miles from the crossroads. It has to be a prearranged meeting, sir."

"Get going," Peter Fungabera ordered. "Follow them!"

136

Now Timon Nbebi drove fast, using the glow of his parking-lights to hold the verge of the road.

"There's the turning!" Peter snapped, as the unmade road showed dusty pale out of the dark.

Timon slowed and swung onto it. A sergeant of the Third Brigade stepped out of the darkness of the encroaching bush. He jumped up onto the footboard and managed to salute with his free hand.

"They passed here a minute ago, General," he blurted. "The truck is just ahead. We have set up a road-block behind it and we will block here as soon as you have passed, sir. We have them bottled up."

"Carry on, Sergeant." Peter nodded, then turned to Timon Nbebi. "The road drops steeply down from here to the drift. Have the trucks cut their engines as soon as we are rolling. We'll coast down."

The silence was eerie after the growl of heavy engines. The only sound was the squeak of the Land-Rover's suspension, the crunch of the tyres over gravel, and the rustle of the wind around their ears.

The twists in the rough track sprang at them out of the night with unnerving speed, and Timon Nbebi wrenched the wheel through them as they careered down the first drop of the great escarpment. The two trucks were guided by their tail-lights. They made monstrous black shapes looming out of the darkness close behind. Sally-Anne reached out for Craig's hand as they were thrown together into the turns, and she hung on to it tightly all the way down.

"There they are!" Peter Fungabera snarled abruptly, his voice roughened with excitement.

Below them they saw the headlights of the Mercedes flickering beyond the trees. They were closing up swiftly. For a few seconds the headlights were blanketed by another turn in the winding road, and then they burst out again—two long beams burning the pale dust surface of the track, to be answered suddenly by another glaring pair of headlights facing in the opposite direction, even at this range, blindingly white. The second pair of headlights flashed three times, obviously a recognition signal, and immediately the Mercedes slowed.

"We've got them," Peter Fungabera exulted, and switched off the parking lights.

Below, a canopied truck was trundling slowly from the verge where it had been parked in darkness into the middle of the road. Its headlights flooded the Mercedes, which pulled to a halt. Two men climbed out of the Mercedes and crossed to the cab of the truck. One of them carried a rifle. They spoke to the driver through the open window.

The Land-Rover raced silently in blackness towards the brightly lit tableau in the valley below. Sally-Anne was clinging to Craig's hand with startling strength.

In the road below, one of the men began to walk back towards the rear of the parked truck and then paused and looked up the dark road towards the racing Land-Rover. They were so close now that, even over the engine noise of the Mercedes and truck, he must have heard the crunch of tyres.

Peter Fungabera switched on the headlights of the Land-Rover. They blazed out with stunning brilliance and at the same moment he lifted an electronic bull-horn to his mouth.

"Do not move!" his magnified voice bellowed into the night and came crashing back in echoes form the close-pressed hills. "Do not attempt to escape!"

The two men whirled and dived back towards the Mercedes. Timon Nbebi started the engine with a roar and the Land-Rover jerked forward.

"Stay where you are! Drop your weapons!"

The men hesitated, then the armed one threw down his rifle and they both raised their hands in surrender, blinking into the dazzle of headlights.

Timon Nbebi swung the Land-Rover in front of the Mercedes, blocking it. Then he jumped down and ran to the open window and pointed his Uzi submachine-gun into the interior.

"Out!" he shouted. "Everybody out!"

Behind them the two trucks came to a squealing halt, clouds of dust boiling out from under their double rear wheels. Armed troopers swarmed out of them, rushing forward to club down the two unarmed men onto the gravel of the road. They surrounded the Mercedes, tearing open the doors and dragging out the driver and another man from the back seat.

There was no mistaking the tall, wide-shouldered figure. The headlights floodlit his craggy features and exaggerated the rocky strength of his jaw. Tungata Zebiwe shrugged off the grip of his captors and glared about him, forcing them to fall back involuntarily.

"Back, you yapping jackals! Do you dare touch me?"

He was dressed in slacks and a white shirt. His cropped head was round and black as a cannon ball.

"Do you know who I am?" he demanded. "You'll wish your twenty-five fathers had taught you better manners."

His arrogant assurance drove them back another pace, and they looked towards the Land-Rover. Peter Fungabera stepped from behind the headlights, and Tungata Zebiwe recognized him instantly.

"You!" he growled. "Of course, the chief butcher."

"Open the truck," Peter Fungabera ordered, without taking his eyes off the other man. They stared at each other with such terrible hatred that it rendered insignificant everything else around them. It was an elemental confrontation, seeming to embody all the savagery of a continent, two powerful men stripped of any vestige of civilized restraint, their antagonism so strong as to be barely supportable to them.

Craig had jumped down from the Land-Rover and started forward, but now he stopped beside the Mercedes in astonishment. He had not expected anything remotely like this. This almost tangible hatred was not a thing of that moment. It seemed that the two of them would launch themselves at each other like embattled animals, tearing with bare hands at each other's throats. This was a passion of deep roots, a mutual rage based on a monumental foundation of long-standing hostility.

From the back of the captured truck the troopers were hurling out bales and crates. One of the crates burst open as it hit the road, and long yellow shafts of ivory glowed like amber in the headlights. A trooper hooked open one of the bales and pulled out handfuls of precious fur, the golden dappled skin of leopard, the thick red pelts of lynx.

"That's it!" Peter Fungabera's voice was choking with triumph and loathing and vindictive gloating. "Seize the Matabele dog!"

"Whatever this is will rebound on your own head," Tungata growled at him, "you son of a Shona whore!"

"Take him!" Peter urged his men, but they hesitated, held at bay by the invisible aura of power that emanated from this tall imperial figure.

In the pause, Sally-Anne jumped down from the Land-Rover

and started towards the treasure of fur and ivory lying in the road. For a second she screened Tungata Zebiwe from his captors, and he moved with a blur of speed, like the strike of an adder, almost too fast to follow with the eye.

He seized Sally-Anne's arm, twisted and lifted her off her feet, holding her as a shield in front of him as he ducked low and scooped up the discarded rifle from the dust at his feet. He had chosen the moment perfectly. They were all crowded in upon each other. The troopers pressed so closely that none of them could fire without hitting one of their own.

Tungata's back was protected by the Land-Rover, his front by Sally-Anne's body.

"Don't shoot!" Fungabera bellowed at his men. "I want the Matabele bastard for myself."

Tungata swung the barrel of the rifle up under Sally-Anne's armpit, holding it by the pistol-grip single-handed, and he aimed at Peter Fungabera, as he fell back towards the Land-Rover, dragging Sally-Anne with him. The Land-Rover's engine was still running.

"You'll not escape," Peter Fungabera gloated. "The road is blocked, I have a hundred men. I've got you, at last."

Tungata slipped the rate-of-fire selector across with his thumb and dropped his aim to Peter Fungabera's belly. Craig, standing diagonally behind his left shoulder, saw the slight deflection of the rifle barrel at the instant before Tungata fired. Craig realized that he had deliberately aimed an inch to one side of Peter's hip. The clattering roar of automatic fire was deafening, and the group of men leaped apart as they went for cover.

The rifle rode up high in Tungata's single-handed grip. Bullets smashed into the parked truck, leaving rents through the body-work, each surrounded by a halo of bright bare metal. Peter Fungabera hurled himself aside, spinning away along the truck body to fall flat in the road and wriggle frantically behind the truck wheels.

Gunsmoke and dust shrouded the blazing headlights, and troopers scattered, blanketing each other's field of fire, while in the chaos, Tungata lifted Sally-Anne bodily and threw her into the passenger seat of the Land-Rover. In the same movement, he vaulted up into the driver's seat, threw the vehicle into gear and the engine roared as it leaped forward.

"Don't shoot!" Peter Fungabera shouted again. There was a

140

desperate urgency in his voice. "I want him alive!"

A trooper jumped in front of the Land-Rover, in a futile attempt to stop it. The impact sounded like a lump of bread dough dropped on the kneading board, as the hood hit him squarely in the chest and he fell. There was a series of jolting bumps as he was dragged under the chassis, then he rolled out into the road and the Land-Rover was boring away up the hill.

Without conscious thought, Craig jerked open the driver's door of the abandoned ministerial Mercedes and slipped into the seat. He locked the wheel into a hard 180-degree turn and gunned her into it. The Mercedes' tail crabbed around, tyres spinning, and he hit the high earth bank a glancing blow with a right front wing, which swung her nose through the last few degrees of the turn. Craig lifted his foot off the accelerator, met the skid, centred the wheel, and then trod down hard. The Mercedes shot forward, and through the open window he heard Peter Fungabera shout, "Craig! Wait!"

He ignored the call and concentrated on the first sharp bend of the escarpment road as it flashed up at him. The Mercedes' steering was deceptively light—he almost oversteered—and the off-wheels hammered over the rough verge. Then he was through the bend and ahead the red tail-lights of the Land-Rover were almost obscured in their own boiling white dust cloud.

Craig dropped the automatic transmission to sports mode, the engine shrieked and the needle of the rev-counter spun up into the red sector above 5000, and she arrowed up the hill, gaining swiftly on the Land-Rover.

It was swallowed by the next turn, and the dust blinded Craig so that he was forced to lift his right foot and grope through the turn. Again he almost missed it and his rear wheels tore at the steep drop, inches from disaster before he took her through.

He was getting the feel of the machine, and four hundred yards ahead he had a brief glimpse of the Land-Rover through the dust. His headlights spotlit Sally-Anne. She was half-twisted over the side, trying to climb out and throw herself from the fleeing vehicle, but Tungata shot out a long arm and caught her shoulders, plucking her back and forcing her down into the seat.

The scarf flew off her head, winging up like a night-bird to be lost in the darkness, and her thick hair broke out and tangled about her head and face. Then dust obscured the Land-Rover again— and Craig felt his anger hit him in the chest with a force that made

141

him choke. In that moment, he hated Tungata Zebiwe as he had never hated another human being in his life before. He took the next bend cleanly, tracking neatly through and pouring on full power again at the moment he was clear.

The Land-Rover was three hundred yards ahead, the gap shrinking at the rush of the Mercedes, then Craig was braking for the next twist of the road and when he came out the Land-Rover was much closer. Sally-Anne was craning around, looking back at him. Her face was white, almost luminous, in the headlights, her hair danced in a glossy tide around it, seeming at moments almost to smother her, and then the next bend snatched her away. Craig followed them into it, meeting the break of the tail as she floated in the floury dust, and then as he came through he saw the road-block ahead.

There was a three-ton army truck parked squarely across the road, and the gaps between it and the bank had been filled with recently felled thorn trees. The entwined branches formed a solid mattress and the heavy trunks had been chained together. Craig saw the steel links glinting in the headlights. The barrier would stop a bulldozer.

Five troopers stood before the barrier, waving their rifles in an urgent command to the Land-Rover to halt. That they hadn't already opened fire made Craig hope that Peter Fungabera had reached them on the radio, yet he felt a nauseating rush of anxiety when he saw how vulnerable Sally-Anne was in the open vehicle. He imagined a volley of automatic fire tearing into that lovely young body and face.

"Please don't shoot," he whispered and pressed so hard on the accelerator that the cup of his artificial leg bit painfully into his stump. The nose of the Mercedes was fifty feet from the Land-Rover's tail and gaining.

A hundred yards from the solid barrier across the road was a low place in the right-hand bank. Tungata swerved into it and the ugly blunt-nosed vehicle flew up it, all four wheels clawing as it went over the top and tore like a combine-harvester into the high yellow stand of elephant grass beyond.

Craig knew he could not follow him. The low-slung Mercedes would tear her guts out on the bank. He raced past it and then hit the brakes as the road-block loomed up and filled his windshield. The Mercedes broadsided to a dead stop in a storm of its own dust and Craig threw his weight on the door and tumbled out into the road.

He caught his balance and scrambled up the right-hand bank. The Land-Rover was twenty yards away, engine roaring in low gear, crashing and bouncing over the broken ground, mowing down the dense yellow grass whose stems were thick as a man's little finger and taller than his head, weaving between the forest trees, its speed reduced by the terrain to that of a running man. Craig saw that Tungata would succeed in detouring around the road-block, and he ran to head off the Land-Rover. Anger and fear for Sally-Anne seemed to guide his feet. He stumbled only once on the rough footing.

Tungata Zebiwe saw him coming and lifted the rifle one-handed, aiming over the hood of the jolting, roaring Land-Rover, but Sally-Anne threw herself across the weapon, clinging to it with both arms, her weight forcing the barrel down, and Tungata could not take his other hand from the wheel as it kicked and whipped in his grip. They were past the road-block now, and Craig was losing ground to them. Realizing with a slide in his chest that he could not catch them, he floundered along behind the roaring vehicle.

Sally-Anne and Tungata were struggling confusedly together until the big black man tore his arm free and, using the hand as a blade, chopped her brutally under the ear. She slumped face forward onto the dashboard, and Tungata swung the wheel over. The vehicle swerved, giving Craig a few precious yards' advantage, and then it seemed to hover for an instant on the high bank beyond the road-block before it leaped over the edge and dropped into the roadway with a clangour of metal and spinning tyres.

Craig used the last of his reserves of strength and determination and raced forward to reach the place on the bank an instant after it had disappeared.

Ten feet below him, the Land-Rover was miraculously still upright, and Tungata, badly shaken, his mouth bleeding from impact with the steering-wheel, was struggling for control.

Craig did not hesitate. He launched himself out over the bank, and the drop sucked his breath away. The Land-Rover was accelerating away, and he dropped half over the tail-gate. He felt his ribs crunch on metal, his breath whistling in his throat as it was driven from his lungs, and his vision starred for an instant—but he found a grip on the radio set and hung on blindly.

He felt the Land-Rover surging forward under him and heard Sally-Anne whimper with pain and terror. The sound steeled him, his vision cleared. He was hanging over the back of the tail-gate, his feet dangling and dragging.

Behind him the army truck was swinging out of the road-block, engine thundering and headlights glaring in pursuit, while just ahead the main-road T-junction was coming up with a rush as the Land-Rover built up to top speed again.

Craig braced himself for the turn, but even so, when it came, his upper arms were almost torn from their shoulder sockets, as Tungata took the left fork on two wheels. Now he was heading north. Of course, the Zambian border was only a hundred miles ahead. The road went down into the great escarpment, and there was no human settlement in that tsetse-fly-infested, heat-baked wilderness before the border post and the bridge over the Zambezi at Chirundu. With a hostage it was just possible he could reach it. If Craig gave up, he could reach it—or get himself and Sally-Anne killed in the attempt.

By inches Craig dragged himself into the Land-Rover. Sally-Anne was crumpled down in the seat, her head lolling from side to side with each jerk and sway of the vehicle, and Tungata was tall and heavy-shouldered beside her, his white shirt gleaming in the reflected glare of the headlights.

Craig released his grip with one hand and made a grab for the back of the seat. Instantly the Land-Rover swerved violently and in that same instant he saw the glint of Tungata's eyes in the rear-view mirror. He had been watching Craig, waiting to catch him off-balance and throw him.

The centrifugal force rolled Craig over and out over the side of the vehicle. He had a hold with his left hand only, and the muscles and tendons crackled with the strain as his full weight was thrown on it. He gasped with the agony as it tore up his arm into his chest, but he held on, hanging overboard with the steel edge catching him in his injured ribs again.

Tungata swerved a second time, running his wheels over the verge, and Craig saw the bank rushing at him in the headlights. Tungata was attempting to wipe him off the Land-Rover on the bank, trying to shred him to pieces between shaly rock and sharp metal. Craig screamed involuntarily with the effort as he jack-knifed his knees up and over. There was a rushing din of metal and stone as the Land-Rover brushed the bank. Something struck his leg a blow that jarred him to his hip and he heard the straps part as his leg was torn away. If it had been flesh and bone he would have been fatally maimed. Instead, as the Land-Rover swung back onto the road he used the momentum to roll across the back seat and whip his free arm around Tungata's neck from behind.

It was a stranglehold and as he threw all his strength into it, he felt the give of Tungata's larynx in the crook of his elbow, and the loaded feel of the vertebrae, like the tension of a dry twig on the point of snapping. He wanted to kill him, he wanted to tear his head off his body, but he could not anchor himself to apply those last few ounces of pressure.

Tungata lifted both hands off the wheel, tearing at his wrist and elbow, making a glottal, cawing sound, and the untended steering-wheel spun wildly. The Land-Rover charged off the road, plunged over the unprotected verge onto the steep rocky slope and, with a rending screech of metal, crashed end over end.

Craig's grip was torn open and he was flung clear. He hit hard earth, cart-wheeled, and lay for a second, his ears humming and his body crushed and helpless until, slowly, he rallied and pulled himself to his knees.

The Land-Rover lay on its back. The headlights still blazed, and thirty paces down the slope, full in their beam, lay Sally-Anne. She looked like a little girl asleep, her eyes closed and her mouth relaxed, the lips very red against her pallor, but from her hair-line a thin maroon-black serpent of blood crawled down across her pale brow.

He started to crawl towards her, when another figure rose out of the intervening darkness, a great, dark, wide-shouldered figure. Tungata was stunned, staggering in a half-circle, clutching his injured throat. At the sight of him Craig went berserk with grief and rage.

He hurled himself at Tungata and they came together, chest to chest. Long ago, as friends, they had often wrestled, but Craig had forgotten the sheer bull strength of the man. His muscles were hard and resilient and black as the cured rubber of a transcontinental truck tyre, and, one-legged, Craig was unbalanced. Dazed though he was, Tungata heaved him off his foot.

As he went down, Craig held on. Despite his own strength, Tungata could not break the grip. They went down together, and

Craig used his stump, driving up with the hard rubbery pad at the end of it, using the swing of it and Tungata's own falling weight to slog into Tungata's lower body.

Tungata grunted and the strength went out of him. Craig rolled out from under him, reared back onto his shoulders, and used all his body to launch himself forward again to hit with the stump. It sounded like an axe swung double-handed against a tree trunk, and it caught Tungata in the middle of his chest right over the heart.

Tungata dropped over backwards and lay still. Craig crawled to him and reached for his unprotected throat with both hands. He felt the ropes of muscle framing the sharp hard lump of the thyroid cartilage and he drove his thumbs deeply into it, and, at the feel of ebbing life under his hands, his rage fell away—he found he could not kill him. He opened his hands and drew away, shaking and gasping.

He left Tungata lying crumpled on the rocky earth and crawled to where Sally-Anne lay. He picked her up and sat with her in his lap, cradling her head against his shoulder, desolated by the slack and lifeless feel of her body. With one hand he wiped away the trickle of blood before it reached her eyes.

Above them on the road the following truck pulled up with a metallic squeal of brakes and armed men came swarming down the slope, baying like a pack of hounds at the kill. In his arms like a child waking from sleep, Sally-Anne stirred and mumbled softly.

She was alive, still alive, and he whispered to her, "My darling, oh my darling, I love you so!"

•   •   •

Four of Sally-Anne's ribs were cracked, her right ankle was badly sprained, and there was serious bruising and swelling on her neck from the blow she had received. However, the cut in her scalp was superficial and the X-rays showed no damage to the skull. Nevertheless, she was held for observation in the private ward that Peter Fungabera had secured for her in the overcrowded public hospital.

It was here that Abel Khori, the public prosecutor assigned to the Tungata Zebiwe case, visited her. Mr. Khori was a distinguished-looking Shona who had been called to the London bar and still affected the dress of Lincoln's Inn Fields, together

146

with a penchant for learned, if irrelevant, Latin phrases.

"I am visiting you to clarify in my own mind certain points in the statement that you have already made to the police. For it would be highly improper of me to influence in any way the evidence that you will give," Khori explained.

He showed Craig and Sally-Anne the reports of spontaneous Matabele demonstrations for Tungata's release, which had been swiftly broken up by the police and units of the Third Brigade, and which the Shona editor of the *Herald* had relegated to the middle pages.

"We must always bear in mind that this man is *ipso jure* accused of a criminal act, and he should not be allowed to become a tribal martyr. You see the dangers. The sooner we can have the entire business settled *mutatis mutandis*, the better for everybody."

Craig and Sally-Anne were at first astonished and then made uneasy at the dispatch with which Tungata Zebiwe was to be brought to trial. Despite the fact that the rolls were filled for seven months ahead, his case was given a date in the Supreme Court ten days hence.

"We cannot *nudis verbis* keep a man of his stature in jail for seven months," the prosecutor explained, "and to grant him bail and allow him liberty to inflame his followers would be suicidal folly."

Apart from the trial, there were other lesser matters to occupy both Craig and Sally-Anne. Her Cessna was due for its thousand-hour check and "certificate of airworthiness." There were no facilities for this in Zimbabwe, and they had to arrange for a fellow pilot to fly the machine down to Johannesburg for her. "I will feel like a bird with its wings clipped," she complained.

"I know the feeling." Craig grinned ruefully and banged his crutch on the floor.

"Oh, I'm sorry, Craig."

"No, don't be. Somehow I no longer mind talking about my missing pin. Not with you, anyway."

"When will it be back?"

"Morgan Oxford sent it out in the diplomatic bag and Henry Pickering has promised to chase up the technicians at Hopkins Orthopaedic. I should have it back for the trial."

The trial. Everything seemed to come back to the trial. Even the running of King's Lynn and the final preparations for the opening of the lodges at Zambezi Waters could not seduce Craig away from Sally Anne's bedside and the preparations for the trial. He was fortunate to have Hans Groenewald at King's Lynn, and Peter Younghusband, the young Kenyan manager and guide whom Sally-Anne had chosen, had arrived to take over the daily running of Zambezi Waters. Though he spoke to these two every day on either telephone or radio, Craig stayed on in Harare close to Sally-Anne.

Craig's leg arrived back the day before Sally-Anne's discharge from the hospital. He pulled up his trouser-cuff to show it to her.

"Straightened, panel-beaten, lubricated and thoroughly reconditioned," he boasted. "How's your head?"

She laughed. "The same as your leg. Although the doctors have warned me off bouncing on it again for at least the next few weeks."

She was using a cane for her ankle, and her chest was still strapped when he carried her bag down to the Land-Rover the following morning.

"Ribs hurting?" He saw her wince as she climbed into the vehicle.

"As long as nobody squeezes them, I'll pull through."

"No squeezing. Is that a rule?" he asked.

"I guess—" She paused and regarded him for a moment before she lowered her eyes and murmured demurely, "But then rules are for fools, and for the guidance of wise men."

And Craig was considerably heartened.

* * *

Number Two Court of the Mashonaland division of the Supreme Court of the Republic of Zimbabwe still retained all the trappings of British justice.

The elevated bench with the coat of arms of Zimbabwe above the judge's seat dominated the courtroom, the tiers of oaken benches faced it, and the witness-box and the dock were set on either hand. The prosecutors, the assessors and the attorneys charged with the defence wore the long black robes, while the judge was splendid in scarlet. Only the colour of the faces had changed, their blackness accentuated by the tight snowy curls of their wigs and the starched white swallow-tail collars.

The courtroom was packed, and when the standing room at the back was filled, the ushers closed the doors, leaving the crowd overflowing into the passages beyond. The crowds were orderly and grave, almost all of them Matabele who had made the long bus journey across the country from Matabeleland, many of them wearing the rosettes of the ZAPU party. Only when the accused was led into the dock was there a stir and murmur, and at the rear of the court a woman dressed in ZAPU colours cried hysterically, "Bayete, Nkosi Nkulu!" and gave the clenched-fist salute.

The guards seized her immediately and hustled her out through the doors. Tungata Zebiwe stood in the dock and watched impassively, by his sheer presence belittling every other person in the room. Even the judge, Mr. Justice Domashawa, a tall, emaciated Mashona, with a delicately bridged atypical Egyptian nose and small, bright, birdlike eyes, although vested in all the authority of his scarlet robes, seemed ordinary in comparison. However, Mr. Justice Domashawa had a formidable reputation, and the prosecutor had rejoiced in his selection when he told Craig and Sally-Anne of it.

"Oh, he is indeed *persona grata*, and now it is very much *in gremio legis*, we will see justice done, never fear."

While the country had still been Rhodesia, the British jury system had been abandoned. The judge would reach a verdict with the assistance of the two black-robed assessors who sat with him on the bench. Both these assessors were Shona: one was an expert on wildlife conservation, and the other a senior magistrate. The judge could call upon their expert advice if he so wished, but the final verdict would be his alone.

Now he settled his robes around him, the way an ostrich shakes out its feathers as it settles on the nest, and he fixed Tungata Zebiwe with his bright eyes while the clerk of the court read out the charge-sheet in English.

There were eight main charges: dealing in and exporting the products of scheduled wild animals, abducting and holding a hostage, assault with a deadly weapon, assault with intent to do grievous bodily harm, attempted murder, violently resisting arrest, theft of a motor vehicle, and malicious damage to state property. There were also twelve lesser charges.

"By God," Craig whispered to Sally-Anne, "they are throwing the bricks from the walls at him."

"And the tiles off the floor," she agreed. "Good for them, I'd love to see the bastard swing."

"Sorry, my dear, none of them is a capital charge." And yet all through the prosecution's opening address, Craig was overcome by a sense of almost Grecian tragedy, in which an heroic figure was surrounded and brought low by lesser, meaner men.

Despite his feelings, Craig was aware that Abel Khori was doing a good businesslike job of laying out his case in his opening address, even displaying restraint in his use of Latin maxims. The first of a long list of prosecution witnesses was General Peter Fungabera. Resplendent in full dress, he took the oath and stood straight-backed and martial with his swagger-stick held loosely in one hand. His testimony was given without equivocation, so direct and impressive that the judge nodded his approval from time to time as he made his notes.

The Central Committee of the ZAPU party had briefed a London barrister for the defence, but even Mr. Joseph Petal, Q.C., could not shake General Fungabera and very soon realized the futility of the effort, so he retired to wait for more vulnerable prey.

The next witness was the driver of the truck containing the contraband. He was an ex-ZIPRA guerrilla, recently released from one of the rehabilitation centres, and his testimony was given in the vernacular and translated into English by the court interpreter.

"Had you ever met the accused before the night you were arrested?" Abel Khori demanded of him after establishing his identity.

"Yes. I was with him in the fighting."

"Did you see him again after the war?"

"Yes."

"Will you tell the court when that was?"

"Last year in the dry season."

"Before you were placed in the rehabilitation centre?"

"Yes, before that."

"Where did you meet Minister Tungata Zebiwe?"

"In the valley, near the great river."

"Will you tell the court about that meeting?"

"We were hunting elephant—for the ivory."

"How did you hunt them?"

"We used tribesmen, Batonka tribesmen, and a helicopter, to drive them into the old minefield."

"I object to this line of questioning, my lord." Mr. Petal, Q.C., jumped up. "This has nothing to do with the charges."

"It has reference to the first charge."

"Your objection is overruled, Mr. Petal. Please continue, Mr. Prosecutor."

150

"How many elephant did you kill?"

"Many, many elephant."

"Can you estimate how many?"

"Perhaps two hundred elephant, I am not sure."

"And you state that the Minister Tungata Zebiwe was there?"

"He came after the elephant had been killed. He came to count the ivory and take it away in his helicopter—"

"What helicopter?"

"A government helicopter."

"I object, your lordship, the point is irrelevant."

"Objection overruled, Mr. Petal, please continue."

When his turn came for cross-examination, Mr. Joseph Petal went into the attack immediately.

"I put it to you that you were never a member of Minister Tungata Zebiwe's resistance fighters. That you never, in fact, met the minister until the night on the Karoi road—"

"I object, your lordship," Abel Khori shouted indignantly. "The defence is trying to discredit the witness in the knowledge that no records of patriotic soldiers exist and that the witness cannot, therefore, prove his gallant service to the cause."

"Objection sustained. Mr. Petal, please confine your questions to the matter in hand and do not bully the witness."

"Very well, your lordship." Mr. Petal was rosy-faced with frustration as he turned back to the witness. "Can you tell the judge when you were released from the rehabilitation centre?"

"I forget. I cannot remember."

"Was it a long time or a short time before your arrest?"

"A short time," the witness replied sulkily, looking down at his hands in his lap.

"Were you not released from the prison camp on the condition that you drove the truck that night, and that you agreed to give evidence—"

"My lord!" shrieked Abel Khori, and the judge's voice was as shrill and indignant.

"Mr. Petal, you will not refer to state rehabilitation centres as prison camps."

"As your lordship pleases." Mr. Petal continued, "Were you made any promises when you were released from the rehabilitation centre?"

"No." The witness looked about him unhappily.

"Were you visited in the centre, two days before your release

151

by a Captain Timon Nbebi of the Third Brigade?"

"No."

"Did you have any visitors in the camp?"

"No! No!"

"No visitors at all, are you sure?"

"The witness has already answered that question," the judge stopped him, and Mr. Petal sighed theatrically, and threw up his hands.

"No further questions, my lord."

"Do you intend calling any further witnesses, Mr. Khori?"

Craig knew that the next witness should have been Timon Nbebi, but unaccountably Abel Khori passed over him and called instead the trooper who had been knocked down by the Land-Rover. Craig felt an uneasy little chill of doubt at the change in the prosecution's tactics. Did the prosecutor want to protect Captain Nbebi from cross-examination? Did he want to prevent Mr. Petal from pursuing the question of a visit by Timon Nbebi to the rehabilitation centre? If this was so, the implications were unthinkable, so Craig forced himself to put his doubts aside.

The necessity for all questions and replies to be translated made the entire court process long-drawn-out and tedious, so it was only on the third day that Craig was called to the witness stand.

*   *   *

After Craig had taken the oath, and before Abel Khori had begun his examination, he glanced towards the dock. Tungata Zebiwe was watching him intently, and as their eyes locked, Tungata made a sign with his right hand.

In the old days when they had worked together as rangers in the Game Department, Craig and Tungata had developed this sign language to a high degree. During the dangerous work of closing in a breeding herd to begin the bloody elephant cullings during which it had been their duty to destroy surplus animals that were overpopulating the reserves, or when they were stalking a marauding cattle-killing pride of lions, they had communicated silently and swiftly with this private language.

Now Tungata gave him the clenched fist, his powerful black fingers closing over the pink of his palm in the sign that said "Beware! Extreme danger."

The last time Tungata had given him that sign, he had had only microseconds to turn and meet the charge of the enraged lung-wounded lioness as she came grunting in bloody pink explosive gasps of breath out of heavy brush cover, launching herself like a golden thunderbolt upon him, so that even though the bullet from his .458 magnum had smashed through her heart, her momentum had hurled Craig off his feet.

Now Tungata's sign made his nerves tingle and the hair on his forearm rise, at the memory of danger past and the promise of danger present. Was it a threat—or a warning, Craig wondered, staring at Tungata. He could not be certain, for Tungata was now expressionless and unmoving. Craig gave him the signal, "Query? I do not understand," but Tungata ignored it, and Craig abruptly realized that he had missed Abel Khori's opening question.

"I'm sorry—will you repeat that?"

Swiftly Abel Khori led him through his questions.

"Did you see the driver of the truck make any signal as the Mercedes approached?"

"Yes, he flashed his lights."

"And what was the response?"

"The Mercedes stopped and two of the occupants left the vehicle and went to speak with the driver of the truck."

"In your opinion, was this a pre-arranged meeting?"

"Objection, your lordship, the witness cannot know that."

"Sustained. The witness will disregard the question."

"We come now to your gallant rescue of Miss Jay from the evil clutches of the accused."

"Objection—the word 'evil.'"

"You will discontinue the use of the adjective 'evil.'"

"As your lordship pleases."

After the hand-signal, and during the rest of Craig's testimony, Tungata Zebiwe sat immovable as a figure carved in the granite of Matabeleland, with his chin sunk in his chest, but his eyes never left Craig's face.

As Mr. Petal rose to cross-examine, Tungata moved for the first time, leaning forward to rumble a few terse words. Mr. Petal seemed to protest, but Tungata made a commanding gesture.

"No questions, your lordship," Mr. Petal acquiesced, and sank back in his seat, freeing Craig to leave the witness-box without harassment.

Sally-Anne was the last of the prosecution witnesses and, after Peter Fungabera, perhaps the most telling.

She was still limping with her sprained ankle, so that Abel

Khori hurried forward to help her into the witness-box. The shadow of the bruise on her neck was the only blemish on her skin, and she gave her evidence without hesitation in a clear, pleasing voice.

"When the accused seized you, what were your feelings?"

"I was in fear of my life."

"You say the accused struck you. Where did the blow land?"

"Here on my neck—you can see the bruise."

"You state that the accused aimed the stolen rifle at Mr. Mellow. What was your reaction?"

"Will you tell the court whether you sustained any other injuries."

Abel Khori made the most of such a lovely witness, and very wisely, Mr. Petal once again declined to cross-examine. The prosecution closed its case on the evening of the third day, leaving Craig troubled and depressed.

He and Sally-Anne ate at her favourite steak-house, and even a bottle of good Cape wine did not cheer him.

"That business about the driver never having met Tungata before, and being released only on a promise to drive the truck—"

"You didn't believe that?" Sally-Anne scoffed. "Even the judge made no secret of how far-fetched he thought that was."

After he dropped her at her apartment, Craig walked alone through the deserted streets, feeling lonely and betrayed—though he could not find a logical reason for the feeling.

*　　*　　*

Mr. Joseph Petal, Q.C., opened his defence by calling Tungata Zebiwe's chauffeur.

He was a heavily built Matabele, and although young, already running to fat, with a round face that should have been jovial and smiling but was now troubled and clouded. His head had been freshly shaved, and he never looked at Tungata once during his time on the witness stand.

"On the night of your arrest, what orders did Minister Zebiwe give you?"

"Nothing. He told me nothing."

Mr. Petal looked genuinely puzzled and consulted his notes.

"Did he not tell you where to drive? Did you not know where you were going?"

"He said, 'Go straight,' 'Turn left here,' 'Turn right here,'" the driver muttered. "I did not know where we were going."

154

Obviously Mr. Petal was not expecting this reply.

"Did Minister Zebiwe not order you to drive to Tuti Mission?"

"Objection, your lordship."

"Do not lead the witness, Mr. Petal."

Mr. Joseph Petal was clearly thinking on his feet. He shuffled his papers, glanced at Tungata Zebiwe, who sat completely impassive, and then switched his line of questioning.

"Since the night of your arrest, where have you been?"

"In prison."

"Did you have any visitors?"

"My wife came."

"No others?"

"No." The chauffeur ducked his head defensively.

"What are those marks on your head? Were you beaten?"

For the first time Craig noticed the dark lumps on the chauffeur's shaven pate.

"Your lordship, I object most strenuously," Abel Khori cried plaintively.

"Mr. Petal, what is the purpose of this line of questioning?" Mr. Justice Domashawa demanded ominously.

"My lord, I am trying to find why the witness's evidence conflicts with his previous statement to the police."

Mr. Petal struggled to obtain a clear reply from the sulky and uncooperative witness, and finally gave up with a gesture of resignation.

"No further questions, your lordship." And Abel Khori rose smiling to cross-examine.

"So the truck flashed its lights at you?"

"Yes."

"And what happened then?"

"I do not understand."

"Did anybody in the Mercedes say or do anything when you saw the truck?"

"My lord—" Mr. Petal began.

"I think that is a fair question—the witness will answer."

The chauffeur frowned with the effort of recall and then mumbled, "Comrade Minister Zebiwe said, 'There it is—pull over and stop.'"

"'There it is!'" Abel Khori repeated slowly and clearly. "'Pull over and stop!' That is what the accused said when he saw the truck, is that correct?"

"Yes. He said it."

"No further questions, your lordship."

• • •

"Call Sarah Tandiwe Nyoni," Mr. Joseph Petal introduced his surprise witness, and Abel Khori frowned and conferred agitatedly with his two assistant prosecutors. One of them rose, bowed to the bench and hurriedly left the court.

Sarah Tandiwe Nyoni entered the witness stand and took the oath in perfect English. Her voice was melodious and sweet, her manner as reserved and shy as the day that Craig and Sally-Anne had first met her at Tuti Mission. She wore a lime-green cotton dress with a white collar and simple low-heeled white shoes. Her hair was elaborately braided in traditional style, and the moment she finished reading the oath, she turned her soft gaze onto Tungata Zebiwe in the dock. He neither smiled nor altered his expression, but his right hand, resting on the railing of the dock, moved slightly, and Craig realized that he was using the secret sign-language to the girl.

"Courage!" said that signal. "I am with you!" And the girl took visible strength and confidence from it. She lifted her chin and faced Mr. Petal squarely.

"Please state your name."

"I am Sarah Tandiwe Nyoni," she replied. *Tandiwe Nyoni*, her Matabele name, meant "Beloved Bird" and Craig translated softly to Sally-Anne.

"It suits her perfectly," she whispered back.

"What is your profession?"

"I am the headmistress of Tuti State Primary School."

"Will you tell the court your qualifications."

Joseph Petal established swiftly that she was an educated and responsible young woman. Then he went on:

"Do you know the accused, Tungata Zebiwe?"

She looked at Tungata again before answering, and her face seemed to glow. "I do, oh yes, I do," she whispered huskily.

"Please speak up, my dear."

"I know him."

"Did he ever visit you at Tuti Mission Station?"

She nodded. "Yes."

"How often?"

156

"The Comrade Minister is an important and busy man, I am a schoolteacher—"

Tungata made a small gesture of denial with his right hand. She saw it and a little smile formed on her perfectly sculptured lips.

"He came as often as he could, but not as often as I would have wished."

"Were you expecting him on the night in question?"

"I was."

"Why?"

"We had spoken together, on the telephone, the previous morning. He promised me he would come. He said he would drive up, and arrive before midnight." The smile faded from her lips, and her eyes grew dark and desolate. "I waited until daylight—but he did not come."

"As far as you know was there any particular reason that he was going to visit you that week-end?"

"Yes." Sarah's cheeks intensified in color, and Sally-Anne was fascinated. She had never seen a black girl blush before. "Yes, he said he wished to speak to my father. I had arranged the meeting."

"Thank you, my dear," said Joseph Petal gently.

During Mr. Petal's examination, the prosecutor's assistant had slipped back into his seat and handed Abel Khori a handwritten sheet of notes. Abel Khori was holding these in his hand as he rose to cross-examine.

"Miss Nyoni, can you tell the court the meaning of the Sindebele word *isifebi*?"

Tungata Zebiwe growled softly and began to rise, but the police guard laid a hand on his shoulder to restrain him.

"It means a harlot," Sarah answered quietly.

"Does it not also mean an unmarried woman who lives with a man—"

"My lord!" Joseph Petal's plea was belated but outraged, and Mr. Justice Domashawa sustained it.

"Miss Nyoni," Abel Khori tried again, "do you love the accused? Please speak up. We cannot hear you."

This time Sarah's voice was firm, almost defiant. "I do."

"Would you do anything for him?"

"I would."

"Would you lie to save him?"

Joseph Petal leaped to his feet. "I object, your lordship."

"And I withdraw the question." Abel Khori forestalled the judge's intervention. "Let me rather put it to you, Miss Nyoni, that the accused had asked you to provide a warehouse at your school where illegal ivory and leopard-skins could be stored!"

"No." Sarah shook her head. "He never would—"

"And that he had asked you to supervise the loading of those tusks into a truck, and the dispatch of the truck—"

"No! No!" she cried.

"When you spoke to him on the telephone, did he not order you to prepare a shipment of—"

"No! He is a good man," Sarah sobbed. "A great and good man. He would never have done that."

"No further questions, your lordship." Looking very pleased with himself, Abel Khori sat down and his assistant leaned over to whisper his congratulations.

"I call the accused, the Minister Tungata Zebiwe, to the stand."

That was a risky move on Mr. Petal's part. Even as a layman Craig could see that Abel Khori had shown himself to be a hardy scrapper.

Joseph Petal began by establishing Tungata's position in the community, his services to the revolution, his frugal life-style.

"Do you own any fixed property?"

"I own a house in Harare."

"Will you tell the court how much you paid for it?"

"Fourteen thousand dollars."

"That is not a great deal to pay for a house, is it?"

"It is not a great deal of house." Tungata's reply was dead-pan, and even the judge smiled.

"A motor car?"

"I have a ministerial vehicle at my disposal."

"Foreign bank accounts?"

"None."

"Wives?"

"None—" he glanced in the direction of Sarah Nyoni, who sat in the back row of the gallery—"yet," he finished.

"Common-law wives? Other women?"

"My elderly aunt lives in my home. She supervises my household."

"Coming now to the night in question. Can you tell the court why you were on the Karoi road?"

158

"I was on my way to Tuti Mission Station."

"For what reason?"

"To visit Miss Nyoni—and to speak to her father on a personal matter."

"Your visit had been arranged?"

"Yes, in a telephone conversation with Miss Nyoni."

"You had visited her before—on more than one occasion?"

"That is so."

"What accommodation did you use on those occasions?"

"There was a thatched *indlu* set aside for my use."

"A hut? With a sleeping-mat and open fire?"

"Yes."

"You did not find such lodgings beneath you?"

"On the contrary, I enjoy the opportunity of returning to the traditional ways of my people."

"Did anyone share these lodgings with you?"

"My driver and my bodyguards."

"Miss Nyoni—did she visit you in these lodgings?"

"That would have been contrary to our custom and tribal law."

"The prosecutor used the word *isifebi*—what do you make of that?"

"He might aptly apply that word to women of his acquaintance. I know nobody whom it might fit."

Again the judge smiled, and the prosecutor's assistant nudged Abel Khori playfully.

"Now, Mr. Minister, was anybody else aware of your intention of visiting Tuti Mission?"

"I made no secret of my intention. I wrote it down in my desk-diary."

"Do you have that diary?"

"No. I requested my secretary to hand it over to the defence. It is, however, missing from my desk."

"I see. When you ordered your chauffeur to prepare the car, did you inform him of your destination?"

"I did."

"He says you did not."

Tungata shrugged. "Then his memory is at fault—or has been affected."

"Very well. Now, on the night that you were driving on the road between Karoi and Tuti Mission, did you encounter any other vehicle?"

"Yes. There was a truck parked in darkness, off the road, but facing in our direction."

"Will you tell the court what transpired then?"

"The truck-driver switched on his lights and then flicked them three times. At the same time he drove forward into the road."

"In such a way as to force your car to halt?"

"That is correct."

"What did you do then?"

"I said to my driver, 'Pull over—but be careful. This could be an ambush.'"

"You were not expecting to meet the truck then?"

"I was not."

"Did you say, 'There it is! Pull over!'?"

"I did not."

"What did you mean by the words 'This could be an ambush'?"

"Recently, many vehicles have been attacked by armed bandits, *shufta*, especially on lonely roads at night."

"So what were your feelings?"

"I was anticipating trouble."

"What happened then?"

"Two of my bodyguards left the Mercedes and went to speak to the driver of the truck."

"From where you were seated in the Mercedes, could you see the truck-driver?"

"Yes. He was a complete stranger to me. I had never seen him before."

"What was your reaction to this?"

"I was by this time extremely wary."

"Then what happened?"

"Suddenly there were other headlights on the road behind us. A voice on a bull-horn ordering my men to surrender and throw down their arms. My Mercedes was surrounded by armed men and I was forcibly dragged from it."

"Did you recognize any of these men?"

"Yes. When I was pulled from the Mercedes, I recognized General Fungabera."

"Did this allay your suspicions?"

"On the contrary, I was now convinced that I was in danger of my life."

"Why was that, Mr. Minister?"

160

"General Fungabera commands a brigade which is notorious for its ruthless acts against prominent Matabele——"

"I object, your lordship—the Third Brigade is a unit of the regular army of the state, and General Fungabera a well-known and respected officer," Abel Khori cried.

"The prosecution is totally justified in its objection." The judge was suddenly trembling with anger. "I cannot allow the accused to use this courtroom to attack a prominent soldier and his gallant men. I cannot allow the accused to stand before me and disseminate tribal hatreds and prejudices. Be warned—I will not hesitate to find you guilty of gross contempt if you continue in this vein."

Joseph Petal took fully thirty seconds to let his witness recover from this tirade.

"You say you felt that your life was in danger?"

"Yes," said Tungata quietly.

"You were strung up and on edge?"

"Yes."

"Did you see the soldiers unloading ivory and furs from the truck?"

"I did."

"What was your reaction?"

"I believed that these would somehow, I was not certain how, but I believed they would incriminate me, and be used as an excuse to kill me."

"I object, your lordship," Abel Khori called out.

"I will not warn the accused again," Mr. Justice promised threateningly.

"What happened then?"

"Miss Jay left the vehicle in which she was travelling and she came near me. The soldiers were distracted. I believed that this would be my last chance. I took hold of Miss Jay to prevent the soldiers' firing and attempted to escape in the Land-Rover."

"Thank you, Mr. Minister." Mr. Joseph Petal turned to the judge. "My lord, my witness has had a tiring examination. May I suggest that the court rise until tomorrow morning to allow him a chance to recover?"

Abel Khori was instantly up on his feet, lusting for blood.

"It is barely noon yet, and the accused has been on the stand for less than thirty minutes, and his counsel has dealt with him *recte et sauviter*. For a trained and hardened soldier, that is a mere

161

bagatelle *per se*." Abel Khori, in his agitation, lapsed into Latin.

"We will continue, Mr. Petal," said the judge. And Joseph Petal shrugged.

"Your witness, Mr. Khori."

Abel Khori was in his element, becoming lyrical and poetic. "You testified that you were in fear of your life—but I put it to you that you were attacked by guilt, that you were in deadly fear of retribution, that you were terrified by the prospect of facing the exemplary processes of this very people's court, of facing the wrath of that learned and just scarlet-clad figure you now see before you."

"No."

"That it was nothing more than craven guilty conscience that made you embark on a series of heinous and callous criminal actions—"

"No. That is not so."

"When you seized the lovely Miss Jay, did you not use excessive physical force to twist her young and tender limbs? Did you not rain brutal blows upon her?"

"I struck her once to prevent her hurling herself from the speeding vehicle and injuring herself seriously."

"Did you not aim a deadly weapon—to wit, a military assault rifle—which you knew to be loaded, at the person of General Peter Fungabera?"

"I threatened him with the rifle—yes, that is true."

"And then you fired deliberately at his nether regions—to wit, his abdomen?"

"I did not fire at Fungabera. I aimed to miss him."

"I put it to you that you tried to murder the general, and only his marvellous reflexes saved him from your attack."

"If I had tried to kill him," said Tungata softly, "he would be dead."

"When you stole the Land-Rover, did you realize that it was state property?"

"Did you aim the rifle at Mr. Craig Mellow? And were you only prevented from murdering him by Miss Jay's brave intervention?"

For almost another hour Abel Khori flew at the impassive figure in the dock, extracting from him a series of damning admissions, so that when at last Abel Khori sat down, preening like a victorious gamecock, Craig judged that Mr. Joseph Petal had paid in heavy coin for any small advantage he might have gained by placing his client on the witness stand.

However, Mr. Petal's closing address was finely pitched to incite sympathy, and to explain and justify Tungata Zebiwe's actions on that night, without flouting the judge's patriotic or tribal instincts in the process.

"I will reserve my judgement until tomorrow," Mr. Justice Domashawa announced, and the court rose, the spectators humming with excited comment as they streamed out into the passage.

Over dinner Sally-Anne admitted, "For the first time in this whole business, I felt sorry when Sarah went on the stand—she is such a sweet child."

Craig chuckled. "Child? I guess she is a year or two older than you. That makes you a babe in arms."

She ignored his levity and went on seriously, "She so obviously believes in him that for a moment or two even I began to doubt what I knew. Then, of course, Abel Khori brought me back to earth."

•   •   •

Mr. Justice Domashawa read out his judgement in his precise, old-maidish voice that somehow did not suit the gravity of the subject. First, he covered the events that were common cause between prosecution and defence, and then went on, "The defence has based its case on two main pillars. The first of these is the testimony of Miss Sarah Nyoni that the accused was on his way to what, for want of a better word, we are led to believe was a love-tryst, and that his meeting with the truck was a coincidence or contrived in some unexplained manner by persons unknown.

"Now Miss Nyoni impressed this court as being a naïve and unworldly young lady, and by her admission is completely under the influence of the accused. The court has had, perforce, to consider the prosecution's postulation that Miss Nyoni might even have been, in fact, so influenced by the accused as to consent to act as an accomplice in arranging the consignment of contraband.

"In view of the foregoing, the court has rejected the testimony of Miss Nyoni as potentially biased and unreliable.

"The second pillar of the defence's case rests on the premise that the life of the accused was threatened, or that he believed it to be threatened, by the arresting officers, and in this belief embarked on a series of unreasoned and unreasoning acts of self-protection.

163

"Brigadier General Peter Fungabera is an officer of impeccable reputation, a high official of the state. The Third Brigade is an elite unit of the state's regular army, its members, although battle-hardened veterans, are disciplined and trained soldiers.

"The court, therefore, categorically rejects the accused's contention that either General Fungabera or his men could have, even in the remotest possibility, constituted a threat to his safety, let alone his life. The court also rejects the contention that the accused *believed* this to be the case.

"Accordingly, I come to the first charge. Namely, that of trading or dealing in the products of scheduled wild animals. I find the accused guilty as charged and I sentence him to the maximum penalty under the law. Twelve years at hard labour.

"On the second charge of abducting and holding a hostage, I find the accused guilty as charged and I sentence him to ten years at hard labour.

"On the third charge of assault with a deadly weapon, I find the accused guilty and sentence him to six years at hard labour.

"Assault with intent to do grievous bodily harm—six years at hard labour.

"Attempted murder—six years at hard labour.

"I order that these sentences run consecutively and that no part of them be suspended."

Even Abel Khori's head jerked up at that. The sentences totalled forty years. With full remission for good behaviour, Tungata could still expect to serve over thirty years, the rest of his useful life.

At the back of the court a black woman shrieked in Sindebele, "Baba! The father! They are taking our father from us!" Others took up the cry. "Father of the people! Our father is dead to us."

A man began to sing in a soaring baritone voice:

> "Why do you weep, widows of the Shangani . . .
> Why do you weep, little sons of the Moles,
> When your fathers did the king's bidding?"

It was one of the ancient fighting songs of the impis of King Lobengula, and the singer was a man in his prime with a strong intelligent face and a short-cropped, spade-shaped beard barely speckled with grey. As he sang, the tears ran down his cheeks into his beard. In another time he might have been an induna of one of the royal impis. His song was taken up by the men around him, and Mr. Justice Domashawa came to his feet in a fury.

"If there is not silence this instant, I will have the court cleared and the offenders charged with contempt," he shouted over the singing, but it was five minutes more of pandemonium before the ushers could restore order.

Through it all, Tungata Zebiwe stood quietly in the dock, with just the barest hint of a mocking smile on his lips. When at last it was over, but before his guards led him away, he gazed across the courtroom at Craig Mellow and he made a last hand-signal. They had only used it playfully before, perhaps after a hard-contested bout of wrestling or some other friendly competition. Now Tungata used it in deadly earnest. The sign meant: "We are equal—the score is levelled," and Craig understood completely. Craig had lost his leg and Tungata had lost his freedom. They were equal.

He wanted to call out to the man who had once been his friend that it was a sorry bargain, not of his choosing, but Tungata had turned away. His wardens were trying to lead him out of the dock, but Tungata pulled back, his head turning as he searched for someone else in the crowded court.

Sarah Nyoni climbed up onto her bench, and over the heads of the crowd she reached out both hands towards him. Now Tungata made his last hand-signal to her. Craig read it clearly. "Take cover!" Tungata ordered her. "Hide yourself. You are in danger."

By the altered expression on her face, Craig saw that the girl had understood the command, and then the warders were dragging Tungata Zebiwe down the stairs that led to the prison cells below ground.

· · ·

Craig Mellow shoved his way through the singing, lamenting crowds of Matabele who overflowed the buildings of the Supreme Court and disrupted the lunch-hour traffic in the broad causeway that it fronted. He dragged Sally-Anne by her wrist and brusquely shouldered aside the press photographers who tried to block his way.

In the car-park he boosted Sally-Anne into the front seat of the Land-Rover and ran round to the driver's side, threatening with a raised fist the last and most persistent photographer in his path. He drove directly to her apartment and halted at the front door. He did not turn off the engine.

"And now?" Sally-Anne asked.

"I don't understand the question," he snapped.

"Hey!" she said. "I'm your friend—remember me?"

"I'm sorry." He slumped over the wheel. "I feel rotten—plain bloody rotten."

She did not reply, but her eyes were full of compassion for him.

"Forty years," he whispered. "I never expected that. If only I'd known—"

"There was nothing you could do then, or now."

He balled his fist and hammered it on the steering-wheel. "The poor bastard—forty years!"

"Are you coming up?" she asked softly, but he shook his head.

"I have to get back to King's Lynn. I've neglected everything while this awful bloody business has been going on."

"You're going right now?" She was startled.

"Yes."

"Alone?" she asked, and he nodded.

"I want to be alone."

"So you can torture yourself." Her voice firmed. "And I'll be damned if I'll allow that. I'm coming with you. Wait! I am going to throw some things in a bag—you needn't even kill the engine, I'll be that quick."

She was five minutes, and then ran back down the stairs lugging her rucksack and her camera bag. She slung them into the back of the Land-Rover.

"Okay, let's go."

They spoke very little on the long journey, but soon Craig was thankful to have her beside him, grateful for her smile when he glanced at her, for the touch of her hand on his when she sensed the black mood too strong upon him, and for her undemanding silence.

They drove up the hills of King's Lynn in the dusk. Joseph had seen them from afar and was waiting on the front veranda.

"I see you, Nkosazana." From their first meeting Joseph had taken an instant liking to Sally-Anne. Already she was his "little mistress" and his welcoming grin kept breaking through his solemn dignity as he ordered his servants to unload her meagre luggage.

"I run bath for you—very hot."

"That will be marvellous, Joseph."

After her bath she came back to the veranda and Craig went

to the drinks table and mixed a whisky for her the way she liked it, and another one for himself that was mainly Scotch and very little soda.

"Here's to Judge Domashawa"—he lifted his glass ironically—"and to Mashona justice. All forty years of it."

Sally-Anne refused wine at dinner despite his protest. "Baron Rothschild would be frightfully affronted. His very best stuff. My last bottle, smuggled in personally." Craig's gaiety was forced.

After dinner he lifted the brandy decanter and, as he was about to pour, she said, "Craig, please don't get drunk."

He paused with the decanter over the snifter and studied her face.

"No"—she shook her head—"I'm not being bossy. I'm being entirely selfish. Tonight I want you sober."

He set down the decanter, pushed back his chair and came round the table to her. She stood up to meet him.

He paused in front of her. "Oh, my darling, I've waited so long."

"I know," she whispered. "Me too."

He took her carefully into his arms, something precious and fragile, and felt her changing slowly. She seemed to soften, and her body became malleable, shaping itself to his own, so he could feel her against him from knees to firm young bosom, the heat of her soaking quickly through their thin clothing.

He bowed his head as she lifted her chin and their mouths came together. Her lips were cool and dry, but almost immediately he felt the heat rising in them and they parted, moist and sweet as a sun-warmed fig freshly plucked and splitting open with its ripe juices.

He looked into her eyes as he kissed her, and marvelled at the colours and the patterns that formed a nimbus around her pupils, green shot through with golden arrowheads, and then her eyelids fluttered down over them, and her long crisp lashes interlocked. He closed his own eyes. The earth seemed to tilt and swing under him and he rode it easily, holding her to him, but not trying yet to explore her body, content with the wonder of her mouth, and the velvet feel of her tongue against his.

Joseph opened the door from the kitchen and stood for a moment with the coffee tray in his hands. Then he smiled smugly and drew back, closing the door behind him. Neither of them had heard

167

him come or go. When she took her mouth away, Craig felt deprived and cheated, and reached for it again. She laid her fingers across his lips, restraining him for a moment, and her whisper was so husky that she had to clear her throat and start again.

"Let's go to your bedroom, darling," she said.

There was one awkward moment when he sat naked on the edge of the bed to remove his leg, but she knelt quickly in front of him, naked also, pushing his hands away and undid the straps herself. Then she bowed her head and kissed the neat hard pad of flesh at the extremity of his leg.

"Thank you," he said. "I'm glad you could do that."

"It's you," she said, "and part of you," and she kissed it again, and then ran her lips gently up to his knee and beyond.

He woke before she did, and lay with his eyes closed, surprised at the sense of wonder that possessed him, not knowing why, until suddenly he remembered and joy came upon him, and he opened his eyes and rolled his head, for an instant terrified that she would not be there—but she was.

She had thrown her pillow off the bed and kicked the sheet aside. She was curled up like a baby, with her knees almost under her chin. The dawn light, filtered by the curtains, cast pearly highlights on her skin and shaded the dips and hollows of her body. Her hair was loose, covering her face and undulating to each long slow breath she drew.

He lay very still so as not to disturb her and gloated over her, wanting to reach out, but denying himself, so as to make the ache of wanting more poignant, waiting for it to become unbearable. She must have sensed his attention, for she stirred and straightened out her legs, rolled over onto her back and arched in a slow voluptuous catlike stretch.

He leaned across and with one finger lifted the shiny dark hair off her face. Her eyes swivelled towards him, came into focus, and she stared at him in comic astonishment. Then she crinkled her nose in a roguish grin.

"Hey, mister," she whispered, "you are something pretty damned special. Now I'm sorry I waited so long."

And she reached out both brown arms towards him. Craig, however, did not share her regrets. He knew it had been perfectly timed—even a day earlier would have been too soon. Later, he told her so, as they lay clinging to each other, glued lightly together with their own perspiration.

168

"We learned to like each other first; that was the way I wanted it to be."

"You're right," she said, and drew back a little to look at his face so that her breasts made a delightfully obscene little sucking sound as they came unstuck from his chest. "I do like you, I really do."

"And I—" he started, but hastily she covered his lips with her fingertips.

"Not yet, Craig darling," she pleaded. "I don't want to hear that—not yet."

"When?" he demanded.

"Soon, I think—" And then with more certainty, "Yes," she said, "soon, and then I'll be able to say it back to you."

*　　*　　*

The great estate of King's Lynn seemed to have waited as they had waited for this to happen again.

Long ago it had been hewn from the wilderness. The love of another man and woman had been the main inspiration in the building of it, and over the decades since then it had taken the love of the men and women who followed that first pair to sustain and cherish it. They and the generations who had followed them lay now in the walled cemetery on the kopje behind the homestead, but while they had lived, King's Lynn had flourished. Just as it had sickened when it fell into the hands of uncaring foreigners in a far land, had been stripped and desecrated and deprived of the vital ingredient of love.

Even when Craig rebuilt the house and restocked the pastures, that vital element had been lacking still. Now at last love burgeoned on King's Lynn, and their joy in each other seemed to radiate out from the homestead on the hill and permeate the entire estate, breathing life and the fecund promise of more life into the land.

The Matabele recognized it immediately. When Craig and Sally-Anne in the battered Land-Rover rode the red dust tracks that linked the huge paddocks, the Matabele women straightened up from the wooden mortars in which they were pounding maize, or turned stiff-necked under the enormous burden of firewood balanced upon their heads to call a greeting and watch them with a fond and knowing gaze. Old Joseph said nothing, but made up the bed in Craig's room with four pillows, put flowers on the table at the side of the bed that Sally-Anne had chosen, and placed four of his special biscuits on the early morning tea-tray when he brought it in to them each dawn.

For three days Sally-Anne restrained herself, and then one morning, sitting up in bed, sipping tea, she told Craig, "As curtains, those make fine dishrags." She pointed a half-eaten biscuit at the cheap unbleached calico that he had tacked over the windows.

"Can you do better?" Craig asked with concealed cunning, and she walked straight into the trap. Once she was involved in choosing curtains, she was immediately involved in everything else, from designing furniture for Joseph's relative, the celebrated carpenter, to build, to laying out the new vegetable garden and replanting the rose-bushes and shrubs that had died of neglect.

Then Joseph entered the conspiracy by bringing her the proposed dinner menu for the evening. "Should it be a roast tonight, Nkosazana, or chicken curry?"

"Nkosi Craig likes tripe." Sally-Anne had made this discovery during casual discussion. "Can you do tripe and onions?"

Joseph beamed. "The old governor-general before the war, whenever he came to Kingi-Lingi I make him tripe and onions, Nkosazana. He tell me, 'Very good, Joseph, best in world!'"

She laughed. "Okay, Joseph, tonight we'll have your 'best-in-world tripe and onions.'" Only when Joseph formally handed over to her the pantry keys did she realize what a serious pronouncement that had been.

She was there at midnight when the first new calf was born on King's Lynn, a difficult birthing with the calf's head twisted back so that Craig had to soap his arm and thrust it up into the mother to free it while Shadrach and Hans Groenewald held the head riems and Sally-Anne held the lantern high to light the work.

When at last it came in a slippery rush, it was a heifer, beige and wobbly on its long ungainly legs. As soon as it began to nurse from its mother's udder, they could leave it to Shadrach and go home to bed.

"That was one of the most marvelous experiences of my life, darling. Who taught you to do that?"

"Bawu, my grandfather." He held her close to him in the bedroom. "You didn't feel sick?"

"I loved it, birth fascinates me."

He chuckled. "Like Henry the Eighth, I prefer it in the abstract."

"You rude boy," she whispered. "But aren't you too tired?"

"Are you?"

"No," she admitted. "I can't truthfully say that I am."

She made one or two half-hearted attempts to break out and leave.

"I had a telegram today. The 'C. of A.' on the Cessna is complete, and I should go down to Johannesburg to collect her."

"If you can wait two or three weeks or so, I'll come down with you. They are having a terrible drought in the south and stock prices are rock bottom. We could fly around the big ranches together and pick up a few bargains."

So she let it pass, and the days telescoped into each other, filled for both of them with love and work—work on the photographic book, on the new novel, on collating her field research material for the Wildlife Trust, on the final preparations for the opening of Zambezi Waters, and on the daily running and embellishing of King's Lynn.

With each week that passed, her will to resist the spell that Craig and King's Lynn were weaving about her weakened, the exigencies of her previous life faded, until one day she caught herself referring to the house on the hill as "home" and was only slightly shocked at herself.

A week later a registered letter was forwarded from her address in Harare. It was a formal application form for the renewal of her research grant from the Wildlife Trust. Instead of filling it in and returning it immediately, she slipped it into her camera bag.

"I'll do it tomorrow," she promised herself, but deep inside she saw the crossroads in her life. The prospect of flying about Africa alone with her only possessions a change of clothes and a camera, sleeping where she lay down and bathing when she could, was no longer as attractive as it had always been to her.

That night at dinner she looked around the huge, almost bare dining-room, the new curtains its only glory, and touched the refectory table of Rhodesian teak that, under her guidance, Joseph's relative had fashioned, and she anticipated the patina of use and care it would soon acquire. Then she looked past the burning candles to the man who sat opposite her and she was afraid and strangely elated. She knew she had made the decision.

They took their coffee onto the veranda and listened to the cicadas whining in the jacaranda trees, and the squeak of the flying bats hunting below a yellow moon.

She snuggled against his shoulder and said, "Craig, darling, it's time to tell you, I do love you—so very dearly."

* * *

Craig wanted to rush into Bulawayo and take the magistrate's court by storm, but she restrained him laughingly.

"My God, you crazy man, it isn't like buying a pound of cheese. You can't just up and get married, just like that."

"Why not? Lots of people do."

"I don't," she said firmly. "I want it to be done properly." She did some counting on her fingers and pencilling on the calendar at the back of her notebook, and then decided, "February sixteenth."

"That's four months away," Craig groaned, but his protests were ridden down ruthlessly.

Joseph, on the other hand, was in full accord with Sally-Anne's plans for a formal wedding.

"You get married on Kingi-Lingi, Nkosikazi."

It was a statement rather than a question, and Sally-Anne's Sindebele was now good enough to recognize that she had been promoted from "little mistress" to "great lady."

"How many people?" Joseph demanded. "Two hundred, three hundred?"

"I doubt we can raise that many," Sally-Anne demurred.

"When Nkosana Roly get married Kingi-Lingi, we have four hundred, even Nkosi Smithy he come!"

"Joseph," she scolded him, "you really are a frightful old snob, you know!"

* * *

For Craig the pervading unhappiness that he had felt at Tungata's sentence slowly dissipated, swamped by all the excitement and activity at King's Lynn. In a few months he had all but put it from his mind; only at odd and unexpected moments his memory of his one-time friend barbed him. To the rest of the world, Tungata Zebiwe might never have existed. After the extravagant coverage by press and television of his trial, it seemed that a curtain of silence was drawn over him like a shroud.

Then abruptly, once again the name Tungata Zebiwe was blazed from every television screen and bannered on every front page across the entire continent.

Craig and Sally-Anne sat in front of the television set, appalled and disbelieving, as they listened to the first reports. When they ended, and the programme changed to a weather report, Craig stood up and crossed to the set. He switched it off and came back to her side, moving like a man who was still in deep shock from some terrible accident.

The two of them sat in silence in the darkened room, until Sally-Anne reached for his hand. She squeezed it hard, but her shudder was involuntary, racking her whole body.

"Those poor little girls—they were babies. Can you imagine their terror?"

"I knew the Goodwins. They were fine people. They always treated their black people well," Craig muttered.

"This proves—as nothing else possibly could—that they were right to lock him away like a dangerous animal." Her horror was beginning to turn to anger.

"I can't see what they could possibly hope to gain by this—" Craig was still shaking his head incredulously, and Sally-Anne burst out.

"The whole country, the whole world must see them for what they are. Bloodthirsty, inhuman—" Her voice cracked and became a sob. "Those babies—of Christ in heaven, I hate him. I wish him dead."

"They used his name—that doesn't mean Tungata ordered it, condoned it, or even knew about it." Craig tried to sound convincing.

"I hate him," she whispered. "I hate him for it."

"It's madness. All they can possibly achieve is to bring Shona troops sweeping through Matabeleland like the wrath of all the gods."

"The little one was only five years old." In her outrage and sorrow, Sally-Anne was repeating herself.

"Nigel Goodwin was a good man—I knew him quite well, we were in the same special police unit during the war. I liked him." Craig went to the drinks table and poured two whiskies. "Please God, don't let it all start again. All the awfulness and cruelty and horror—please God, spare us that."

•   •   •

Although Nigel Goodwin was almost forty years of age, he had one of those beefy pink faces unaffected by the African sun that made him look like a lad. His wife, Helen, was a thin, brown-haired girl, her plainness alleviated by her patent good nature and her sparkly, toffee-brown eyes.

The two girls were weekly boarders at the convent in Bulawayo. At eight years, Alice Goodwin had ginger hair and gingery freckles and, like her father, she was plump and pink. Stephanie, the baby, was five, really too young for boarding-school. However, because she had an elder sister at the convent, the Reverend Mother made an exception in her case. She was the pretty one, small and chirpy as a little bird with her mother's bright eyes.

Each Friday morning, Nigel and Helen Goodwin drove in seventy-eight miles from the ranch to town. At one o'clock they picked up the girls from the convent, had lunch at the Selborne Hotel, sharing a bottle of wine, and then spent the afternoon shopping. Helen restocked her groceries, chose material to make into dresses for herself and the girls, and then, while the girls went to watch a matinée at the local cinema, had her hair washed, cut and set, the one extravagance of her simple existence.

Nigel was on the committee of the Matabele Farmers Union and spent an hour or two at the Union's offices in leisurely discussion with the secretary and those other members who were in town for the day. Then he strolled down the wide sun-scorched streets, his slouch hat pushed back on his head, hands in pockets, puffing happily on a black briar, greeting friends and acquaintances both white and black, stopping every few yards for a word or a chat.

When he arrived back where he had left the Toyota truck outside the Farmers Co-operative, his Matabele headman, Josiah, and two labourers were waiting for him. They loaded the purchases of fencing and tools and spare parts and cattle medicines and other odds and ends into the truck, and as they finished, Helen and the girls arrived for the journey home.

"Excuse me, Miss," Nigel accosted his wife, "have you seen Mrs. Goodwin anywhere?" It was his little weekly joke, and Helen giggled delightedly and preened her new hairdo.

For the girls he had a bag of liquorice all-sorts. His wife protested, "Sweets are so bad for their teeth, dear," and Nigel winked at the girls and agreed, "I know, but just this once won't kill them."

Stephanie, because she was the baby, rode in the truck cab

between her parents, while Alice went in the back with Josiah and the other Matabele.

"Wrap up, dear, it will be dark before we get home," Helen cautioned her.

The first sixty-two miles were on the main road, and then they turned off on the farm track, and Josiah jumped down to open the wire gate and let them through.

"Home again," said Nigel contentedly, as he drove onto his own land. He always said that and Helen smiled and reached across to lay her hand on his leg.

"It's nice to be home," she agreed.

The abrupt African night fell over them, and Nigel switched on the headlights. They picked up the eyes of the cattle in little points of light, fat contented beasts, the smell of their dung sharp and ammoniacal on the cool night air.

"Getting dry," Nigel grunted. "Need some rain."

"Yes, dear." Helen picked little Stephanie onto her lap, and the child cuddled sleeping against her shoulder.

"There we are," Nigel murmured. "Cooky has lit the lamps."

He had been promising himself an electric generator for the last ten years, but there was always something else more important, so they were still on gas and paraffin. The lights of the homestead flickered a welcome at them between the stems of the acacia trees.

Nigel parked the truck beside the back veranda and cut the engine and headlights. Helen climbed down carrying Stephanie. The child was asleep now with her thumb in her mouth, and her skinny bare legs dangling.

Nigel went to the back of the truck and lifted Alice down.

"*Longile*, Josiah, you can go off now. We will unload the truck tomorrow morning," he told his men. "Sleep well!"

Holding Alice's hand, he followed his wife to the veranda, but before they reached it the dazzling beam of a powerful flashlight struck them and the family stopped in a small compact group.

"Who is it?" Nigel demanded irritably, shielding his eyes from the beam with one hand, still holding Alice's hand with the other.

His eyes adjusted and he could see beyond the flashlight, and suddenly he felt sick with fear for his wife and his babies. There were three black men, dressed in blue denim jeans and jackets. Each of them carried an AK 47 rifle. The rifles were pointed at the family group. Nigel glanced behind him quickly. There were other strangers, he was not sure how many. They had come out of the night, and under their guns Josiah and his two labourers were huddled fearfully.

Nigel thought of the steel gun safe in his office at the end of the veranda. Then he remembered that it was empty. At the end of the war, one of the first acts of the new black government had been to force the white farmers to hand in all their weapons. It didn't really matter, he realized. He could never have reached the safe, anyway.

"Who are they, Daddy?" Alice asked, her voice small with fear. Of course she knew. She was old enough to remember the war days.

"Be brave, my darlings," Nigel said to all of them, and Helen drew closer to his bulk, still holding baby Stephanie in her arms.

The muzzle of the rifle was thrust into Nigel's back. His hands were pulled behind him, and his wrists bound together. They used galvanized wire. It cut into his flesh. Then they took Stephanie from her mother's arms and set her down. Her legs were unsteady from sleep and she blinked like an owlet in the flashlight beam, still sucking her thumb. They wired Helen's hands behind her back. She whimpered once as the wire cut in and then bit down on her lip. Two of them took the wire to the children.

"They are babies," Nigel said in Sindebele. "Please do not tie them, please do not hurt them."

"Be silent, white jackal," one of them replied in the same language and went down on one knee behind Stephanie.

"It's sore, Daddy," she began to cry. "He's hurting me. Make him stop."

"You must be brave," Nigel repeated, stupidly and inadequately, hating himself. "You're a big girl now."

The other man went to Alice.

"I won't cry," she promised. "I'll be brave, Daddy."

"That's my own sweet girl," he said, and the man tied her.

"Walk!" commanded the one with the flashlight, who was clearly the leader of the group, and with the barrel of his automatic rifle he prodded the children up the back steps onto the kitchen veranda.

Stephanie tripped and sprawled. With her hands tied behind her she could not regain her feet. She wriggled helplessly.

"You bastards," whispered Nigel. "Oh, you filthy bastards."

One of them took a handful of the child's hair and lifted her

176

to her feet. She stumbled, weeping hysterically, to where her sister stood against the veranda wall.

"Don't be a baby, Stephy," Alice told her. "It's just a game." But her voice quavered with her own terror, and her eyes in the lamplight were huge and brimming with tears.

They lined up Nigel and Helen beside the girls, and the flashlight played back and forth into each face in turn, blinding them so they could not see what was happening out in the yard.

"Why are you doing this?" Nigel asked. "The war is over— we have done you no harm."

There was no reply at all, just a beam of brilliant light moving across their pale faces, and the sound of Stephanie weeping, a racking piteous sobbing. Then there was the murmur of other voices, many subdued frightened voices, women and children and men.

"They have brought our people to watch," said Helen softly. "It's just like the war days. It's going to be an execution." She spoke so the girls could not hear her. Nigel could think of nothing to say. He knew she was right.

"I wish I had told you how much I love you, more often," he said.

"That's all right," she whispered. "I knew all along."

They could make out a throng of Matabele from the farm village now, a mass of them beyond the glaring torch, and then the voice of the leader was raised in Sindebele.

"These are the white jackals that feed upon the land of the Matabele. These are the white offal that are in league with the Mashona killers, the eaters-of-dirt in Harare, the sworn enemies of the children of Lobengula—"

The orator was working himself up into the killing frenzy. Already Nigel could see that the other men guarding them were beginning to sway and hum, losing themselves in that berserker passion where no reason exists. The Matabele had a name for it, "the divine madness." When old Mzilikazi had been king, one million human beings had died from his divine madness.

"These white lickers of Mashona faeces are the traitors who delivered Tungata Zebiwe, the father of our people, to the death camps of the Mashona," screamed the leader.

"I embrace you, my darlings," Nigel Goodwin whispered.

Helen had never heard him say anything so tender before, and it was that, not fear, that made her begin to weep. She tried to force back the tears, but they ran down and dripped from her chin.

"What must we do with them?" howled the leader.

"Kill them!" cried one of his own men, but the massed farm Matabele were silent.

"What must we do with them?" the question was repeated.

This time the leader leaped down from the veranda and shouted it into the faces of the farm people. Still they were silent.

"What must we do with them?" Again the question, and this time the sound of blows, the rubbery slap of a rifle-barrel against black flesh.

"What must we do with them?" The same question for the fourth time.

"Kill them!" An uncertain terrified response, and more blows.

"Kill them!" The cry was taken up.

"Kill them!"

"Abantwana kamina!" A woman's voice. Nigel recognized it as that of fat old Martha, the girls' nanny. "My babies," she cried, but then her voice was lost in the rising chorus, "Kill them! Kill them!" as the madness spread.

Two men, both denim-clad, stepped into the torchlight. They seized Nigel by his arms and turned him to face the wall, before forcing him to his knees.

The leader handed the flashlight to one of his men and he took the pistol from the belt of his jeans and pulled back the slide, forcing a round into the chamber. The breech made a sharp snapping rattle. He put the muzzle of the pistol to the back of Nigel's head and fired a single shot. Nigel was thrown forward onto his face. The contents of his skull were dashed against the white wall, and then began to run down it in a jelly-like stream to the floor.

His feet were still kicking and dancing as they forced Helen down to her knees facing the wall beside her husband's corpse.

"Mummy!" screamed Alice as the next pistol bullet tore out through her mother's forehead and her skull collapsed inwards. Alice's pathetic little show of courage was over. Her legs gave way, and she crumpled to the veranda floor. With a soft spluttery sound her bowels voided involuntarily.

The leader stepped up to her. Her forehead was almost touching the floor. Her gingery curls had parted, exposing the back of her neck. The leader extended his right arm full length, and touched the muzzle of the pistol to the tender white skin at the nape. His arm jerked to the recoil and the shot was muffled to a jarring thud. Blue tendrils of gunsmoke spiralled upwards in the beam of the flashlight.

Little Stephanie was the only one who struggled, until the leader clubbed her with the barrel of the pistol. Even then she wriggled and kicked, lying on the veranda floor in the spreading puddle of her sister's blood. The leader placed his foot between her shoulder-blades to hold her still for the shot. The bullet came out through Stephanie's temple just in front of her right ear, and it gouged a hole not much larger than a thimble in the concrete of the veranda floor. The hole filled swiftly with the child's blood.

The leader stooped and dipped his forefinger into the cup of dark blood and with it wrote on the white veranda wall in large erratic letters, "TUNGATA ZEBIWE LIVES."

Then he jumped down off the veranda and, like a leopard, padded silently away into the night. His men followed him in Indian file at an easy swinging trot.

• • •

"I give you my solemn promise," said the prime minister, "these so-called dissidents will be destroyed, completely destroyed."

His eyes behind the lens of his spectacles had a steely, blind look. The poor quality of the television projection added haloes of ghost silhouettes to his head but did not diminish his anger, which seemed to spill over from the set and flood the living-room of King's Lynn.

"I've never seen him like that," said Craig.

"He's usually such a cold fish," Sally-Anne agreed.

"I have ordered the army and the police force to move in to hunt down and apprehend the perpetrators of this terrible outrage. We will find them, and their supporters, and they will feel the full force of the people's anger. We will not endure these dissidents."

Sally-Anne nodded. "Good for him. I can't say I've ever liked him very much—until now."

"Darling, don't be too happy about it," Craig cautioned her. "Remember this is Africa, not America or Britain. This land has a different temper. Words have a different meaning here—words like 'apprehend' and 'hunt down.'"

"Craig, I know that your sympathy is always with the Matabele, but this time surely—"

"All right"—he held up one hand in agreement—"I admit it.

179

The Matabele are special, my family has always lived with them, we've beaten and exploited them, we've fought them and slaughtered them—and been slaughtered by them in return. Yet, also, we have cherished and honoured them and come to know them and, yes, to love them. I don't know the Mashona. They are secretive and cold, clever and tricky. I can't speak their language, and I don't trust them. That's why I choose to live in Matabeleland."

"You are saying the Matabele are saints—that they are incapable of committing an atrocity like this?" She was getting irritable with him now, her tone sharpening, and he was quick to placate her.

"Good God, no! They are as cruel as any other tribe in Africa, and a hell of a lot more warlike than most. In the old days when they raided a foreign tribe, they used to toss the infants in the air and catch them on the points of their assegais, and throw the old women in the watch-fires and laugh to see them burn. Cruelty has a different value in Africa. If you live here you have to understand that from the beginning."

He paused and smiled. "Once I was discussing political philosophy with a Matabele, an ex-guerrilla, and I explained the concept of democracy. His reply was, 'That might work in your country, but it doesn't work here. It doesn't work here.' Don't you see? That's the crux. Africa makes and keeps her own rules, and I lay you a million dollars to a pinch of elephant dung that we're going to see a few pretty things in the weeks ahead that you wouldn't see in Pennsylvania or Dorset! When Mugabe says, 'Destroy,' he doesn't mean, 'Take into custody and process under the laws of evidence.' He's an African and he means precisely that—destroy!"

That was on the Wednesday, and when Friday came round it was market day at King's Lynn, the day to go into Bulawayo for shopping and socializing. Craig and Sally-Anne left early on that Friday morning. The new five-ton truck followed them, filled with Matabele from the ranch, taking advantage of the free ride into town for the day. They were dressed in their best and singing with excitement.

Craig and Sally-Anne came up against the road-block just before they reached the crossroads at Thabas Indunas. The traffic was backed up for a hundred yards, and Craig could see that most of the vehicles were being turned back.

"Hold on!" he told Sally-Anne, left her in the Land-Rover and jogged up to the head of the line of parked vehicles.

The road-block was not a casual, temporary affair. There were heavy-machine-guns in sandbagged emplacements on both sides of the highway, and light machine-guns set back in depth beyond it to cover a breakthrough by a speeding vehicle.

The actual barricade was of drums filled with concrete and spiked metal plates to puncture pneumatic tyres, and the guards were from the Third Brigade in their distinctive burgundy berets and silver cap-badges. Their striped camouflage battle-jackets gave them a tigerish air.

"What is happening, Sergeant?" Craig asked one of them.

"The road is closed, mambo," the man told him politely. "Only military permit-holders allowed to pass."

"I have to get into town."

The man shook his head. "Not today. Bulawayo is not a good place to be today."

As if to confirm this, there was a faint popping sound from the direction of the town. It sounded like green twigs in a fire, and the hair on Craig's forearms lifted instinctively. He knew that sound so well, and it brought nightmarish memories from the war days crowding back. It was the sound of distant automatic-rifle fire.

"Go back home, mambo," said the sergeant in a kindly tone. "This is not your *indaba* any more."

Suddenly Craig was very anxious to get the truck-load of his people safely back to King's Lynn.

He ran back to the Land-Rover and swung it out of the line of parked vehicles in a hard 180-degree turn.

"What is it, Craig?"

"It has started," he told her grimly and thrust the accelerator flat to the floorboards.

They met the King's Lynn truck barrelling merrily along towards them, the women singing and clapping, their dresses fluttering brightly in the wind. Craig flagged them down, and jumped up onto the running-board. Shadrach, in the cast-off grey suit that Craig had given him was sitting up in his place of honour beside the driver.

"Turn around," Craig ordered. "Go back to Kingi-Lingi. There is big trouble. Nobody must leave Kingi-Lingi until it is over."

"Is it the Mashona soldiers?"

181

"Yes," Craig told him. "The Third Brigade."

"Jackals and sons of dung-eating jackals," said Shadrach, and spat out of the open window.

• • •

"To say that thousands of innocent persons have been killed by the state security forces is a nonsense—" The Zimbabwean minister of justice looked like a successful stockbroker in his grey suit and white shirt. He smiled blandly out of the television screen, his face shining with a light sheen of sweat from the brute arc lamps which only enhanced the coaly blackness of his skin. "One or two civilians have been killed in the cross-fire between the security forces and the outlaw Matabele dissidents—but thousands! Ha, ha, ha!" he chuckled jovially. "If thousands have been killed, then I wish somebody would show me the bodies—I know nothing about them."

Craig switched it off. "Well, that's all you are going to get from Harare." He checked his wrist-watch. "Almost eight o'clock. Let's see what the B.B.C. has to say."

During the rule of the Smith regime, with its draconian censorship, every thinking man in central Africa had made sure he had access to a short-wave radio receiver. It was still a good rule to follow. Craig's set was a Yaesu Musen, and he got the African service of B.B.C. on 2171 kilohertz.

"The Zimbabwe government has expelled all foreign journalists from Matabeleland. The British high commissioner has called on the prime minister of Zimbabwe to express Her Majesty's government's deep concern at the reports of atrocities being committed by security forces—"

Craig switched to Radio South Africa, and it came through sharp and clear: "—the arrival of hundreds of illegal refugees across the northern border from Zimbabwe. The refugees are all members of the Matabele tribe. A spokesman for one group described a massacre of villagers and civilians that he had witnessed. 'They are killing everybody,' he said. 'The women and the children, even the chickens and the goats.' Another refugee said, 'Do not send us back. The soldiers will kill us.'"

Craig searched the bands and found Voice of America.

"The leader of the ZAPU party, the Matabele faction of Zimbabwe, Mr. Joshua Nkomo, has arrived in the neighbouring state

182

of Botswana after fleeing the country. 'They shot my driver dead,' he told our regional reporter. 'Mugabe wants me dead. He's out to get me.'

"With the recent imprisonment and detention of all other prominent members of the ZAPU party, Mr. Nkomo's departure from Zimbabwe leaves the Matabele people without a leader or a spokesman.

"In the meantime, the government of Mr. Robert Mugabe has placed a total news blackout over the western part of the country, all foreign journalists have been expelled, and a request by the international Red Cross to send in observers has been refused."

"It's all so familiar," Craig muttered. "I even have the same sick feeling in the bottom of my stomach as I listen to it."

• • •

The next Monday was Sally-Anne's birthday. After breakfast, they drove across to Queen's Lynn together to fetch her present. Craig had left it in the care of Mrs. Groenewald, the overseer's wife, to preserve the secrecy and surprise.

"Oh, Craig, he's beautiful."

"Now you have two of us to keep you at King's Lynn," he told her.

Sally-Anne lifted the honey-coloured puppy in both hands and kissed his wet nose, and the puppy licked her back.

"He's a Rhodesian lion dog," Craig told her, "or now I suppose you'd call him a Zimbabwean lion dog."

The puppy's skin was too big for him. It hung down in wrinkles over his forehead and gave him a worried frown. His back was crested in the distinctive ridge of his breed.

"Look at his paws!" Sally-Anne cried. "He's going to be a monster. What shall I call him?"

Craig declared a public holiday to mark the occasion of Sally-Anne's birth. They took the puppy and a picnic lunch down to the main dam below the homestead and lay on a rug under the trees at the water's edge. They tried to find a name for the puppy. Sally-Ann vetoed Craig's suggested "Dog."

The black-faced weaver-birds fluttered and shrieked and hung upside-down from their basket-shaped nests above their heads. The puppy chased grasshoppers until he collapsed exhausted on the rug beside Sally-Anne. Joseph had put a cold bottle of white

183

wine in the basket, and when they had finished the wine and made love on the rug, Sally-Anne whispered seriously, "Shh! Don't wake the puppy!"

As they drove back up the hills, Sally-Anne said suddenly, "We haven't spoken about the troubles all day."

"Don't let's spoil our record."

"I'm going to call him Buster."

"Why?"

"The first puppy I was ever given I called Buster."

They gave Buster his supper in the bowl labelled "Dog" that Craig had bought for him, and then made him a bed in an empty wine-crate near the Aga stove. They were both happily tired and that evening left the book and the photographs and went to bed immediately after their own meal.

●　　●　　●

Craig woke to the sound of gun-fire. His residual war reflexes hurled him from the bed before he was fully awake. It was automatic-rifle fire, short bursts, very close, and, he noted instinctively, short bursts meant good, trained riflemen. They were down by the farm village, or the workshop. He judged the distance.

He found his leg and clinched the strap, fully awake now, and his first thought was for Sally-Anne. Keeping low, beneath the sill level of the windows, he rolled back to the bed and dragged her down beside him.

She was naked, and muzzy with sleep.

"What is it?"

He whipped her gown off the foot of the bed. "Here. Get dressed, but keep down."

While she shrugged into the gown, he was trying to marshal his thoughts. There were no weapons in the house, except the kitchen knives and a small hand-axe for chopping firewood on the back veranda. There was no sandbagged fall-back position, no defensive perimeter of wire and floodlights, no radio transmitter—none of even the most elementary defences with which every farm homestead had once been provided.

Another burst of rifle-fire, and somebody screamed—a woman—the faint scream abruptly cut off.

"What's happening? Who are they?" Sally-Anne's voice was level and crisp. She was awake and unafraid. He felt a little lift of pride for her. "Are they dissidents?"

"I don't know, but we aren't going to wait around to find out," he told her grimly.

He glanced up at the new highly inflammable thatch overhead. Their best chance was to get out of the house and into the bush. To do that, they needed a diversion.

"Stay here," he ordered. "Get your shoes on and be ready to run. I'll be back in a minute."

He rolled under the window to the wall, and came to his feet. The bedroom door was unlocked and he darted into the passage. He wasted ten seconds on the telephone—he knew they would have cut the wires, and that was confirmed immediately by the dead, echoless void in the ear-piece. He dropped it dangling on the cord and ran through to the kitchens.

There was only one diversion he could think of—light. He hit the remote-control switch of the diesel generator, and there was the faint ripple of sound from the engine-room across the yard and the overhead bulbs glowed yellow and then flared into full brilliance. He tore open the fuse-box above the control board, tripped out the house lights, and then switched on the veranda and front garden lights. That would leave the back of the house in darkness. They would make their break that way, he decided, and it would have to be quick. The attackers hadn't hit the house yet, but they could only be seconds away.

He ran back out of the kitchen, paused at the door of the lounge, and glanced through it to check the lighting in the front garden and veranda. The lawns were a peculiarly lush green in the artificial light, the jacaranda trees domed over them like the roof of a cathedral. The firing had ceased, but down near the labourers' village a woman was keening, that doleful sound of African mourning. It made his skin creep.

Craig knew that they would be coming up the hill already, and he was turning away to go back to Sally-Anne when he caught a flicker of movement at the edge of the light and he narrowed his eyes and tried to identify it. To know who was attacking would give him some small advantage, but he was wasting precious seconds.

The movement was a running man, coming up towards the house. A black man, naked—no, he was wearing a loincloth. Not really running, but staggering and weaving drunkenly. In the veranda lights half his body glinted as though it had been freshly oiled, and then Craig realized that it was blood. The man was

185

painted with his own blood, and it was falling in scattered drops from him like water from the coat of a retriever when it came ashore with the duck in its jaws.

Then, in a more intense shock of horror, Craig realized that it was old Shadrach and unthinkingly went to help him. He kicked open the french doors of the lounge, went out onto the veranda at a run, and vaulted the low half-wall. He caught Shadrach in his arms just as he was about to fall and lifted him off his feet. He was surprised at the lightness of the old man's body. Craig carried him at a single bound onto the veranda and crouched with him below the low wall.

Shadrach had been hit in the upper arm, just above the elbow. The bone had shattered, and the limb hung by a ribbon of flesh. Shadrach held it to his breast like a nursing infant.

"They are coming," he gasped at Craig. "You must run. They are killing our people. They will kill you also."

It was miraculous that the old man could speak, let alone move and run with such a wound. Crouching below the wall, he ripped a strip of cotton from his loincloth with his teeth and started to bind it around his own arm above the wound. Craig pushed his hand away and tied the knot for him.

"You must run, little master," and before Craig could prevent him, the old man rolled to his feet and disappeared into the darkness beyond the floodlights.

"He risked his life to warn me." Craig looked after him for a second, then roused himself and, doubled over, ran back into the house.

Sally-Anne was where he had left her, crouched below the window. Light fell through it in a yellow square. He saw that she had tied back her hair and pulled on a T-shirt and shorts, and was lacing her soft, leather, running shoes.

"Good girl." He knelt beside her. "Let's go."

"Buster," she replied. "My puppy!"

"For God's sake!"

"We can't leave him!" She had that stubborn look that he had already come to know so well.

"I'll carry you if I have to," he warned fiercely, and raising himself quickly he risked a last glance over the window-sill.

The lawns and gardens were still brightly lit. There were the dark shapes of men coming up from the valley, armed men in disciplined extended order. For a moment he could not believe what he was seeing, and then he sagged with relief.

"Oh, thank you, God!" he whispered. He found that reaction had set in already. He felt weak and shivery, and he took Sally-Anne in his arms and hugged her.

"It's all right now," he told her. "It's going to be all right."

"What has happened?"

"The security forces have arrived," he said. He had recognized the burgundy-coloured berets and silver cap-badges of the men closing in across the lawns. "The Third Brigade is here—we will be all right now."

They went out onto the front veranda to greet their rescuers, Sally-Anne carrying the yellow puppy in her arms, and Craig with his arm about her shoulders.

"I am very glad to see you and your men, Sergeant," Craig greeted the non-commissioned officer who led the advancing line of troopers.

"Please go inside." The sergeant made a gesture with his rifle, imperative if not directly threatening. He was a tall man, with long sinewy limbs. His expression was cold and neutral, and Craig felt his relief shrink. Something was wrong. The line of troopers had closed like a net around the homestead, while skirmishers came forward in pairs, covering each other, the classical tactics of the street fighter, and they went swiftly into the house, breaking through windows and side-doors, sweeping the interior. There was a crash of breaking glass at the rear of the house. It was a destructive search.

"What's going on, Sergeant?" Craig's anger resurfaced, and this time the tall sergeant's gesture was unmistakably hostile.

Craig and Sally-Anne backed off before him into the dining-room and stood in the center of the room beside the teak refectory table, facing the threatening rifle, Craig holding her protectively.

Two troopers slipped in through the front door and reported to the sergeant in a gabble of Shona that Craig could not follow. The sergeant acknowledged with a nod and gave them an order. They spread out obediently along the wall, their weapons turned unmistakably onto the dishevelled couple in the centre of the room.

"Where are the lights?" the sergeant asked, and when Craig told him, he went to the switch and white light flooded the room.

"What is going on here, Sergeant?" Craig repeated, angry and uncertain and starting to be afraid for Sally-Anne again.

The sergeant ignored the question and strode to the door. He called to one of the troopers on the lawn, and the man came at a run. He carried a portable radio transmitter strapped on his back, with the scorpion-tail aerial sticking up over his shoulder. The sergeant spoke softly into the handset of the radio and then came back into the room.

They waited now in an unmoving tableau. To Craig it seemed like an hour passed in silence, but it was less than five minutes before the sergeant cocked his head slightly, listening. Craig heard it, the beat of an engine, in a different tempo from that of the diesel generator. It firmed, and Craig knew that it was a Land-Rover.

It came up the driveway, headlights swept the windows, brakes squeaked and gravel crunched. The engine was cut, doors banged and then there were the footsteps of a group of men crossing the veranda.

General Peter Fungabera led his staff in through the french doors. He wore his beret pulled down over one eye and a matching silk scarf at his throat. Except for the pistol in its webbing holster at his side, he was armed only with the leather-covered swagger-stick.

Behind him Captain Timon Nbebi was tall and round-shouldered, his eyes inscrutable behind the steel-rimmed spectacles. He carried a leather map-case in his hand, and a machine pistol on a sling over his shoulder.

"Peter!" Craig's relief was tempered by wariness. It was all too contrived, too controlled, too menacing. "Some of my people have been killed. My induna is out there somewhere, badly wounded."

Peter Fungabera nodded. "There have been many enemy casualties."

"Enemy?" Craig was puzzled.

Peter nodded again. "Dissidents. Matabele dissidents."

"Dissidents?" Craig stared at him. "Shadrach a dissident? That's crazy—he's a simple, uneducated cattleman, and doesn't give a damn for politics—"

"Things are often not what they seem." Peter Fungabera pulled back the chair at the head of the long table and placed one foot on it, leaning an elbow on his knee. Timon Nbebi placed the leather map-case on the table in front of him and stood back, in a position of guard behind his shoulder, holding the machine pistol by the grip.

"Will somebody please tell me what in hell is happening here, Peter?" Craig was exasperated and nervous. "Somebody attacked my village—they've killed some of my people, God knows how many. Why don't you get after them?"

"The shooting is over," Peter Fungabera told him. "We have cleaned out the vipers' nest of traitors that you were breeding on this colonial-style estate of yours."

"What on earth are you talking about?" Craig was now truly flustered. "You cannot be serious!"

"Serious?" Peter smiled easily. He straightened up and placed both feet back on the floor. He walked across to face them. He was still smiling. "A puppy. How adorable."

He took Buster from Sally-Anne's arms before she realized his intention. He strolled back to the head of the table, fondling the little animal, scratching behind its ear. It was still half-asleep and it made little whimpering sounds, nuzzling against him, instinctively searching for its mother's teat.

"Serious?" Peter repeated the original question. "I want to impress upon you just how serious I am."

He dropped the puppy onto the stone-flagged floor. It fell on its back, and lay stunned. He placed his boot upon its chest and crushed it with his full weight. The puppy screamed once only as its chest collapsed.

"That's how serious I am." He was no longer smiling. "Your lives are as valuable to me as this animal was."

Sally-Anne made a small moaning sound and turned away, burying her face in Craig's chest. She heaved with nausea, and Craig could feel her fighting to control it. Peter Fungabera kicked the soft yellow corpse into the fireplace and sat down.

"We have wasted enough time on the theatricals," he said, and opened the leather map-case, spreading the documents on the table in front of him.

"Mr. Mellow, you have been acting as an *agent provocateur* in the pay of the notorious American C.I.A.—"

"That's a bloody lie!" Craig shouted, and Peter ignored the outburst.

"Your local control was the American agent Morgan Oxford at the United States Embassy, while your central control and pay-master was a certain Henry Pickering, who masquerades as a senior official of the World Bank in New York. He recruited both you and Miss Jay—"

"That's not true!"

"Your remuneration was sixty thousand dollars per annum, and your mission was to set up a center of subversion in Matabeleland, which was financed by C.I.A. monies channelled to you in the form of a loan from a C.I.A.-controlled subsidiary of the World Bank. The sum allocated was five million dollars."

"Christ, Peter, that's nonsense, and you know it."

"During the rest of this interrogation, you will address me as either 'Sir' or 'General Fungabera,' is that clear to you?" He turned away to listen, as there was sudden activity outside the french doors. It sounded like the arrival of a convoy of light trucks, from which more troops were disembarking with orders being called in Shona. Through the glass doors, Craig saw a dozen troopers carrying heavy crates up onto the veranda.

Peter Fungabera glanced inquiringly at Timon Nbebi, who nodded in confirmation of the unspoken question.

"Right!" Peter Fungabera turned back to face Craig. "We can continue. You opened negotiations with known Matabele traitors, using your fluent knowledge of the language and the character of these intractable people——"

"You can't name one, because there weren't any."

Peter Fungabera nodded to Timon Nbebi. He shouted an order.

A man was led into the room between two troopers. He was barefooted, dressed only in ragged khaki shorts, and was emaciated to the point where his head appeared grotesquely huge. His pate was shaven and covered with lumps and fresh scabs, his ribs latticed with the scars of beatings—probably the wicked hippo-hide whips called sjamboks had been used on him.

"Do you know this white man?" Peter Fungabera demanded of him. The man stared at Craig. His eyes had an opaque dullness, as though they had been sprinkled with dust.

"I've never seen him——" Craig started, and then broke off as he recognized him. It was Comrade Dollar, the youngest and most truculent of the men from Zambezi Waters.

"Yes?" Peter Fungabera invited, smiling again. "What were you about to say, Mr. Mellow?"

"I want to see somebody from the British High Commission," Craig said, "and Miss Jay would like to make a telephone call to the United States Embassy."

Peter Fungabera nodded. "Of course. All in good time, but first we must complete what we have already begun." He swung

190

back to Comrade Dollar. "Do you know the white man?"

Comrade Dollar nodded. "He gave us money."

"Take him away," Peter Fungabera ordered. "Care for him well, and give him something to eat. Now, Mr. Mellow, do you still deny any contact with the subversives?" He did not wait for a reply, but went on smoothly, "You built up an arsenal of weapons on this estate to be used against the elected people's government in a *coup d'état* which would place a pro-American dictator—"

"No," Craig said quietly. "I have no weapons."

Peter Fungabera sighed. "Your denials are pointless—and tiresome." Then to the tall Shona sergeant, "Bring the two of them."

He led the way onto the wide veranda, to where his men had stacked the crates.

"Open them," he commanded, and his men knocked back the clips and lifted the lids.

Craig recognized the weapons that were packed into them. They were American Armalite 5.56 mm AR 18 automatic rifles. Six to the case, and brand-new, still in their factory grease.

"These are nothing to do with me." Craig was at last able to deny it with vehemence.

"You are testing my patience." Peter Fungabera turned to Timon Nbebi. "Fetch the other white man."

Hans Groenewald, Craig's overseer, was dragged from the cab of one of the parked trucks and led to the veranda. His hands were manacled behind his back, and he was terrified. His broad tanned face seemed to have deflated into heavy wrinkles and folds of loose skin like a diseased bloodhound, and his suntan had faded to the colour of creamed coffee. His eyes were bloodshot and rheumy, like those of a drunkard.

"You stored these weapons in the tractor sheds on this ranch?" Peter Fungabera asked, and Groenewald's reply was inaudible.

"Speak up, man."

"Yes. I stored them, sir."

"On whose orders?"

Groenewald looked piteously at Craig, and suddenly Craig's heart was sheathed in ice, and the cold spread down into his belly and his loins.

"Whose orders?" Peter Fungabera repeated patiently.

"Mr. Mellow's orders, sir."

"Take him away."

As the guards led him back to the truck, Groenewald's head

was screwed around, his eyes still on Craig's face, his expression harrowed. Suddenly he shouted, "I'm sorry, Mr. Mellow, I've got a wife and kids—"

One of the guards swung the butt of his rifle into Groenewald's stomach, just below the ribs. Groenewald gasped, and doubled over. He would have fallen but they seized his arms and swung him up into the cab. The driver of the truck started the engine and the big machine roared away down the hill.

Peter Fungabera led them back into the dining-room and resumed his seat at the head of the table. While he rearranged and studied the papers from the map-case, he ignored Craig and Sally-Anne. They were forced to stand against the opposite wall, a trooper on each side of them, and the silence stretched out. Even though Craig realized this silence was deliberate, he wanted to break it, to shout out his innocence, to protest against the web of lies and half-truths and distortions in which they were being slowly enmeshed.

Beside him Sally-Anne stood upright, gripping her own hands at waist level to prevent their trembling. Her face had a sick greenish hue under a light sheen of sweat and she kept turning her eyes towards the fireplace where the puppy's crushed carcass lay like a discarded toy.

At last Peter Fungabera pushed the papers aside and rocked back in his chair, tapping lightly on the table-top with his swagger-stick.

"A hanging matter," he said, "a capital offence for both you and Miss Jay—"

"It has nothing to do with her." Craig put protective arm around her shoulders.

"Women's lower organs are less able to withstand the downward shock of the hangman's drop," Peter Fungabera remarked. "The effect can be quite bizarre—or at least, so I am told." It conjured up an image that sickened Craig, saliva and nausea flooding his mouth. He swallowed it down and could not speak.

"Fortunately, it need not come to that. The choice will be yours."

Peter rolled the swagger-stick lightly between his fingers. Craig found himself staring fixedly at Peter's hands. The palms and insides of his long powerful fingers were a soft delicate pink.

"I believe that you are the dupes of your imperialistic capitalist masters." Peter smiled again. "I'm going to let you go."

192

Both their heads jerked up, and they watched his face.

"Yes, you look disbelieving, but I mean it. Personally, I have grown quite fond of both of you. To have you hanged would give me no special pleasure. Both of you possess artistic talents which it would be wasteful to terminate, and from now on you will be unable to do any further harm."

Still they were silent, beginning to hope, and yet fearful, sensing that it was all part of a cruel cat's game.

"I am prepared to make you an offer. If you make a clean breast of it, a full and unreserved confession, I will have you escorted to the border, with your travel documents and any readily portable possessions and items of value you choose. I will have you set free, to go and trouble me and my people no more."

He waited, smiling, and the swagger-stick went tap tap tap on the table-top, like a dripping faucet. It distracted Craig. He found himself unable to think clearly. It had all happened too swiftly. Peter Fungabera had kept him off balance, shifting and changing his attack. He had to have time to pull himself together, and to begin thinking clearly and logically again.

"A confession?" he blurted. "What kind of confession? One of your exhibitions—before a people's court? A public humiliation?"

"No, I don't think we need go that far," Peter Fungabera assured him. "I will need only a written statement from you, an account of your crimes and the machinations of your masters. The confession will be properly witnessed, and then you will be escorted to the border and set at liberty. All very straightforward, simple and, if I may be allowed to say so, very civilized and humane."

"You will, of course, prepare my confession for me to sign?" Craig asked bitterly, and Peter Fungabera chuckled.

"How very perceptive of you." He selected one of the documents from the pile in front of him. "Here it is. You need only fill in the date and sign it."

Even Craig was surprised at that.

"You've had it typed already?"

Nobody replied, and Captain Nbebi brought the document to him.

"Please read it, Mr. Mellow," he invited.

There were three typewritten foolscap sheets, and much of them filled with denunciations of his "imperialistic masters" and the hysterical cant of the extreme left. But in this mishmash, like plums in a stodgy pudding, were the hard facts of which Craig stood accused.

He read through it slowly, trying to force his numbed brain to function clearly, but it was all somehow dreamlike and unreal, seeming not really to affect him personally—until he read the words that jerked him fully conscious again. The words were so familiar, so well remembered, and they burned like concentrated acid into the core of his being.

"I fully admit that by my actions I have proved myself to be *an enemy of the state and the people of Zimbabwe*."

It was the exact wording used in another document he had signed, and suddenly he was able to see the design behind it all.

"King's Lynn," he whispered, and he looked up from the typewritten confession of Peter Fungabera. "That's what it's all about. You are after King's Lynn!"

There was silence, except for the tap of the swagger-stick on the table-top. Peter Fungabera did not miss a beat with it, and he was still smiling.

"You had it all worked out from the very beginning. The surety for my loan—you wrote in that clause."

The numbness and lethargy sloughed away, and Craig felt his anger rising again within him. He threw the confession on the floor. Captain Nbebi retrieved it and stood with it held awkwardly in both hands. Craig found himself shaking with rage. He took a step forward towards the elegant figure seated before him, his hands reaching out involuntarily, but the tall Shona sergeant barred his way with the barrel of his rifle held across Craig's chest.

"You bloody swine!" Craig hissed at Peter, and there was a little white froth of saliva on his lower lip. "I want the police, I want the protection of the law."

"Mr. Mellow," Peter Fungabera replied evenly, "in Matabeleland, I am the law. It is my protection that you are being offered."

"I won't do it. I won't sign that piece of dung. I will go to hell first."

"That might be arranged," Peter Fungabera mused softly, and then persuasively, "I really do urge you to put aside these histrionics and bow to the inevitable. Sign the paper and we can disperse with any further nastiness."

Crude words crowded to Craig's lips, and with an effort he resisted using them, not wanting to degrade himself in front of them.

194

"No," he said instead. "I'll never sign that thing. You'll have to kill me first."

"I give you one last chance to change your mind."

"No. Never!"

Peter Fungabera swivelled in his chair towards the tall sergeant.

"I give you the woman," he said. "You first and then your men, one at a time until they have all had their turn. Here, in this room, on this table."

"Christ, you aren't human," Craig blurted, and tried to hold Sally-Anne, but the troopers seized him from behind and hurled him back against the wall. One of them pinned him there with the point of a bayonet against his throat.

The other twisted Sally-Anne's wrist up between her shoulder-blades and held her in front of the sergeant. She began to struggle wildly, but the trooper lifted her until just the toes of her running shoes touched the stone-flagged floor, and her face contorted with pain.

The sergeant was expressionless, neither leering nor making any obscene gesture. He took the front of Sally-Anne's T-shirt in both hands and tore it open from neck to waist. Her breasts swung out. They were very white and tender-looking, their pink tips seemed sensitive and vulnerable.

"I have one hundred and fifty men," Peter Fungabera remarked. "It will be some time before they have all finished."

The sergeant hooked his thumbs into the waistband of her shorts and yanked them down. He let them fall in a tangle around her ankles. Craig strained forward, but the point of the bayonet pierced the skin at his throat. A few drops of blood dribbled down his shirt-front. Sally-Anne tried to cover the dark triangular mound of her pudenda with her free hand. It was a pathetically ineffectual gesture.

"I know how fiercely even a so-called white liberal like you resents the thought of black flesh penetrating his woman." Peter Fungabera's tone was almost conversational. "It will be interesting to see just how many times you will allow it to happen."

The sergeant and the trooper lifted Sally-Anne between them and laid her on her back on the refectory table. The sergeant freed the silk shorts that bound her ankles but left the running shoes on her feet, and the tatters of her shirt around her upper body.

Expertly they pulled her knees up against her chest and then forced them down, tucking them under her armpits. They must

195

have done this often before. She was helpless, doubled over, wide open and completely defenceless. Every man in the room was staring into her body's secret depths. The sergeant began to unbuckle his webbing belt with his free hand.

"Craig!" Sally-Anne screamed, and Craig's body bucked involuntarily as though to the stroke of a whip.

"I'll sign it," he whispered. "Just let her go, and I'll sign it."

Peter Fungabera gave an order to Shona, and immediately they released Sally-Anne. The trooper stood back and the sergeant helped her to her feet. Politely, he handed her back her shorts, and she hopped on one foot, sobbing softly and trembling, as she pulled them on.

Then she rushed to Craig and threw both arms about him. She could not speak, but she choked and gulped down her tears. Her body shook wildly and Craig held her close and made incoherent soothing noises to her.

"The sooner you sign, the sooner you can go."

Craig went to the table, still holding Sally-Anne in the curve of his left arm.

Captain Nbebi handed him a pen and he initialled the two top sheets of the confession, and signed the last one in full. Both Captain Nbebi and Peter Fungabera witnessed his signature, and then Peter said, "One last formality. I want both you and Miss Jay to be examined by the regimental doctor for any signs of ill-treatment or undue coercion."

"God damn you, hasn't she had enough?"

"Humour me, please, my dear fellow."

The doctor must have been waiting in one of the trucks outside. He was a small dapper Shona and his manner was brisk and businesslike.

"You may examine the woman in the bedroom, Doctor. In particular, please satisfy yourself that she has not been forcibly penetrated," Peter Fungabera instructed him, and then as they left the dining-room, he turned to Craig. "In the meantime, you may open the safe in your office and take out your passport and whatever other documents you may need for the journey."

Two troopers escorted Craig to his office at the far end of the veranda and waited while he struck the combination of the safe. He took out his passport, the wallet containing his credit cards and World Bank badge, three folders of American Express traveller's checks, and the bundle of manuscript for the new novel.

He stuffed them into a British Airways flight bag and went back to the dining-room.

Sally-Anne and the doctor came back from the bedroom. She had changed into a blue cashmere jersey, shirt and jeans, and she had controlled her hysteria to an occasional gulping sob, though she was still shivering in little convulsive fits. She dragged her camera bag and under one arm carried the art folder of photographs and text for their book.

"Your turn," Peter Fungabera invited Craig to follow the doctor, and when he returned Sally-Anne was seated in the back seat of a Land-Rover parked in front of the veranda. Captain Nbebi was beside her, and there were two armed troopers in the back of the vehicle. The seat beside the driver was empty for Craig.

Peter Fungabera was waiting on the veranda. "Goodbye, Craig," he said, and Craig stared at him, trying to project the full venom he felt for him.

"You didn't really believe that I would allow you to rebuild your family's empire, did you?" Peter asked without rancour. "We fought too hard to destroy that world."

As the Land-Rover drove down the hills in the night, Craig turned and looked back. Peter Fungabera still stood on the lighted veranda, and somehow his tall figure was transformed. He looked as though he belonged there, like a conqueror who has taken possession, like the *patron* of the grand estate. Craig watched him until the trees hid him, and only then did the leaven of his true hatred begin to rise within him.

•   •   •

The headlights of the Land-Rover swung across the signboard:

KING'S LYNN AFRIKANDER STUD
PROPRIETOR: CRAIG MELLOW

It seemed to mock him, then they were past it and rattling across the steel cattle-grid. They left the soil of King's Lynn and Craig's dreams behind them, and swung westwards. The tyres began their monotonous hum as they hit the black top of the main road, and still nobody in the Land-Rover spoke.

Captain Nbebi opened the map-case that he was holding on his knees and took out a bottle of the fiery locally made cane spirits. He passed the bottle over the front seat to Craig. Craig waved it brusquely aside, but Timon Nbebi insisted, and Craig took it with ill grace. He unscrewed the cap and swallowed a mouthful, then exhaled the fumes noisily. It brought tears to his eyes, but immediately the fireball in his belly spread out through his blood, giving him comfort. He took another swig and passed the bottle back to Sally-Anne. She shook her head.

"Drink it," Craig ordered, and meekly she obeyed. She had stopped weeping, but the fits of shivering still persisted. The spirits made her cough and choke, but she got them down, and they steadied her.

"Thank you." She handed the bottle back to Timon Nbebi, and the politeness from a woman who had been so recently degraded and humiliated was embarrassing to all of them.

They reached the first road-block on the outskirts of the town of Bulawayo, and Craig checked his wrist-watch. It was seven minutes to three in the morning. There were no other vehicles waiting at the barrier, and two troopers stepped out from behind the barricade and came to each side of the Land-Rover. Timon Nbebi slid back his window and spoke quietly to one of them, offering his pass at the same time. The trooper examined it briefly in the beam of his flashlight, then handed it back. He saluted, and the barrier lifted. They drove through.

Bulawayo was silent and devoid of life. Very few of the windows were lit. A traffic-light flashed green and amber and red, and the driver stopped obediently, although the streets were completely deserted. The engine throbbed in idle and then above it, far-off and faint, came the sound of automatic-rifle fire.

Craig was watching Timon Nbebi's face in the rear-view mirror and saw him wince slightly at the sound of gunfire. Then the light changed and they drove on, taking the south road through the suburbs. On the edge of the town there were two more road-blocks and then the open road.

They ran southwards in the night, with the whine of the tyres and the buffet of the wind against the cab. The glow from the dashboard gave their faces a sickly greenish hue and once or twice the radio in the back crackled and gabbled distorted Shona. Craig recognized Peter Fungabera's voice on one of the transmissions, but he must have been calling another unit, for Timon Nbebi made no effort to reply and they drove on in silence. The monotonous hum of the engine and tyres and the warmth of the cab lulled

Craig, and in a reaction from anger and fear he found himself dozing.

He awoke with a start as Timon Nbebi spoke for the first time, and the beat of the Land-Rover's engine altered. It was dawn's first light. He could see the silhouette of the tree-tops against the paling lemon sky. The Land-Rover slowed and then swung off the main tarmac road onto a dirt track. Immediately the mushroom smell of talcum dust permeated the cab.

"Where are we?" Craig demanded. "Why are we leaving the road?"

Timon Nbebi spoke to the driver and he pulled to the side of the track and stopped.

"You will please step out," Timon ordered, and as Craig did so, Timon was waiting for him, seeming to help him down—but instead he took Craig's arm, turned it slightly, and before Craig could react to the icy touch of steel on his skin, Timon had hand-cuffed both his wrists. It had been so unexpected and so expertly done that for seconds Craig stood bewildered with his manacled hands thrust out in front of him, staring at them. Then he shouted, "Christ, what is this?"

By then Timon Nbebi had handcuffed Sally-Anne as quickly and efficiently and, ignoring Craig's outburst, was talking quietly to his driver and the two troopers. It was too quick for Craig to follow, although he caught the Shona words "kill" and "hide." One of the troopers seemed to protest and Timon leaned through the open door of the Land-Rover, and lifted the microphone of the radio. He gave a call sign, repeated three times, and after a short wait was patched through to Peter Fungabera. Craig recognized the general's voice despite the V.H.F. distortion. There was a brief exchange, and when Timon Nbebi hung up the micro-phone, the trooper was no longer protesting. Clearly Timon Nbe-bi's orders had been endorsed.

"We will go on," Timon reverted to English, and Craig was roughly hustled back into the front seat. The change in their treat-ment was ominous.

The driver threaded the Land-Rover deeper and deeper into the thorn veld, and the morning light strengthened. Outside the cab, the dawn bird chorus was in full voice. Craig recognized the high clear duet of a pair of collared barbets in an acacia tree beside the track. A brown hare was trapped in the beam of the headlights and lolloped ahead of them with his long pink ears flapping. Then the sky began to burn with the stupendous colours of the African dawn and the driver switched off the headlights.

"Craig, darling. They are going to kill us, aren't they?" Sally-Anne asked quietly. Her voice was clear and firm now. She had conquered her hysteria and was in control of herself again. She spoke as though they were alone.

"I'm sorry." Craig could find nothing else to say. "I should have know that Peter Fungabera would never let us go."

"There is nothing you could have done. Even if you *had* known."

"They'll bury us in some remote place and our disappearance will be blamed on the Matabele dissidents," Craig said, and Timon Nbebi sat silent and impassive, neither admitting nor denying the accusation.

The road forked, the left-hand track barely discernible, and Timon Nbebi indicated it. The driver slowed further and changed to a lower gear. They bumped along it for another twenty minutes. By then it was fully light, the promise of sunrise flaming the tiptops of the acacia.

Timon Nbebi gave another order and the driver turned off the track and drove blindly through the waist-high grass, skirting the edge of a grey granite kopje, until they were entirely screened from even the rudimentary bush track that they had been following. Another short order, and the driver stopped and switched off the engine.

The silence closed in on them, enhancing their sense of isolation and remoteness.

"No one will ever find us here," Sally-Anne said quietly, and Craig could find no word of comfort for her.

"You will remain where you are," Timon Nbebi ordered.

"Don't you feel anything for what you are going to do?" Sally-Anne asked him, and he turned his head to her. Behind the steel-rimmed spectacles his eyes were perhaps shaded with misery and regret, but his mouth was set hard. He did not reply to her question, and after a moment, turned from her and alighted. He gave orders in Shona, and the troopers racked their weapons in the back of the Land-Rover while the driver climbed up onto the roof-rack and brought down three folding trenching-tools.

Timon Nbebi reached through the window and took the keys out of the Land-Rover's ignition, then he led his men a short distance away and with the toe of his boot marked out two oblongs

on the sandy grey earth. The three Shonas shucked off their webbing and battle-jackets and began to dig out the graves. They went
swiftly in the loose soil. Timon Nbebi stood aside watching them.
He lit a cigarette and the grey smoke spiralled straight up in the
still, cool dawn.

"I am going to try to get one of the rifles," Craig whispered.
The weapons were in the back of the vehicle. He would have to
crawl over the backs of both seats, then reach the rifles which
were standing upright in the racks. He would have to open the
clip on the rack, load the weapon, change the rate-of-fire selector
and aim through the back window—all with his hands manacled.

"You won't make it," Sally-Anne whispered.

"Probably not," he agreed grimly, "but can you think of anything else? When I say 'Go,' I want you to throw yourself flat on
the floor."

Craig wriggled around in the seat, his leg hampering him,
catching by the ankle on the lever of the four-wheel-drive selector.
He kicked it free and gathered himself. He took a slow breath,
then glanced out of the rear window at the little group of grave-
diggers.

"Listen," he told her urgently, "I love you. I have never loved
anyone the way I love you."

"I love you, too, my darling," she whispered back.

"Be brave!" he said.

"Good luck!" She was crouching down, and he almost made
his move, but at that moment Timon Nbebi turned towards the
Land-Rover. He saw Craig twisted around in the seat, and Sally-
Anne down below the sill. He frowned and came back to the
vehicle with quick businesslike strides. At the open window he
paused and spoke softly in English.

"Don't do it, Mr. Mellow. We are all of us in great danger.
Our only chance is for you to remain still and not to interfere or
make any unexpected move." He took the ignition keys from his
pocket, and, with his other hand, loosened the flap of the webbing
pistol-holster on his belt. He kept on talking softly, "I have effectively disarmed my men, and their attention is on their work.
When I enter the Land-Rover, do not hamper me or try to attack
me. I am in as great danger as you are. You must trust me. Do
you understand?"

Craig nodded. "Yes." Christ! Do I have any choice, he thought.

Timon opened the driver's door of the Land-Rover and slid in under the wheel. He glanced once at the three soldiers, who were by now waist-deep in the two graves, then Timon slipped the key into the ignition and turned it.

The engine turned over loudly, and the three soldiers looked up, puzzled. The starter-motor whirred and churned, and the engine would not fire. One of the troopers shouted and jumped out of the grave. His chest was snaked with sweat and powdered with grey dust. He started towards the stranded Land-Rover. Timon Nbebi pumped the accelerator and kept turning the engine. He had a desperate, terrified look on his face.

"You'll flood her," Craig told him. "Take your foot off!"

The trooper broke into a run towards them. He was shouting angry questions, and the starter went on—*whirr! whirr! whirr!*—with Timon frozen to the wheel.

The running trooper was almost alongside, and now the others, slower and less alert, began to follow him. They were shouting also, one of them swinging his trenching-tool menacingly.

"Lock the door!" Craig shouted urgently, and Timon pushed down the handle into the lock position just as the trooper threw his weight on it. He heaved at the outside handle with all his weight, and then darted to the rear door and, before Sally-Anne could lock it, jerked it open. He reached in and caught Sally-Anne by the upper arm and began dragging her from the open door.

Craig was still hunched around in the front seat and now he lifted both manacled hands high and brought them down on the trooper's shaven head. The sharp steel edge of the cuffs cut down to the bone of the skull, and the man collapsed half in and half out of the open door.

Craig hit him again, in the centre of the forehead, and had a brief glimpse of white bone in the bottom of the wound before quick bright blood obscured it. The other two soldiers were only paces away, baying like wolfhounds and armed with their spades.

At that moment the engine of the Land-Rover fired and roared into life. Timon Nbebi hit the gear-lever, and with a clash of metal it engaged and the Land-Rover shot forward. Craig was thrown over the seat half on top of Sally-Anne, and the bleeding trooper was caught by his dangling legs in a thorn-bush and ripped out through the rear door.

The Land-Rover swerved and bucked over the rough ground, with the two screeching soldiers running behind it, and the open door flapping and banging wildly. Then Timon Nbebi straightened the wheel and changed gear. The Land-Rover accelerated away, crashing over rock and fallen branches, and the pursuing troopers fell back. One of them hurled the spade despairingly after them. It shattered the rear window, and broken glass spilled over the rear of the cab.

Timon Nbebi picked up their own incoming tracks through the high grass, and at last they were going faster than a man could run. The two troopers gave up and stood panting in the tracks. Their shouts of recrimination and anger dwindled and then were lost. Timon reached the bush track at the point that they had left it and turned onto it, picking up speed.

"Give me your hands," he ordered, and when Craig proffered his manacled hands, Timon unlocked the cuffs. "Here!" he gave Craig the key. "Do the same for Miss Jay."

She rubbed her wrist. "My God, Craig, I truly thought that was the end of the line."

"A close-run thing," Timon Nbebi agreed, with all his attention on the track. "Napoleon said that, I think." And then, before Craig could correct him, "Please to arm yourself with one of those rifles, Mr. Mellow, and place the other beside me."

Sally-Anne passed the short, ugly weapons over to the front seat. The Third Brigade was the only unit of the regular army still armed with AK 47s, a legacy from their North Korean instructors.

"Do you know how to use it, Mr. Mellow?" Timon Nbebi asked.

"I was an armourer in the Rhodesian Police."

"Of course, how stupid of me."

Swiftly Craig checked the curved "banana" magazine and then reloaded the chamber. The weapon was new and well cared for. The weight of it in Craig's hands changed his whole personality. Minutes before, he had been mere flotsam on the stream, swept along by events over which he had no control, confused and uncertain and afraid—but now he was armed. Now he could fight back, now he could protect his woman and himself, now he could shape events rather than be shaped by them. It was the primeval, atavistic instinct of primitive man, and Craig revelled in it. He reached over the seat and took Sally-Anne's hand. He squeezed it briefly, and fervently she returned the pressure.

"Now we have a fighting chance, at least." The new tone of his voice reached her. Her spirits lifted a little, and she gave him the first smile he had seen that night. He freed his hand, found the bottle of cane spirit in the cubby-hole, and passed it to her. After she had drunk, he gave it to Timon Nbebi.

"All right, Captain, what the hell is going on here?"

Timon gasped at sting of the liquor and his voice was roughened by it as he replied.

"You were perfectly correct, Mr. Mellow, my orders from General Fungabera were to take you and Miss Jay into the bush and execute you. And you were also correct in guessing that your disappearance would be blamed on the Matabele dissidents."

"Well, why didn't you obey your orders?"

Before replying, Timon handed the bottle back to Craig, and then glanced over his shoulder at Sally-Anne.

"I am sorry that I had to go through the preparations for your execution without being able to reassure you, but my men speak English. I had to make it look real. It galled me, for I didn't want to inflict more on you, after what you have already suffered."

"Captain Nbebi, I forgive you everything and I love you for what you are doing, but why, in God's name, are you doing it?" Sally-Anne demanded.

"What I am about to tell you, I have never told a living soul before. You see, my mother was a full-blooded Matabele. She died when I was very young, but I remember her well and honour that memory." He did not look at them but concentrated on the track ahead. "I was raised as a Shona by my father, but I have always been aware of my Matabele blood. They are my people, and I can no longer stomach what is being done to them. I am certain that General Fungabera has become aware of my feelings, though I doubt that he knows about my mother, but he knows that I have reached the end of my usefulness to him. Recently there have been small signs of it. I have lived too close to the man-eating leopard for too long not to know its moods. After I had buried you, there would have been something for me also, an unmarked grave—or Fungabera's puppies."

Timon used the Sindebele, *amawundhla ka Fungabera*, and Craig was startled. Sarah Nyoni, the school-teacher at Tuti Mission, had used the same phrase.

"I have heard that expression before—I do not understand it."

"Hyena," Timon explained. "Those who die or are executed at the rehabilitation centres are taken into the bush and laid out for the hyena. The hyena leaves nothing, not a chip of bone or a tuft of hair."

204

"Oh God," said Sally-Anne in a small voice. "We were at Tuti. We heard the brutes but didn't understand. How many have gone that way?"

"I can only guess—many thousands," Timon Nbebi said.

"It's scarcely believable."

"General Fungabera's hatred for the Matabele is a kind of madness, an obsession. He is planning to wipe them out. First it was their leaders, accused of treason—falsely accused, like Tungata Zebiwe—"

"Oh no!" Sally-Anne said miserably. "I can't bear it—was Zebiwe innocent?"

Timon Nbebi confirmed it. "I'm sorry, Miss Jay. Fungabera had to be very careful when he tackled Zebiwe. He knew if he seized him for his political activities, he would have the entire Matabele tribe in revolt. You and Mr. Mellow provided him with the perfect opportunity—a non-political crime. A crime of greed."

"I'm being stupid," said Sally-Anne. "If Zebiwe wasn't the master poacher, was there ever a poacher? And if there was—who was it?"

"General Fungabera himself," said Timon Nbebi simply.

"Are you sure?" Craig was incredulous.

"I was personally in charge of many of the shipments of animal contraband that left the country."

"But that night on the Karoi road?"

"That was easily arranged. The general knew that sooner or later Zebiwe would be going to Tuti Mission again. Zebiwe's secretary informed us of the exact time and date. We arranged for the truck loaded with contraband, driven by a Matabele detainee we had bribed, to be waiting for him on the Tuti road. Of course, we had not anticipated Tungata Zebiwe's violent reaction—that was merely a bonus for us."

Timon drove as fast as the truck would allow, while Sally-Anne and Craig hunched down in their seats, their artificial elation at their escape rapidly giving way to fatigue and shock.

"Where are you heading?" Craig asked.

"Botswana border."

That was the land-locking state to the south and west which had become an established staging post for political fugitives from its neighbours.

"On our way I hope you will have a chance to see what is really happening to my people. No one else will bear witness.

205

General Fungabera has sealed off the whole of south-western Matabeleland. No journalists are allowed in, no clergymen, no Red Cross—"

He slowed for an area where ant-bears had dug their holes in the track, burrowing for the nests of termites, and then he accelerated again.

"The pass I have from General Fungabera will take us a little farther, but not as far as the border. We will have to use side-roads and back roads until we can find a crossing place. Very soon General Fungabera will learn of my defection, and we will be hunted by the whole of the Third Brigade. We must make as much distance as we can before that happens."

They reached the main fork in the track and Timon stopped, but kept the motor running. He took a large-scale map from his leather map-case and studied it attentively.

"We are just south of the railway line. This is the road to Empandeni Mission Station. If we can get through there before the alarm goes out for us, then we can try for the border between Madaba and Matsumi. The Botswana police run a regular patrol along the fence."

"Let's get on with it." Craig was impatient and becoming fearful, the comfort of the weapon across his lap beginning to fade. Timon folded the map and drove on.

"Can I ask you some more questions?" Sally-Anne spoke after a few minutes.

"I will try to answer," Timon agreed.

"The murder of the Goodwins, and the other white families in Matabeleland—were those atrocities ordered by Tungata Zebiwe? Is he responsible for those gruesome murders?"

"No, no, Miss Jay. Zebiwe has been trying desperately to control those killers. I believe that he was on his way to Tuti Mission for just such a reason—to meet with the radical Matabele elements and try to reason with them."

"But the writing in blood, 'Tungata Zebiwe Lives'?"

Now Timon Nbebi was silent, his face contorted as though he fought some inner battle, and they waited for him to speak. At last he sighed explosively, and his voice had changed.

"Miss Jay, please try to understand my position, before you judge me for what I am about to tell you. General Fungabera is a persuasive man. I was carried along by his promises of glory

206

and reward. Then suddenly I had gone too far and I was not able to turn back. I think the English expression is 'riding the tiger.' I was forced to move on from one bad deed to another even worse." He paused, and then, in a rush, "Miss Jay, I personally recruited the killers of the Goodwin family from the rehabilitation centre. I told them where to go, what to do—and what to write on the wall. I supplied their weapons and arranged for them to be driven to the area in transport of the Third Brigade."

There was silence again, broken only by the throb of the Land-Rover engine, and Timon Nbebi had to break in, speaking as though words were an opiate for his guilt.

"They were Matabele, veterans, war-hard men, men who would do anything for the return of their personal liberty, the chance to carry weapons again. They did not hesitate."

"And Fungabera ordered it?" Craig said.

"Of course. It was his excuse to begin the purge of the Matabele. Now perhaps you understand why I am fleeing with you. I could not continue along this path."

"The other murders—the killing of Senator Savage and his family?" Sally-Anne asked.

Timon shook his head. "General Fungabera did not have to order those. Those were copy-cat murders. The bush is still full of wild men from the war. They hide their weapons and come into towns, some even have regular jobs, but at the week-end or on a public holiday they return to the bush, dig up their rifles and go on the rampage. They are not political dissidents, they are armed bandits and the white families are the juiciest, softest targets, rich and helpless, deprived of their weapons by Mugabe's government so they cannot defend themselves."

"And it all plays right into Peter Fungabera's hands. Any bandit is labelled a political dissident, any grisly robbery an excuse to continue the purge, held up to the world as proof of the savagery and intractability of the Matabele tribe," Craig continued for him.

"That is correct, Mr. Mellow."

"And he has already murdered Tungata Zebiwe"—Craig felt old and tired with regret and guilt for his old comrade—"you can be sure of that!"

Timon shook his head. "No, Mr. Mellow. I do not believe that Zebiwe is dead. I believe General Fungabera wants him alive. He has some plans for him."

"What plans?" Craig demanded.

"I do not know for certain, but I believe Peter Fungabera is dealing with the Russians."

"The Russians?" Craig looked his disbelief.

"He has had secret meetings with a stranger, a foreigner, a man who, I believe, is an important member of Russian intelligence."

"Are you sure, Timon?"

"I have seen the man with my own eyes."

Craig thought about that for a few seconds and then reverted to his original question.

"Okay, leave the Russians for the moment—where is Tungata Zebiwe? Where is Fungabera holding him?"

"Again, I do not know. I'm sorry, Mr. Mellow."

"If he is alive, then may the Lord have mercy on his soul," Craig whispered.

He could imagine that Tungata must be suffering. He was silent for a few minutes and then he changed the line of questioning.

"General Fungabera has seized my property for himself, not for the state? I am correct in believing that?"

"The general wanted that land very badly. He spoke of it often."

"How? I mean, even quasi-legally, how will he work it?"

"It is very simple," Timon explained. "You are an admitted enemy of the state. Your property is forfeited. It will be confiscated by the state. The Land Bank will repudiate the suretyship for your loan under the release clause that you signed. The custodian of enemy property will put up your shares of Rholands Company for sale by private tender. General Fungabera's tender will be accepted—his brother-in-law is custodian of enemy property. The tender price will be greatly advantageous to the general."

"I bet," said Craig bitterly.

"But why should he go to such lengths?" Sally-Anne demanded. "He must be a millionaire many times over. Surely he has enough already?"

"Miss Jay, for some men there is no such thing as enough."

"He cannot hope to get away with it, surely?"

"Who is there to prevent him doing so, Miss Jay?" And when she did not reply, Timon went on, "Africa is going back to where it was before the white man intruded. There is only one criterion for a ruler here and that is strength. We Africans do not trust anything else. Fungabera is strong, as Tungata Zebiwe was once strong." Timon glanced at his wrist-watch. "But we must eat. I

208

think we will have a long day ahead of us."

He pulled off the track and drove the Land-Rover into a patch of second-growth scrub. He climbed onto the hood and arranged branches to cover the vehicle, hiding it from detection from the air, and then opened the case of emergency rations from the locker under the passenger seat. There was water in the tank under the floorboards.

Craig filled a metal canteen with sand and soaked the sand with gasoline from the reserve tank. It made a smokeless burner on which to brew tea. They ate the unappetizing cold rations with little conversation.

Once Timon turned up the volume on the radio to listen to a transmission, then shook his head.

"Nothing to do with us." He came back to squat beside Craig.

"How far to the border, do you reckon?" Craig asked with a mouth full of cold, sticky bully beef.

"Forty miles, or a little more."

The radio cracked to life again, and Timon jumped up and stooped over it attentively.

"There is a unit of the Third Brigade just a few miles ahead of us," he reported. "They are at the mission station at Empandeni. There has been action against dissidents, but they have dealt with them and are moving out. Perhaps this way. We must be careful."

"I will check that we are hidden from the road." Craig stood up. "Sally-Anne douse the fire! Captain, cover me!"

He picked up the AK 47 and ran back to the track. Critically he examined the patch of scrub that concealed the Land-Rover and then brushed over his own tracks and those of the vehicle with a leafy twig. He carefully straightened the grass that the Land-Rover had flattened where it left the road. It wasn't perfect, but it would bear a cursory examination from a speeding vehicle, he thought, and then there was a faint vibration on the windless air. He listened. The sound of truck motors, strengthening. Craig ran back to the Land-Rover and climbed into the front seat beside Timon.

"Put your rifle back in the rack," Timon said, and, when Craig hesitated, "Please do as I say, Mr. Mellow. If they find us, it will be useless to fight. I will have to try and talk our way through. I couldn't explain if you were armed."

Reluctantly Craig passed the weapon back to Sally-Anne. She racked it and Craig was left feeling naked and vulnerable. He clenched his fists in his lap. The sound of motors grew swiftly, and then over them the voices of men singing. The song grew louder. Despite his tension Craig felt the hair prickle on the nape of his neck to the peculiar beauty of African voices raised in song.

"Third Brigade," Timon said. "That is the 'Song of the Rain Winds,' the praise song of the regiment."

Neither of them replied, and Timon hummed the tune to himself, and then began to sing softly. He had a startling true and thrilling voice:

> "When the nation burns, the rain winds bring relief.
> When the cattle are drought-stricken, the rain winds lift them up.
> When your children cry with thirst,
>   the rain winds slake them,
> We are the winds that bring the rain,
> We are the good winds of the nation."

Timon translated from the Shona for their benefit, and now Craig could see the grey dust of the trucks smoking up above the scrub, and the singing was close and clear.

There was a flash of reflected sunlight off metal. Through the foliage Craig caught quick glimpses of the passing convoy. There were three trucks, painted a dull sand colour, and the backs were crowded with soldiers in battle camouflage and bush hats, their weapons held ready at the high port position. On the cab of the last truck rode an officer, the only one of them wearing the red beret and silver cap-badge. He looked directly at Craig, and seemed very close, the screen of foliage suddenly very sparse. Craig shrank down in his seat.

Then, thankfully, the convoy was past, the rumble of engines and the singing dwindling, the dust settling.

Timon Nbebi exhaled a long breath. "There will be others," he cautioned, and, with his fingers on the ignition key, waited until the silence was complete once again. Then he started the Land-Rover, reversed out of the scrub and turned back onto the track.

He swung the Land-Rover in the opposite direction from the convoy, and they drove over the lugged tracks that the trucks had imprinted deeply into the sandy earth. They drove for another twenty minutes before Timon ducked down abruptly in his seat, to peer up at the sky through the windshield.

"Smoke," he said. "Empandeni is just ahead. Will you have your camera ready, Miss Jay? I believe the Third Brigade will have left something for you."

They came to the maize fields that surrounded the mission village. The maize stalks had dried; the cobs in their yellow sheaths were beginning to droop heavily, ready for the harvest. There had been women working in the fields. One of them lay beside the track. She had been shot in the back as she ran; the bullet had exited between her breasts. The unweaned child that she carried on her back had been bayoneted many times. The flies rose up in a blue hum as they passed and then settled again.

Nobody spoke. Sally-Anne reached into her camera-bag and brought out her Nikon. She was bloodless grey under her freckles.

The other women lay farther from the road, mere bundles of gay cloth, heavily stained. There were possibly fifty huts in the village, all of them burning, the thatched roofs touching up to the clear blue morning sky. They had thrown most of the corpses into the burning huts, leaving black puddles drying where they had fallen and drag marks in the dust. The smell of seared flesh was very strong; it coated the roofs of their mouths like congealed pork fat. Craig's stomach heaved, and he covered his mouth and nose with his hand.

"These are dissidents?" Sally-Anne whispered. Her lips were icy white. The motor drive of her Nikon whirred as she shot through the open window.

They had killed the chickens. The loose feathers rolled on the light breeze, like the stuffing from a burst pillow.

"Stop!" Sally-Anne ordered.

"It is dangerous to stay," said Timon.

"Stop," Sally-Anne repeated.

She left the door open, and went among the huts, working swiftly, changing roll after roll of film with practised nimble fingers, while her white lips trembled and her eyes behind the lens were huge with horror.

"We must move on," said Timon.

"Wait." Sally-Anne moved quickly forward, doing her job like the professional she was. She moved behind a group of huts. The smell of burning flesh nauseated Craig, and the heat from the fires came at him in great furnace gusts as the breeze veered.

Sally-Anne screamed and the two men jumped from the Land-Rover and ran, cocking their rifles, diverging to give each other covering fire, Craig finding his old training returning instinctively. He came around the side of a hut.

Sally-Anne stood in the open, no longer able to use her camera. A naked black woman lay at her feet. The woman's upper body was that of a comely, healthy young woman, below her navel she was a pink skinless monstrosity. She had dragged herself back out of the fire into which they had thrown her. There were places on her lower body where the burning was not deep; here the flesh was piebald pink and weeping lymph. Then in other places the bone was exposed; her hip-bone, charred black as charcoal, protruded obscenely from the scorched meat of her pelvic area. The lining of her stomach had burned through and her entrails bulged from the opening. Miraculously, she was still alive. Her fingers raked the dust with a repetitive, mechanical movement. Her mouth opened and closed convulsively, making no sound, and her eyes were wide open, aware and suffering.

"Go back to the Land-Rover, please, Miss Jay," Timon Nbebi said. "There is nothing you can do to help her."

Sally-Anne stood stiffly, unable to move. Craig put his arm around her shoulders and turned her away. He led her back towards the Land-Rover.

At the corner of the burning hut Craig glanced back. Timon Nbebi had moved up close to the maimed woman; he stood over her with the AK 47 held ready on his hip, his whole attention focused upon her and his face almost as riven with suffering as was the woman's.

Craig took Sally-Anne around the hut. Behind them there was the whip-crack of a single shot, muted by the crackle of flames all around them. Sally-Anne stumbled and then caught her balance. When they reached the Land-Rover, Sally-Anne leaned against the cab and doubled over slowly. She vomited in the dust and then straightened up and wiped her mouth with the back of her hand.

Craig took the bottle of cane spirit from the cubby-hole. There was an inch of the clear liquor remaining. He gave it to Sally-Anne and she drank it like water. Craig took the empty bottle back from her and then abruptly and savagely hurled it into the burning hut.

Timon Nbebi came round the hut. Wordlessly he climbed behind the steering-wheel and Craig helped Sally-Anne into the rear seat. They drove slowly through the rest of the village, their heads turning from side to side as each fresh horror was revealed.

As they passed the little church of red brick, the roof collapsed in upon itself, and the wooden cross on the spire was swallowed in a belch of sparks and flames and blue smoke. In the bright sunlight the flames were almost colourless.

·　　·　　·

Timon Nbebi used the radio the way a navigator uses an echo sounder to find the channel through shoal water.

The Third Brigade road-blocks and ambushes were reporting over the V.H.F. net to their area headquarters, giving their positions as part of their routine reports, and Timon pin-pointed them on his map.

Twice they avoided road-blocks by taking side-tracks and cattle paths, groping forward carefully through the acacia forest. Twice more they came to small villages, mere cattle stations, homes of two or three Matabele families. The Third Brigade had preceded them, and the crows and vultures had followed, picking at the partially roasted carcasses in the warm ashes of the burned-out huts.

They kept moving westwards, when the tracks allowed. At each prominence that afforded a view ahead, Timon parked in cover and Craig climbed to the crest to scout ahead. In every direction he looked, the towering blue of the sky above the horizon was marred by standing columns of smoke from burning villages. Westwards still they crawled, and the terrain changed swiftly as they approached the edge of the Kalahari Desert. There were fewer and still fewer features. The land levelled into a grey, monotonous plain, burning endlessly under the high merciless sun. The trees became stunted, their branches heat-tortured as the limbs of cripples. This was a land able to support only the most rudimentary human needs, the beginning of the great wilderness. Still they edged westwards into it.

The sun made its noon and slid down the sky, and they had made a mere thirty miles since dawn. Still at least another twenty miles to reach the border, Craig estimated from the map, and all three of them were exhausted from the unremitting strain and the heat in the unlined metal cab.

In the middle of the afternoon, they stopped again for a few minutes. Craig brewed tea. Sally-Anne went behind a low clump of thorn scrub nearby and squatted out of view, while Timon hunched over the radio.

213

"There are no more villages ahead," Timon said as he retuned the set. "I think we are clear, but I have never been farther than this. I am not sure what to expect."

"I worked here with Tungata when we were in the Game Department. That was back in '72. We followed a pride of cattle-killing lions nearly a hundred miles across the border. It's bad country— no surface water, soft going with salt-pans and—" He broke off as Timon signalled him urgently to silence.

Timon had picked up another voice on the radio. It was more authoritative, more cutting than the reports of the platoon he had been monitoring. Clearly it was demanding priority and clearing the net for an urgent flash. Timon Nbebi stiffened, and exclaimed under his breath.

"What is it?" Craig could not contain his forebodings, but Timon held up a hand for silence and listened to the long staccato transmission that followed in Shona. When the carrier beam of the radio went mute, he looked up at them.

"A patrol has picked up the three men we marooned this morning. That was an alert to all units. General Fungabera has given top priority to our recapture. Two spotter aircraft have been diverted to this area. They should be overhead very soon. The general has calculated our position with great accuracy; he has ordered the punitive units to the east of us to abandon their missions and to move in this direction immediately. He has guessed that we are trying to reach the border south of Plumtree and the railway-line. He is rushing two platoons down from the main border-post at Plumtree to block us." He paused, took off his spectacles and polished the lens on the tail of his silk cravat. Without his spectacles, he was as myopic as an owl in daylight.

"General Fungabera has given the 'leopard' code to all units—" He paused again, and then almost apologetically explained, "The 'leopard' code is the 'kill on sight' order, which is rather bad news, I'm afraid."

Craig snatched the map and unrolled it on the hood. Sally-Anne came back and stood close behind him.

"We are here," he said, and Timon nodded agreement. "This is the only track from here on, and it angles northwards, about west northwest," Craig muttered to himself. "The patrol from Plumtree must come down it to meet us, and the punitive groups must come up it behind us."

Again Timon nodded. "This time they won't drive past us. They'll be on the lookout."

The radio came alive again and Timon darted back to it. His expression became even more lugubrious as he listened.

"The punitive unit behind us has picked up the tracks of our Land-Rover. They are not far behind and they are coming up fast," he reported. "They have contacted the patrol on the road ahead of us. We are boxed in. I don't know what to do, Mr. Mellow. They'll be here in a few minutes." And he looked appealingly at Craig.

"All right." Craig took control quite naturally. "We'll go for the border cross-country."

"But you said this is bad country—" Timon began.

"Put her into four-wheel drive and get going," Craig snapped. "I'll ride on the roof-rack to guide you. Sally-Anne, take the front seat."

Perched on the roof-rack, the AK 47 slung over one shoulder, Craig took a sight with the hand-bearing compass from Timon's map-case, made a rough calculation of the magnetic deflection, and called down to Timon.

"Right, turn right—that's it. Hold that course." He was lined up on the white glare of a small salt-pan a few miles ahead, and the surface under them seemed firm and reasonably fast. The Land-Rover accelerated away, barging through the low thorn scrub, weaving only when they came to coarser thorn or one of the stunted trees. Craig called corrections after every deviation.

They were making twenty-five miles an hour, and it was clear as far as the horizon. The pursuing trucks, heavy and cumbersome, couldn't outrun them, Craig was sure, and the border was less than an hour ahead, darkness not far off. That cup of tea had cheered him, and Craig felt his spirits lift.

"All right, you bastards, come and get us!" he challenged the unseen enemy and laughed into the wind. He had forgotten the way adrenalin buzzed in the blood when danger was close. Once he had thrived on the feel of it, and the addiction was still there, he realized.

He swivelled and looked back, and saw it immediately—like a little willy-willy, the dust devils that dance on the desert in the hot stillness of midday. But this dust cloud was moving with purpose, and it was exactly where he had expected to find it, due east of them and coming fast down the road they had just left.

"I have one patrol in sight," he leaned out and shouted down to the open driver's window. "They are about five miles behind."

Then he looked back again and grimaced at their own dust cloud thrown up by the four-wheel drive. It followed them like a bridal train and hung for minutes after they had passed, a long smear above the scrub. They could hardly miss it. He was watching the dust when he should have been looking ahead. The ant-bear hole was screened from the driver's view by the pale desert grass. They hit it at twenty-five miles an hour, and it stopped them dead.

Craig was hurled forward off the roof, flying out over the hood to hit the earth with his elbows and his knees and the side of his face. He lay in the dust, stunned and hurting. Then he rolled into a sitting position and spat muddy blood from his mouth. He checked his teeth with his tongue, and they were all firm. There was no skin on his elbows, and blood seeped through the knees of his jeans. He fumbled at the strap of his leg and it was intact. He dragged himself to his feet.

The Land-Rover was down heavily on her left front, chassis deep in the hole. He limped to the passenger side, cursing his own inattention, and jerked the door open. The windscreen was cracked and starred where Sally-Anne's head had hit, and she was slumped forward in the seat.

"Oh God!" he whispered, and lifted her head gently. There was a lump the size of a blue acorn over her eye, but when he touched her cheek, her vision focused and she looked at him.

"Are you hurt badly?"

She struggled upright. "You are bleeding," she mumbled, like a drunk.

"It's a graze," he reassured her, and squeezed her arm, looking across her at Timon.

His mouth had struck the steering-wheel, his upper lip was cut through and one of his incisors had broken off at the gum. His mouth was full of blood, but he staunched it with the silk scarf.

"Get her in reverse," Craig ordered him, and pulled Sally-Anne from the cab to lighten the vehicle. She staggered a few paces and flopped down on her backside, still groggy and confused from the head blow.

The engine had stalled, and it balked at the starter while Craig fretted and watched the dust cloud behind them. It was no longer distant, and it was coming on fast. At last the engine caught, stuttered and then roared as Timon trod too heavily on the pedal. He let out the clutch with a bang, and all four wheels spun wildly.

"Easy, man, you'll break a half-shaft," Craig snarled at him.

Timon tried again, more gently, but again the wheels spun, blowing out dust behind them, and the vehicle rocked crazily but remained bogged down.

"Stop it!" Craig pounded Timon's shoulder to make him obey. The spinning wheels in the soft earth were digging the Land-Rover into its own grave. Craig dropped on his belly and peered under the chassis. The left front wheel had dropped into the hole and was turning in air; the weight of the vehicle rested on the blades of the front suspension.

"Trenching-tool," Craig called to Timon.

"We left them," Timon reminded him, and Craig went at the earth on the rim of the hole with his bare hands.

"Find something to dig with!" He kept on digging frantically.

Timon hunted in the back locker and brought him the jack handle and a broad-bladed panga. Craig attacked the edge of the hole with them, grunting and panting, his own sweat stinging the open graze on his cheek.

The radio jabbered. "They have found the spot where we left the road," Timon translated.

"Christ!" Craig sobbed with effort. That was less than two miles back.

"Can I help you?" Timon was lisping through the gap in his teeth.

Craig did not bother to reply. There was only room for one man at a time to work under the chassis. The earth crumbled and the Land-Rover subsided a few inches, and then the free tyre found purchase in the bottom of the hole. Craig turned his attention to the sharp edge of the hole, cutting it away in a ramp so that it would not block the wheel.

"Sally-Anne, you get behind the steering-wheel." He spoke jerkily between each blow with the panga. "Timon and I will try to lift the front." He crawled out from under the body and wasted a second to look back. The dust of the pursuit was clearly visible from ground level. "Come on, Timon."

They stood shoulder to shoulder in front of the radiator and bent their knees to get a good grip on the front fender. Sally-Anne sat behind the dust-smeared windscreen. The lump on her forehead looked like a huge, blue, blood-sucking tick clinging to her skin. She stared at Craig through the glass, her eyes and her expression desperate.

"Hit it!" Craig grunted and they straightened together, lifting with their knees and all the strength of their bodies. Craig felt the front end come up a few inches on the suspension and he nodded at Sally-Anne. She let out the clutch and the engine blustered, the wheel spun, and she jerked back and then stuck fast, blocking on the edge of the hole.

"Rest!" Craig grunted, and they slumped gasping over the hood. Craig saw the dust of the pursuit was so close that he expected the trucks to appear beneath it as he watched.

"Okay, we'll bounce her," he told Timon. "Hit it! One! Two! Three!"

While Sally-Anne raced the engine, they flung their weight on the fender in a short regular rhythm. "One! Two! Three!" Craig gasped, and the vehicle started surging and bounding wildly against the rim of the hole.

"Keep her going!"

Dust boiled around them, and the voice on the radio yelped exultantly like a lead hound taking the scent. They had seen the dust.

"Keep it up!"

Craig found strength and reserves that he had never known were there. His teeth ground together, his breath whined in his throat, his face swelled dark angry red, and his vision starred and filled with shooting light. Still he heaved, and knew that the sinew and muscle in his back was tearing, his spine felt as though it was crushing—and suddenly the Land-Rover's wheels bounced over the rim and it shot backwards, clear and free.

Deprived of support, Craig fell on his knees and thought he did not have the strength to rise again.

"Craig! Hurry!" Sally-Anne yelled at him. "Get in!"

With another vast effort, he heaved himself upright and staggered to the moving Land-Rover. He dragged himself up onto the hood. Sally-Anne accelerated. For long seconds Craig clung to the hood, as strength oozed back into his limbs. He crawled up onto the roof-rack and peered over the back of the cab.

There was only one truck behind them, a five-ton Toyota painted the familiar sand colour. Through the shimmer of heat mirage, it appeared monstrous, seeming to float towards him, disembodied from the earth. *Craig blinked the sweat out* of his eyes. How close was it? Hard to tell over level ground and through the mirage.

His vision cleared, and he saw that the ungainly black super-structure above the Toyota's cab was a heavy-machine-gun on a ring mount with the gunner's head behind it. It looked at this distance to be the modified Goryunov Stankovy, a nasty weapon.

"Sweet Jesus!" he whispered, as for the first time he became aware of the Land-Rover's altered motion. She was vibrating and shaking brutally, and there was the shrill protest of metal bearing on metal from the left end where she had hit—and the speed was down, way down.

Craig leaned out and yelled into the driver's window.

"Speed up!"

Sally-Anne stuck her head out of the window. "She's busted up front. Any faster and she'll tear herself to pieces."

Craig looked back. The truck was closing, not rapidly, but inexorably. He saw the gunner on the cab roof traverse his weapon slightly.

"Go for it, Sally-Anne!" he shouted. "Take a chance of its holding. They've got a heavy-machine-gun and they're coming into range."

The Land-Rover lumbered forward, and now there was a heavy clattering combined with the whine of metal. The vibration clattered Craig's teeth and he looked back. They were holding the truck off—and then he saw the pursuing vehicle judder to the recoil of the heavy weapon on the cab.

No sound of gunfire yet. Craig watched with an academic interest. Abruptly dust fountained close down their left flank, jumping six feet into the heated air in a diaphanous curtain, appearing ethereal and harmless, but the sound of passing shot spranged viciously like a copper telegraph wire hit with an iron bar.

"Turn left!" Craig yelled. Always turn towards the fall of shot. The gunner will be correcting the opposite way, and the dust will help obscure his aim.

The next burst fell right and very wide.

"Turn right!" Craig shouted.

Sally-Anne stuck her head out again. "Shoot back at them!" She was obviously recovering from the head knock, and getting fighting mad.

"I'm giving the orders," he told her. "You keep driving."

The next burst was wide again, a hundred feet out.

219

"Turn left!"

Their weaving was confusing the gunner's aim, and their dust obscuring the range, but it was costing them ground. The truck was gaining on them again.

The salt-pan was close ahead, hundreds of bare acres shimmering silver in the path of the sun. Craig narrowed his eyes against the glare and picked up the tracks where a small herd of zebra had crossed the smooth surface. Their hooves had broken through the salt crust into the yellow mush beneath. It would bog any vehicle that attempted that deceptively inviting crossing.

"Angle to miss the right edge of the pan—left! More! More! Okay, hold that," he shouted.

There was a narrow horn of salt-pan extending out toward them. Perhaps he could tempt the pursuit to take the cut across it. He stared back over their own dust cloud and said, "Shit!" softly.

The truck commander was too canny to try to cut across the horn. He was following them around, and a burst of machine-gun fire fell all around them. Three rounds crashed into the metal of the cab, leaving jagged craters rimmed with shiny metal where the camouflage paint flaked off.

"Are you okay?"

"Okay!" Sally-Anne called back, but the tone of her voice was no longer so cocky. "Craig, I can't keep her going. I've got my foot flat and she is slowing down. Something is binding up!"

Now Craig could smell red-hot metal from the damaged front end.

"Timon, hand me up a rifle!"

They were still well out of range of the AK 47, but the burst he fired made him feel less helpless, even though he could not even mark the fall of his bullets. They roared around the horn of the salt-pan, in the stink of hot metal and dust, and Craig looked ahead while he reloaded the rifle.

How far to the border now? Ten miles perhaps? But would a punitive patrol of the Third Brigade, given the "leopard" code, stop at an international border? The Israelis and South Africans had long ago set a precedent for "hot pursuit" into neutral territory. He knew they would follow them to the death.

The Land-Rover lurched rhythmically now to her unbalanced suspension and for the first time Craig knew that they weren't going to make it. The realization made him angry. He fired the second magazine in short-spaced bursts, and at the third burst the

Toyota swerved sharply and stopped in a billow of its own dust.

"I got him!" he bellowed exultantly.

"Way to go!" Sally-Anne shouted back. "Geronimo!"

"Well done, Mr. Mellow, jolly well done."

The truck stood massively immobile while the wreaths of dust subsided around it.

"Eat that!" Craig howled. "Stick that up your rear end, you sons of porcupines!" And he emptied the rifle at the distant vehicle.

Men were swarming around the cab of the truck like black ants around the carcass of a beetle, and the Land-Rover limped away from them gamely.

"Oh, no," Craig groaned.

The silhouette of the truck altered as it turned back toward them, once again dust rose in a feathery tail behind it.

"They are coming on!"

Perhaps he had fluked a hit on the driver, but whatever damage he had inflicted, it was not permanent. It had stopped them for less than two minutes and now, if anything, the truck was coming on faster than before. As if to emphasize that fact, another burst of heavy-machine-gun fire hit the Land-Rover with a crash.

In the cab, somebody screamed, and the sound was shrill and feminine. Craig went cold, not daring to ask, clinging to the roof-rack, frozen with dread.

"Timon's been hit." Sally-Anne's voice—and Craig's heart raced with relief.

"How bad?"

"Bad. He's bleeding all over."

"We can't stop. Keep going."

Craig looked desperately ahead, and there was a great nothingness stretched before him. Even the stunted trees had disappeared. It was flat and featureless, the reflection from the white pans turned the sky milky pale and smudged the horizon so that there was no clear dividing line between earth and air, nothing to hold the eye.

Craig dropped his gaze, and shouted, "Stop!"

To enforce the order he stamped on the roof of the cab with all his strength. Sally-Anne reacted instantly and locked the brakes. The crippled Land-Rover skidded broadside, and came up short.

The cause of Craig's urgency was an apparently innocuous little yellow ball of fur, not as big as a football. It hopped in front of the vehicle, on long kangaroo back legs, totally out of proportion to the rest of its body, and then abruptly disappeared into the earth.

"Spring hare!" Craig called. "A huge colony, right across our front."

"Kangaroo rats!" Sally-Anne leaned out of the window, the engine idling, turning her face up to his for guidance.

They had been fortunate. The spring hare was almost entirely nocturnal, the single animal outside the burrows was an exceptional warning in daylight. Only now, under close scrutiny, could Craig make out the extent of the colony. There were tens of thousands of burrows, the entrances inconspicuous little mounds of loose earth, but Craig knew that the sandy soil beneath them would be honeycombed with the interlinking burrows, the entire area undermined to a depth of four feet or so.

That ground would not bear the weight of a mounted man, let alone the Land-Rover. With the engine idling, Craig could clearly hear the roar of the truck behind them, and machine-gun fire whiplashed over them, so close that Craig ducked instinctively.

"Turn left!" he shouted. "Back towards the pan."

They turned at right angles across the front of the approaching truck, machine-gun fire goading them on, Timon's groans reaching Craig above the engine beat. He closed his ears to them.

"There is no way through!" Sally-Anne called. The spring-hare burrows were everywhere.

"Keep going," Craig answered her. The truck had swung to cut them off, closing very swiftly now.

"There!" Craig cried with relief. As he had guessed, the spring-hare colony stopped short of the salt-pan's edge, avoiding the brackish seepage from the pan. There was a narrow bridge through, and Craig guided Sally-Anne into it. Within five hundred paces they were over the bridge with the ground firm ahead. Sally-Anne pushed the Land-Rover to its limit, directly away from the pursuit.

"No! No!" Craig called. "Turn right, hard right." She hesitated. "Do it, damn you!" And suddenly she saw what he intended, and she spun the steering-wheel, running back in the opposite direction across the front of the approaching truck.

Immediately the truck turned to head them off again, turning away from the pan, and from the bridge of firm ground through the subterranean maze of burrows. It was so close that they could see the heads of the troopers in the open back, catch the colour of a burgundy-red beret and the spark of the silver cap-badge,

222

hear the fierce, bloodthirsty yells, see an AK 47 rifle brandished triumphantly.

Machine-gun fire ploughed up the earth ten feet ahead of the Land-Rover and they tore into the standing dust.

Craig was blazing away with the AK 47, trying to keep the driver's attention off the ground ahead of the truck.

"Please! Please, let it happen," he pleaded as he changed the magazine on the hot rifle. And the gods were listening. The truck went into the undermined ground at full bore.

It was like an elephant running into a pitfall. The earth opened and swallowed her down, and as she went in she toppled to one side hurling the load of armed men out of the back. When the dust rolled aside, she was half-buried, lying on her side. Human bodies were strewn around her, some of them beginning to drag themselves upright, others lying where they had been thrown.

"That's it!" Craig shouted down. "They'll need a bulldozer to get out of that."

"Craig!" she called back. "Timon is in a bad way. Can't you help him?"

"Stop for a second."

Craig dropped off the roof and scrambled into the back seat, and immediately Sally-Anne drove on.

Timon was lying sprawled half off the seat, his head thrown back and pillowed against the door. He had lost his glasses. His breathing gargled in his throat, and the back of his battle-jacket was a soggy mess of blood. Craig eased him cautiously back into the seat and unzipped his jacket.

He was appalled. The bullet must have come in through the metal cab and been deformed by the impact into a primitive dum-dum. It had torn a hole the size of a demi-tasse coffee cup in Timon's back. There was no exit wound. The bullet was still in there.

There was a first-aid box clamped to the dashboard. Craig took out two field dressings, stripped the wrappers and wadded them over the wound. Hampered by the Land-Rover's erratic and violent motion, he strapped them tightly.

"How is he?" Sally-Anne took her eyes off the ground ahead for a moment.

"He's going to be okay," Craig said for Timon's benefit, but to Sally-Anne he shook his head and mouthed a silent denial.

Timon was a dead man. It was merely a matter of an hour or two. Nobody could survive a wound like that. The smell of hot metal in the cab was suffocating.

"I can't breathe," Timon whispered, and sawed for breath.

Craig had hoped he was unconscious, but Timon's eyes were focusing on his face. Craig knocked out the Perspex pane of the window above Timon's head with his fist, to give him more air.

"My glasses," Timon said. "I can't see."

Craig found the steel-rimmed spectacles on the floor between the seats and placed them on the bridge of his nose, hooking the side frames over his ears.

"Thank you, Mr. Mellow." Incredibly, Timon smiled. "It doesn't look as though I'll be coming with you, after all."

Craig was surprised by the strength of his own regret. He gripped Timon's shoulder firmly, hoping that physical contact might comfort him a little.

"The truck?" Timon asked.

"We knocked it out."

"Good for you, sir."

As he spoke, the cab filled with the smell of burning rubber and oil.

"We're on fire!" Sally-Anne cried, and Craig whipped around in the seat.

The front end of the Land-Rover was burning. Red-hot metal from the damaged bearing had ignited the grease and rubber of the front tyre. Almost immediately the bearing seized up completely, and although the engine roared vainly, they ground to a halt. The slipping clutch burned out, more smoke spewing out from under the chassis.

"Switch off!" Craig ordered and banged open the door, grabbing the fire-extinguisher from its rack on the doorpost.

He sprayed a white cloud of powder over the burning front end, snuffing out the flames almost instantly, and then unhitched and lifted the hood, scalding his fingers on hot metal. He sprayed the engine compartment to prevent a resurgence of the fire, and then stood back.

"Well," he said with finality. "This bus isn't going anywhere any more!"

The silence after the engine roar and the gunfire was overpowering. The pinking of cooling metal from the body of the Land-Rover sounded loud as cymbals. Craig walked to the rear

224

of the cab and looked back. The bogged truck was out of sight behind them in the heat haze. The silence buzzed in his ears and the loneliness of the desert bore down upon him with a physical weight and substance, seeming to slow his movements and his thinking.

His mouth felt chalky dry from the adrenalin hangover.

"Water!" He went quickly to the reserve tank under the seat, unscrewed the cap and checked the level.

"At least twenty-five litres."

There was an aluminum canteen hanging beside the AK 47 in the rack left by one of the grave-diggers. Craig topped it up from the tank and then took it to Timon.

Timon drank gratefully, gulping and choking in his haste to swallow. Then he lay back panting. Craig passed the canteen to Sally-Anne and then drank himself. Timon seemed a little easier. Craig checked the dressings. The bleeding was staunched for the moment.

"The first rule of desert survival," Craig reminded himself: "Stay with the vehicle."

But it didn't apply here. The vehicle would draw the pursuit like a beacon. Timon had mentioned spotter aircraft. On this open plain they would see the Land-Rover from thirty miles. Then there was the second patrol coming down from the Plumtree border-post. They would be here in a few hours.

They couldn't stay. They had to go on. He looked down at Timon, and understanding flashed between them.

"You'll have to leave me," Timon whispered.

Craig could not hold his eyes, or reply. Instead he climbed onto the roof again and looked back.

Their tracks showed very clear on the soft earth, filled with shadow by the lowering angle of the sun. He followed them with the eye towards the hazy horizon, and then started with alarm.

Something moved on the very edge of his vision. For long seconds he hoped it was a trick of light. Then it swelled up again, like a wriggling caterpillar, floated free of earth on a lake of mirage, changed shape once more, anchored itself to earth again and became a line of armed men, running in Indian file, coming in on their tracks. The men of the Third Brigade had not abandoned the chase. They were coming on foot, trotting steadily across the plain. Craig had worked with crack black troops before. He knew that they could keep up that pace for a day and a night.

225

He jumped down and found Timon's binoculars in the cubby beside the driver's seat.

"There is a foot patrol following us," he told them.

"How many?" Timon asked.

On the roof he focused the binoculars. "Eight of them—they took casualties when the truck overturned."

He looked back at the sun. It was reddening and losing its heat, sinking into the ground haze. Two hours to sunset, he guessed.

"If you move me into a good place, I'll give you delaying fire," Timon told him. And as Craig hesitated, "Don't waste time arguing, Mr. Mellow."

"Sally-Anne, refill the canteen," Craig ordered. "Take the chocolate and high-protein slabs from the emergency rations. Take the map and the compass and these binoculars."

He was surveying the fields of fire around the stranded vehicle. No advantage to be wrung from that flat terrain. The only strong point was the Land-Rover itself. He knocked the drain plug out of the bottom of the gasoline tank and let the remaining fuel run into the sandy soil, to prevent a lucky shot torching the vehicle and Timon with it. Swiftly he built a rudimentary screen around the back wheels, placing the spare wheels and the steel tool-box to cover Timon's flanks when they started to enfilade him.

He helped Timon out of the back seat and laid him belly down behind the rear wheels. The bleeding started again, soaking the dressing, and Timon was grey as ash and sweating in bright little bubbles across his upper lip. Craig placed one of the AK 47s in his hands and arranged a seat cushion as an aiming rest in front of him. The box of spare magazines he set at Timon's right hand, five hundred rounds.

"I'll last until dark," Timon promised in a croak. "But leave me one grenade."

They all knew what that was for. Timon did not want to be taken alive. At the very end he would hold the grenade to his own chest and blow it away.

Craig took the remaining five grenades and packed them into one of the rucksacks. He placed the British Airways bag that contained his papers and the book manuscript on top of them. From the tool-box he took a roll of light gauze wire and a pair of side cutters; from the ammunition box, six spare magazines for the AK 47. He divided the contents of the first-aid box, leaving two field dressings, a blister pack of pain-killers and a disposable syringe of morphine for Timon. The rest he tipped into his rucksack.

He glanced quickly around the interior of the Land-Rover. Was there anything else he might need? A rolled plastic groundsheet in camouflage design lay on the floorboards. He stuffed that into the bag, and hefted it. That was all he could afford to carry. He looked across at Sally-Anne. She had the canteen slung on one shoulder, and the second rucksack on the other. She had rolled the portfolio of photographs and crammed them into the rucksack. She was very pale and the lump on her forehead seemed to have swelled even larger.

"Right?" Craig asked.

"Okay."

He squatted beside Timon. "Goodbye, Captain," he said.

"Goodbye, Mr. Mellow."

Craig took his hand and looked into his eyes. He saw no fear there, and he wondered again at the equanimity with which the African can accept death. He had seen it often.

"Thank you, Timon—for everything," he said.

"*Hamba gashle,*" said Timon gently. "Go in peace."

"*Shala gashle,*" Craig returned the traditional response. "Stay in peace."

He stood up and Sally-Anne knelt in his place.

"You are a good man, Timon," she said, "and a brave one."

Timon unfastened the flap of his holster and drew the pistol. It was a Chinese copy of the Tokarev type 51. He reversed it, and handed it to her, butt first. He said nothing, and after a moment she took it from him.

"Thank you, Timon."

They all knew that, like the grenade, it was for the very end— the easier way out. Sally-Anne pushed the weapon into the belt of her jeans and then impulsively stooped and kissed Timon.

"Thank you," she said again, and stood up quickly and turned away.

Craig led her away at a trot. He looked back every few yards, keeping the vehicle directly between them and the approaching patrol. If they suspected that two of them had left the vehicle, they would simply leave half their men to attack it, and circle back onto the spoor again with the rest of the force.

Thirty-five minutes later they heard the first burst of automatic fire. Craig stopped to listen. The Land-Rover was just a little black pimple in the distance, with the dusk darkening and drooping down over it. The first burst was answered by a storm of gunfire, many weapons firing together furiously.

"He's a good soldier," Craig said. "He would have made sure of that first shot. There aren't eight of them any more. I'd bet on that."

With surprise he saw that the tears were running down her cheeks, turning to muddy brown in the dust that coated her skin.

"It's not the dying," Craig told her quietly, "but the manner of it."

She flared at him angrily. "Keep that literary Hemingway crap to yourself, buster! It's not you that's doing the dying." And then, contrite immediately, "I'm sorry, darling, my head hurts and I liked him so much."

The sound of gunfire became fainter as they trotted on, until it was just a whisper like footsteps in dry bush far behind them.

"Craig!" Sally-Anne called, and he turned. She had fallen back twenty paces behind him and her distress was apparent. As soon as he stopped, she sank down and put her head between her knees.

"I'll be all right in a moment. It's just my head."

Craig split open a blister pack of pain-killers from the first aid box. He made her take two of them and swallow them with a mouthful of water from the canteen. The lump on her forehead frightened him. He put his arm around her and held her tightly.

"Oh, that feels good." She slumped against him.

On the silence of the desert dusk came the distant woof of an explosion, muted by distance, and Sally-Anne stiffened.

"What's that?"

"Hand grenade," he told her, and checked his wrist-watch. "It's over, but he gave us a start of fifty-five minutes. Bless you, Timon, and God speed you."

"We mustn't waste it," she told him determinedly and pulled herself to her feet. She looked back. "Poor Timon," she said, and then set off again.

It would take them only minutes to discover that there was but one man defending the Land-Rover. They would find the outgoing tracks almost immediately, and they would follow. Craig wondered how many Timon had taken out and how many there were left.

"We'll find out soon enough," he told himself, and the night came down with the swiftness of a theatre fire-curtain.

New moon three days past, and the only light was from the

228

stars. Orion stood tall on one hand, and the great cross blazed on the other. Through the dry desert air their brilliance was marvelous, and the Milky Way smeared the heavens like the phosphorescence from a firefly crushed between a child's fingers. The sky was magnificent, but when Craig looked back he saw that it gave enough light to pick out their footprints.

"Rest!" he told Sally-Anne, and he stretched out full-length on the ground. With the bayonet from the AK 47 he chopped a bunch of scrub, wired it together and fastened the wire to the back of his belt.

"Lead!" he told her, saving energy with economy of words. She went ahead of him, no longer at a trot, and he dragged the bunch of dry scrub behind him. It swept the earth, and when he checked again, their footprints had dissolved.

Within the first mile the weight of the scrub dragging like an anchor from his belt was beginning to take its toll of his strength. He leaned forward against it. Three times in the next hour Sally-Anne asked for water. He grudged it to her. Never drink on the first thirst, one of the first survival laws. If you do, it will become insatiable, but she was sick and hurting from the head injury, and he did not have the heart to deny her. He did not drink himself. Tomorrow, if they lived through it, would be a burning hell of thirst. He took the canteen from her, to removed temptation.

A little before midnight, he untied the wire from his belt. The dragging weight of the scrub thorn-brush was too much for him, and if the Shona were still on their spoor, it would not serve much further purpose. Instead, he lifted the rucksack from Sally-Anne's back and slung it over his own shoulder.

"I can manage it," she protested, although she was reeling like a drunkard. She had not complained once, although her face in the starlight was silver as the salt-pan they were crossing.

He tried to think of something to comfort her.

"We must have crossed the border hours ago," he said.

"Does that mean we are safe?" she whispered, and he could not bring himself to lie. She shivered.

The night wind cut through their thin clothing. He unfolded the nylon groundsheet and spread it over her shoulders, then he took her weight on his arm and led her on.

A mile farther on they reached the far edge of the salt-pan, and he knew she could go no farther that night. There was a crusty bank eighteen inches high, and then firm ground again.

"We'll stop here." She sagged to the ground and he covered her with the groundsheet.

"Can I have a drink?"

"No. Not until morning."

The water canteen was light, sloshing more than half-empty as he lowered the pack.

He cut a pile of scrub to break the wind and keep it off her head, and then pulled off her jogging shoes, massaging her feet and examining them by touch.

"Oh, that stings." Her left heel was rubbed raw. He lifted it to his mouth and licked the abrasion clean, saving water. Then he dripped Mercurochrome on it and strapped it with a Band-Aid from the first-aid kit. He changed her socks from foot to foot and then laced up her shoes.

"You're so gentle," she murmured, as he slipped under the groundsheet and took her in his arms, "and so warm."

"I love you," he said. "Go to sleep."

She sighed and snuggled, and he thought she was asleep until she said softly, "Craig, I'm so sorry about King's Lynn."

Then, at last, she did sleep, her breathing swelling deeply and evenly against his chest. He eased out from under the groundsheet and left her undisturbed. He went to sit on the low bank with the AK 47 across his knees, keeping the open pan under surveillance, waiting for them to come.

While he kept the watch, he thought about what Sally-Anne had said. He thought about King's Lynn. He thought of his herds of great red beasts, and the homestead on the hill. He thought about the men and the women who had lived there and bred their families there. He thought about the dreams he had fashioned from their lives and how he had planned to do with this woman what they had done.

My woman. He went back to where she lay and knelt over her to listen to her breathing, and he thought about her spread naked and open on the long table under the cruel scrutiny of many eyes.

He went back to wait at the edge of the pan and he thought about Tungata Zebiwe, and remembered the laughter and comradeship they had shared. He saw again the hand-signal from the dock as they led Tungata away.

"We are equal—the score is levelled," and he shook his head.

He thought about once being a millionaire, and the millions he

230

now owed. From a man of substance he had been reduced in a single stroke to something worse than a pauper. He did not even own the bundle of paper in the British Airways bag. The manuscript would be forfeit, his creditors would take that also. He had nothing, nothing except this woman and his rage.

Then the image of General Peter Fungabera's face filled his imagination—smooth as hot chocolate, handsome as mortal sin, as powerful and evil as Lucifer—and his rage grew within him, until it threatened to consume him.

He sat through the long night without sleep, hating with all the strength of his being. Every hour he went back to where Sally-Anne slept and squatted beside her. Once he adjusted the ground-sheet over her, another time he touched the lump on her forehead lightly with his fingertips and she whimpered in her sleep, then he went back to his vigil.

Once he saw shapes out on the pan, and his stomach turned over queasily, but when he put Timon's binoculars on them, he saw they were gemsbok, huge desert gazelle, large as horses, the diamond-patterned face masks that give them their name showing clearly in the starlight. They passed silently upwind of where he sat and merged into the night.

Orion hunted down the sky and faded at dawn's first glimmering. It was time to go on, but he lingered, reluctant to put Sally-Anne to the terrors and the trials that day would bring, giving her just those last few minutes of oblivion.

Then he saw them, and his guts and his loins filled with the molten lead of despair. They were still far out across the pan, a darkness too large to be one of the desert animals, a darkness that moved steadily towards him. The scrub brush that he had dragged must have been effective to delay them so long. But once he had abandoned it, they would have come on swiftly down the deeply trodden spoor.

Then his despair changed shape. If it had to come, it might as well be now, he thought. This was as good a place as any to make their last stand. The Shona must come across the open pan, and he had the light advantage and that afforded by the bank and the sparse cover of knee-high scrub, but little time in which to exploit them.

He ran back to where he had left his rucksack, keeping doubled over so as to show no silhouette against the lightening sky. He stuffed the five grenades down the front of his shirt, snatched up the roll of wire and the side cutters, and hurried back to the edge of the bank.

He peered out at the advancing patrol. They were in single file because the pan was so open, but he guessed they would spread out into skirmishing line as soon as they reached the bank, adopting the classic arrowhead running formation that would give them overlapping cover and prevent their being enfiladed by ambush.

Craig began to place his fragmentation grenades on that assumption. He sited them along the top of the bank; that slight elevation would spread the blast out a little more.

He wired each grenade securely to the stem of a bush, twenty paces apart, and then used a haywire twist to secure a single strand to each of the split pins that held down the firing-handles. Then he led the strands back one at a time to where Sally-Anne slept and secured them to the flap of his rucksack.

He was down on his knees now, for the light was coming up strongly and the patrol was closer each minute. He readied the fifth and last grenade, and this time wriggled back on his belly. The strands of wire were spread out fanlike from where he lay behind the screen of cut brush. He checked the load of the AK 47 and placed the spare magazines at his right hand.

It was time to wake her. He kissed her softly on the lips, and she wrinkled her nose and made little mewing sounds, then she opened her eyes and love dawned green in them for an instant, to be replaced by dismay as she remembered their circumstances. She started to sit up, but he held her down with an arm over her chest.

"They are here," he warned her. "I'm going to fight."

She nodded.

"Have you got Timon's pistol?"

She nodded again, groping for it in the waistband of her jeans.

"You do know how to use it?"

"Yes."

"Keep one bullet for the end."

She stared at him.

"Promise you won't hesitate."

"I promise," she whispered.

He lifted his head slowly. The patrol was four hundred yards out from the edge of the pan, and they were already spreading into the arrowhead hunting formation.

As they separated from a single amorphous blot in the poor light, he was able to count them. Five! His spirits dropped again sharply. Timon had not done as well as he had hoped for. He had culled out only three of the original pursuit. Five was too many for Craig. Even with all the advantages of surprise and concealment, it was just too many.

"Keep your face down," he whispered. "It can shine like a mirror." Obediently she dropped it into the crook of her arm. He pulled up his shirt to cover his own mouth and nose, and watched them come on.

Oh God, they are good, he thought. Look at them move! They have been going all night, and they are still as sharp and wary as lynx. The point was a tall Shona who moved like a reed in the wind. He carried his AK 47 low on the right hip, and he was charged with a deadly intensity of concentration. Once the light of coming dawn caught his eyes and they flashed like distant cannon-fire in the blackness of his face. Craig recognised him as the main man.

His drags, two on each side of him, were sombre, stocky figures, full of menace and yet subservient to the man who led. They reacted like puppets to the hand-signals that the tall Shona gave them. They came on silently towards the edge of the pan, and Craig arranged the wires across the palm of his left hand and ran them out between his fingers.

Fifty paces from the bank the Shona stopped them with a cut-out signal, and the line froze. The Shona's head turned slowly from side to side as he surveyed the low bank and the scrub beyond it. He took five paces forward, stepping lightly, and stopped again. His head turned once more, back and forth—and then back again. He had seen something. Craig instinctively held his breath as the seconds drew out.

Then the Shona moved again. He swivelled and picked out his flanks, marking them with a stab of his forefinger, and then a pumped fist. Their formation changed into a reversed arrowhead— the Shona had adopted the traditional fighting formation of the Nguni tribes, the "bull's horns" that King Chaka had used to such terrible effect, and now the horns were moving to invest Craig's position.

Craig felt a surge of relief at his own foresight in spreading the grenades so widely. The two flank men would walk almost on top of his outside grenades. He sorted the wires in his hand, taking

233

up the slack, and watching the flank men come on. He wished it had been the tall Shona, the danger man, but he had not moved again. He was still way back out of blast range, watching and directing the flanking movement.

The man on the right reached the bank and gingerly stepped up onto it, but the man on the left was still ten paces out on the pan.

"Together," Craig whispered. "I've got to take them together."

The man on the bank must have almost brushed the hidden grenade with his knee as Craig let him overrun it. The man on the left reached the bank; there was a bloody bandage around his head, Timon's work. The grenade would be at about the level of his navel. Craig heaved with all his weight on the two outside wires, and heard the firing handles fly off the grenades with a metallic Twang! Twang!

Three seconds' delay on the primers, and the Shona were reacting with trained reflexes. The man on the bank dropped from sight, but Craig judged he was too close to the grenade to survive. The three others out on the pan went down also, firing as they dropped, rolling sideways as they hit the crust, firing again, raking the top of the bank.

Only the trooper out on the left, the wounded man, perhaps slowed by his injury, stayed on his feet those fatal seconds. The grenade exploded with the brilliance of a flashbulb, and the man was hit by fragmenting shrapnel. He was lifted off his feet as the blast tore into his belly. On the right the other grenade burst in brief thunder, and Craig heard the taut, drumlike sound of shrapnel slapping into flesh.

Two of the bastards, he thought, and tried for the tall Shona, but his aim was through scrub and over the lip of the bank, and the Shona was rolling. Craig's first burst kicked white salt inches short, but on line; his second burst was a touch left, and the Shona fired back and kept rolling.

One of the other troopers jumped up and charged the bank, jinking like a quarter-back with the ball, and Craig swung onto him. He hit him cleanly with a full burst, starting at the level of his crotch and pulling up across his belly and chest. The AK 47 was notorious for the way she rode up in automatic and Craig had compensated for it. The trooper dropped his rifle and spun around sharply, fell onto his knees and then toppled forward on his face like a Muslim at prayer.

The tall Shona was up, coming in, shouting an order, the second man followed him, twenty paces behind. Craig switched his aim back to him exultantly. He couldn't miss now. The AK 47 kicked once, and then snapped on an empty chamber. The Shona kept on coming, untouched.

Craig was not as quick on the reload as he had once been; just that microsecond too late he swung back onto the Shona, and as he squeezed the trigger, the man dropped out of sight, below the rim of the bank, and Craig's burst flew high and harmless.

Craig swore, and swung left onto the last trooper who was just five paces from the safety of the bank. It was snap shooting, but a single lucky bullet out of the long burst hit him in the mouth and snapped his head back like a heavy punch. The burgundy-red beret, glowing like a pretty bird in the dawn light, flew high in the air, and the trooper collapsed.

Four out of five in the first ten seconds—it was more than Craig could possibly have hoped for—but the fifth man, the danger man, was alive down there below the bank, and he must have marked Craig's muzzle flashes. He had Craig pinpointed.

"Keep under the sheet," Craig ordered Sally-Anne, and pulled the wires on the other three grenades. The explosions were almost simultaneous, a thunderous roll like the broadside of a man-of-war, and in the dust and flame Craig moved.

He went forward and right, thirty running paces, doubled over, with the reloaded AK in his hand, and he dived forward and rolled and then waited, belly down, covering the spot below the bank where the Shona had disappeared, but darting quick glances left and right.

The light was better, the dawn coming up fast, and the Shona moved. He came up over the bank, a brief silhouette against the white pan, quick as a mamba, but where Craig had not expected him. He must have elbow-walked under the bank, and he was way out on Craig's left.

Craig swung the AK onto him but held his fire, that quick chance not good enough to betray his new position, and the Shona disappeared into the low brush fifty paces away. Craig crawled forward to intercept, slowly as an earthworm, making no noise, raising no dust, and listening and staring with all his being. Long seconds drew out, slow as treacle, and Craig inched forward, knowing that the Shona must be working towards where he had left Sally-Anne.

Then Sally-Anne screamed. The sound raked his nerve ends like an emery wheel, and out of the brush they rose together, Sally-Anne fighting and clawing like a cat and the Shona holding her by the hair, down on his knees, but holding her easily, turning with her to frustrate any chance of a shot.

Craig charged. It was not a conscious decision. He found himself on his feet, hurling forward, swinging the AK 47 like a club. The Shona saw him, released Sally-Anne, and she staggered backwards and fell. The Shona ducked under the swinging rifle and hit Craig in the ribs with his shoulder as he came off his knees. The rifle flew from Craig's hands. He grappled, holding desperately as he fought to regain the breath that had been driven out of him. The Shona, realizing that his rifle was useless in hand-to-hand contact, let it fall, and used both arms.

Craig knew in that first moment of contact that the Shona was simply too strong for him. He had height and weight and he was trained to the hardness of anthracite. He whipped a long arm around the back of Craig's neck, but Craig, instead of resisting, put all his own weight into the direction of the Shona's pull. It took him by surprise, and they cart-wheeled. As he went over, Craig kicked out with the metal leg—but he didn't connect cleanly.

The Shona twisted and struck back at him. Craig smothered it and they locked, chest to chest, rolling first one on top, then the other, flattening the coarse scrub, their breath hissing into each other's face. The Shona snapped like a wolf at Craig's face with his square white teeth. If he got a grip, he would bite off Craig's nose or rip his cheek away. Craig had seen it done before in beer-hall brawls.

Instead of pulling his head back, Craig butted forward with his forehead, and hit him in the mouth. One of the Shona's incisors snapped off at the gum and his mouth glutted with blood. Craig reared back to butt him again, but the Shona shifted over him and suddenly had the trench-knife out of his scabbard on his belt. Craig grabbed his wrist desperately, only just smothering the stab.

They rolled and the Shona came out on top, straddling Craig, the knife in his right hand probing with the bright silver point for Craig's throat and face. Craig got both hands to it, one on the Shona's wrist, the other into the crook of his elbow, but he couldn't hold him. The knife point descended slowly towards him, and the Shona kicked his legs and locked one between Craig's, pinning him like a lover.

236

Down came the knife, and behind it, the Shona's face, swollen with effort, his broken tooth pink with blood, blood running from his chin and dripping into Craig's upturned face, his eyes mottled with tiny brown veins, bulging from their sockets—and the knife came down.

Craig put all his remaining, failing strength against him. The knife point checked for a second, then moved down to touch Craig's skin in the notch where his collar-bones met. It stung like a hypodermic needle as it pierced the skin. With a sense of horror, Craig felt the Shona's body gathering for the final thrust that would force the silver steel through his larynx—and knew that he could not prevent it.

Miraculously, the Shona's head changed shape, distorting like a rubber Halloween mask, collapsing upon itself, the contents of the skull bursting in a liquid fountain from his temple—and the sound of a shot dinned in on Craig's eardrums. The strength went out of the Shona's body and he rolled off and flopped on the ground like a fresh-caught catfish.

Craig sat up. Sally-Anne was only feet away, kneeling facing him, the Tokarev pistol held double-handed, the barrel still pointing skywards where the recoil had thrown it. She must have placed the muzzle against the Shona's temple before she fired.

"I killed him," she breathed gustily and her eyes were filled with horror.

"Thank God for it!" Craig gasped, using the collar of his shirt to dry the nick on his throat.

"I . . . never . . . killed anything before," Sally-Anne whispered. "Not even a rabbit or a fish—nothing."

She dropped the pistol and started to dry-wash her hands, scrubbing one with the other, staring at the Shona's corpse. Craig crawled to her and took her in his arms. She was shaking wildly.

"Take me away," she pleaded. "Please, Craig. I can smell the blood, take me away from here."

"Yes. Yes." He helped her to her feet, and in a frenzy of haste rolled the groundsheet and buckled the straps of the rucksacks.

"This way." Burdened by both packs and the rifle, Craig led her away from the killing ground towards the west.

They had been going for almost three hours and had stopped for the first sparing drink before Craig realized his terrible oversight. *The water bottles*! In his panicky haste, he had forgotten to take the water-bottles from the dead Shona.

He looked back longingly. Even if he left Sally-Anne here and went back alone, it would cost him four hours, and the Third Brigade patrols would surely be coming up. He weighed the water-bottle in his hand. A quarter full. Barely enough to see out this day, even if they laid up now and waited for nightfall and the cool. Not nearly enough if they kept going—and they had to keep going.

The decision was made for him. The sound of a single-engined aircraft throbbing down from the north. Bitterly he stared up into the sky, feeling the helplessness of the rabbit below the towering falcon.

"Spotter plane," he said, and listened to the beat of the engine. It receded for a while and then grew stronger again.

"They are flying a grid search."

As he spoke, he saw it. It was closer than he had thought, and much lower. He forced Sally-Anne down with a hand on her shoulder and spread the cape over her, glancing back as he did so. It was coming on swiftly, a low-winged, single-engined mon-oplane. It altered course slightly, heading directly, towards him. He dropped down beside Sally-Anne and crawled under the groundsheet beside her.

The engine roared louder. The pilot had spotted them. Craig lifted a corner of the groundsheet and looked out.

"Piper Lance," said Sally-Anne softly.

It carried Zimbabwe air-force roundels, and incongruously the pilot was a white man, but there was a black man in the right-hand seat, and he wore the dreaded burgundy-red beret and silver cap-badge. They both stared down expressionlessly as the Piper made a steep turn, with one wing-tip pointed like a knife directly at where Craig lay. The black officer was holding the radio micro-phone to his lips. The wings of the Piper levelled and she came out of her turn, heading back the way she had come. The throb of the engine receded and was lost in the desert silence.

Craig pulled Sally-Anne to her feet.

"Can you go on?"

She nodded, pushing back the sweat-damp wisp of hair from her forehead. Her lips were flaking, and the lower one had cracked through. A drop of blood sat on it like a tiny ruby.

"We must be well inside Botswana. The border road can't be far ahead. If we can find a Botswana police patrol—"

The road was single width, two continuous ruts running north and south, swerving now and then to avoid a spring-hare colony or a soft pan. It was patrolled regularly by the Botswana police on anti-poaching and illegal entry duties.

Craig and Sally-Anne reached the road in the middle of the afternoon. By this time Craig had discarded the rifle and ammunition, and stripped the pack of all but essentials. He had even considered for a while burying his manuscript for later retrieval. It weighed eight pounds, but Sally-Anne had dissuaded him in a hoarse whisper.

The water-bottle was empty. They had had their last drink, a blood-warm mouthful each, just before noon. Their speed was reduced to little more than a mile an hour. Craig was no longer sweating. He could feel his tongue beginning to swell and his throat closing as the heat sucked the moisture out of him.

They reached the road. Craig's gaze was fastened grimly on the heat-smudged horizon ahead, all his being concentrated on lifting one foot and placing it ahead of the other. They crossed the road without seeing it and kept going on into the dessert. They were not the first to walk past the chance of succour and go on to death by thirst and exposure. They staggered onwards for two hours more before Craig stopped.

"We should have reached the road by now," he whispered, and checked the compass heading again. "The compass must be wrong! North isn't there." He was confused and doubting. "Damaged the bloody thing. We are too far south," he decided, and began the first aimless circle of the lost and totally disorientated, the graveyard spiral that precedes death in the desert.

An hour before sunset Craig stumbled over a dried brown vine growing in the grey soil. It bore only a single green fruit the size of an orange. He knelt and plucked it as reverently as if it had been the Cullinan diamond. Mumbling to himself through cracked and bleeding lips, he split the fruit carefully with the bayonet. It was as warm as living flesh from the sun.

"Gemsbok melon," he explained to Sally-Anne as she sat and watched him with dull, uncomprehending eyes.

He used the point of the bayonet to mash the white flesh of the melon, and then held the half-shell to Sally-Anne's mouth.

Her throat pumped in the effort of swallowing the clear warm juice, and she closed her eyes in ecstasy as it spread over her swollen tongue.

Working with extreme care, Craig wrung a quarter of a cupful of liquid from the fruit and fed it to her. His own throat ached and contracted at the smell of the liquid as he made her drink. She seemed to recharge with strength before his eyes, and when the last drop had passed between her lips, she suddenly realized what he had done.

"You?" she whispered.

He took the hard rind and squeezed-out pith, and sucked on them.

"Sorry." She was distraught at her own thoughtlessness, but he shook his head.

"Cool soon. Night."

He helped her up, and they stumbled onwards.

Time telescoped in Craig's mind. He looked at the sunset and thought it was the dawn.

"Wrong." He took the compass and hurled it from him. It did not fly very far. "Wrong—wrong way." He turned, and led Sally-Anne back.

Craig's head filled with shadows and shapes. Some faceless and terrifying and he shouted soundlessly at them to drive them away. Some he recognized. Ashe Levy rode past on the back of a huge shaggy hyena. He was brandishing Craig's new manuscript, and his gold-rimmed spectacles glinted blindly in the sunset.

"Can't make a paperback sale," he gloated. "Nobody wants it, baby, you're finished. One-book man, Craig baby—that's you."

Then Craig realized that it was not his manuscript, but the winelist from the Four Seasons.

"Shall we try the Corton-Charlemagne?" Ashe taunted Craig. "Or a magnum of the Widow?"

"Only witch-doctors ride hyena," Craig yelled back, no sound issuing from his desiccated throat. "Always knew you were—"

Ashe hooted with malicious laughter, spurred the hyena into a gallop, and threw the manuscript in the air. The white pages fluttered to the earth like roosting egrets, and when Craig went down on his knees to gather them, they turned to handfuls of dust and Craig found he could not rise. Sally-Anne was down beside him and, as they clung to each other, the night came down upon them.

When he woke it was morning. He could not rouse Sally-Anne. Her breathing snored and sawed through her nose and open mouth.

On his knees he dug the hole for a solar still. Though the soil was soft and friable, it went slowly. Laboriously, still on his knees, he gathered an armful of the scattered desert vegetation. There seemed to be no moisture in the woody growth when he chipped it finely with the bayonet and laid it in the bottom of his hole.

He cut the top off the empty aluminium water-bottle and placed the cup this formed in the centre of the hole. It required enormous concentration to perform even these simple tasks. He spread the plastic groundsheet over the hole and anchored the edges with heaped earth. In the centre of the sheet he gently laid a single round of ammunition, so that it was directly above the aluminium cup.

Then he crawled back to Sally-Anne and sat over her so that his shadow kept the sun off her face.

"It's going to be all right," he told her. "We'll find the road soon. We must be close—"

He did not realize that no sound came from his throat, and that she would not have been able to hear him even it had.

"That little turd Ashe is a liar. I'll finish the book, you'll see. I'll pay off what I owe. We'll get a movie deal—I'll buy King's Lynn. It will be all right. Don't worry, my darling."

He waited out the baking heat of the morning, containing his impatience, and at noon by his wrist-watch he opened the still. The sun beating down on the plastic sheet had raised the temperature in the covered hole close to the boiling point. Evaporation from the chopped plants had condensed on the under-side of the plastic sheet and run down it towards the sag of the bullet. From there it had dropped into the aluminium cup.

He had collected half a pint. He took it up between both hands, shaking so violently that he almost spilled it. He took a small sip and held it in his mouth. It was hot, but it tasted like honey and he had to use all his self-control to prevent his swallowing.

He leaned forward and placed his mouth over Sally-Anne's blackened and bleeding lips. Gently he injected the liquid between them.

"Drink, my sweet, drink it up." He found he was giggling stupidly as he watched her swallow painfully.

He passed the precious fluid, a few drops at a time, from his own mouth into hers and she swallowed each sip more easily. He

241

kept the last mouthful for himself and let it trickle down his throat. It went to his head like strong drink and he sat grinning stupidly through fat, scaly black lips, his face swollen and sun-baked purple red, the abrasions on his cheek covered with a crusty weeping scab, and his bloodshot eyes gummed with dried mucus.

He rebuilt the still and lay down beside Sally-Anne. He covered her face from the sun with the tail torn from his shirt and whispered, "All right—find help—soon. Don't worry—my love—"

But he knew that this was their last day. He could not keep her alive for another. Tomorrow they would die. It would be either the sun or the men of the Third Brigade—but tomorrow they would die.

● ● ●

At sunset the still gave them another half cup of distilled water, and after they had drunk it, they fell into a heavy, deathlike sleep in each other's arms.

Something woke Craig. For a moment he thought it was the night wind in the scrub. With difficulty he pushed himself into a sitting position and cocked his head to listen, not sure whether he was still hallucinating or whether he was truly hearing that soft rise and fall of sound. It must be nearly dawn, he realized. The horizon was a crisp line beneath the velvet drape of the sky.

Then abruptly the sound firmed, and he recognized it. The distinctive beat of a four-cylinder Land-Rover engine. The Third Brigade had not abandoned the hunt. They were coming on relentlessly, like hyenas with the reek of blood in their nostrils.

He saw a pair of headlights, far out across the desert, their pale beams swinging and tilting as the vehicle covered the rough ground. He groped for the AK 47. He could not find it. Ashe Levy must have stolen it, he thought bitterly, taken it off with him on the hyena. "I never did trust the son-of-a-bitch."

Craig stared helplessly at the approaching headlights. In their beams danced a little pixie-like figure, a diminutive yellow manikin. "Puck," he thought. "Fairies. I never believed in fairies. Don't say that—when you do, one dies. Don't want to kill fairies. I believe in them." His mind was going, fantasy mixed with flashes of lucidity.

Suddenly he recognized that the little half-naked yellow manikin was a Bushman, one of the pygmy desert race. A Bushman tracker. The Third Brigade was using a Bushman tracker to hunt them down. Only a Bushman could have run on their spoor all night, tracking by the headlights of the Land-Rover.

The headlights flashed over them, like a stage spotlight, and Craig lifted his hand to shade his eyes. The light was so bright that it hurt. He had the bayonet in his other hand behind his back.

I'll get one of them, he told himself. *I'll take one of them*.

The Land-Rover stopped only a few paces away. The little Bushman tracker was standing near them, clicking and clucking in his strange birdlike language. Craig heard the door of the Land-Rover open behind the blinding lights, and a man came towards them. Craig recognized him instantly. *General Peter Fungabera*— he seemed as tall as a giant in the back lighting of the headlights as he strode towards where Craig huddled on the desert floor.

Thank you, God, Craig prayed, *thank you for sending him to me before I died*, and he gripped the bayonet. *In the throat*, he told himself, *as he stoops over me*. He marshalled all his remaining strength, and General Peter Fungabera stooped toward him. *Now!* Craig made the effort. *Drive the point into his throat!* But nothing happened. His limbs would not respond. He was finished. There was nothing left.

"I have to inform you that you are under arrest for illegal entry into the republic of Botswana, sir," said General Fungabera—but he had changed his voice. He was using a deep, gentle, caring voice, in heavily accented English.

He won't fool me, Craig thought, *the tricky bastard*, and he saw that Peter Fungabera was wearing the uniform of a sergeant of the Botswana police.

He went down on one knee. "You are lucky. We found where you were crossing the road." He was holding a felt-covered water-bottle to Craig's mouth. "We have been following you since three o'clock yesterday."

Cool, sweet water gushed into Craig's mouth and ran down his chin. He let the bayonet drop and grabbed for the bottle with both hands. He wanted to gulp it all down at once, he wanted to drown in it. It was so marvellous that his eyes flooded with tears.

Through the tears he saw the Botswana police crest on the open door of the Land-Rover.

"Who?" he stared at Fungabera, but he had never seen his face before. It was a broad, flat-nosed face, puckered now with worry and concern, like that of a friendly bulldog.

"Who?" he croaked.

"Please not to talk, we must get you and the lady to hospital at Francistown pretty bloody quickly. Plenty people die in desert— you goddamned lucky."

"You aren't General Fungabera?" he whispered. "Who are you?"

"Botswana police, border patrol. Sergeant Simon Mafekeng at your honour's service, sir."

●   ●   ●

As a boy, before the great patriotic war, Colonel Nikolai Bukharin had accompanied his father on the wolf hunts, hunting the packs that terrorized their remote village in the high Urals during the long harsh winter months.

Those expeditions into the vast gloomy Taiga forests had nurtured in him a deep passion for the hunt. He enjoyed the solitude of wild places and the primeval joy of pitting all his senses against a dangerous animal. Eyesight, hearing, smell, and the other extraordinary sense of the born hunter that enabled him to anticipate the twists and evasions of his quarry—all those the colonel still possessed in full strength, despite his sixty-two years. Together with a memory for facts and faces that was almost computerlike, they had enabled him to excel at his work, had seen him elevated to the head of his department of the Seventh commissariat where he had hunted professionally the most dangerous game of all— man.

When he hunted boar and bear on the great estates reserved for the recreations of high officers of the G.R.U. and K.G.B., he had alarmed his comrades and the gamekeepers by scorning to fire from the prepared hides and by going on foot alone into the thickest cover. The thrill of great physical danger had satisfied some deep need in him.

When the assignment on which he was now engaged had been channelled through to his office on the second floor of the central headquarters on Dzerzhinsky Square, he had recognized its importance immediately and taken control of it personally. With careful cultivation, that first potential was gradually being realized, and when the time had come for Colonel Bukharin at last to meet his subject face to face on the ground over which they would manoeuvre, he had chosen the cover which best suited his tastes.

Russians, especially Russians of high rank, were objects of hostile suspicion in the new republic of Zimbabwe. During the *chimurenga*, the war of independence, Russia had chosen the

244

wrong horse and given her support to Joshua Nkomo's ZIPRA—the Matabele revolutionary wing. As far as the government in Harare was concerned, the Russians were the new colonialist enemy, while it was China and North Korea who were the true friends of the revolution.

For these reasons, Colonel Nikolai Bukharin had entered Zimbabwe on a Finnish passport, bearing a false name. He spoke Finnish fluently, as he did five other languages, including English. He needed a cover under which he could freely leave the city of Harare, where his every move would be watched over, and go out into the unpopulated wilderness where he could meet his subject without fear of surveillance.

Although many of the other African republics under pressure from the World Bank and the International Monetary Fund had banned big-game hunting, Zimbabwe still licensed professional hunters to operate their elaborate safaris in the designated "controlled hunting areas." These were large earners of foreign exchange for the embattled economy.

It amused the colonel to pose as a prosperous timber merchant from Helsinki, and to indulge his own love of the hunt in this decadent manner reserved almost exclusively for the financial aristocrats of the capitalist system.

Of course, the budget that had been allocated for this operation could not stand such extravagance. However General Peter Fungabera, the subject of the operation, was a wealthy and ambitious man. He had made no difficulties when Colonel Bukharin had suggested that they use a big-game hunting safari as a cover for their meeting, and that General Fungabera should be allowed the honour of acting as host and of paying the thousand dollars *per diem* that the safari cost.

Standing in the centre of the small clearing now, Colonel Bukharin looked at his man. The Russian had deliberately wounded the bull. Nikolai Bukharin was a fine shot with pistol, rifle and shotgun, and the range had been thirty yards. If he had chosen, he could have placed a bullet in either of the bull's eyes, in the very centre of the bright black pupil. Instead, he had shot the animal through the belly, a hand's width behind the lungs so as not to impair its wind, but not far enough back to damage the hindquarters and so slow it down in the charge.

It was a marvellous bull, with a mountainous boss of black horn that would stretch fifty inches or more around the curve from point to point. A fifty-inch bull was a trophy few could match, and as he had drawn first blood it would belong to the colonel no matter who delivered the *coup de grâce*. He was smiling at Peter Fungabera as he poured vodka into the silver cup of his hip-flask.

"Na Zdorovye!" he saluted Peter, and tossed it down without blinking, refilled the silver cup and offered it to him.

Peter was dressed in starched and crisply ironed fatigues with his name tag on the breast, and a khaki silk scarf at his throat, but he was bareheaded with no insignia to sparkle in the sunlight and alarm the game.

He accepted the silver cup and looked over the rim at the Russian. The man was as tall as Peter, but even slimmer, erect as a man thirty years younger. His eyes were a peculiarly pale, cruel blue. His face was riven with the scars of war and of other ancient conflicts, so that it was a miniature lunar landscape. His skull was shaven, the fine stubble of hair that covered it was silver and shone in the sun like glass fibres.

Peter Fungabera enjoyed this man. He enjoyed the aura of power that he wore like an emperor's cloak. He enjoyed the innate cruelty in him that was almost African, and which Peter understood perfectly. He enjoyed his deviousness, the layering of lies and truths and half-truths, so that they became indistinguishable. He was excited by the sense of danger that exuded from him so powerfully that it had almost an odour of its own. "We are the same breed," Peter thought, as he lifted the silver cup and returned the salute. He drank down the pungent spirit at one swallow. Then, breathing carefully so as not to show the smallest sign of distress, he handed back the cup.

"You drink like a man," Nikolai Bukharin admitted. "Let us see if you hunt like one."

Peter had guessed correctly. It had been a test: the vodka and the buffalo bull, both of them. He shrugged to show his indifference, and the Russian beckoned to the professional hunter who stood respectfully out of earshot.

The hunter was a Zimbabwe-born white man, in his late thirties, dressed for the part in wide-brimmed hat and khaki gilet with heavy-calibre cartridges in the loops across his breast. He had a thick curly beard and an extremely unhappy expression on his face, as befits a man who is about to follow a gut-shot buffalo bull into dense riverine bush.

"General Fungabera will take the .458," Colonel Bukharin said, and the hunter nodded miserably. How had this strange old bastard managed to make a muck-up of a sitting shot like that? He had been shooting like a Bisley champion up to now. Christ, but that bush looked really nasty. The hunter suppressed a shiver and snapped his fingers for the number two gunbearer to bring up the other heavy rifle.

"You will wait here with the bearers," said the Russian quietly.

"Sir!" the hunter protested quickly. "I can let you go in alone. I'd lose my licence. It's just not on—"

"Enough," said Colonel Bukharin.

"But, sir, you don't understand—"

"I said, enough!" The Russian never raised his voice, but those pale eyes silenced the younger man completely. The hunter found suddenly that he was more afraid of this man than of losing his licence, or of the wounded bull in the bush ahead. He subsided and stepped back thankfully.

The Russian took the .458 from the gunbearer, shot the bolt back to check that it was loaded with soft-tipped bullets, and then handed it to Peter Fungabera. Peter took it from him, smiling slightly, hefted it, then handed it back to the gunbearer. General Bukharin raised one silver eyebrow and smiled also. The smile was mockery shaded with contempt.

Peter spoke sharply in Shona to the bearer, *"Eh he, mambo!"*

The man ran and snatched another weapon from one of the other black bearers. He brought it back to Peter, clapping softly to show his respect.

Peter weighed his new weapon in his hands. It was a short-shafted stabbing assegai. The handle was of hardwood bound with copper wire. The blade was almost two feet long and four inches broad. Carefully Peter shaved the hairs off the back of his thumb with the edge of the silver blade, then, deliberately, he shrugged off his jacket and stripped his trousers and jungle boots.

Dressed only in a pair of olive-green shorts and carrying the stabbing assegai, he said, "This is the African way, Colonel." The Russian was no longer smiling. "But I do not expect a man of your years to hunt the same way." Peter excused him courteously. "You may use your rifle again."

The Russian nodded, conceding the exchange. He had lost that one, but now let's see if this black *mujik* can make good his boast. Bukharin looked down at the spoor. The great hoof prints were the size of soup plates, and the thin watery gouts of blood were tinged with greenish-yellow dung from the ruptured bowels.

"I will track," he said. "You will watch for the break."

They moved off easily, with the Russian five paces ahead, stooped attentively to the blood spoor, and Peter Fungabera drifting behind him, the assegai held underhand, and his eyes covering the bush ahead, with a steady rhythmic sweep, trained eyes not expecting to see the whole animal, searching for the little things, perhaps the shine of a wet muzzle or the drooping curve of a great horn.

Within twenty paces the bush closed in around them. It was sultry green as a hothouse, dank vegetation pressing breathlessly around them. The air stank of the rotting leaf mould that deadened their footfalls. The silence was oppressive, so that the drag of a thorny branch across the Russian's leather leggings sounded loud as a truck engine. He was sweating; perspiration soaked his shirt in a patch between the shoulderblades and sparkled like dew-drops on the back of his neck. Peter could hear his breathing, deep and harsh, but knew instinctively that it was not fear that worked in the Russian, but the pervading excitement of the hunter.

Peter Fungabera did not share it. There was a coldness in him where his own fear should have been. He had trained himself to that during the *chimurenga*. This was a necessary task, this thing with the assegai. It was to impress the Russian only, and with all fear and feeling anaesthetized by the coldness. Peter Fungabera prepared himself. He felt his muscles charging, felt the tension build in his sinews and nerves until he was like an arrow, notched against the curve of the longbow.

With his eyes he swept the bush directly in the run of the spoor only lightly and concentrated his main attention on the flanks. This beast that they were hunting was the most cunning of all the dangerous game of Africa, except perhaps the leopard. But it was possessed of the brute strength of a hundred leopards. The lion will growl before he charges, the elephant will turn under the punishment of heavy bullets in the chest, but the Cape buffalo comes in silence, and only one thing will stop his charge—and that is death.

A big, metallic-blue fly settled on Peter Fungabera's lip and crawled into his nostril. So complete was his concentration that he did not feel it, or brush it away. He watched the flanks, he concentrated the very essence of his being on the flanks.

The Russian checked, examining the change in the spoor, the plant of solid hooves, the puddle of loose bloody dung. This was where the bull had stood, after his first, wild run. Peter Fungabera could imagine him, standing massive and black, with his nose held high, looking back towards the hunters with the spreading agony in his guts and liquid faeces from his torn intestines beginning to ooze uncontrollably down his quarters. Here he had stood and listened and heard their voices, and the hatred and anger had begun to seethe in him. Here the killing rage had begun. He had dropped his head and gone on, humping his back against the agony in his bowels, sustained by the rage within him.

The Russian glanced back at Peter, and they did not have to speak. In unison they moved forward.

The bull was acting on an atavistic memory. Everything he did had been done countless times before by his ancestors. From that first wild gallop as he received the bullet, the stop to listen and peer back, the gathering of great muscles, and now the more sedate trot, angling to present his haunches to the fitful breeze so that the scent of the hunters would be borne down to him, huge armoured head swinging from side to side as he began the search for the ambush point, it was all part of a pattern.

The bull crossed a narrow clearing ten paces across, forced his head into the wall of glossy green leaves on the far side, leaving it smeared with fresh bright blood, and went on another fifty yards. Then he turned sharply aside and started back in a wide circle. Now he moved with deliberate stealth, insinuating his bulk gently through the intertwined creeper and branch a single pace at a time—until he came back to the clearing again.

Here he stopped, hidden on the far edge of the clearing, covering from the side his own bloody tracks across the narrow opening, his body screened entirely by dense growth, and a terrible stillness settled upon him. He let the stinging flies feast on his open wound without shuddering his skin or swinging his tail. He did not twitch either of his large, cup-shaped ears but strained them forward. Not even his eyes blinked as he peered back along the blood spoor and waited for the hunters to come.

The Russian stepped lightly into the clearing, his gaze darting ahead to where blood-painted branches hung on the far side and a large body had forced its way through into the forest beyond. He started forward quietly. Peter Fungabera followed him, watching the flanks, moving like a dancer, his body glowing with a light sheen of sweat, the flat, hard muscle in his chest and arms changing shape at his slightest movement.

He saw the bull's eye. It caught the light like a new coin, and Peter froze. He snapped the fingers of his left hand, and the Russian froze with him. Peter Fungabera stared at the bull buffalo's eye, not quite sure what he was seeing, but knowing that it was in the right place—thirty yards out on the left. If the bull had doubled, that was where he would be.

Peter blinked his eyes, and suddenly the image cleared. He was no longer focused only on the eye, and so he could see the curve of one horn held so still that it could have been a branch. He saw the crenellations of the boss meeting above the bull's eye, and now he looked into the eye itself—and it was like a glimpse into hell.

The bull charged. The forest burst open before his rush, branches crackled and broke, the leaves shook and fluttered as though struck by a hurricane and the bull came out into the clearing. He came out crabbing sideways, a deceptive but characteristic feint that had lulled many a hunter until the sudden direct lunge at the end.

He came fast. It seemed impossible that any beast so enormous could move so fast. He was broad and tall as a granite kopje, his back and shoulder crusted with dried mud from the wallow, and there were obscene silvery bald patches on his shoulders and neck, criss-crossed with the long-healed scars of thorn and lions' claws.

From his open jaws drooled silver ropes of saliva, and tears had tracked wet lines down his hairy cheeks. A man could barely have encompassed that neck with both arms, or matched the spread of those horns with arms extended. In the skin folds of his throat were huge bunches of blue ticks like ripe grapes, and the rank bovine smell of him was choking in the hothouse of the forest.

He came on, majestic in his killing rage, and Peter Fungabera went out to meet him. He passed in front of the Russian just as Colonel Bukharin swung up the stubby heavy-calibre rifle, screening the shot, forcing him to throw the barrel up towards the sky. Peter moved like a dark forest wraith, crossing the bull at the opposite angle to his crabbing charge, taking him off balance so that the bull hooked at him like a boxer punching as he moves away, not timing the swing of horns, not sighting true, and Peter swayed away from it with his upper body only, letting the curved point hiss past his ribs by the breadth of a hand and then swaying

250

back as the bull's head was flung high at the finish of the stroke.

In that instant the bull was open, from his reaching chin to the soft folds of skin between his forelegs, and Peter Fungabera put the full weight of his body and all the momentum of his run behind the silver blade.

The bull ran onto the point. It went into him with the sucking sound of a foot in mud, and the blade was swallowed by living flesh. It went in until the fingers of Peter's right hand on the shaft followed the blade into the wound, and spurting blood drenched him to the shoulder. Peter released his grip on the assegai, and pirouetted away, spinning clear while the bull bucked stiff-legged against the long steel in his chest cavity. He tried to follow Peter round but came up short and stood with his thick stubby forelegs braced, staring at the naked man with a glaze spreading over his eyes.

Peter Fungabera posed before him, with both arms lifted gracefully. "Ha, earth-shaker!" he called in Shona. "Ha, you sky thunder!"

The bull made two plunging strides forward and something burst inside him. Blood erupted in a double gush from his flaring nostrils. He opened his jaws and bellowed, and blood shot up his throat in a frothing bright cascade and drenched his chest. The great bull reeled, fighting to keep his balance.

"Die, spawn of the black gods!" Peter taunted. "Feel the steel of a future king—and die!"

The bull went down. The earth jumped beneath their feet as the weight of him struck.

Peter Fungabera stepped up to the huge bossed head in which the smouldering eyes were fading. He went down on one knee and, with his cupped hands, scooped up the rich hot blood as it streamed from the bull's gaping mouth, and he lifted his hands to his mouth and drank the blood like wine. It streamed down his arms and dribbled from his chin, and Peter laughed, a sound that made even the Russian's vinegary blood chill.

"I have drunk your living blood, oh great bull. Now your strength is mine!" he shouted, as the bull arched his final spasm of death.

•   •   •

Peter Fungabera had showered and changed into mess-jacket. His trousers were black with a burgundy watered-silk side stripe.

251

His short bumfreezer jacket was in the regimen's same distinctive burgundy-red with black silk lapels. His white shirt was starch-fronted and wing-collared, with a black bow-tie, and he wore a double row of miniature decorations.

The camp servants had set a table under the spread branches of a mhoba-hoba tree, on the edge of an open vlei of short lush green grass, out of sight and earshot of the main camp. On the table was a bottle of Chivas Regal whisky and another of vodka, a bucket of ice and two crystal glasses.

Colonel Nikolai Bukharin sat opposite Peter. His long loose cotton shirt hung outside his baggy Cossack pants and was belted at the waist. His feet were thrust into boots of soft glove-leather. He leaned forward and filled the glasses, then passed one to Peter.

This time there was no flamboyant tossing back of liquor. They drank slowly, watching the African sky turn mauve and smouldering gold. The silence was the companionable accord of two men who have risked their lives together and have each found the other worthy, a comrade to die with, or an adversary to fight to the death.

At last Colonel Bukharin placed his glass back on the table with a click.

"And so, my friend, tell me what you want," he invited.

"I want this land," said Peter Fungabera simply.

"All of it?" the colonel asked.

"All of it."

"Not just Zimbabwe?"

"Not just Zimbabwe."

"And we are to help you take it?"

"Yes."

"In exchange?"

"My friendship."

"Your friendship unto death?" the colonel suggested drily. "Or until you have what you want and find a new friend?"

Peter smiled. They spoke the same language, they understood each other.

"What tangible signs of this eternal friendship will you give us?" the Russian insisted.

"A poor little country like mine," Peter shrugged, "a few strategic minerals—nickel, chrome, titanium, beryllium—a few ounces of gold."

The Russian nodded sagely. "They will be useful to us."

"Then, once I am the Monomatapa of Zimbabwe, my eyes will become restless, naturally—"

"Naturally." The Russian watched his eyes. He did not like black men—this racist bigotry was a common Russian trait—he did not like their colour or their smell. But this one!

"My eyes might turn southwards," Peter Fungabera said softly. Ha! Colonel Bukharin hid his glee behind a doleful expression. This one is different!

"The direction in which your own eyes have been focused all along," Peter went on, and the Russian could have chortled.

"What will you see in the south, Comrade General?"

"I will see a people enslaved and ripe for emancipation."

"And what else?"

"I will see the gold of the Witwatersrand and the Free State fields, I will see the diamonds of Kimberley, the uranium, the platinum, the silver, the copper—in short, I will see one of the great treasure-houses of this earth."

"Yes?" the Russian probed with delight. This one is quick, this one has brains, and this one has the courage that it would take.

"I will see a base that divides the western world, a base that controls both the south Atlantic and the Indian oceans, that sits upon the oil lines between the Gulf and Europe, between the Gulf and the Americas.

The Russian held up a hand. "Where will these thoughts lead you?"

"It will be my duty to see this land to the south elevated to its true place in the community of nations, in the tutelage of and under the protection of that greatest of all lovers of freedom, the Union of Soviet Socialist Republics."

The Russian nodded, still watching his eyes. Yes, this black man had seen the design behind it all. The south was the grand prize, but to win it they needed to take it in the strangler's grasp. To the east they already had Mozambique, to the west Angola was theirs and Namibia would soon be also. They needed only the north to isolate the prize. The north was Zimbabwe, like the strangler's thumb on the windpipe, and this man could deliver it to them.

Colonel Bukharin sat forward in his canvas camp-chair and became businesslike and brisk.

"Opportunity?"

"Economic chaos, and intertribal warfare, the breakdown of

253

central government." Peter Fungabera counted them off on his fingers.

"The present government is meeting you more than halfway in creating its own economic breakdown," the Russian observed, "and you are already doing fine work in fanning tribal hatreds."

"Thank you, comrade."

"However, the peasants must begin to starve a little before they become manageable—"

"I am pushing in the cabinet for the nationalization of the white-owned farms and ranches. Without the white farmers I can promise you a goodly measure of starvation." Peter Fungabera smiled.

"I hear you have already made a start. I congratulate you on the recent acquisition of your own estates. King's Lynn? That is the name, is it not?"

"You are well-informed, Colonel."

"I take pains to ensure that I am. But when the moment comes to seize the reins of state, what kind of man will the people look to?"

"A strong man," Peter answered without hesitation. "One whose ruthlessness has been demonstrated."

"As yours was during the *chimurenga*, and more recently in Matabeleland."

"A man of charisma and presence, a man well known to the people."

"The women sing your praises in the streets of Harare. Not a single day passes without your image on the television screens or your name on the front page of the newspapers."

"A man with force behind him."

"The Third Brigade"—the Russian nodded—"and the blessing to the people of the U.S.S.R. However," he paused significantly, "two questions need answers, Comrade General."

"Yes?"

"The first is a mundane and distasteful question to raise between men such as you and I—money. My paymasters become restless. Our expenses have begun to exceed by a considerable amount the shipments of ivory and animal products that you have sent us—" He held up his hand again to forestall argument. It was an old man's hand, dappled with withered dark spots and criss-crossed with prominent blue veins. "I know that we should do these things merely for the love of freedom, that money is a capitalist obscenity, but nothing is perfect in this world. In short, Comrade General, you are reaching the limits that Moscow has set on your credit."

Peter Fungabera nodded. "I understand. What is your second question?"

"The Matabele tribe. They are a warlike and difficult people. I know that you have been forced to stir up enmity, to cause dissension and strife and to bring upon the present government the disapproval of the western powers by your campaign in Matabeleland. But what happens afterwards? How do you control them once you yourself have seized power?"

"I answer both questions with a single name," Peter Fungabera replied.

"The name?"

"Tungata Zebiwe."

"Ha! Yes! Tungata Zebiwe. The Matabele leader. You had him put away. I presumed that by now he had been liquidated."

"I am holding him in great secrecy and safety at one of my rehabilitation centres near here."

"Explain."

"First, the money."

"From what we know, Tungata Zebiwe is not a rich man," the Russian demurred.

"He has the key to a fortune which might easily exceed two hundred million U.S. dollars."

The Russian raised a silver eyebrow in the gesture of disbelief that Peter was coming to know well, and which was beginning to irritate him.

"Diamonds," he said.

"The mother country is one of the world's largest producers." The Russian spread his hands disparagingly.

"Not industrial rubbish, not black bort, but gem stones of the first water, large stones, huge stones, some of the finest ever mined anywhere."

The Russian looked thoughtful. "If it is true—"

"It is true! But I will not explain further. Not yet."

"Very well. At least I can hold out some sort of promise to the money-sucking leeches in our Treasury Department? And the second question. The Matabele? You cannot plan to obliterate them, man, woman and child?"

Peter Fungabera shook his head regretfully. "No. Though it would be the better way, America and Britain would not allow it. No, my answer is Tungata Zebiwe again. When I take over the country, he will reappear—it will be almost miraculous. He will come back from the dead. The Matabele tribe will go wild with joy and relief. They will follow him, they will dote upon him, and I will make him my vice-president."

"He hates you. You destroyed him. If you ever free him, he will seek to revenge that."

Peter shook his head. "No. I will send him to you. You have special clinics for difficult cases, do you not? Institutes where a mentally sick man can be treated with drugs—and other techniques to make him rational and reasonable once more?"

This time the Russian actually began to chortle, and he poured himself another vodka, shaking with silent laughter. When he looked up at Peter, there was respect in those pale eyes for the first time.

"I drink to you, Monomatapa of Zimbabwe. May you reign a thousand years!"

He set down his glass and turned to stare down the long open vlei to the distant water-hole. A herd of zebra had come to drink. They were nervous and skittish, for the lions lie in ambush at the water. At last they waded in, knee-deep and in a single rank, dipped their lips to touch the surface in unison. They formed an overlapping frieze of identical heads like an infinity of mirror images until the old stallion sentinel snorted in nervous alarm and the pattern exploded in foaming water and wildly galloping forms.

"The treatment of which you speak is drastic." Colonel Bukharin watched the zebra herd tear away into the forest. "Some patients do not survive it. Those who do are"—he searched for the word—"altered."

"Their minds are destroyed," Peter said it for him.

"In plain terms—yes," the colonel nodded.

"I need his body, not his brain. I need a puppet, not a human being."

"We can arrange that. When will you send him to us?"

"The diamonds first," Peter replied.

"Of course, the diamonds first. How long will that take?"

Peter shrugged. "Not long."

"When you are ready I will send a doctor to you, with the appropriate medications. We can bring this Tungata Zebiwe out on the same route as the ivory: Air Zimbabwe to Dar-es-Salaam and one of our freighters from there to Odessa."

"Agreed."

"You say that he is being held near here? I would like to see him."

"Is it wise?"

"Indulge me, please!" From Colonel Bukharin it was an order rather than a request.

•   •   •

Tungata Zebiwe stood in the flat white glare of the noonday sun. He stood facing a whitewashed wall that caught the sun's rays and flung them back like a huge mirror. He had stood there since before the rise of the sun, when the frost had crusted the sparse brown grass at the edge of the parade-ground.

Tungata was stark naked, as were the two men who flanked him. All three of them were so thin that every rib showed clearly, and the crests of their spines stood out like the beads of a rosary down the centre of their backs. Tungata had his eyes closed to slits to keep out the glare of sunlight off the wall, but he concentrated on a mark in the plaster to counter the effects of giddy vertigo which had already toppled the men on each side of him more than once. Only heavy lashing by the guards had forced them to their feet again. They were still swaying and reeling as they stood.

"Courage, my brothers," Tungata whispered in Sindebele. "Do not let the Shona dogs see you beaten."

He was determined not to collapse, and he stared at the dimple in the wall. It was the mark of a bullet strike, painted over with lime-wash. They lime-washed the wall after every execution— they were meticulous about it.

"Amanzi," husked the man on his right, "water!"

"Do not think of it," Tungata ordered him. "Do not speak of it, or it will drive you mad."

The heat came off the wall in waves that struck with physical weight.

"I am blind," whispered the second man. "I cannot see." The white glare had seared his eyeballs like snow-blindness.

"There is nothing to see but the hideous faces of Shona apes," Tungata told him. "Be thankful for your blindness, friend."

Suddenly from behind them brusque orders were shouted in Shona and then came the tramp of feet from across the parade-ground.

"They are coming," whispered the blinded Matabele, and Tun-

257

gata Zebiwe felt a vast regret rising within him.

Yes, they were coming at last. This time for him.

During every day of the long weeks of his imprisonment, he had heard the tramp of the firing-squad crossing the parade-ground at noon. This time it was for him. He did not fear death, but he was saddened by it. He was sad that he had not been able to help his people in their terrible distress, he was saddened that he would never again see his woman, and that she would never bear him the son for whom he longed. He was sad that his life which had promised so much would end before it had delivered up :ts fruits, and he thought suddenly of a day long ago when he had stood at his grandfather's side and looked out over the maize fields that had been scythed by a brief and furious hailstorm.

"All that work for nothing. What a waste!" his grandfather had murmured, and Tungata repeated his words softly to himself as rude hands turned him and hustled him to the wooden stake set in the ground before the wall.

They tied his wrists to the stake and he opened his eyes fully. His relief from the glare of the wall was soured by the sight of the rank of armed men who faced him.

They brought the two other naked Matabele from the wall. The blind one fell to his knees, weak with exposure and terror, and his bowels voided involuntarily. The guards laughed and exclaimed with disgust.

"Stand up!" Tungata ordered him harshly. "Die on your feet like a true son of Mashobane!"

The man struggled back to his feet.

"Walk to the stake," Tungata ordered. "It is a little to your left."

The man went, groping blindly, and found the stake. They bound him to it.

There were eight men in the firing-squad and the commander was a captain in the Third Brigade. He went slowly down the rank of executioners, taking each rifle and checking the load. He made little jokes in Shona that Tungata could not follow, and his men laughed. Their laughter had an unrestrained quality, like men who had taken alcohol or drugs. They had done this work before, and enjoyed it. Tungata had known many men like them during the war. Violence and blood had become their addictions.

The captain came back to the head of the rank and from his breast-pocket took a sheet of typescript which was grubby and dog-eared from much handling. He read from it, stumbling over the words and mispronouncing them like a schoolboy, his English only barely intelligible.

"You have been condemned as enemies of the state and the people," he read. "You have been declared incorrigible. Your death warrant has been approved by the vice-president of the republic of Zimbabwe—"

Tungata Zebiwe lifted his chin and began to sing. His voice soared, deep and beautiful, drowning out the thin tones of the Shona captain:

> "The Moles are beneath the earth,
> 'Are they dead?' asked the daughters of Mashobane."

He sang the ancient fighting song of the Matabele, and at the end of the first verse he snarled at the two condemned men who flanked him.

"Sing! Let the Shona jackals hear the Matabele lion growl."
And they sang with him:

> "Like the black mamba from under a stone
> We milked death with a fang of silver steel—"

Facing them, the captain gave an order, and as one man the squad advanced a right foot and lifted their rifles. Tungata sang on, staring into their eyes, defying them, and the men beside him fed on his courage and their voices firmed. A second order and the rifles were levelled. The eyes of the executioners peered over their sights, and the three naked Matabele sang on in the sunlight.

Now, marvellously, there was the sound of other voices, distant voices, lifted in the war-song. They came from the prison huts beyond the parade-ground. Hundreds of imprisoned Matabele were singing with them, sharing the moment of their deaths, giving them strength and comfort.

The Shona captain lifted his right hand, and in the last instants of his life Tungata's sadness fell away to be replaced by a soaring pride. *These are men*, he thought; *with or without me they will resist the tyrant*.

The captain brought his hand down sharply, as he bellowed the command, "Fire!"

The volley was simultaneous. The line of executioners swayed to the sharp recoil of rifles—and the blast dinned in on Tungata's eardrums so that he flinched involuntarily.

He heard the vicious slap of bullets into living flesh and, from the corners of his vision, saw the men beside him jerk as though from the blows of invisible sledge-hammers and then fall forward against their bonds. The song was cut off abruptly on their lips. Yet the song still poured from Tungata's throat and he stood erect.

The riflemen lowered their weapons, laughing and nudging each other as though at some grand joke. From the prison huts the war-song had changed to the dismal ululation of mourning, and now at last Tungata's voice dried and he faltered into silence.

He turned his head and looked at the men beside him. They had shared the volley between them, and their torsos were riddled with shot. Already the flies were swarming to the wounds.

Now suddenly Tungata's knees began to buckle, and he felt his sphincter loosening. He fought his body, hating its weakness. Gradually he brought it under control.

The Shona captain came to stand in front of him and said in English, "Good joke, hey? Heavy, man, heavy!" and grinned delightedly. Then he turned and shouted, "Bring water, quickly!"

A trooper brought an enamel dish, brimming with clear water, and the captain took it from him. Tungata could smell the water. It is said that the little Bushmen can smell water at a distance of many miles, but he had not truly believed it until now. The water smelled sweet as a freshly sliced honeydew melon, and his throat convulsed in a spasmodic swallowing reflex. He could not take his eyes off the dish.

The captain lifted the dish with both hands to his own lips and took a mouthful, then he rinsed his mouth and gargled with it noisily. He spat the mouthful and grinned at Tungata, then held the dish up before his face. Slowly and deliberately he tipped the dish and the water spilled into the dust at Tungata's feet. It splashed his legs to the knees. Each drop felt cold as ice chips and every cell of Tungata's body craved for it with a strength that was almost madness. The captain inverted the dish and let the last drops fall.

"Heavy, man!" he repeated mindlessly, and turned to shout an order at his men. They doubled away across the parade-ground, leaving Tungata alone with the dead and the flies.

They came for him at sunset. When they cut his wrist bonds, he groaned involuntarily at the agonizing rush of fresh blood into his swollen hands and fell to his knees. His legs could not support him. They had to half-carry him to his hut.

The room was bare, except for an uncovered toilet bucket in the corner and two bowls in the centre of the baked-mud floor. One dish contained a pint of water, the other a handful of stiff white maize cake. The cake was heavily oversalted. On the morrow, he would pay for eating it in the heavy coin of thirst, but he had to have strength.

He drank half the water and set the rest aside for the morning, and then he stretched out on the bare floor. Residual heat beat down on him from the corrugated-iron roof, but by morning he knew he could be shivering with cold. He ached in every joint of his body, and his head pounded with the effects of the sun and the glare until he thought his skull would pop like a ripe cream-of-tartar pod on a baobab tree.

Outside in the darkness beyond the wire, the hyena packs disputed the feat that had been laid for them. Their cries and howls were a lunatic bedlam of greed, punctuated by the crunch of bone in great jaws.

Despite it all, Tungata slept, and woke to the tramp of feet and shouted orders in the dawn. Swiftly he gulped down the remains of the water to fortify himself and then squatted over the bucket. His body had so nearly played him false the day before. He would not let it happen today.

The door was flung open.

"Out, you Matabele dog! Out of your stinking kennel!"

They marched him back to the wall. There were three other naked Matabele facing it already. Irrelevantly he noticed that they had lime-washed the wall. He stood with his face two feet from the pristine white surface and steeled himself for the day ahead.

They shot the three other prisoners at noon. This time Tungata could not lead them in the singing. He tried, but his throat closed up on him. By the middle of the afternoon, his vision was breaking up into patches of darkness and stabbing white light. However, every time his legs collapsed and he fell forward against his bound wrists, the pain in his shoulder sockets as his arms twisted upwards revived him.

The thirst was unspeakable.

The patches of blackness in his head became deeper and lasted longer, the pain could no longer revive him completely. Out of one of the dark areas a voice spoke.

"My dear fellow," said the voice, "this is all terribly distasteful to me."

The voice of Peter Fungabera drove away the blackness and gave Tungata new strength. He struggled upright, lifted his head and forced his vision to clear. He looked at Fungabera's face and his hatred came to arm him. He cherished his hatred as a life-giving force.

Peter Fungabera was in fatigues and beret. He carried his swagger-stick in his right hand. At his side was a white man whom Tungata had never seen before. He was tall and slim and old. His head was freshly shaven, his skin ruined with cicatrices and his eyes were a strange shade of blue that Tungata found as repulsive and chilling as the stare of a cobra. He was watching Tungata with clinical interest, devoid of pity or other human sentiment.

"I regret that you are not seeing Comrade Minister Zebiwe at his best," Peter told the white man. "He has lost a great deal of weight, but not here——"

With the tip of the swagger-stick, Peter Fungabera lifted the heavy black bunch of Tungata's naked genitalia.

"Have you ever seen anything like that?" he asked, using the swagger-stick with the same dexterity as a chopstick. Bound to the stake, Tungata could not pull away. It was the ultimate degradation, this arrogant mauling and examination of his private parts.

"Enough for three ordinary men," Peter estimated with mock admiration, and Tungata glared at him wordlessly.

The Russian made an impatient gesture and Peter nodded.

"You are right. We are wasting time."

He glanced at his wrist-watch and then turned to the captain who was close by, waiting with his squad.

"Bring the prisoner up to the fort."

They had to carry Tungata.

•   •   •

Peter Fungabera's quarters in the blockhouse on the central rock kopje were spartanly furnished, but the dirt floor had been freshly swept and sprinkled with water. He and the Russian sat on one side of the trestle-table that served as a desk. There was a wooden bench on the opposite side, facing them.

The guards helped Tungata to the bench. He pushed their hands away and sat upright, staring silently at the two men opposite him. Peter said something to the captain in Shona, and they brought a cheap grey blanket and draped it over Tungata's shoulders. Another

262

order, and the captain carried in a tray on which stood a bottle of vodka and another of whisky, two glasses, an ice-bucket and a pitcher of water.

Tungata did not look at the water. It took all his self-control, but he kept his eyes on Peter Fungabera's face.

"Now, this is much more civilized," Peter said. "The Comrade Minister Zebiwe speaks no Shona, only the primitive Sindebele dialect, so we will use the language common to all of us—English."

He poured vodka and whisky and as the ice clinked into the glasses Tungata winced but kept his gaze fixed on Peter Fungabera.

"This is a briefing," Peter explained. "Our guest," he indicated the old white man, "is a student of African history. He has read, and remembered, everything ever written about this country. While you, my dear Tungata, are a sprig of the house of Kumalo, the old robber chiefs of the Matabele, who for a hundred years raided and terrorized the legitimate owners of this land, the Mashona people. Therefore both of you might already know something of what I am about to relate. If that is so, I beg your indulgence." He sipped his whisky, and neither of the other two moved or spoke.

"We must go back a hundred and fifty years," said Peter, "to when a young field commander of the Zulu king Chaka, a man who was the king's favourite, failed to render up to Chaka the spoils of war. This man's name was Mzilikazi, son of Mashobane of the Kumalo subtribe of Zulu, and he was to become the first Matabele. In passing, it is interesting to note that he set a precedent for the tribe which he was to found. Firstly, he was a master of rapine and plunder, a famous killer. Then he was a thief. He stole from his own sovereign. He failed to render to Chaka the king's share of the spoils. Then Mzilikazi was a coward, for when Chaka sent for him to face retribution, he fled." Peter smiled at Tungata. "Killer, thief and coward—that was Mzilikazi, father of the Matabele, and that description fits every member of the tribe from then until the present day. Killer! Thief! Coward!" He repeated the insults with relish, and Tungata watched his face with eyes that glowed.

"So this paragon of manly virtues, taking with him his regiment of renegade Zulu warriors, fled northwards. He fell upon the weaker tribes in his path and took their herds and their young

263

women. This was the *umfecane*, the great killing. It is said that one million defenceless souls perished under the Matabele assegais. Certainly Mzilikazi left behind him an empty land, a land of bleached skulls and burned-out villages.

"He blazed this path of destruction across the continent until he met, coming from the south-west, a foe more bloodthirsty, more avaricious even than he, the white men, the Boers. They shot down Mzilikazi's vaunted killers like rabid dogs. So Mzilikazi, the coward, ran again. Northwards again."

Peter gently agitated the ice cubes in his glass, a soft tinkling that made Tungata blink, but he did not look down at the glass.

"Bold Mzilikazi crossed the Limpopo River and found a pleasant land of sweet grass and clear waters. It was inhabited by a gentle, pastoral people, descendants of a race who had built great cities of stone, a comely people whom Mzilikazi contemptuously named the 'eaters of dirt' and referred to as his cattle. He treated them like cattle, killing them for sport or husbanding them to provide his indolent warriors with slaves. The young women of the Mashona, if they were nubile, were mounted for pleasure and used as breeding-stock to provide more warriors for his murderous impis—but then you know all this."

The old white man nodded. "The broad facts, yes, but not your interpretation of them. Which proves that history is merely propaganda written by the victors."

Peter laughed. "I hadn't heard it put that way before. However, it's true. Now we, the Shona, are the ultimate victors, so it is our right to redraft history."

"Go on," the white man invited. "I find this instructive."

"Very well. In the year 1868, as white men measure time, Mzilikazi, this great fat debauched and diseased killer, died. It is amusing to recall that his followers kept his corpse fifty-six days in the heat of Matabeleland before committing it to burial, so he stank in death as powerfully as he did in life. Another endearing Matabele trait." He waited for Tungata to protest and, when he did not, went on.

"One of his sons succeeded him, Lobengula, 'the one who drives like the wind', as fat and devious and bloodthirsty as his illustrious father. However, at almost the same time as he took the chieftainship of the Matabele, two seeds were sown that would soon grow into great creeping vines that would choke and finally bring the fat bull of Kumalo crashing to earth." He paused for

264

effect, like a practised story-teller, and then held up one finger. "First, far to the south of his plundered domains, the white men had found on a desolate kopje in the veld a little shiny pebble, and second, from a dismal island far to the north a sickly young white man embarked on a ship, seeking clean dry air for his weak lungs.

"The kopje was soon dug away by the white ants and became a hole a mile across and four hundred feet deep. The white men called it Kimberley, after the foreign secretary in England who condoned its theft from the local tribes.

"The sickly white man was named Cecil John Rhodes, and he proved to be even more devious and cunning and unprincipled than any Matabele king. He simply ate up the other white men who had discovered the kopje of shiny stones. He bullied and bribed and cheated and wheedled until he owned it all. He became the richest man in the world.

"However, the winning of these shiny pebbles called for enormous amounts of physical labour by tens of thousands of men. Whenever there is hard work to be done, where does the white man in Africa look?" Peter chuckled and left his rhetorical question unanswered.

"Cecil Rhodes offered simple food, a cheap gun and a few coins for three years of a black man's life. The black men, unsophisticated and naïve, accepted those wages, and made their master a multimillionaire many times over.

"Among the black men who came to Kimberley were the young *amadoda* of the Matabele. They had been sent by Lobengula—have I mentioned that Lobengula was a thief? His instruction to his young men was to steal the shiny pebbles and bring them back to him. Tens of thousands of Matabele made the long journey southwards to the diamond diggings and they brought back diamonds.

"The diamonds they picked were the largest and the brightest, the ones that showed up most clearly in the washing and processing. How many diamonds? One Matabele whom the white police caught had swallowed 348 carats of diamonds worth £3,000 in the coin of those days—say £300,000 in today's terms. Another had slit open his thigh and pouched in his own flesh a single diamond that weighed 200 carats." Peter shrugged. "Who can say what its present value might have been? Perhaps £2,000,000."

The old white man who had been aloof, even disinterested,

during the first part of this recital, was now leaning forward intently, his head twisted to watch Peter Fungabera's lips.

"Those were the few that the white police caught, but there were thousands upon thousands of Matabele diamond-smugglers who were never caught. Remember, in the early days of the diggings, there was virtually no control over the black labourers. They came and went as the fancy moved them. So some stayed a week before drifting away, others worked a full three-year contract before leaving, but when they went, the shiny pebbles went with them—in their hair, in the heels of their new boots, in their mouths, in their bellies, stuffed up their anuses or in the vaginas of their women—the diamonds went out in thousands upon thousands of carats.

"Of course, it could not last. Rhodes introduced the compound system. The labourers were locked up in barbed-wire compounds for the full three years of their contract. Before they left they were stripped naked and placed in special quarantine huts for ten days, during which time their heads and pudenda were shaved, and their bodies minutely examined by the white doctors. Their rear ends were thoroughly probed and any recently healed scars sounded and, if necessary, reopened with a surgeons's scalpel.

"They were given massive doses of castor oil, and finely meshed screens were placed under the latrines so that their droppings could be washed and processed as though they were the blue earth of the diggings. However, the Matabele were crafty thieves, and they still founds ways to get the stones out of the compounds. The river of diamonds had been reduced to a trickle, but the trickle went northwards still to Lobengula.

"Again you ask how many? We can only guess. There was a Matabele named Bazo, the Axe, who left Kimberley with a belt of diamonds around his waist. You have heard of Bazo, son of Gandang, my dear Tungata. He was your great-grandfather. He became a notorious Matabele induna and slew hundreds of defenceless Mashona during his depredations. The belt of diamonds that he laid before Lobengula, so legend tells us, weighed the equivalent of ten ostrich eggs. As a single ostrich egg has the same capacity as two dozen domestic hens' eggs, and even allowing for legend's exaggerations, we come to a figure in excess of five million pounds sterling in today's inflated currency.

"Another source tells us that Lobengula had five pots full of first-water diamonds. That is five gallons of diamonds, enough to

266

rock the monopoly of De Beers' central diamond-selling organization.

"Yet another verbal history talks of the ritual *khombisile* that Lobengula held for his indunas, his tribal counsellors. *Khombisile* is the Sindebele word for a showing, or putting on display," Peter explained to the white man. "In the privacy of his great hut, the King would strip naked and his wives would anoint his bloated body with thick beef grease. Then they would stick diamonds onto the grease, until his entire body was covered in a mosaic of precious stones, a living sculpture covered with a hundred million pounds' worth of diamonds.

"So that is the answer to your question, gentlemen. Lobengula probably had more diamonds than have ever been assembled in one place at one time, other than in the vaults of De Beers' central selling organization in London.

"While this was happening, Rhodes, the richest man in the world, sitting in Kimberley and obsessed with the concept of empire, looked northwards and dreamed. Such was the strength of his obsession that he began to speak of 'my north.' In the end, he took it as he had done the diamond diggings of Kimberley—a little at a time. He sent his envoys to negotiate with Lobengula a concession to prospect and exploit the minerals of his domains, which included the land of the Mashona.

"From the white queen in England, Rhodes obtained approval for the formation of a Royal Charter Company, and then he sent a private army of hard and ruthless men to occupy these concessions. Lobengula had not expected anything like this. A few men digging little holes, yes, but not an army of brutal adventurers.

"Firstly Lobengula protested to no avail. The white men pressed him harder and harder, until they forced him to a fatal error of judgement. Lobengula, feeling his very existence threatened, assembled his impis in a warlike display.

"This was the provocation for which Rhodes and his henchmen had worked and planned. They fell upon Lobengula in a savage and merciless campaign. They machine-gunned his famous impis and shattered the Matabele nation. Then they galloped to Lobengula's kraal at GuBulawayo. However, Lobengula, that wily thief and coward, had already fled northwards, taking with him his wives, his herds, what remained of his fighting impis—and his diamonds.

"A small force of white men pursued him for part of the way, until they ran into a Matabele ambush and were slaughtered to a man. More white men would have followed Lobengula, but the rains came and turned the veld to mud and the rivers to torrents. So Lobengula escaped with his treasure. He wandered on northwards without a goal, until the will to go on deserted him.

"In a wild and lonely place, he called Gandang, his half-brother, to him. He entrusted to him the care of the nation and, coward to the very end, ordered his witch-doctor to prepare a poisonous potion and drank it down.

"Gandang sat his body upright in a cave. Around his body he placed all Lobengula's possessions: his assegais and regimental plumes and furs, his sleeping-mat and head-stool, his guns and knives and beer-pots—and his diamonds. Lobengula's corpse was wrapped in a sitting position in the green skin of a leopard and at his feet were placed the five gallon beer-pots of diamonds. Then the entrance to the cave was carefully sealed and disguised, and Gandang led the Matabele nation back to become the slaves of Rhodes and his Royal Charter Company.

"You ask when this occurred? It was in the rainy season of the year 1894. Not long ago—barely ninety years ago.

"You ask where? The answer is—very close to where we now sit. Probably within twenty miles of us. Lobengula travelled directly northwards from GuBulawayo and had almost reached the Zambezi River before he despaired and committed suicide.

"You ask if any living man knows the exact location of the treasure cave? The answer is yes!"

Peter Fungabera stopped and then exclaimed, "Oh, *do* forgive me, my dear Tungata, I have neglected to offer you any refreshment." He called for another glass, and when it came, filled it with water and ice and, with his own hands, carried it to Tungata.

Tungata held the glass in both hands and drank with careful control, a sip at a time.

"Now, where was I?" Peter Fungabera returned to his chair behind the desk.

"You were telling us about the cave." The white man with the pale eyes could not resist.

"Ah, yes, of course. Well, it seems that before Lobengula died, he charged this half-brother of his, Gandang, with the guardianship of the diamonds. He is supposed to have told him, "There will come a day when my people will need these diamonds. You and your son and his sons will keep this treasure until that day."

268

"So the secret was passed on in the Kumalo family, the so-called royal family of the Matabele. When a chosen son reached his manhood he was taken by his father or his grandfather on a pilgrimage."

Tungata was so reduced by his ordeal that he felt weak and feverish. His mind floated and the iced water in his empty stomach seemed to drug him, so that fantasy became mixed with reality, and the memory of his own pilgrimage to Lobengula's tomb was so vivid that he seemed to be reliving it as he listened to Peter Fungabera's voice.

It had been during his first year as an undergraduate at the University of Rhodesia. He had gone home to spend the long vacation with his grandfather. Gideon Kumalo was the assistant headmaster at Khami Mission School, just outside the town of Bulawayo.

"I have a great treat for you," the old man had greeted him, smiling through the thick lenses of his spectacles. He still had a little of his eyesight left, though within the following five years he would lose the last vestiges of it.

"We are going on a journey together, Vundla." It was the old man's pet name for him. *Vundla*, the hare, the clever lively animal always beloved by the Africans. The slaves had taken him with them in legend to America in the form of Brer Rabbit.

The two of them took the bus northwards, changing half a dozen times at lonely trading-stores or remote crossroads, sometimes waiting for forty-eight hours at a stop, when their connection was delayed. However, the delay did not rankle. They made a picnic of it, sitting at night round their camp-fire and talking.

What marvellous stories old grandfather Gideon could tell—fables and legends and tribal histories—but it was the histories that fascinated Tungata. He could hear them repeated fifty times without tiring of them: the story of Mzilikazi's exodus from Zululand, and the *umfecane*, the war with the Boers, and the crossing of the Limpopo River. He could recite the names of the glorious impis and the men who had commanded them, the campaigns they had waged and the battle honours they had won.

Most especially, he learned from the old man the history of the "Moles who burrowed under a mountain," the impi that had been founded and commanded by his great-grandfather, Bazo, the Axe. He learned to sing the war-songs and the praise-songs of the Moles, and he dreamed that in a perfect world he would himself have

269

commanded the Moles one day, wearing the regimental head-band of mole-skin and the furs and the feathers.

So the pair, the greybeard with failing eyesight and the stripling, travelled together for five leisurely companionship-filled days, until at the old man's request the rackety, dusty old bus set them down on a rutted dirt track in the forest.

"Mark this spot well, Vundla," Gideon instructed. "Here, the watercourse with the fall of rock, and the kopje over there shaped like a sleeping lion—this is the starting point."

They set off northwards through the forest, following a succession of landmarks that the old man made him recite in the form of a rhyming poem. Tungata found he could still recite it without hesitation: "The beginning is the lion that sleeps, follow his gaze to the crossing place of the elephant—"

It was another three days' travel at Gideon's reduced pace before he toiled up the steep hillside with Tungata handing him over the worst places, and they stood before the tomb of Lobengula at last.

Tungata remembered kneeling before the tomb, sucking blood from the self-inflicted cut on his wrist and spitting the blood on the rocks that blocked the entrance and repeating after his grandfather the terrible oath of secrecy and guardianship. Of course neither the old man nor the oath had mentioned diamonds or treasure. Tungata had merely sworn to guard the secret of the tomb, passing it to his chosen son until the day when "the children of Mashobane cry out for succour, and the stones are burst open to free the spirit of Lobengula, and it shall come forth like fire— Lobengula's fire!"

After the ceremony the old man had lain down in the shade of the *ficus* tree that grew beside the entrance and, exhausted by the long journey, had slept until nightfall. Tungata had remained awake, examining the tomb and the area around it. He had found certain signs that had led him to a conclusion that he did not confide to his grandfather, not then or during the journey homewards. He had not wanted to alarm and disturb Gideon, his love for him was too great and protective.

Peter Fungabera's voice intruded on his reverie, jerking him back to the present.

"In fact, we are privileged to have with us at this very moment an illustrious member of the Kumalo clan, and the present guardian of the old robber's tomb, the honourable Comrade Minister Tungata Zebiwe."

The white man's cruel eyes riveted him, and Tungata stiffened on the hard wooden bench. Tungata tried his voice and found that even the small quantity of water that he had taken had eased his throat. His voice was deep and measured, only slightly ragged at the edges.

"You delude yourself, Fungabera." He made the name into an insult, but Peter's smile never slipped. "I know nothing of this nonsense that you have dreamed up, and even if I did—" Tungata did not have to finish the sentence.

"You will find my patience inexhaustible," Peter promised him. "The diamonds have lain there ninety years. A few more weeks will not spoil them. I have brought with me a doctor to supervise your treatment. We will find just how much you can bear before your Matabele courage fails you. On the other hand, you have the option at any time to make an end to this unpleasantness. You can elect to take us to Lobengula's burial site, and immediately after you have done so, I will arrange to have you flown out of the country to any destination of your choice"—Peter paused before adding the final sweetener to his proposition—"and with you will go the young woman who so gallantly defended you in the courtroom, Sarah Nyoni."

This time there was a flash of emotion behind the contemptuous mask of Tungata's features.

Peter nodded. "Oh yes, we have her safely taken care of."

"Your lies need no denial. If you had her, you would have used her already." Tungata forced himself to believe that Sarah would have obeyed him. She had read and understood the hand-sign that he had flashed to her across the courtroom as he was being led away. "Take cover! Hide yourself. You are in danger!" he had ordered and she had acknowledged and agreed. She was safe. He had to believe that; it was all he had to believe in.

"We shall see," Peter Fungabera promised.

"Not that it matters." Tungata had to try and protect her, now that it was clear that the Shona were hunting for Sarah. "She is a mere woman—do what you will to her. It will mean little to me."

Fungabera raised his voice. "Captain!" The guard commander came immediately. "Take the prisoner back to his quarters. His

271

treatment will be ordered and supervised by the doctor. Do you understand?"

When they were alone, Colonel Bukharin said quietly, "He will not be easy. He has physical strength and something else beyond that. Some men simply will not bend, even under the most extreme coercion."

"It may take a little time, but in the end—"

"I am not so certain," Bukharin sighed morosely. "Do you indeed have the woman you spoke of, this Sarah Nyoni?"

Peter hesitated. "Not yet. She has disappeared, but again, it's only a matter of time. She cannot hide for ever."

"Time," Colonel Bukharin repeated. "Yes, there is a time for everything, but your time is passing. This thing must be done soon, or not at all."

"Days only, not weeks," Peter promised, but his voice had become thin and Colonel Bukharin, the consummate hunter of men, sensed his advantage.

"This Zebiwe is a hard man. I am not sure he will respond to the treatment at our clinic. I do not like this business of a diamond treasure. It smacks too much of a story for young boys. And I do not like the fact that you have let this Matabele woman elude you. This whole business begins to depress me."

"You are unduly pessimistic—everything is going well. I need just a little time to prove to you."

"You already know that I cannot remain here much longer. I must return to Moscow. And what must I tell them there—that you are digging for treasure?" Bukharin threw up both hands. "They will believe that I am turning senile."

"A month," Peter Fungabera said. "I need another month."

"Today is the tenth. You have until the last day of the month to deliver both money and the man to us."

"That is cutting it too fine," Peter protested.

"On the first of next month, I will return. If on that date you cannot deliver, I will recommend to my superiors that this entire project be aborted."

. . .

The adder was almost six feet long and seemed as gross as a pregnant sow. It was coiled upon itself in a corner of the mesh cage, and the patterning of its scales was in soft purples and golds, in russet and madder, all the colours of autumn enclosed in perfect diamonds, each of which was outlined in the black of mourning.

However, the colours and patterns were not sufficiently spectacular to divert attention from the creature's hideous head. It was the size of a poisonous gourd, but shaped like the ace of spades, flattening and tapering to the snout with its nostril slits. The adder's eyes were bright as beads of polished jet and its tongue was bifurcated and feathery light as it slipped in and out between the grinning lips.

"I can claim no credit for this," said Peter Fungabera. "The good doctor is responsible for this little entertainment." He smiled at Tungata. "It is many days since last we spoke and, frankly, your time is up. So is mine. I must have your agreement today or else it does not matter. After today you are expendable, Comrade Zebiwe."

Tungata was strapped to a sturdy chair of red Rhodesian teak. The mesh cage stood on the table before him.

"You were once in the Game Department," Peter Fungabera went on, "so you will recognize this reptile as *Bitis gabonica*, the Gaboon adder. It is one of the most venomous of African snakes, its toxicity exceeded only by the mamba. However, its sting is more agonizing than either mamba or cobra. It is said that the pain drives men mad before they die."

He touched the cage with the tip of his swagger-stick, and the adder struck at him. The coils propelled the monstrous head across the cage in a liquid blur of movement, half its gross body aerialized by the power of the strike; the jaws gaped to expose the butter-yellow lining of the throat, and the long recurved fangs were gleaming white as polished porcelain, as it crashed into the wire mesh with a force that shook the table. Even Fungabera jumped back involuntarily and then chuckled apologetically.

"I cannot stand snakes," he explained. "They make my flesh crawl. What about you, Comrade Minister?"

"Whatever you are planning, it is a bluff," Tungata answered. His voice was weaker now. Since their last meeting, he had spent many days at the wall in the sun. His body seemed to have shrunk until it was too small for his head. His skin had a grey tone and looked dusty and dry. "You cannot afford to let that thing sting me. I expect you have removed the poison sacs."

"Doctor." Peter Fungabera turned to the regimental doctor who sat at the far end of the table. He rose immediately and left the room.

273

"We were quite fortunate to find a specimen of the Gaboon," Peter Fungabera went on conversationally. "They are really rather rare, as you know."

The doctor returned. He now wore thick gloves that reached to his elbows, and carried a large striped bush-rat the size of a kitten. The rat squealed piercingly and struggled in his gloved hands. Gingerly the doctor opened the door in the top of the mesh cage, dropped the rat through it and immediately snapped the sprung door closed. The furry little animal scampered around the cage, testing the mesh walls with its nose and whiskers until suddenly it saw the adder in the corner. It leaped high and landed on stiff legs and then retreated into the opposite corner and crouched there, staring across the cage.

The adder began to uncoil, its scales glowing with an unearthly loveliness as it slid silently over the sanded floor towards the cornered rat. An unnatural stillness overcame the small animal. Its nose no longer twitched and wriggled. It sank down on its belly, fluffed out its fur and watched with mesmeric fascination as repulsive death slid inexorably towards it.

Two feet from the rat the adder stopped, its neck arched into a taut "S", and then, so swiftly that the eye could not record it, it struck.

The rat was hurled back against the mesh, and immediately the adder withdrew, its coils flowing back upon itself. Now there were tiny droplets of blood on the rat's russet fur, and its body began to pulsate rapidly. The limbs twitched and jumped without coordination and then, abruptly, it squealed, a shrill cry of unbearable agony, and rolled over on its back in the final convulsion of death.

The doctor lifted the carcass out of the cage with a pair of wooden tongs and carried it from the room.

"Of course," said Peter Fungabera, "you have many times the body mass of that rodent. With you it would take much longer."

The doctor had returned and with him were the guard captain and two troopers.

"As I said, the doctor has designed the apparatus. I think he has done excellent work, given the limited materials and shortage of time."

They lifted Tungata's chair and placed him closer to the cage. One of the troopers carried another smaller mesh cage. It was shaped like an oversized fencing helmet, and it fitted over Tungata's head, closing snugly around his throat. From the front of the encompassing helmet protruded a mesh tube that resembled the thickened and shortened trunk of a deformed elephant.

The two troopers stood behind Tungata's chair and forced him forward until the open tube of mesh aligned with the door of the adder's cage. Dexterously the Shona doctor clipped the tube of Tungata's helmet and the cage together.

"When the door of the cage is raised, you and the Gaboon will be sharing the same living-space." Tungata stared down the mesh tube to the door at its extremity. "But we can stop this at any time you say the word."

"Your father was a dung-eating Shona hyena," said Tungata softly.

"We will induce the adder to leave its cage and join you in yours by applying heat to the far wall. I do advise you to be sensible, Comrade. Take us to old Lobengula's tomb."

"The king's tomb is sacred—" Tungata broke off. He was weaker than he had realized. It had slipped out. Up to now he had stubbornly denied the existence of the tomb.

"Good," said Peter happily. "At least we have now agreed that there is a tomb. Now agree to take us there, and this will all end. A safe flight to another land, for you and the woman—"

"I spit on you, Fungabera, and I spit on the diseased whore that was your mother."

"Open the cage," ordered Fungabera.

It rattled up in its runners—and Tungata stared down the tube as though down the barrel of a rifle. The adder was coiled on the far side of the cage, staring back at him with those bright black eyes.

"There is still time, Comrade."

Tungata did not trust his voice to speak again. He steeled himself, and stared into the adder's eyes, trying to dominate it.

"Proceed," said Peter, and one of the troopers placed a small charcoal brazier on the table. Tungata could feel the heat from it even where he sat. Slowly the soldier pushed the glowing stove closer to the far mesh of the cage, and the adder hissed explosively and uncoiled its body. To escape the heat, it began to slither towards the opening of the mesh tube.

"Quickly, Comrade," Peter urged him, "say you will do it. There are only seconds left. I can still close the door."

Tungata felt the sweat prickle as it burst out on his forehead and slid down his naked back. He wanted to shout a curse at Fungabera, to consign him to a fate as horrid as this, but his pulse was pounding in his own ears, deafening him.

The adder hesitated at the mouth of the tube, reluctant to enter.

"There is still time," Peter whispered. "You do not deserve such a loathsome death. Say it! Say you will do it!"

Tungata had not realized how huge the adder was. Its eyes were only eighteen inches from his, and it hissed again as loudly as a punctured truck tyre, a vast exhalation of air that dinned in his eardrums. The trooper pushed the glowing charcoal brazier hard up against the mesh, and the adder thrust its head into the opening of the tube and its belly scales made a dry rasping sound against the wire.

"It's not too late yet." Peter Fungabera unbuckled the flap of his holster and drew his pistol. He placed the muzzle against the wire, only inches from the adder's head. "Say the word, and I will blow its head off."

"Damn you to your own stinking Shona hell," whispered Tungata. He could smell the adder now, not a strong odour, a faint mousy sweetness tinged with corruption. He felt vomit rise and scald the back of his throat. He swallowed it down and began to struggle against the straps that held him. The cage shook with his efforts, but the two troopers held his shoulders, and the great adder, alarmed by his movements, hissed again and arched its neck into the "S" of the strike.

Tungata stopped struggling and forced himself to remain still. He could feel his sweat pouring down his body, tickling coldly down his flanks and puddling under him on the seat of his chair.

Gradually the adder uncocked its neck and crept forward towards his face, six inches from his eyes, and Tungata sat still as a statue in his own sweat and loathing and horror. It was so close now that he could not focus on it. It was merely a blur that filled all his vision—and then the adder shot out its tongue and explored his face with feather-light strokes of the black forked tongue.

Every nerve in Tungata's body was screwed up to snapping point, and his weakened body was overdosed with adrenalin so that he felt he was suffocating. He had to cling to consciousness with all his remaining strength or he would have slipped over the edge into the black void of oblivion.

The adder moved on slowly. He could feel the cool slippery touch of coils across his cheek, under his ear, around the back of his neck, and then, in a final orgasm of horror, he realized that the huge reptile was throwing coil after coil of its body about his head, enveloping him, covering his mouth and his nose. He dared not scream or move, and the seconds drew out.

"He likes you." Peter Fungabera's voice had thickened with excitement and anticipation. "He's settling down with you."

Tungata swivelled his eyes and Peter was on the periphery of his field of vision, blurred by the fine mesh of the cage.

"We can't have that," Peter gloated, and Tungata saw his hand reach out towards the charcoal brazier. For the first time Tungata noticed that a thin steel rod, like a poker, had been thrust into the burning charcoal. When Peter drew it out, the tip glowed red-hot.

"This is your absolutely final chance to agree," he said. "When I touch the creature with this, it will go crazy."

He waited for a reply. "You cannot speak, of course. If you agree, just blink your eyes rapidly."

Tungata stared fixedly at him through the mesh, trying to convey to him the universe of hatred that he experienced.

"Ah well, we tried," said Peter Fungabera. "Now you have only yourself to blame."

He slipped the point of the glowing poker through the mesh and touched the adder with it. There was a sharp hiss of searing flesh, a tiny puff of stinking smoke and the adder went berserk.

Tungata felt the coils enfold his head, pumping and swelling and then the great body whipped and slashed, filling the confined space of the cage with crazy uncoordinated convulsions. The cage banged and jarred and clattered, and Tungata lost control. He heard himself screaming as terror engulfed him.

Then the snake's head filled his vision. Its jaws flared open, and its bright yellow throat gaped at him, as it struck into his face. The force of the strike stunned him. It hit him in the cheek below the eye, a heavy punch that jarred him so his teeth clashed together and he bit through his own tongue. Blood filled his mouth and he felt the long curved fangs snag into his flesh like fish-hooks tugging and jerking, as they spurted jets of deadly toxin into his flesh— and then, mercifully, darkness took possession and Tungata slumped unconscious against the straps that held him.

• • •

"You've killed him, you bloody idiot!" Peter Fungabera's voice was shrill and petulant with panic.

"No, no." The doctor was working quickly. With the help of the troopers, he pulled the mesh helmet off Tungata's head. One of the troopers hurled the maimed adder against the wall and then crushed its head under the butt of an AK 47. "No. He's passed out, that's all. He was weak from the wall."

Between them they lifted Tungata and carried him to the camp-bed against the far wall. With exaggerated care they laid him on it, and swiftly the doctor checked his pulse.

"He's all right." He filled a disposable syringe from a glass ampoule and shot it into Tungata's sweat-slicked upper arm. "I've given him a stimulant—ah, there!" The doctor's relief was obvious. "There! He is coming round already."

The doctor swabbed the deep punctures in Tungata's cheek from which watery lymph was oozing.

"There is always risk of infection from these bites," the doctor explained anxiously. "I will inject an antibiotic."

Tungata moaned and muttered, and then began to struggle weakly. The troopers restrained him until he came fully conscious and then they helped him into a sitting position. His eyes focused with difficulty on Fungabera, and his confusion was obvious.

"Welcome back to the land of the living, Comrade." The voice was once more smooth and richly modulated. "You are now one of the privileged few who have had a glimpse of the beyond."

The doctor still fussed over him, but Tungata's eyes never left Peter Fungabera's face.

"You do not understand," Peter said, "and nobody can blame you for that. You see, the good doctor *had* removed the creature's poison sacks, as you suggested he might have."

Tungata shook his head, unable to speak.

"The rat!" Peter spoke for him. "Yes, of course, the rat. That was rather clever. While he was out of the room the doctor gave it a little injection. He had tested the dosage on other rodents to get the correct delay. You were right, my dear Tungata, we aren't ready to let you go just yet. Maybe next time, or the time after that—you will never know for certain. Then, of course, we might miscalculate. There might, for instance, have been a little residual toxin in that adder's fangs—" Peter shrugged. "It's all very delicate—this time, next time—who knows? How long can you keep it up, Comrade, before your mind snaps?"

"I can keep it up as long as you can," Tungata whispered huskily. "I give you my oath on that."

278

"Now, now, no rash promises," Peter scolded him mildly. "The next little production that I am planning involves my puppies—you have heard Fungabera's puppies, every night you have heard them. I am not sure how we can control them. It will be interesting—you could easily lose an arm or a foot—it only takes one snap of those jaws." Peter played with his swagger-stick, rolling it between his fingers. "The choice is yours, and of course it only takes one word from you to end it all." Peter held up one hand. "No, please don't tax yourself. There is no need to give an answer now. We'll let you have another few days at the wall to recuperate from this ordeal, and then—"

* * * *

Tungata had lost track of time. He could not remember how many days he had spent at the wall, how many men he had seen executed, how many nights he had lain and listened to the hyena.

He found it difficult to think further ahead than the next bowl of water. The doctor had judged the amount required to keep him alive with precision. Thirst was a torment that never ceased, not even when he slept, for his nightmares now were filled with images of water—lakes and running streams which he could not reach, rain that fell all around him and did not touch him, and raging, intolerable thirst.

Added to the thirst, Peter Fungabera's threat of delivering him to the hyena pack festered in his imagination and became more potent for every day that it was delayed. Water and hyena—they were beginning to drive him beyond the borders of sanity. He knew that he could not hold out much longer, and he wondered confusedly why he had held out this long. He had to keep reminding himself that Lobengula's tomb was all that was keeping him alive. While he had the secret, they could not kill him. He did not entertain for even a moment the hope that Peter Fungabera would keep his promise of sending him to safety once he led them to the tomb.

He had to stay alive, it was his duty. As long as he lived, there was still hope, however faint, of delivery. He knew that with his death his people would sink deeper into the tyrant's coils. He was their hope of salvation. It was his duty to them to live. Even though death would now be a blessing and a release, he could not die. He must live on.

He waited in the icy darkness of pre-dawn, his body too stiff and weak to rise. This day they would have to carry him to the wall, or to whatever they had planned for him. He hated that thought. He hated to show such weakness in front of them.

He heard the camp beginning to stir. The march of the guards, the orders shouted with needless violence, the sound of blows and the cries of a prisoner in the adjoining cell being dragged to the execution wall.

Now soon they would come for him. He reached out for the waterbowl and his disappointment hit him in a cold gust as he remembered that the previous evening he had not been able to control himself. The bowl was empty. He crouched over it and licked the enamel like a dog, in case a drop remained of the precious fluid. It was dry.

The bolts shot back and the door was flung open. The day had begun. Tungata tried to rise. He lurched up onto his knees. A guard entered and placed a large object on the threshold and then quietly withdrew. The door was bolted again and Tungata was left alone.

This had never happened before. Tungata was stupefied and uncomprehending. He crouched in the darkness and waited for something more to happen, but nothing did. He heard the other prisoners being led away, and then silence beyond the door of his cell.

The light began to strengthen and cautiously he examined the object that had been left by the guard. It was a plastic bucket, and in the dawn light the contents shimmered.

Water. A full gallon of water. He crawled to it and examined it, not yet beginning to hope. Once before, they had tricked him. They had doctored his water-bowl and he had gulped down a mouthful before he realized that it was heavily laced with salt and bitter alum. The thirst that followed had driven him delirious and shaking as though in malarial crisis.

Gingerly he dipped his forefinger into the liquid in the bucket and tasted a drop. It was sweet, clean water. He made a little whining sound in his throat and scooped the empty bowl full of the precious fluid. He tilted back his head and poured the water down his throat. He drank with a terrible desperation, expecting that at any moment the door would crash open and a guard would kick the bucket over. He drank until his empty belly bulged, and pangs of colic stabbed through it. Then he rested for a few minutes, feeling the fluid flowing into his desiccated tissues, feeling them recharge with strength, and then he drank again, and rested and drank again. After three hours he urinated copiously in the toilet bucket for the first time in as long as he could remember.

When they finally came for him at noon, he could stand up unaided and curse them with fluency and artistry.

They led him towards the execution wall, and he felt almost cheerful. With his belly sloshing with water, he knew he could resist them for ever. The execution stake had no terror for him any longer. He had stood there too long and too often. He welcomed it as a part of the routine which he understood. He had reached the point where he feared only the unknown.

Halfway across the parade-ground he realized that something was different. They had built a new structure facing the wall. A neatly thatched sun-shelter. Under the shelter two chairs were set and a table had been laid for lunch.

Seated at the table was the dreadfully familiar figure of Peter Fungabera. Tungata had not seen him for days, and his new-found courage faltered; weakness came back over him. He felt a rubbery give to his knees and he stumbled. What had they planned for today? If only he knew, he could meet it. The uncertainty was the one truly unbearable torture.

Peter Fungabera was lunching and he did not even look up as Tungata was led past the thatched shelter. Peter ate with his fingers in the African manner, taking the stiff white maize cake and moulding it into bite-sized balls, pressing a depression into it with his thumb and then filling it with a sauce of stewed greens and salted kapenta fish from Lake Kariba. The smell of the food flooded Tungata's mouth with saliva, but he trudged on towards the wall and the execution stake.

There was only one other victim today, he noticed, narrowing his eyes against the glare. He was already strapped to one of the stakes. Then, with a small shock of surprise, Tungata realized that it was a woman.

She was naked—a young woman. Her skin had a velvety sheen in the sunlight, like polished amber. Her body was graciously formed, her breasts symmetrical and firm, their aureolas were the colour of ripe mulberries, the nipples upturned and out-thrust. Her legs were long and willowy, the bare feet small and neat. Bound as she was, she could not cover herself. Tungata sensed her shame

281

at her naked sex, nestled dark and fluffy in the juncture of her thighs like a tiny animal with separate life. He averted his eyes, looked up at her face—and at last he despaired.

It was all over. The guards released his arms, and he tottered towards the young woman at the stake. Though her eyes were huge and dark with terror and shame, her first words were for him. She whispered softly in Sindebele, "My lord, what have they done to you?"

"Sarah." He wanted to reach over and touch her dear and lovely face, but he would not do so under the lewd gaze of his guards.

"How did they find you?" He felt very old and frail. It was all over.

"I did as you commanded," she told him in soft apology. "I went into the hills. But then a message reached me—one of my children from the school was dying—dysentery and no doctor. I could not ignore the call."

"Of course, it was a lie," he guessed flatly.

"It was a lie," she admitted. "The Shona soldiers were waiting for me. Forgive me, lord."

"It does not matter any longer," he answered.

"Not for me, lord," she pleaded. "Do not do anything for me. I am a daughter of Mashobane. I can bear anything these Shona animals can do to me."

He shook his head sadly and at last reached out and touched her lips with the tips of his fingers. His hand was trembling like that of a drunkard. She kissed his fingers. He dropped his hand and, turning, trudged wearily back to the thatched shelter. The soldiers made no effort to prevent him.

Peter Fungabera looked up as he approached and motioned to the empty canvas chair. Tungata sat down and his body slumped.

"First," Tungata said, "the woman must be untied and clothed."

Fungabera gave the order. They covered her and led her away to one of the hutments.

"My lord—" She strained back against their grip, her face turned piteously to him.

"She must not be ill-treated in any way."

"She has not been," he said. "She will not be, unless you make it necessary."

He pushed a bowl of maize cake towards Tungata, who ignored it.

"She must be taken out of the country and delivered to a rep-

282

resentative of the international Red Cross in Francistown."

"There is a light aircraft waiting at Tuti airfield. Eat, Comrade, we must have you strong and well."

"When she is safe, she will speak to me—radio telephone— and give me a code-word that I will arrange with her before she leaves."

"Agreed." He poured hot sweet tea for Tungata.

"We will be left alone together to agree on the code."

Fungabera nodded. "You may speak to her, of course, but in the middle of this parade-ground. None of my men will be closer than a hundred yards to you, but there will be a machine-gun trained upon you at all times. I will allow you precisely five minutes with the woman."

      •   •   •

"I have failed you," Sarah said, and Tungata had forgotten how beautiful she was. His whole being ached with longing for her.

"No," he told her, "it was inevitable. There is no blame to you. It was for duty, not for yourself that you came out of hiding."

"My lord, what can I do now?"

"Listen," he said, and spoke quietly and quickly, "some of my trusted people have escaped from the scourge of Fungabera's Third Brigade. You must find them. I believe they are in Botswana." He gave her the names and she repeated them faithfully. "Tell them—" She memorized all that he told her and repeated it to him perfectly.

From the corner of his eye Tungata saw the guards at the edge of the parade-ground start towards where they stood alone in the centre. Their five minutes together was up.

"When you are safe, they will allow us to speak on the radio. To let me know that all is well, you will repeat to me: 'Your beautiful bird has flown high and swiftly.' Repeat it."

"Oh my lord," she choked.

"Repeat it!"

She obeyed and then flung herself into his arms. She clung to him, and he to her.

"Will I ever see you again?"

"No," he told her. "You must forget me."

"Never!" she cried. "Not if I live to be an old woman—never, my lord."

The guards dragged them apart. A Land-Rover drove out onto the parade-ground. They hustled Sarah into it.

The last he saw of her was her face in the rear window, looking back at him—her beautiful beloved face.

•   •   •

On the third day, they came to fetch Tungata from his cell and take him up to Peter Fungabera's command post on the central kopje.

"The woman is ready to speak to you. You will converse only in English. Your conversation will be recorded." Peter indicated the transistor tape-deck beside the radio apparatus. "If you do attempt to slip in any Sindebele message, it will be translated later."

"The code we have arranged is in Sindebele," Tungata told him. "She will have to repeat it."

"Very well. That is acceptable, but nothing else." He looked Tungata over critically. "I am delighted to see you looking so well again, Comrade. A little good food and rest have worked wonders."

Tungata wore faded suntans, but they were freshly laundered and pressed. He was still gaunt and wasted, but his skin had lost the dusty grey look and his eyes were clear and bright. The swelling of the adder bite on his cheek had abated, and the scab covering it looked dry and healthy.

Peter Fungabera nodded to the guard captain, who passed the radio microphone to Tungata and pressed the "record" button on the tape-deck.

"This is Tungata Zebiwe."

"My lord, this is Sarah." Her voice was scratchy and distorted by static, but he would have known it anywhere. The ache of longing filled his chest.

"Are you safe?"

"I am in Francistown. The Red Cross is caring for me."

"Do you have a message?"

She replied in Sindebele. "Your beautiful bird has flown high and swiftly." Then she added, "I have met others here. Do not despair."

"That is good—I want you to—"

Fungabera reached across and took the microphone from his hand. "Excuse me, Comrade, but I am paying for the call." He held the microphone to his lips and depressed the transmit button.

284

"Transmission ends," he said, and broke the connection.

He tossed the microphone casually to the guard captain. "Have the tape translated—by one of the Matabele trustees—and bring me a copy immediately." Then he turned back to Tungata.

"Your little holiday is over, Comrade. Now you and I have work to do. Shall we go?"

• • •

How long would he be able to draw out the search for Lobengula's grave, Tungata wondered. For every hour he could gain would have value—another hour of life, another hour of hope.

"It is almost twenty years since my grandfather took me to visit the site. My memory is unclear—"

"Your memory is as brilliant as that sun up there," Peter told him. "You are renowned for your ability to remember places and faces and names, Comrade, you forget that I have heard you speak in the Assembly, without notes. Besides which, you will have a helicopter to ferry you directly to the site."

"That will not work. The first time I went was on foot. I must go back the same way. I would not recognize the landmarks from the air."

So they went back along the dirt roads that Tungata and old Gideon had bussed over so many years before, and Tungata genuinely could not find the starting place—the fall of rocks in the old river-course and the kopje shaped like an elephant's head. They spent three days searching, with Fungabera becoming more and more short-tempered and disbelieving, before they stopped at the tiny village and trading-store that was the last reference point that Tungata could remember.

"Hau! The old road. Yes, the bridge was washed away many years ago. It was never used again. Now the new road goes so and so—"

They found the overgrown track at last and four hours later reached the dry river-bed. The old bridge had collapsed into a heap of shattered concrete already overgrown with lianas, but the rock wall upstream was exactly as Tungata had remembered it and he experienced a pang of nostalgia. Suddenly old Gideon seemed very close to him, so much so that he glanced around and made a small sign with his right hand to appease the ancestral spirits and whispered, "Forgive me, Baba, that I am going to betray the oath."

285

Strangely the presence that he sensed was benign and fondly indulgent, as Old Gideon had always been. "The path lies this way." They left the Land-Rover at the broken bridge and continued on foot.

Tungata led with two armed troopers at his back. He set an easy pace, which chafed Peter Fungabera, who followed behind the guards. As they went, Tungata could allow his imagination to wander freely. He seemed to be part of the exodus of the Matabele people of almost a hundred years before, an embodiment of Gandang, his great-great-grandfather, faithful and loyal to the end. He felt again the despair of a defeated people and the terror of the hard-riding white pursuit that might appear at any instant from the forest behind them, with their chattering three-legged machine guns. He seemed to hear the lament of the women and the small children, the lowing of herds as they faltered and fell in this hard and bitter country.

When the last of the draught oxen were dead, Gandang had ordered the warriors of his famous Inyati regiment into the traces of the king's remaining wagon. Tungata imagined the king, obese and diseased and doomed, sitting up on the rocking wagon-box staring into the forbidden north, a man caught up in the millstones of history and destiny and crushed between them.

"And now the final betrayal," Tungata thought. "I am leading these Shona animals to disturb his rest once again."

Three times, deliberately, he took the wrong path, drawing it out to the very limit of Fungabera's patience. The third time, Fungabera ordered him stripped naked and his wrists and ankles bound together, then he had stood over him with a cured hippo-hide whip, the vicious kiboko that the Arab slave-traders had introduced to Africa, and he thrashed Tungata like a dog until his blood dripped into the sandy grey earth.

It was the shame and humiliation of the beating rather than the pain that had made Tungata turn back and pick up his landmarks again. When he reached the hill at last, it appeared ahead of them with all the suddenness that Tungata recalled so vividly from his first visit.

They had been following a deep gorge of black rock, polished by the roaring torrential spates of the millennia. The depths were studded with stagnant green pools in which giant whiskered cat-fish stirred the scummy surface as they rose to feed, and lovely swallow-tailed butterflies floated in the heated air above, gems of scarlet and iridescent blue.

They came around a bend in the gorge, clambering over boulders the size and the colour of elephants, and abruptly the surrounding cliffs opened and the forest fell back. Before them, like a vast monument to dwarf the pyramids of the pharaohs, the hill of Lobengula rose into the sky.

The cliffs were sheer and daubed with lichens of twenty different shades of yellow and ochre and malachite. There was a breeding colony of vultures in the upper ledges, the parent birds sailing gracefully out over the heated void, tipping their wings in the rising thermals as they banked and spiralled.

"There it is," Tungata murmured. "*Thabas Nkosi*, the hill of the King."

The natural pathway to the summit followed a fault in the rockface where limestone overlaid the country rock. At places it was steep and daunting and the troopers, weighted with packs and weapons, glanced nervously over the drop and hugged the inner wall of rock as they edged upwards, but Peter Fungabera and Tungata climbed easily and surefooted over even the worst places, leaving the escort far below.

"I could throw him over the edge," Tungata thought, "if I can take him unawares." He glanced back and Peter was ten paces below him. He had the Tokarev pistol in his right hand and he smiled like a mamba.

"No," he warned, and they understood each other without further words. For a moment Tungata put away the thought of vengeance and went on upwards. He turned a corner in the rock and they came out onto the crown of the hill, five hundred feet above the gorge.

Standing a little apart, both of them sweating lightly in the white sunlight, they looked down into the deep wide valley of the Zambezi. On the edge the wide waters of the man-made lake of Kariba glinted softly through the haze of heat and blue smoke from the first bush-fires of the dry season. The troopers came off the path with transparent relief, and Peter Fungabera looked expectantly at Tungata.

"We are ready to go on, Comrade."

"There is not much farther to go," Tungata answered.

Over the crest of the cliff the rock formation had eroded and broken up into buttress and tumbled ramparts, the trees that had found purchase in the cracks and crevices had intertwined their root systems over the rock-face like mating serpents, while their stems were thickened and deformed by the severe conditions of heat and drought.

Tungata led them through the broken rock and tortured forest into the mouth of a ravine. At the head of the ravine grew an ancient *Ficus natalensis*, the strangler fig-tree, its fleshy limbs of blotched yellow loaded with bunches of bitter fruit. As they approached it a flock of brown parrots, green wings flagged with bright yellow, that had been feasting on the wild figs, exploded into flight. At the base of the *ficus* tree, the cliff was segmented, and the roots had found the cracks and forced them apart.

Tungata stood before the cliff and Fungabera, suppressing an exclamation of impatience, glanced at him and saw his lips were moving silently, in prayer or entreaty. Fungabera began to examine the cliff-face more carefully and realized with rising excitement that the cracks in the rock were too regular to be natural.

"Here!" he shouted to his troopers, and then they hurried forward; he pointed out one of the blocks in the face, and they set to work on it with bayonets and bare hands.

Within fifteen minutes of sweaty labour, they had worked the block free, and it was now clear that the face was in reality a wall of carefully fitted masonry. In the depths of the aperture left by the block, they could make out a second wall of masonry.

"Bring the prisoner," Fungabera ordered. "He will work in the front rank."

By the time it was too dark to go on, they had opened an aperture just wide enough for two men to work shoulder to shoulder in the outer wall, and had begun on the inner wall. In the forefront, Tungata was able to confirm what he had guessed on his first visit to the tomb so long ago. The signs that he had noticed then and concealed from old grandfather Gideon were even more apparent on the inner wall of the tomb. They helped salve his conscience and ease the pain of oath-breaking.

Reluctantly Fungabera called a halt on the work for the night. Tungata's hands were raw from contact with the rough blocks and he had lost a fingernail where it had been trapped and torn off in a slide of masonry. He was handcuffed to one of the Third Brigade troopers for the night, but even this could not keep him from dreamless exhaustion-drugged sleep. Peter Fungabera had to kick both him and his guard awake the next morning.

It was still dark and they ate their meagre rations of cold maize cake and sweet tea in silence. They had barely gulped it down before Fungabera ordered them back to the masonry wall.

Tungata's torn hands were clumsy and stiff. Peter Fungabera stood behind in the opening and, when Tungata faltered, slashed him with the kiboko around the ribs, in the soft and sensitive flesh below the armpit. Tungata growled like a wounded lion and lifted a hundred-weight block out of the wall.

The sun cleared the crown of the hill, and its golden rays illuminated the cliff-face. With a branch of dead wood, Tungata and one of the Shona troopers levered up another lump of rock, and as it began to move, there was a rumble and a harsh grating sound and the inner wall collapsed towards them. They jumped clear and stood coughing in the swirl of dust, peering into the aperture that they had made.

The air from the cave stank like a drunkard's mouth, stale and sour, and the blackness beyond was forbidding and menacing.

"You first," Peter Fungabera ordered, and Tungata hesitated. He was overcome with a superstitious awe. He was an educated and sophisticated man, but beneath that he was African. The spirits of his tribe and his ancestors guarded this place. He looked at Peter Fungabera and knew that he was experiencing the same dread of the supernatural, even though armed with a flashlight, whose batteries he had conserved zealously for this moment.

"Move!" Fungabera ordered. His harsh tone could not disguise his disquiet, and Tungata, to shame him, stepped cautiously over the rockfall into the cave.

He stood for a while until his eyes adjusted to the gloom and he could make out the configuration of the cave. The floor beneath his feet was smooth and worn, but it sloped downwards at a steep angle. Obviously this cave had been the lair of animals and the home of primitive man for tens of thousands of years before it became the tomb of a king.

Fungabera, standing behind Tungata, played the beam of his flashlight over walls and roofs. The roof was crusted with the soot of ancient cooking-fires, and the smooth walls were rich with the art of the little yellow Bushmen who had lived here. There were depictions of the wild game that they had hunted and observed so minutely: herds of black buffalo, and tall, dappled giraffe, rhinoceros and horned antelope in glowing colours, all delightfully caricatured. With them the artists had drawn their own people, sticklike figures with buttocks as pronounced as a camel's hump and imperial erections to boast of their manhood. Armed with bows, they pursued the herds across the rock wall.

Peter Fungabera flicked the torch beam over this splendid gallery and then held it steady into the inner recesses of the cave where the throat narrowed and the rocky passage turned upon itself and was shrouded in mysterious shadow far below them.

"Forward!" he ordered, and Tungata moved cautiously down the sloping floor of the chamber.

They reached the throat of the cave and were forced to stoop under the low roof. Tungata turned the corner of the rocky passage and went on for fifty paces before he stopped short.

He had come out into a capacious cavern with a domed roof twenty feet above their heads. The floor was level, but cluttered with rock fallen from above. Fungabera flashed his beam around the cavern. Against the far wall was a ledge the height of a man's shoulder and he held the beam on a jumble of objects that were stacked upon it.

For a moment Tungata was puzzled, and then he recognized the shape of a wagon wheel design from a hundred years before, a wheel taller than the oxen that drew it; then he made out the wagon bed and frames. The vehicle had been broken down into its separate parts and carried up to the cave.

"Lobengula's wagon," he whispered. "His most cherished possession, the one his warriors pulled when the oxen failed—"

Fungabera prodded him with the barrel of the Tokarev and they picked their way forward through the litter of fallen rock.

There were rifles, stacked like wheat-sheaves, old Lee-Enfields, part of the payment that Cecil Rhodes had made to Lobengula for his concessions. Rifles and a hundred gold sovereigns every month—the price of a land and a nation sold into slavery, Tungata recalled bitterly. There were other objects piled upon the ledge, salt-bags of leather, stools and knives, beads and ornaments and snuff-horns and broad-bladed assegais.

Peter Fungabera exclaimed with avarice and impatience, "Hurry! We must find his corpse—the diamonds will be with the body."

Bones. They gleamed in the torchlight. A pile of them below the ledge.

290

A skull! It grinned mirthlessly up at them, a cap of matted wool still covering the pate.

"That's him!" cried Peter jubilantly. "There is the old devil." He dropped to his knees beside the skeleton.

Tungata stood aloof. After the first pang of alarm, he had realized that it was the skeleton of a small and elderly man, not much larger than a child, with teeth missing in the front upper jaw. Lobengula had been a big man with fine flashing teeth. Everyone who had met him in life had commented on his smile. This skeleton was still decked in the gruesome paraphernalia of the witch-doctor's trade: beads and shells and bones, plugged duiker-horns of medicine and skulls of reptiles belted about the bony waist. Even Fungabera recognized his mistake, and he jumped to his feet.

"This isn't him!" he cried anxiously. "They must have sacrificed his witch-doctor and placed him here as a guardian." He was playing the torch wildly about the cave.

"Where is he?" he demanded. "You must know. They must have told you."

Tungata remained silent. Above the skeleton of the witch-doctor, the ledge jutted out, rather like a large pulpit of rock. The king's possessions were laid out neatly around this prominence, the human sacrifice laid below it. The entire focus of the cavern was on this spot. It was the logical and natural position in which to place the king's corpse. Peter Fungabera sensed that also and slowly turned the beam back to it.

The rock pulpit was empty.

"He isn't here," Fungabera whispered, his voice tense with disappointment and frustration. "Lobengula's body is gone!"

The signs that Tungata had noticed at the outer wall, the place where the masonry wall had been opened and resealed with less meticulous workmanship, had led him to the correct conclusion. The old king's tomb had obviously been robbed many years previously. The corpse had long ago been spirited away and the tomb resealed to hide the traces of this desecration.

Fungabera clambered up onto the rock pulpit and searched it frantically on his hands and knees. Standing back impassively, Tungata marvelled at how ludicrous greed could render even such a dangerous and impressive man as Peter Fungabera. He was muttering incoherently to himself as he strained the dusty detritus from the floor through his hooked fingers.

"Look! Look here!" He held up a small object, and Tungata stepped closer. In the torchlight he recognized that it was a shard from a clay pot, a piece of the rim decorated in the traditional diamond pattern used on the Matabele beer-pots.

"A beer-pot." Peter turned it in his hands. "One of the diamond pots—broken!" He dropped the fragment and scratched in the dirt, stirring up a soft cloud of dust that undulated in the torch beam.

"Here!" He had found something else. Something smaller. He held it up between thumb and forefinger. It was the size of a small walnut. He turned the torch beam full upon it, and immediately the light was shattered into the rainbow hues of the spectrum. Shafts of coloured light were reflected in Fungabera's face, like sunlight off water.

"Diamond," he breathed with religious awe, turning it slowly in his fingers so that it shot out arrows and blades of light.

It was an uncut stone, Tungata realized, but the crystal had formed in such symmetry and each plane was so perfect as to catch and reflect even the meagre beam of the torch.

"How beautiful!" the man murmured, bringing it closer still to his face.

This diamond was a perfect natural octahedron and its colour, even in artificial light, was clear as snow melt in a mountain stream.

"Beautiful," Fungabera repeated, and then gradually his face lost its dreamy, gloating expression.

"Only one!" he whispered. "A single stone dropped in haste, when there should have been five beer-pots brimming with diamonds."

His eyes swivelled from the diamond to Tungata. The torch was held low, and it cast weird shadows across his face, giving him a demoniacal look.

"You knew," he accused. "I sensed all along you were holding something back. You knew the diamonds had been taken, and you knew where."

Tungata shook his head in denial, but Fungabera was working himself into a fury. His features contorted; his mouth worked soundlessly and a thin white froth coated his lips.

"You knew!"

He launched himself from the ledge with all the fury of a wounded leopard.

"You'll tell me!" he shrieked. "In the end you'll tell me."

He hit Tungata in the face with the barrel of the Tokarev.

"Tell me!" he screamed. "Tell me where they are!" And the steel thudded into Tungata's face as he struck again and again.

"Tell me where the diamonds are!"

The barrel crunched against Tungata's cheek-bone, splitting the flesh, and he fell to his knees. Peter Fungabera pulled himself away and braced himself against the rocky ledge to contain his own fury.

"No," he told himself. "That is too easy. He is going to suffer—"

He folded his own arms tightly across his chest to restrain himself from attacking Tungata again.

"In the end you will tell me—you will plead with me to allow you to take me to the diamonds. You will plead with me to kill you—"

•   •   •

"Babes in the fornicating woods," said Morgan Oxford, "that's what you two are! By God, you have dropped us in this cesspool as well, right up to the eyebrows."

Morgan Oxford had flown down from Harare as soon as he had heard that a Botswana border patrol had brought Craig and Sally-Anne in from the desert.

"Both the American ambassador and the Brits have had notes from Mugabe. The Brits are hopping up and down and frothing at the mouth also. They know nothing about you, Craig, and you are a British subject. I gather that they'd like to lock you up in the Tower and chop your head off."

Morgan stood at the foot of Sally-Anne's hospital bed. He had declined the chair that Craig offered him.

"As for you, missy, the ambassador has asked me to inform you that he would like to see you on the next plane back to the States."

"He can't order me to do that." Sally-Anne stopped his flow of bitter recriminations. "This isn't Soviet Russia, and I'm a free citizen."

"You won't be for long. No, by God, not if Mugabe gets his hands on you: murder, armed insurrection and a few other charges—"

"Those are all a frame-up!"

293

"You and your boy-friend here left a pile of warm bodies behind you like empty beer-cans at a Labor Day picnic. Mugabe has started extradition proceedings with the Botswana government—"

"We are political refugees," Sally-Anne flared.

"Bonnie and Clyde, sweetheart, that's the way the Zimbabweans are telling it."

"Sally-Anne," Craig intervened mildly, "you are not supposed to get yourself excited—"

"Excited!" cried Sally-Anne. "We've been robbed and beaten, threatened with rape and a firing-squad—and now the official representative of the United States of America, the country of which I happen to be a citizen, barges in here and calls us criminals."

"I'm not calling you anything," Morgan denied flatly. "I'm just warning you to get your cute little ass out of Africa and all the way home to mommy."

"He calls us criminals, and then patronizes me with his male chauvinistic—"

Morgan Oxford held up one hand wearily. "Throttle back, Sally-Anne. Let's start again. You are in big trouble—we are in big trouble. We've got to work something out."

"Now will you sit down?" Craig pushed the empty chair towards him and Morgan slumped into it and lit a Chesterfield.

"How are you, anyway?" he asked.

"I thought you'd never ask, sweetheart," Sally-Anne snapped tersely.

"She was badly desiccated. They suspected renal failure, but they've had her on a drip and liquids for three days. She is okay that end. They were also worried about the crack on her head but the X-rays are negative, thank God. It was only a mild concussion. They have promised to discharge her tomorrow morning."

"So she's fit to travel?"

"I thought your concern was too touching—"

"Look, Sally-Anne, this is Africa. If the Zimbabweans get hold of you, there will be nothing we can do to help. It's for your own good. You've got to get out. The ambassador—"

"Screw the ambassador," said Sally-Anne with relish, "and screw you, Morgan Oxford."

"I can't speak for His Excellency," Morgan said, grinning for the first time, "but for myself, when can we begin?" And even Sally-Anne laughed.

Craig took advantage of the softening of attitudes.

"Morgan, you can rely on me to see she does the right thing—"

Immediately Sally-Anne puffed up in the high bed, preparatory to fending off another chauvinistic onslaught, but Craig gave her a tiny frown and shake of the head and she subsided reluctantly. Morgan turned on Craig instead.

"As for you, Craig, how the hell did they find out you were working for the Agency?" Morgan demanded.

"Was I?" Craig looked stunned. "If I was, nobody told me."

"Who the hell do you think Henry Pickering is anyway—Santa Claus?"

"Henry, he is a vice-president of the World Bank!"

"Babes," moaned Morgan, "babes in the tupping woods." He braced up. "Well, anyway, that is over. Your contract is terminated. If there was anything sooner than immediately, that would be the date of termination."

"I sent Henry a full report three days ago—"

Morgan nodded resignedly. "Yeah! About Peter Fungabera being the Moscow candidate. Peter is a Shona. The Ruskies would never touch him. Just so you put it out of your head, General Fungabera is a Russian-hater from way back and we have a very good relationship with Peter Fungabera—very good indeed. Enough said."

"For God's sake, Morgan, then he is playing a double game. I had it from his own aide, Captain Timon Nbebi!"

"Who is now conveniently dead," Morgan reminded him. "If it makes you feel better, we've put your report into the computer— with a D-minus credibility rating. Henry Pickering sends you his sincere thanks."

Sally-Anne cut in, "Morgan, you have seen my photographs of the burned villages, the dead children, the devastation caused by the Third Brigade—"

"Like the man said: Eggs to make omelettes," Morgan interrupted. "Naturally we don't like the violence, but Fungabera is anti-Russian. The Matabele are pro-Russian. We have to support the anti-communist regimes, even if we don't like some of their methods. There are women and kids taking a beating in El Salvador, so does that mean that we must stop aid to that country?

Must we back out of any situation where our people aren't sticking precisely to the rules of the Geneva Convention? Grow up, Sally-Anne, this is the real world."

There was silence in the tiny ward, except for the pinking of the galvanized-iron roof as it expanded in the noon heat. On the parched brown lawn beyond the window, the walking patients were dressed in a uniform of pink bathrobes stamped across the back with the initials of the Botswana Health Department.

"That's all you came to tell us?" Sally-Anne asked at last.

"Isn't it enough?" Morgan stubbed out his cigarette and stood up. "There is one other thing, Craig. Henry Pickering asked me to tell you that the Land Bank of Zimbabwe has repudiated its suretyship for your loan. Their grounds are that you have been officially declared an enemy of the people. Henry Pickering asked me to tell you they will be looking to you for repayment of capital and interest. Does this make sense to you?"

Craig nodded glumly. "Unfortunately."

"He said he would try to work something out with you when you reach New York, but in the meantime they have been forced to freeze all your bank accounts and serve your publishers with a restraining order to withhold all future royalty payments."

"That figures."

"Sorry, Craig. It sounds real tough." Morgan held out his hand. "I liked your book, I really did, and I liked you. I'm just sorry it all had to end this way."

Craig walked with him as far as the green Ford with diplomatic registration plates that Morgan Oxford was driving.

"Will you do me one last favour?"

"If I can." Morgan looked suspicious.

"Can you see that a package is delivered to my publisher in New York?" And when Morgan's suspicions were unabated, "It's only the final pages of my new manuscript, I give you my word."

"Okay, then," said Morgan Oxford dubiously. "I'll see he gets it."

Craig fetched the British Airways bag from the rented Land-Rover at the far end of the car-park. "Look after it," he pleaded. "It's my heart's blood and my hope of salvation."

He watched the green Ford drive away and went back into the hospital building.

"What was all that about the banks and loans?" Sally-Anne asked as he entered her ward.

"It means that when I asked you to marry me I was a millionaire." Craig came back to sit on the edge of her bed. "Now I'm just about as broke as anybody who has no assets and owes a couple of million bucks can be."

"You've got the new book. Ashe Levy says it's a winner."

"Darling, if I wrote a best-seller every year for the rest of my life, I would just about keep level with the interest payments on what I owe to Henry Pickering and his banks."

She stared at him.

"So what I am trying to say is this—my original offer is up for review. You've got a chance to change your mind. You don't *have* to marry me."

"Craig," she said, "lock the door and close the shutters."

"You've got to be joking—not here, not now! It's probably a serious offence in this country, illicit cohabitation or something."

"Listen, mister, when you are wanted for murder and armed insurrection, a little bit of illicit nip and tuck with your future husband, even if he is a pauper, sits pretty lightly on the conscience."

• • •

Craig picked Sally-Anne up from the hospital the following morning. She wore the same jeans, shirt and trainers as she had when she was admitted.

"Sister had them washed and mended—" She stopped as she saw the Land-Rover. "What's this? I thought we were broke."

"The computer hasn't had the happy news yet. They are still honouring my American Express card."

"Is that kosher?"

"When you owe five big Ms, lady, another couple of hundred bucks sits pretty lightly on the conscience." He grinned at her as he turned the ignition key, and when the engine fired, said cheerfully, "Eat your heart out, Mr. Hertz."

"You're taking it very well, Craig." She slid across the seat to him.

"We are both alive—that is cause for fireworks and general rejoicing. As for the money—well, I don't think I was truly cut out to be a millionaire. When I've got money I spend all my time worrying about losing it. It saps my energy. Now that I've lost it, I feel free again in a funny sort of way."

"You're happy to have lost everything you ever owned?" She

turned sideways in the seat to look at him. "Even for you, that's cuckoo!"

"I'm not happy, no," he denied the charge. "What I truly regret is losing King's Lynn and Zambezi Waters. We could have made something wonderful out of them, you and I. I regret that very much—and I regret Tungata Zebiwe."

"Yes. We destroyed him." Both of them were sobered and saddened. "If there was only something we could do for him."

"Not a damned thing." Craig shook his head. "Despite Timon's assurances, we don't know that he is still alive, and even if he is, we don't have the faintest idea where he is, or how to find him."

They rattled across the railway lines and into the main street of Francistown.

"'Jewel of the north,'" said Craig. "Population two thousand, main industry consumption of alcoholic beverage, reason for existing uncertain."

He parked outside the single hotel. "As you can see, total population now in permanent residence in the public bar."

However, the young Botswana receptionist was pretty and efficient.

"Mr. Mellow, there is a lady waiting to see you," she called, as Craig entered the lobby. Craig did not recognize his visitor, not until Sally-Anne ran forward to embrace her.

"Sarah!" she cried. "How did you get here? How did you find us?"

Craig's room had two single beds with a dressing table between them, a threadbare imitation Persian rug on the shiny red-painted cement floor and a single wooden chair. The two girls sat on one bed, with their legs curled up under them in that double-jointed feminine attitude.

"They told me at the Red Cross that you had been found in the desert and brought in by the police, Miss Jay."

"My name is Sally-Anne, Sarah."

Sarah smiled softly in acknowledgement. "I wasn't sure if you would want to see me again, not after the trial. But then my friends here told me how you had been ill-treated by Fungabera's soldiers. I thought you might have realized that I was right all along, that Tungata Zebiwe was not a criminal, and that he needs friends now."

She turned towards Craig. "He was your friend, Mr. Mellow. He told me about you. He spoke of you with respect and great

298

feeling. He was afraid for you, when he heard that you had returned to Zimbabwe. He realized that you wanted to take up your family land in Matabeleland, and he knew there were going to be terrible troubles and that you would be caught up in them. He said that you were too gentle for the hard times that were coming. He called you 'Pupho,' the dreamer, the gentle dreamer, but he said that you were also stubborn and obstinate. He wanted to save you from being hurt again. He said, 'Last time he lost his leg—this time he could lose his life. To be his friend, I must make myself his enemy. I must drive him out of Zimbabwe.'"

Craig sat in the straight-backed wooden chair and remembered his stormy meeting with Tungata when he had come to him for assistance in acquiring King's Lynn. Had it been an act, then? Even now he found that hard to believe. Tungata's passion had been so real, his fury so convincing.

"I am sorry, Mr. Mellow. These are very rude things that I am saying about you. I am telling you only what Tungata said. He was your friend. He still is your friend."

"It doesn't really matter any more, what he thought of me," Craig murmured. "Sam is probably dead by now."

"No!" For the first time Sarah raised her voice, her tone vehement, almost angry. "No, do not say that, never say that! He is alive. I have seen and spoken to him. They can never kill a man like that!"

The chair creaked under Craig as he leaned forward eagerly. "You have seen him? When?"

"Two weeks ago."

"Where? Where was he?"

"Tuti—at the camp."

"Sam alive!" Craig changed as he said it. The despondent slump of his shoulders squared out, he held his head at a more alert angle and his eyes were brighter, more eager. He wasn't really looking at Sarah. He was looking at the wall above her head, trying to marshal the torrent of emotions and ideas that came at him, so he did not see that Sarah was weeping.

It was Sally-Anne who put a protective and comforting arm about her, and Sarah sobbed. "Oh, my lord Tungata. The things they have done to him. They have starved and beaten him. He is like a village cur, all bones and scars. He walks like a very old man. Only his eyes are still proud."

Sally-Anne hugged her wordlessly. Craig jumped up from the

chair and began to pace. The room was so small, he crossed it in four strides, turned and came back. Sally-Anne dug in her pocket and found a crumpled tissue for Sarah.

"When will the Cessna be ready?" Craig asked, without pausing in his stride. His artificial leg made a tiny click each time he swung it forward.

"It's been ready since last week. I told you, didn't I?" Sally-Anne replied distractedly, fussing over Sarah.

"What is her all-up capacity?"

"The Cessna? I've had six adults in her, but that was a squeeze. She's licensed for—" Sally-Anne stopped. Slowly her head turned from Sarah towards him and she stared at him in total disbelief.

"In the love of all that's holy, Craig, are you out of your mind?"

Craig ignored the question. "Range fully loaded?"

"Twelve hundred nautical miles, throttle setting for maximum endurance—but you can't be serious."

"Okay." Craig was thinking aloud. "I can get a couple of drums in the Land-Rover. You can land and refuel on a pan right on the border—I know a spot near Panda Matenga, five hundred kilometres north of here. That is the closest point of entry—"

"Craig, do you know what they'd do if they caught us?" Sally-Anne's voice was husky with shock.

Sarah had the tissue over her nose, but her eyes swivelled between the two of them as they spoke.

"Weapons," Craig muttered. "We'd need arms. Morgan Oxford? No, damn it, he's written us off."

"Guns?" Sarah's voice was muffled by tears and tissue.

"Guns and grenades," Craig agreed. "Explosives, whatever we can get."

"I can get guns. Some of our people have escaped. They are here in Botswana. They had guns hidden in the bush from the war."

"What kind?" Craig demanded.

"Banana guns and hand grenades."

"AKs." Craig rejoiced. "Sarah, you are a star."

"Just the two of us?" Sally-Anne paled as she realized that he truly meant it. "Two of us, against the entire Third Brigade—is that what you are thinking about?"

"No, I'm coming with you." Sarah put aside the tissue. "There will be three of us."

"Three of us, great!" said Sally-Anne. "Three of us—marvellous!"

Craig came back and stood in front of them.

"Number one: we are going to draw up a map of Tuti camp. We are going to put down every detail we can remember."

He started pacing again, unable to stand still.

"Number two: we meet with Sarah's friends and see how much help they can give us. Number three: Sally-Anne takes the commercial flight down to Johannesburg and brings back the Cessna— how long will that take?"

"I can be back in three days." Colour was coming back into Sally-Anne's cheeks. "That's if I decide to go!"

"Okay! Fine!" Craig rubbed his hands together. "Now we can start on the map."

Craig ordered sandwiches and a bottle of wine sent to the room and they worked through until 2 A.M., when Sarah left them with a promise to return at breakfast time. Craig folded the map carefully and then he and Sally-Anne climbed into one of the narrow beds together, but they were so keyed up that neither of them could sleep.

"Sam was trying to protect me," Craig marvelled. "He was doing it for me, all along."

"Tell me about him," Sally-Anne whispered and she lay against his chest and listened to him talk of their friendship. When at last he fell silent, she asked softly, "So you are serious about this thing?"

"Deadly serious, but will you do it with me?"

"It's crazy," she said. "It's plain dumb. But let's do it then."

• • •

The sooty black smoke from the beacon fires of oily rags that Craig had set climbed straight up in two columns into the clear desert sky. Craig and Sarah stood together on the hood of the Land-Rover, staring into the south. This was the dry wild land of north-eastern Botswana. The Zimbabwe border was thirty kilometres east of them, the flat arid plain between pimpled with camel-thorn trees and blotched with the leprous white salt-pans.

The mirage shimmered and tricked the eye so that the stunted trees on the far side of the pan seemed to swim and change shape like amoeba under a microscope. A spinning dust devil jumped

301

up from the white pan surface and swirled and swayed sinuously as a belly dancer, rising two hundred feet into the hot air until it collapsed again as suddenly as it had risen.

The sound of the Cessna engine rose and fell and rose again on the heat-flawed air. "There!" Sarah pointed out the mosquito speck, low on the horizon.

Craig made a last anxious appraisal of his makeshift landing-strip. He had lit the beacon fires at each end of it as soon as they had picked up the first throb of the Cessna's motor. He had driven the Land-Rover back and forth between the beacons to mark the hard crust at the edge of the pan. Fifty metres out, the surface was treacherously soft.

Now he looked back at the approaching aircraft. Sally-Anne was banking low over the baobab trees, lining up with the strip he had set out for her. She made a prudent precautionary pass along it, her head twisted in the cockpit window as she examined it, then she came around again and touched down lightly, and taxied towards the Land-Rover.

"You were gone for ever." Craig seized her as she jumped down from the cockpit.

"Three days," she protested with her feet off the ground.

"That's for ever," he said and kissed her.

He set her down but kept one arm around her as he led her to the Land-Rover. After she had greeted Sarah, Craig introduced her to the two Matabele who were squatting in the shade of the Land-Rover.

They rose courteously to meet her.

"This is Jonas, and this is Aaron. They led us to the arms cache and they are giving us all the help they can."

They were reserved and unsmiling young men with old eyes that had seen unspeakable things, but they were willing and quick.

They pumped the Avgas from the forty-four gallon drums on the back of the Land-Rover directly into the Cessna's wing-tanks, while Craig stripped out the seats from the rear of the cockpit to reduce weight and give them cargo space.

Then they began loading. Sally-Anne weighed each item of cargo on the spring balance that she had brought for the purpose and entered it on her loading table. The ammunition was the heaviest part of the load. They had eight thousand rounds of 7.62 mm ball Ps. Craig had repacked it in black plastic garbage-bags to save weight and space. It had been buried for years and many of the rounds were so corroded as to be useless. However, Craig had hand-sorted it, and test-fired a few rounds from each case without a single misfire.

Most of the rifles had also been corroded and Craig had worked through the nights by gas lantern, stripping and cannabalizing until he had twenty-five good weapons. There were also five Tokarev pistols and two cases of fragmentation grenades which seemed in better condition than the rifles. Craig had set off one grenade from each case, popping them down an ant-bear hole to a satisfactory crump and cloud of dust. That had left forty-eight from the original fifty. Craig packed them in five cheap canvas haversacks that he had bought from a general dealer in Francistown.

The rest of the equipment he had also purchased there. Wire-cutters and bolt-cutters, nylon rope, pangas that Jonas and Aaron sharpened to razor edges, flashlights and extra batteries, canteens and water-bottles and a dozen or so other items which might prove useful. Sarah had been appointed medical orderly and had made up a first-aid kit with items purchased at the Francistown pharmacy. The food rations were spartan—raw maize meal packed in five-kilo plastic bags, the best nourishment-to-weight ratio available, and a few bags of coarse salt.

"Okay, that's it," Sally-Anne called a halt to the loading. "Another ounce and we won't get off the ground. The rest of it will have to wait for the second trip."

When darkness fell, they sat round the camp-fire and gorged on the steaks and fresh fruit that Sally-Anne had brought with her from Johannesburg.

"Eat hearty, my children," she encouraged them. "It could be a long time."

Afterwards Craig and Sally-Anne carried their blankets away from the fire, out of earshot of the others, and they lay naked in the warm desert air and made love under the silver sickle of the moon, both of them poignantly aware that it might be for the last time.

They ate breakfast in the dark, after the moon had set and before the first glimmering of the dawn. They left Jonas and Aaron to guard the Land-Rover and help with loading and refuelling for the second trip and Sally-Anne taxied out to the end of the strip when it was just light enough to make out the tracks.

Even in the cool of night it took the overloaded Cessna forever to unstick, and they climbed away slowly towards the glow of the sunrise.

"Zimbabwe border," Sally-Anne murmured. "And I still can't believe what we are doing."

Craig was perched up beside her on the bags of ammunition, while Sarah was curled up like a salted anchovy on top of the load behind them.

Sally-Anne banked slightly as she picked up her landmarks from the map on her lap. She had laid out a course to cross the railway line fifteen miles south of the coal-mining town of Wankie, and then to cross the main road a few miles beyond, avoiding all human habitation. The terrain below them changed swiftly, the desert falling away and becoming densely forested with open glades of golden grass. There were some high fair-weather cumulus clouds in the north, otherwise the sky was clear. Craig squinted ahead down the track of the rising sun.

"There is the railway."

Sally-Anne closed the throttle and they descended sharply. Fifty feet above the tree-tops they roared over the deserted railway tracks and minutes later crossed the main road. They had a glimpse of a truck crawling along the blue-grey tarmac ribbon, but crossed behind it and were visible to it for only seconds. Sally-Anne pulled a face.

"Let's hope they make nothing of us—there must be quite a lot of light aircraft traffic around here." She glanced at her wrist-watch. "Expected time of arrival, forty minutes."

"All right," Craig said. "Let's go over it one more time. You drop Sarah and me, then clear out again as quickly as possible. Back to the pan. Reload and refuel. Two days from now you come back. If there is a smoke-signal, you land. No signal and you head back to the pan. Give it two more days and then the last trip. If there is no smoke-signal on the second trip, that's it. You head out and don't come back."

She reached out and took his hand. "Craig, don't even say it. Please, darling, come back to me."

They held hands for the rest of the trip, except for the brief moments when she needed both for the controls.

"There it is!"

The Chizarira River was a green python across the vast brown land, and there was a glint of water through the trees.

"Zambezi Waters—just up there."

They were keeping well clear of the camps that they had built with so much loving labour, but both of them stared longingly upstream to where the dreaming blue hills studded the line of the horizon.

Sally-Anne dropped lower and still lower until she was shaving the tree-tops, and then she turned slowly back in a wide circle, keeping the hills between them and the buildings on Zambezi Waters.

"There it is," Craig called, and pointed out under the port wing-tip, and they had a glimpse of white beads at the edge of the trees.

"They are still there!" The bones of Craig's poached rhinoceros had been picked over by the scavengers and bleached by the sun.

Sally-Anne ran her landing-check and then lined up for the narrow strip of grassland along the head of the gorge where she had landed before.

"Just pray the wart-hog and ant-bear haven't been digging around," she murmured, and the overloaded Cessna wallowed sluggishly and the stall warning bleeped and flashed intermittently at the reduced-power setting.

Sally-Anne dropped in steeply over the tree-tops and touched down with a jarring thud. The Cessna pitched and bounced over the rough ground, but maximum safe braking and the coarse grass wrapping the undercarriage pulled them up quickly, and Sally-Anne let out her breath.

"Thank you, Lord."

They off-loaded with frenzied haste, piling everything in a heap and spreading over it the green nylon nets designed for shading young plants from the sun that Craig had found in Francistown.

Then Sally-Anne and Craig looked at each other miserably.

"Oh God, I hate this," she said.

"Me too—so go! Go quickly, damn it."

They kissed and she broke away and ran back to the cockpit. She taxied to the end of the clearing, flattening the grass, and then came back at full throttle in her own tracks. The lightened aircraft leaped into the air, and the last he saw of her was her face in the side-window turning back towards him, and then the tree-tops cut them off from each other.

Craig waited until the last vibration of the engine died away and the silence of the bush closed in again. Then he picked up the rifle and haversack and slung them over his shoulders. He looked at Sarah. She wore denims and blue canvas shoes. She carried the food-bag and water-bottles, with a Tokarev holstered on her belt.

"Ready?"

She nodded, fell in behind him, and stayed with the forcing pace he set. They reached the kopje in the early part of the afternoon, and from the summit Craig looked towards the camps of Zambezi Waters on the river.

This would be the dangerous part now, but he lit the signal-fire and then, taking Sarah with him, moved out and set up an ambush on the approach path, just in case the smoke-signal brought unwanted visitors.

He and Sarah lay up in good cover, and neither of them moved or spoke for three hours. Only their eyes were busy, sweeping the slopes below and above and the bush all around.

Even so, they were taken unawares. The voice was a harsh, raw whisper in Sindebele, close—very close by.

"Ha! Kuphela. So you have brought my money." Comrade Lookout's scarred visage peered at them. He had crept up to within ten paces without alerting them. "I thought you had forgotten us."

"No money for you—but hard and dangerous work," Craig told him.

•   •   •

There were three men with Lookout, lean, wolflike men. They extinguished the signal-fire and then spread back into the bush in an extended scouting order that would cover their march.

"We must go," Comrade Lookout explained. "Here in the open the Shona *kanka* press us like hunting-dogs. Since we last met, we have lost many good men. Comrade Dollar has been taken by them."

"Yes." Craig remembered him, beaten and bedraggled, giving evidence against him on that terrible night at King's Lynn.

They marched until two hours after darkness, northwards into the bad and broken land along the escarpment of the great river. The way was cleared for them and guarded by the scouts who were always invisible in the forest ahead. Only their bird-calls guided and reassured them.

They came at last to the guerrilla camp. There were women at the small smokeless cooking-fires and one of them ran to embrace Sarah as soon as she recognized her.

"She is my aunt's youngest daughter," Sarah explained. She and Craig spoke only Sindebele to each other now.

The camp was an uncomfortable and joyless place, a series of rude caves, hacked out of the steep bank of a dried watercourse and screened by the overhang of the trees. It had a temporary air about it. There were no luxuries and no items of equipment that could not be packed within minutes and carried on a man's back. The guerrilla women were as unsmiling as their men.

"We do not stay at one place," Comrade Lookout explained. "The *kanka* see the signs from the air if we do. Even though we never walk the same way, not even to the latrines, in a short time our feet form pathways and that is what they look for. We must move again soon."

The women brought them food and Craig realized how hungry and tired he was, but before he ate he opened his pack and gave them the cartons of cigarettes he had carried in. For the first time he saw these embittered men smile as they passed a single butt around the circle.

"How many men in your group?"

"Twenty-six." Comrade Lookout puffed on the cigarette and passed it on. "But there is another group nearby."

Twenty-six, Craig brooded. If they could exploit the element of surprise, it would be just enough.

They ate with their fingers from the communal pot and then Comrade Lookout allowed them to share another cigarette.

"Now, Kuphela, you said you had work for us."

"The Comrade Minister Tungata Zebiwe is the prisoner of the Shona."

"This is a terrible thing. It is a stab in the heart of the Matabele people—but even here in the bush we have known of this for many months. Did you come to tell us something that all the world knows?"

"They are holding him alive at Tuti."

"Tuti. Hau!" Comrade Lookout exclaimed violently and every man spoke at once.

"How do you know this?"

"We heard he was killed—"

"This is old women's talk—"

Craig called across to where the women sat apart.

"Sarah!" She came to them.

"You know this woman?" Craig asked.

"She is my wife's cousin."

"She is the teacher at the mission."

"She is one of us."

"Tell them," Craig ordered her.

They listened in attentive silence while Sarah related her last meeting with Tungata, their eyes glittering in the firelight, and when she had finished, they were silent. Sarah rose quietly and went back to the other women, and Comrade Lookout turned to one of his men.

"Speak!" he invited.

The one chosen to give his opinion first was the youngest, the most junior. The others would speak in their ascending order of seniority. It was the ancient order of council and it would take time. Craig composed himself to patience; this was the tempo of Africa.

After midnight Comrade Lookout summed up for them. "We know the woman. She is trustworthy and we believe what she tells us. Comrade Tungata is our father. His blood is the blood of kings, and the stinking Shona hold him. On this we are all agreed." He paused. "But there are some who would try to wrest him from the Shona child-rapers, and others who say we are too few, and that we have only one rifle between two men, and only five bullets for each rifle. So we are divided." He looked at Craig. "What do you say, Kuphela?"

"I say that I have brought you eight thousand rounds of ammunition and twenty-five rifles and fifty grenades," said Craig. "I say that comrade Tungata is my friend and my brother. I say that if there are only women and cowards here and no men to go with me, then I will go alone with this woman, Sarah, who has the heart of a warrior, and I will find men somewhere else."

Comrade Lookout's face puckered up with affront, pulled out of true by the scar, and his tone was reproachful.

"Let there be no more talk of women and cowards, Kuphela. Let there be no more talking at all. Let us rather go to Tuti and do this thing that must be done. That is what I say."

•   •   •

They lit the smoke-signal as soon as they heard the Cessna and extinguished it as soon as Sally-Anne flashed her landing-lights to acknowledge. Comrade Lookout's guerrillas had cut the grass

308

in the clearing with pangas and filled in the holes and rough spots, so Sally-Anne's landing was confident and neat.

The guerrillas unloaded the rest of the ammunition and the weapons in disciplined silence, but they could not conceal their grins of delight as they handed down the bags of ammunition and the haversacks of grenades, for these were the tools of their trade. The loads disappeared swiftly into the forest. Within fifteen minutes Craig and Sally-Anne were left alone under the wing of the empty Cessna.

"Do you know what I prayed for?" Sally-Anne asked. "I prayed that you wouldn't be able to find the gang, and if you did, that they would refuse to go with you, and that you had been forced to abort and had to come back with me."

"You aren't very good at praying, are you?"

"I don't know. I'm going to get in a lot of practice in the next few days."

"Five days," Craig corrected her. "You come in again on Tuesday morning."

She nodded. "Yes. I will take-off in the dark and be over Tuti airfield at sunrise—that's at 0522 hours."

"But you are not to land until I signal that we have secured the strip. Now, for the love of God, don't run yourself short on fuel to get back to the pan. If we don't show up, don't stay on hoping."

"I will have three hours' safe endurance overhead Tuti. That means you will have until 0830 hours to get there."

"If we don't make it by then, we aren't going to make it. It's time for you to go now, my love."

"I know," Sally-Anne said, and made no move.

"I have to go," he said.

"I don't know how I'm going to live through the next few days, sitting out there in the desert, not knowing a thing, just living with my fears and imagination."

He took her in his arms and found she was trembling.

"I'm so very afraid for you," she whispered against his throat.

"See you Tuesday morning," he told her. "Without fail."

"Without fail!" she agreed, and then her voice quavered. "Come back to me, Craig. I don't want to live without you. Promise me you'll come back."

"I promise." He kissed her.

"There now, I feel much better." She gave him that cheeky grin of hers, but it was all soft around the edges.

She climbed up into the cockpit and started the engine.

"I love you." Her lips formed the words that the engine drowned, and she swung the Cessna round with a burst of throttle and did not look back.

* * *

It was only sixty miles on the map and from the front seat of an aircraft it had not looked like hard-going. On the ground it was different.

They were crossing the grain of the land. The watershed dropped away from their right to their left, towards the escarpment of the Zambezi valley. They were forced to follow the switchback of hills and the intervening valleys so they were never on level ground.

The guerrillas had hidden their own women in a safe place and only reluctantly consented to Sarah's accompanying the raiding party, but she carried a full load and kept up with the hard pace that Comrade Lookout set for them.

The ironstone hills soaked up the heat of the sun and bounced it back at them as they toiled up the steep hillsides and dropped again into the next valley. The descents were as taxing as the climbs, and heavy loads jarring their spines and straining the backs of their legs and their Achilles tendons. The old elephant trails that they were following were littered with round pebbles washed out by the rains that rolled underfoot like ball-bearings and made each pace fraught with danger.

One of the guerrillas fell, and his ankle swelled so that they could not get his boot back on his foot. They distributed his load among them and left him to find his own way back to where they had left the women.

The tiny mopani bees plagued them during the day, clouding around their mouths and nostrils and eyes in their persistent search for moisture, and in the nights the mosquitoes from the stagnant pools in the valleys took over. At one stage of the trek they passed through the edge of the fly-belt, and the silent, light-footed tsetse-flies joined the torment, settling so softly that the victim was unaware until a red-hot needle stabbed into the soft flesh at the back of the ear or under the armpit.

Always there was danger of attack. Every few miles either the scouts out ahead or the rearguard dragging the trail behind them would signal an alert, and they would be forced to dive into cover and wait with fingers on triggers until the all-clear signal was passed down the line.

It was slow and gruelling and nerve-racking—two full days' marching from freezing dawn through burning noon into night again—to reach Sarah's father's village. Vusamanzi was his name and he was a senior magician, soothsayer and rain-maker of the Matabele tribe. Like all his kind, he lived in isolation, with only his wives and immediate family around him. However great their respect for them, ordinary mortals avoided the practitioners of the dark arts; they came to them only for divination or treatment, paid the goat or beast that was the fee, and hurried thankfully away again.

Vusamanzi's village was some miles north of Tuti Mission Station. It was a prosperous little community on a hilltop, with many wives and goats and chickens and fields of maize in the valley.

The guerrillas lay up in the forest below the kopje, and they sent Sarah in to make certain all was safe and to warn the villagers of their presence. Sarah returned within an hour, and Craig and Comrade Lookout went back to the village with her.

Vusamanzi had earned his name, "Raise the Waters," from his reputed ability to control the Zambezi and its tributaries. As a much younger man he had sent a great flood to wash away the village of a lesser chief who had cheated him of his fees, and since then a number of others who had displeased him had drowned mysteriously at fords or bathing-holes. It was said that at Vusamanzi's behest the surface of a quiet pool would leap up suddenly in a hissing wave as the marked victim approached to drink or bathe or cross, and he would be sucked in. No living man had actually witnessed this terrible phenomenon—nevertheless, Vusamanzi, the magician, did not have much trouble with bad debts from his patients and clients.

Vusamanzi's hair was a cap of pure white and he wore a small beard, also white, dressed out to a spade shape in the fashion of the Zulus. Sarah must have been a child of his old age, but she had inherited her fine looks from him, for he was handsome and dignified. He had put aside his regalia. He wore only a simple loincloth and his body was straight and lean, and his voice, when he greeted Craig courteously, was deep and steady.

Clearly Sarah revered him, for she took the beer-pot from one

311

of his junior wives and knelt to offer it to him herself. In her turn, Sarah obviously had a special place in the old man's affections, for he smiled at her fondly, and when she sat at his feet, he fondled her head casually as he listened attentively to what Craig had to tell him. Then he sent her to help his wives to prepare food and beer and take it down to the guerrillas hidden in the valley before he turned back to Craig.

"The man you call Tungata Zebiwe, the Seeker after Justice, was born Samson Kumalo. He is in direct line of succession from Mzilikazi, the first king and father of our people. He is the one upon whom the prophecies of the ancients descend. On the night he was taken by the Shona soldiers, I had sent for him to appraise him of his responsibility and to make him privy to the secrets of the kings. If he is still alive, as my daughter tells us he is, then it is the duty of every Matabele to do all in his power to seek his freedom. The future of our people rests with him. How can I assist you? You have only to ask."

"You have already helped us with food," Craig said and thanked him. "Now we need information."

"Ask, Kuphela. Anything that I can tell you, I will."

"The road between Tuti Mission and the camp of the soldiers passes close to this place. Is that correct?"

The old man pointed. "Beyond those hills."

"Sarah tells me that every week the trucks come along this road on the same day, taking food to the soldiers and the prisoners at the camp."

"That is so. Every week, on the Monday late in the afternoon, the trucks pass here loaded with bags of maize and other stores. They return empty the following morning."

"How many trucks?"

"Two or, rarely, three."

"How many soldiers to guard them?"

"Two in front beside the driver, three or four more in the back. One stands on the roof with a big gun that shoots fast." A heavy-machine-gun, Craig translated for himself. "The soldiers are very watchful and alert and the trucks drive fast."

"They came last Monday, as usual?" Craig asked.

"As usual." Vusamanzi nodded his cap of shiny white wool. He must believe then that the routine was still in operation, Craig decided, and bet everything on it.

"How far is it to the mission station from here?" he asked.

"From there to there." The witch-doctor swept his arm through a segment of the sky, about four hours of the sun's passage. Reckoned as the pace of a man on foot, that was approximately fifteen miles.

"And from here to the camp of the soldiers?" Craig went on.

Vusamanzi shrugged. "The same distance."

"Good." Craig unrolled his map. They were equidistant between the two points; that gave him a fairly accurate fix. He began calculating times and distances and scribbling them in the margin of the map.

Craig looked up at last. "We have a day to wait. The men will rest and ready themselves."

"My women will feed them," Vusamanzi agreed.

"Then on Monday I will need some of your people to help me."

"There are only women here," the old man demurred.

"I need women—young women, comely women," Craig told him.

•   •   •

The next morning, leaving before dawn, Craig and Comrade Lookout, taking a runner with them, reconnoitred the stretch of road that lay just beyond the line of low hills. It was as Craig remembered it, a crude track into which heavy trucks had ground deep ruts, but the Third brigade had cleared the brush on both sides to reduce the risk of ambush.

A little before noon they reached the spot where Peter Fungabera had stopped during their first drive to Tuti, the causeway where the road crossed the timber bridge across the green river, and where they had eaten that lunch of baked maize cobs.

Craig found that his memory was accurate. The approaches to the bridge, first down the steep slope of the valley and then across the narrow earthen causeway, must force the supply convoy to slow down and engage low gear. It was the perfect spot for an ambush, and Craig sent the runner back to Vusamanzi's village to bring up the rest of the force. While they waited, Craig and Comrade Lookout went over their plans and adapted them to the actual terrain.

The main attack would take place at the bridge, but if that failed, they must have a back-up plan to prevent the convoy's getting through. As soon as the main force of guerrillas arrived,

Craig sent Comrade Lookout with five men along the road beyond the bridge. Out of sight from the bridge, they felled a large mhoba-hoba tree so that it fell across the track, as an effective road-block. Comrade Lookout would command here, while Craig coordinated the attack at the bridge.

"Which are the men who speak Shona?" Craig demanded.

"This one speaks it like a Shona, this one not as well."

"They are to be kept out of any fighting. We cannot risk losing them," Craig ordered. "We will need them for the camp."

"I will hold them in my hand," Comrade Lookout agreed.

"Now the women."

Sarah had chosen three of her half-sisters from the villag∍, ranging in age from sixteen to eighteen years.

They were the prettiest of the old witch-doctor's multitudinous daughters, and when Craig explained their role to them, they giggled and hung their heads, and covered their mouths with their hands and went through all the other motions of modesty and maidenly shyness. But they were obviously relishing the adventure hugely; nothing so exciting and titillating had happened to them in all their young lives.

"Do they understand?" Craig asked Sarah. "It will be danger-ous—they must do exactly as they are told."

"I will be with them," Sarah assured him. "All the time—tonight as well, especially tonight." This last was for the benefit of the girls; Sarah had been fully aware of mutual ogling between her sisters and the young guerrillas. She shooed them away, still giggling, to the rough shelter of thorn branches that she had made them build for themselves, and settled herself across the entrance.

"The thorns are sharp enough to keep out a man-eating lion, Kuphela," she had told Craig, "but I do not know about a buck with an itchy spear and a maid determined to scratch it for him. I will have little sleep tonight."

In the end, Craig spent a sleepless night as well. He had the dreams again, those terrible dreams that had almost driven him mad during his long, slow convalescence from the minefield and the loss of his leg. He was trapped in them, unable to escape back into consciousness, until Sarah shook him awake, and when he came awake, he was shaking so violently that his teeth chattered and sweat had soaked his shirt as though he had stood under a warm shower.

Sarah understood. Compassionately she sat beside him and held his hand until the tremors stilled, and then they talked the night away, keeping their voices to a whisper so as not to disturb the camp. They talked of Tungata and Sally-Anne, and what each of them wanted from life and their chances of getting it.

"When I am married to the Comrade Minister, I will be able to speak for all the women of Matabele. Too long they have been treated like chattels by their men. Even now I, a trained nursing sister and teacher, must eat at the women's fire. After this, there will be another campaign to wage. A fight to win for the women of my tribe their rightful place and to have their true worth recognized."

Craig found his respect for Sarah beginning to match his liking. She was, he realized, a fitting woman for a man like Tungata Zebiwe. While they talked, he managed to subdue his fear for the morrow, and the night passed so swiftly that he was surprised when he checked his wristwatch.

"Four o'clock. Time to move," he whispered. "Thank you, Sarah. I am not a brave man. I needed your help."

She rose to her feet with a lithe movement and for a moment stood looking down at him. "You do yourself injustice. I think you are a very brave man," she said softly and went to rouse her sisters.

• • •

The sun was high, and Craig lay in the cleft between two black water-polished boulders on the far bank of the stream. The AK 47 was propped in front of him, covering the causeway and the far banks on each side of the timber bridge. He had paced out the ranges. It was one hundred and twenty yards from where he lay to the end of the handrail. Off a dead rest, he could throw in a six-inch group at that range.

"Please let it not be necessary," he thought, and once more ran a restless eye over his stake-out. There were four guerrillas under the bridge, stripped to the waist. Although their rifles were propped against the bridge supports close at hand, they were armed with the five-foot elephant bows. Craig had been dubious of these weapons until he had watched a demonstration. The bows were of hard, elastic wood, bound with strips of green kudu hide which had been allowed to dry and shrink on the shaft until they were hard as iron. The bowstring was of braided sinew, almost as tough as monofilament nylon. Even with all his strength, Craig had been

315

unable to draw one of the bows to his full reach. The pull must have been well over one hundred pounds. To draw it required calloused fingertips and specially developed muscle in chest and arm.

The arrowheads were barbless mild steel, honed to a needle-point for penetration, and one of the guerrillas had stood off thirty paces and sunk one of these arrows twenty inches into the fleshy fibrous trunk of a baobab tree. They had been forced to cut it free with an axe. The same arrow would have flown right through an adult human being, from breast to backbone with hardly a check, or pierced the chest cavity of a full-grown bull elephant from side to side.

So there were now four bowmen under the bridge, and ten other men crouching in knee-deep water below the bank. Only the tops of their heads showed, and they were screened from anyone on the far side by the sharp drop-off of the bank and the growth of fluffy-topped reeds.

The engine beat of the approaching trucks altered as they changed gear on the up-slope before cresting and dropping down this side to the causeway and the bridge. Craig had walked down that slope himself looking for give-away signs, all his old training in the Rhodesian police coming back to him, looking for litter or disturbed vegetation, for the shine of metal, for footprints on the white sandbanks of the river or the verge of the road, and he had found no give-away signs.

"We must do it now," said Sarah. She and her sisters were squatting behind the rock at his side. She was right—it was too late to alter anything, to make any other arrangements. They were committed.

"Go," he told her and she stood up and let the denim shirt slip off her shoulders and drop to the sand. Quickly her younger sisters followed her example, letting drop their loincloths as they stood.

All four of them were naked, except for the tiny beaded aprons suspended from their waists by a string of beads. The aprons hung down over their *mons pubis* but bounced up revealingly with every movement as they ran to the water's edge. Their plump young buttocks were bared, swelling enticingly below the hourglass nip of their waists.

"Laugh!" Craig called after them. "Play games."

They were totally unashamed of their nudity. In the rural areas the beaded apron was still the traditional casual dress of the unsophisticated unmarried Matabele girl. Even Sarah had worn it until she had gone in to the town to begin her schooling.

They splashed each other. The water sparkled on their glossy dark skins, and their laughter had an excited, breathless quality that must attract any man. Yet, Craig saw that his guerrillas were unaffected. They had not even turned their heads to watch. They were professionals at work, all their attention focused on the dangerous job in hand.

The lead truck crested the far rise. It was a five-ton Toyota, similar to the one that had pursued them across the Botswana border. It was painted the same sandy colour. There was a trooper behind the ring-mounted heavy-machine-gun on the cab. A second truck, heavily laden and armed, came over the rise behind it.

"Not a third. Please, only two," Craig breathed, and cuddled the butt of the AK 47 into his shoulder. The barrel was festooned with dried grass to disguise its shape, and his own face and hands were thickly smeared with black clay from the river-bank.

There were only two trucks. They came trundling out onto the causeway and Sarah and her sisters stood knee-deep in the green waters below the handrail of the bridge and waved to them. The lead truck slowed, and the girls swung their hips, shrieked with provocative laughter and joggled their wet and shiny breasts.

There were two men in the cab of the lead truck. One was a subaltern, Craig could make out his cap-badge and the glitter of his shoulder pips even through the dusty windscreen. He was grinning and his teeth were almost as bright as his badges. He spoke to the driver and, with a squeal of brakes, the lead truck pulled up on the threshold of the bridge. The second truck was forced to pull up behind it.

The young officer opened the door and stood on the running-board. The troopers in the back of the truck and the heavy-machine-gunner craned forward, grinning and calling ribald comment. The girls, following Sarah's example, sank down coyly to cover their lower bodies and answered the suggestions and comments with dissembling coyness. Some of the troopers in the second truck, not to be outdone, jumped down and came forward to join the fun.

One of the older girls made a slyly obscene gesture with thumb and forefinger and there was an appreciative bellow of raunchy masculine laughter from the bank. The young officer replied with an even more specific gesture, and the rest of his troopers left the trucks and crowded up behind him. Only the two heavy-machine-gunners were still at their posts.

Craig darted a glance at the under-side of the bridge. On their bellies the bowmen were wriggling up the far side of the bank, keeping the timber balks of the bridge between them and the bunch of troopers.

In the river Sarah stood up. She had loosened the string of her apron and now carried the minuscule garment in her hand, swinging it with artful provocation. She waded towards the men on the bank, with the water swirling around her thighs, and the laughter choked off as they stared at her. She walked slowly, the pull of water exaggerating the churning movement of her pelvis. She was as sleek and beautiful as a wet otter, the sunlight on her body gave it a plastic sheen, an unearthly glow, and even from where he lay, Craig could feel the jocular mood of the men watching her thicken with lust and begin to steam with the stirring of sexual fury.

Sarah paused below them, cupped her hands under her breasts and lifted them, pointing her nipples up at them. Now they were totally concentrated upon her; even the machine-gunners high up on the ring mounts of the trucks were rapt and enchanted.

Behind them the four bowmen had slid up under the lee of the causeway. They were not more than ten paces from the side of the leading truck as they came up onto their knees in unison and drew. The bows arched, their right hands came back to touch their lips, wet muscle bulged in their backs as they sighted along the shafts, and then one after the other they let their arrows fly.

There was no sound, not even the softest fluting, but one of the machine-gunners slid gently forward and hung over the side of the cab with head and arms dangling. The other arched his back, his mouth wide open but no sound coming from it, and tried to reach back over his own shoulder to the shaft that stood stiffly out between his shoulder-blades. Another arrow hit him, a hands-breadth lower, and he convulsed in agony and dropped from view.

The bowmen changed their target and the silent arrows flew into the bunch of troopers on the river-bank — and a man screamed. In the same instant the guerrillas hiding below the bank burst from the water, and went up through the reeds, just as the troopers whirled to face the bowmen. The naked guerrillas took them from behind, and this time Craig heard the explosive grunts as they swung the long-bladed pangas, each like a tennis-player hitting a hard forehand volley. A panga blade cleaved through the subaltern's burgundy-red beret and split his skull to the chin.

Sarah whirled and raced back, gathering the other girls. One of the younger ones was screaming as they floundered over the submerged sandbanks.

There was a single shot, and then all the troopers were down, scattered along the edge of the bank, but the guerrillas were still working over them, swinging and chopping and hacking.

"Sarah," Craig called to her as she reached the bank, "get the girls back into the bush!" She snatched up her shirt and pushed her sisters ahead, shepherding them away.

Carrying the AK, Craig ran across the bridge. The guerrillas were already stripping and looting the dead men. They worked with the dexterity of much practice, wrist-watches first and then the contents of pockets and webbing pouches.

"Was anyone hit?" Craig demanded. That single shot had worried him, but there were no casualties. Craig gave them two minutes to finish with the corpses and then sent a patrol back to the crest to cover them against surprise. He turned back to the dead Shona. "Bury them!" They had prepared the mass grave the previous afternoon, and they dragged the naked bodies away.

There was blood down the side of one truck where the machine-gunner had hung. "Wash that off!" One of the guerrillas dipped a canteen of water from the river. "And wash off those uniforms." They would dry out in an hour or less.

Sarah returned before the burial party had finished. She was fully dressed again.

"I have sent the girls back to the village. They know the country well. They will be safe."

"You did well," Craig told her and climbed into the cab of the leading truck. The keys were in the ignition.

The burial party returned from out of the thick bush, and Craig called in his pickets. The guerrilla detailed to drive the second truck started it, and then the rest of them climbed aboard. The two trucks crossed the bridge and growled up the far slope. The entire operation had taken less than thirty-five minutes. They reached the felled mhoba-hoba tree and Comrade Lookout stepped into the track and directed them off the road. Craig parked in thick cover, and immediately a gang of guerrillas covered both vehicles with cut branches, and another gang began unloading the cargo and clearing the road-block.

There were two-hundred-pound sacks of maize meal, cases of canned meat, blankets, medicines, cigarettes, ammunition, soap, sugar, salt—all of it priceless to the guerrillas. It was all carried away, and Craig knew it would be hidden and retrieved later whenever the opportunity occurred. There were a dozen kitbags containing the dead troopers' personal gear, a treasure trove of Third Brigade uniforms, even two of the famous burgundy berets. While the guerrillas dressed in these uniforms, Craig checked the time. It was a little after five o'clock.

Craig had noted that the radio operator at Tuti camp started the generator and made his routine report at seven o'clock every evening. He checked the radio in the leading truck. It had a fifteen-amp output, more than enough to reach Tuti camp but not sufficient power to reach Harare headquarters. That was good.

He called Comrade Lookout and Sarah to the cab and they went over their notes. Sally-Anne would be over Tuti airstrip at five-twenty tomorrow morning, and she could stay in the circuit until eight-thirty. Craig allowed three hours for the journey from Tuti camp back to the airstrip at the mission station—that would take into account any minor delays or mishaps. Ideally they should leave the camp at two-thirty, but not later than five.

That meant they must time their arrival at the gates of the camp for midnight, or close to it. Two and a half hours to secure the position, refuel the trucks from the storage tank, release the prisoners, find Tungata and start back.

"All right," Craig said, "I want each group to go over their duties. First you, Sarah—"

"I take my two with the bolt-cutters, and we go straight to Number One hutment—" He had given her two men. Tungata might be so weak as to be unable to walk unassisted. Number One hutment was set a little apart from the others behind its own wire and was obviously used as the highest security cell. Sarah had seen them lead Tungata from it to their last meeting on the parade-ground.

"When we find him, we bring him back to the assembly point at the main gate. If he can walk on his own I will leave my two men to open the other cells and release the prisoners."

"Good." She had it perfectly.

"Now the second group."

"Five men for the perimeter guard-towers—" Comrade Lookout went through his instructions.

"That's it, then." Craig stood up. "But it all depends on one thing. I've said this fifty times already, but I'm going to say it again. We must get the radio before they can transmit. We have about five minutes from the first shot to do it, two minutes for the operator to realize what is happening, two minutes to start the electric generator and run up to full power, another minute to make his contact with Harare headquarters and pass the warning. If that happens, we are all dead men." He checked his watch. "Five minutes past seven—we can make the call now. Where is your man who speaks Shona?"

Carefully Craig coached the man in what he had to say and was relieved to find him quick-witted.

"I tell them that the convoy is delayed on the road. One of the trucks has broken down, but it will be repaired. We will arrive much later than usual, in the night," he repeated.

"That's it."

"If they begin asking questions, I reply, 'Your message not understood. Your transmission breaking up and unreadable.' I repeat, 'Arriving late,' and then I sign off."

Craig stood by anxiously while the guerrilla made the radio transmission, listening to the unintelligible burst of Shona from the operator at Tuti camp, but he was unable to detect any trace of suspicion or alarm in the static-distorted voice.

The guerrilla impostor signed off and handed the microphone back to Craig. "He says it is understood. They expect us in the night."

"Good. Now we can eat and rest."

However, Craig could not eat. His stomach was queasy with tension for the night ahead and from reaction to the ghastly violence at the bridge. Those pangas, wielded with pent-up hatred, had inflicted hideous mutilation. Many times during the long brush war he had witnessed death in some of its most unlovely forms but had never become accustomed to it. It still made him sick to the guts.

• • •

"There is too much moon," Craig thought as he peered out from under the canvas canopy of the leading truck. It was only four days from full and it rode so high and so bright as to cast hard-edged shadows on the earth. The truck lurched and jolted over the rough tracks, and dust filtered up and clogged his throat.

321

He had not dared to ride in the cab, not even with his face blackened. A sharp eye would have picked him out readily. Comrade Lookout sat up beside the driver, dressed in the subaltern's spare uniform, complete with beret and shoulder-flashes. Beside him was the Shona-speaker wearing the second beret. The heavy-machine-guns were loaded and cocked, each served by a picked man, and eight other men dressed in looted uniforms rode up on the coachwork in plain view, while the remainder crouched with Craig under the canvas canopy.

"So far, everything is going well," Sarah murmured.

"So far," Craig agreed. "But I prefer bad starts and happy endings—"

There were three taps on the cab, beside Craig's head. That was Comrade Lookout's signal that the camp was in sight.

"Well, one way or the other, here we go." Craig twisted round to peer through the peep-hole he had cut in the canvas hood.

He could make out the watch-towers of the camp, looking like oil rigs against the moon-bright sky, and there was a glint of barbed-wire. Then quite suddenly the sky lit up. The floodlights on their poles around the perimeter of the camp glowed and then bloomed with stark white light. The entire compound was illuminated with noonday brilliance.

"The generator," Craig groaned. "Oh, Christ, they've started the generator to welcome us in."

Craig had made his first mistake. He had planned for everything to happen in darkness, with only the truck headlights to dazzle and confuse the camp guards. And yet, he now realized how logical and obvious it was for the guards to light up the camp to check the arrival of the convoy and to facilitate the unloading.

They were committed already. They could only ride on into the glare of floodlights, and Craig was helpless, pinned by the lights beneath the canopy, not even able to communicate with Comrade Lookout in the cab in front of him. Bitterly reviling himself for not having planned for this contingency, he kept his eye to the peep-hole.

The guards were not opening the gates. There was the sand-bagged machine-gun emplacement to one side of the guardhouse, and Craig could see the barrel of the weapon traversing slowly to keep them covered as they approached. The guard was turning out, four troopers and a non-commissioned officer, falling in outside the guardroom.

The sergeant stepped in front of the leading truck as it drove up to the gate and held up one hand. As the truck pulled up he came round to the offside window, asked a question in Shona, and the bereted guerrilla answered him easily. But immediately the sergeant's tone altered; clearly the reply had been incorrect. His voice rose, became hectoring and strident. He was outside Craig's limited circle of vision, but Craig saw the armed guard react. They began to unsling their rifles, started to spread out to cover the truck. The bluff was over before it had begun.

Craig tapped the leg of the uniformed guerrilla standing above him. It was the signal, and the guerrilla lobbed the grenade that he was holding in his right hand with the pin already drawn. It went up in a high, lazy parabola and dropped neatly into the machine-gun emplacement.

At the same instant, Craig said quietly to the men on either side of him, "Kill them."

They thrust the muzzles of their AKs through the firing-slits in the canopy, and the range was less than ten paces. The volley ripped into the unprepared guards before they could bring up their weapons. The sergeant raced back towards the guardroom door, but Comrade Lookout leaned out of the cab with the Tokarev pistol in a stiff-armed double grip and shot him twice in the back.

As the sergeant sprawled, the grenade burst behind the sandbags, and the barrel of the heavy-machine-gun swivelled aimlessly towards the sky as the hidden gunner was torn by flying shrapnel.

"Drive!" Craig stuck his head and shoulders through the slit in the canopy, and yelled at the driver through the open window of the cab. "Smash through the gate!"

The powerful diesel of the Toyota bellowed, and the truck surged forward. There was a rending crash, and the vehicle bucked and shuddered, checked for an instant, and then roared into the brightly lit compound, dragging a tangle of barbed-wire and shattered gate-timbers behind it.

Craig scrambled up beside the machine-gunner on the cab.

"On the left—" He directed his fire at the barrack-room of adobe and thatch beside the gate. The machine-gunner fired a long burst into the knot of half naked troopers as they spilled out of the front door.

"Guard-tower on the right."

They were receiving fire from the two guards in the tower. It hissed and cracked around their heads like the lash of a stock-

323

whip. The machine-gunner traversed and elevated, and the belted ammunition fed into the clattering breech and empty cases poured in a glittering stream from the ejector side. Splinters of timber and glass flew from the walls and windows of the tower, and the two guards were picked up and flung backwards by the solid strike of shot.

"Number One hutment just ahead," Craig warned Sarah with a shout. She and her two men were crouched at the tail-board and, as the Toyota slowed, they jumped over and hit the ground running. Sarah carried the bolt-cutters and the two guerrillas ran ahead of her, jinking and dodging and firing from the hip.

Craig slid over the side of the truck onto the running-board and clung to the cab.

"Drive for the kopje," he shouted at the driver. "We have to take the radio!"

The fortified kopje lay directly ahead, but they had to cross the wide, brightly lit parade-ground, with the whitewashed wall at the far end, to reach the foot of the kopje.

Craig glanced backwards. Sarah and her team were working on the wire with the bolt-cutters. Even as he watched, they completed their opening and broke through, disappearing into the building.

He looked for the second truck. It was roaring around the perimeter, just inside the wire, taking on each guard-tower as they came to it and pouring suppressing fire into it with the heavy-machine-gun. They had knocked out four towers already, only two more to go.

The flash of bursting grenades dragged his attention to the barracks abutting the main prison hutment. The second truck had dropped a group of guerrillas to attack these barracks. Craig could see them crouched below the sills of the barracks, popping grenades through the windows and then, as they exploded, darting forward, flashing like moths in the floodlights, towards the main prison hutment.

In the first few minutes they had taken control of the entire camp. They had knocked out the towers, devastated the guard-house and both barrack blocks—it was all theirs. He felt a surge of triumph, and then he looked ahead across the parade-ground to the kopje. *Everything but the kopje*, and as he thought it, a line of white tracer stretched out towards him from the sandbagged upper slopes of the rocky hillock. It looked like a string of white fire-beads, at first coming quite slowly but accelerating miraculously as they closed, and suddenly there was flying dust and the shriek of ricochets all around them and the jarring crashing of shot into the metal body of the racing truck.

The truck swerved wildly, and Craig screamed at the driver as he clung desperately to the projecting rear-view mirror.

"Keep going—we have to get the radio!"

The driver wrestled with the wrenching, bucking steering-wheel, and the nose of the truck swung back towards the kopje just as the second burst of machine-gun fire hit it. The windscreen exploded in flying diamond chips, and the driver was hurled against the door of the cab, his chest shot half-away. The truck slowed as his foot slipped from the accelerator pedal.

Craig hit the handle and yanked the door open. The driver's body slid out of the seat and tumbled overside. Craig swung himself into his place and jammed his foot flat on the accelerator. The truck lunged forward again.

Beside Craig, Comrade Lookout was firing his AK through the gaping hole where the windscreen had been shot away, and overhead the heavy-machine-gun returned the fire from the kopje with a fluttering ear-numbing clatter. The streams of opposing tracer fire seemed to meet and mingle in the air above the bare earth of the parade-ground, and then Craig saw something else.

From one of the embrasures in the sandbagged walls at the foot of the hill, a black blob, the size of a pineapple, flew towards them on a tiny tail of flame. He knew instantly what it was, but he didn't even have time to shout a warning as the RPG-7 rocket missile hit them.

It hit low into the front end of the truck—that was all that saved them. The main blast was absorbed by the solid engine block but, nevertheless, it tore the front end off the truck and stopped it as though it had run into an ironstone cliff. The Toyota somersaulted over its ruined front-wheel assembly, hurling Craig out of the open cab-door.

Craig crawled up onto his knees, and the machine-gun on the hill traversed back towards him. A stream of bullets showered him with chunks of hard, dried clay from the surface of the parade-ground and he fell flat again.

There were stunned and wounded guerrillas scattered around

the wrecked Toyota. One man was trapped under it, his legs and pelvis crushed by the steel side, and he was screaming like a rabbit in a wire snare.

"Come on," Craig shouted in Sindebele. "Get to the wall—the wall—run for the wall."

He jumped up and started to run. The white execution wall was off to their right seventy yards away, and a handful of men heard him and ran with him.

The machine-gun came hunting back. The whip-crack of passing shot around his head made Craig reel like a drunkard, but he steadied himself. The man just ahead of him went down, both legs shot from under him. As Craig passed him, he rolled on his back and threw his AK up at Craig.

"Here, Kuphela, take it. I am dead."

Craig snatched the rifle from the air without missing a step.

"You are a man," he called to the downed guerrilla and sprinted on. Ahead of him, Comrade Lookout reached the shelter of the wall, but the machine-gunner on the kopje traversed back towards Craig, kicking up curtains of dust and lumps of clay as the stream of bullets reached out for him.

Craig went for the corner of the wall first, sliding like a baseball player for home base, and shots flew close around him. He kept rolling until he hit the wall and lay in a tangle of limbs, fighting for breath. Only Comrade Lookout and two others had made it to the wall—the rest of them were dead in the truck or lying broken and crumpled on the open ground between.

"We have to get that gun," he gasped, and Comrade Lookout gave him a twisted grin.

"Go to it, Kuphela—we will watch you with great interest."

Another RPG rocket missile slammed into the wall, deafening them and covering them with a fine haze of white dust.

Craig rolled on his side and checked the AK 47. It had a full magazine. Comrade Lookout passed him another full magazine from the haversack on his shoulder, and Craig had the Tokarev pistol on his belt and two remaining grenades buttoned into his breast-pockets.

He darted another quick glance around the corner of the wall and instantly a burst of machine-gun fire kicked and jarred into the brickwork around his head. He rolled back. It was only a hundred yards or so to the foot of the kopje, but it could as well have been a hundred miles. They were pinned helplessly, and the gunner up there on the hill commanded the entire compound. Nobody could move under the floodlights without drawing instant fire or a rocket from the RPG launcher.

Craig looked anxiously for the second truck, but sensibly the driver must have parked it behind one of the buildings as soon as the RPG opened up. There was no sign of any of the other guerrillas, they were all under cover, but they had taken more casualties than they could afford.

"It can't end like this—" Craig was consumed by his own sense of frustration and helplessness. "We've got to get that gun!"

The gun up on the hill, without a target, fell silent—and then suddenly in the silence Craig heard the singing begin, low at first, just a few voices, but swelling and growing strong:

> "Why do you weep, widows of Shangani
> When the three-legged guns laugh so loudly?"

Then the ancient fighting chant crashed into the silence, flung out by hundreds of throats:

> "Why do you weep, little sons of the Moles,
> When your fathers did the king's bidding?"

And then from the prison-huts they came, a motley army of naked figures, some of them staggering with weakness, others running strongly, carrying stones and bricks, and poles torn from the roofs of their prison. A few, a very few, had picked up the weapons of the dead guards, but all of them were singing with wild defiance as they charged the hill and the machine-gun.

"Oh, Christ!" whispered Craig. "It's going to be a massacre."

In the front rank of the throng came a tall gaunt figure brandishing an AK 47, looking like a skeletal caricature of death itself, and the army of starvelings and jail-sweepings rallied to him. Even altered as he was, Craig would have recognized Tungata Zebiwe anywhere this side of hell.

"Sam, go back!" he shouted, using the name by which he had known his friend, but Tungata came on heedlessly, and beside Craig Comrade Lookout said phlegmatically, "They will draw fire, that will be our chance."

"Yes, be ready." Lookout was right—they must not let them

die in vain. As he spoke, the machine-gun opened up.

"Wait!" Craig grabbed Comrade Lookout's arm. "He must change belts soon." And while he waited for the gun to fire away its first belt, he watched the terrible havoc it was playing among the throng of released prisoners.

The stream of tracer seemed to wash them away like a fire-hose, but as the front rank fell, the men behind raced forward into the gaps, and still Tungata Zebiwe was coming on, outdistancing his fellows, firing the AK as he ran—and the gunner on the hilltop singled him out and swung the machine-gun onto him so that he was wreathed in smoking dust, still miraculously untouched as the machine-gun abruptly fell silent.

"Gun empty!" Craig shouted. "Go! Go! Go!"

They launched themselves, like sprinters off the blocks, and the open ground seemed to stretch ahead of Craig to the ends of the earth.

Another rocket missile howled over their heads, and Craig ducked on the run, but it was high, aimed in panic. It flew across the parade-ground and it hit the silver bulk-fuel tank next to the guard barracks. The fuel went up with a vast whooshing detonation. The flames shot up two hundred feet in the air, and Craig felt the hot breath of the blast sweep over him, but he kept running and firing.

He had been losing ground steadily to Comrade Lookout and the other guerrillas, his bad leg hampering him in the race for the hill, but while he ran he was counting in his head. A good man might need ten seconds to change ammunition boxes and reload the machine-gun. Since leaving the sheltering wall seven seconds had passed—eight, nine, ten—it must come now! And there were still twenty paces to cover.

Comrade Lookout reached the sandbagged fortifications and shinned up and over.

Then something hit Craig a crushing hammer-blow and he was thrown violently to the ground as bullets flew all around him. He rolled over and came up again running, but the gunner had seen him go down and swung the machine-gun away, back to the charging mob of released prisoners.

Hit but unharmed, Craig ran on as strongly as before, and he realized that he had taken it in the leg, the artificial leg. He wanted to laugh, it was so ridiculous, and he was so terrified.

"You can only do that to me once," he thought, and suddenly he had reached the foot of the kopje. He jumped up, found a hold on the top of the sandbag parapet with one hand, and heaved himself up and over. He dropped onto the narrow, deserted firing platform on the other side.

"The radio," he fixed his will upon it, "got to get the radio." And he jumped down into the communication trench and ran down it to the bend in the passage. There was the sound of a scuffle, and a cry ahead of him, and as he came around the corner, Comrade Lookout was straightening up from the body of the Third Brigade trooper who had been manning the RPG.

"Go for the gun," Craig ordered. "I'll take the radio room."

Craig climbed up the sandbagged passageway, passing the dug-out where he had been quartered on his last visit.

"Now, first on the left—" He dived into the opening, brushing aside the curtain of hessian, and he heard the radio operator in his dugout at the end of the passage shouting frantically. Craig hurled himself down the narrow passage and paused in the door-way.

Too late. His stomach turned over in a despairing convulsion. The radio operator, dressed only in a vest and underpants, was hunched over the radio set on the bench by the far wall of the dugout. He was holding the microphone to his mouth with both hands, shouting his warning into it in English, repeating it for the third time, and, as Craig hesitated, the acknowledgement boomed from the speaker, also spoken in clear English.

"Message received and understood," said the voice of the operator at Brigade headquarters in Harare. "Hold on! We will reinforce you immediately—"

Craig fired a long burst of the AK, and his bullets smashed into the radio, shattering the housing and ripping the wiring out of it in a glittering tangle. The unarmed radio operator dropped the microphone and cowered against the sandbag wall, staring at Craig, blubbering with terror. Craig swung the AK on him but could not force himself to fire.

Instead, the burst of automatic fire came from the passageway behind Craig, startling him, and then for an instant the operator was pinned to the wall by the striking bullets and he slid down into a huddle on the floor.

"You always were too soft, Pupho," said the deep voice beside

329

Craig, and he turned and looked up at the gaunt naked figure that towered over him, into the scarred and desiccated visage, into the dark, hawk-fierce eyes.

"Sam!" Craig said weakly. "By God, it's good to see you again."

*   *   *

The first truck had its entire front section wrecked by the RPG while the rear wheels of the second truck had been destroyed by heavy-machine-gun-fire. The fuel tanks of both vehicles were registering empty.

As briefly as he could, Craig explained to Tungata the plans for getting out of the country.

"Eight o'clock is the deadline. If we don't make it back to the airstrip by then, the only way out will be on foot."

"It's thirty miles to the airstrip," Tungata mused. "There is no other vehicle here. Fungabera took the Land-Rover when he left two days ago."

"I can pull the rear wheels out of the wrecked truck—but fuel! Sam, we need fuel."

They both looked towards the blazing tank. The flames were still towering into the night sky and clouds of dense, black smoke rolled across the parade-ground. In the light of the flames, the dead men lay in wind-rows where the machine-gun had scythed them down, but there were no surviving prison guards either. They had been torn to pieces and beaten to bloody pulp by their prisoners. How many dead, Craig wondered, and shied away from the answer, for every death was his direct responsibility.

Tungata was watching him. He was now dressed in random items of clothing gleaned from the lockers of the barrack room, most of it too small for his huge frame, and the prison stench still hung around him like a cloak.

"You were always like this," Tungata told him softly, "after an unpleasant task, I remember the elephant culls—you would not eat for days afterwards."

"I'll drain the one tank into the other," said Craig quickly. He had forgotten how perceptive Tungata was—he had recognized Craig's remorse. "And I will get them started on changing the wheels. But you must find fuel for us, Sam. You must!" Craig turned and limped towards the nearest truck, thankful to be able to evade Tungata's scrutiny.

Comrade Lookout was waiting for him. "We lost fourteen men, Kuphela," he said.

"I am sorry." *God! How inadequate.*

The guerilla shrugged. "They had to die one day. What do we do now?"

There were heavy wheel-wrenches in the tool-boxes of the trucks, and enough men to lift the rear end bodily and chock it with timber balks while they worked. Craig supervised the swapping of rear axle and wheels, while at the same time he rolled up his trouser leg and stripped off his leg. The machine-gun bullet had ripped through his aluminium shin, leaving a ragged exit hole in the calf, but the articulated ankle was undamaged. He tapped down the sharp petals of torn metal neatly with a hammer from the tool-box and strapped the leg back in place. "Now, you just hold together a little longer," he told it firmly, gave the leg an affectionate pat and took the wheel-wrench away from Comrade Lookout, who had already cross-threaded two of the nuts on the rear wheel of the truck.

An hour later Tungata came striding up to where Craig and his gang were lowering the truck's body onto its cannibalized rear axle. Craig was black to the elbows with thick grease. Sarah hurried to keep up with Tungata. Next to him she seemed thin and girlish, despite the rifle she carried.

"No fuel," Tungata said. "We've searched the camp."

"I reckon we have fifteen litres." Craig straightened up and wiped the sweat off his face with his shirt-sleeve. It left a smear of grease down his cheek. "That might take us twenty miles—if we are lucky." He checked his watch. "Three o'clock—where did the time go? Sally-Anne will be overhead in just over two hours. We aren't going to make it—"

"Craig, Sarah has told me what you have done, the risks, the planning, all of it—" Tungata said quietly.

"We haven't got time for that now, Sam."

"No," he agreed. "I must speak to my people, then we can go."

The prisoners who had survived the slaughter on the parade-ground gathered around him as Tungata stood on the hood of the truck. Their faces were upturned towards him, lit by the harsh glare of the floodlights.

"I must leave you," Tungata told them, and they groaned, "but my spirit stays with you, it remains with you until the day that I

331

return. And I swear to you on the beard of my father and by the milk that I drank from my mother's breast that I shall return to you."

"Baba!" they called to him. "You are our father."

"The Shona *kanka* will be here very soon. You must go into the bush, carry with you all weapons and food you can find and go with these men." Tungata pointed to the little group of guerrillas around Comrade Lookout. "They will lead you to a safe place, and you will wait until I return in strength to lead you to what is rightfully yours." Tungata held his arms extended in blessing. "Go in peace, my friends!"

They reached up to touch him, some of them weeping like children. Then, in little groups, they began to drift away towards the gate of the compound and the blackness beyond.

Comrade Lookout was the last to go. He came to Craig and smiled that cold white wolfish smile.

"Though you were in the forefront of the fighting, you did not kill a single Shona—not here or at the bridge," he said. "Why is that, Kuphela?"

"I leave the killing to you," Craig told him. "You are better at it than I am."

"You are a strange man, oh writer of books—but we are grateful to you. If I live that long I will boast to my grandchildren of the things we did together this day."

"Goodbye, my friend," said Craig, and held out his hand, and when they shook hands it was with the double grip of palm and wrist and palm, a salute of deep significance. Then Comrade Lookout turned and loped away, carrying his rifle at the trail, and the night swallowed him. The three of them, Craig, Tungata and Sarah, stood by the cab of the truck and the loneliness held them mute.

Craig spoke first. "Sam, you heard the radio operator speaking to his headquarters. You know that Fungabera will already have sent in reinforcements. Are there any troopers between here and Harare?"

Tungata shook his head. "I do not think so. A few men in Karoi, but not a large-enough force to respond to an attack like this."

"All right—let's say that it took them an hour to assemble and dispatch a force. It will take them another five hours to reach

Tuti—" He looked at Tungata for confirmation, and he nodded.

"They will hit the mission at approximately six—and Sally-Anne should be overhead at five. It will be close, especially if we have to make the last few miles on foot. Let's get moving."

While the others climbed up into the cab, Craig took a last look around the devastated compound. The flames had died down, but smoke drifted over the deserted hutments and across the parade-ground where the dead men lay. The scene was still brightly lit by the floodlights.

"The lights—" Craig said aloud. There was something about the lights that worried him. The generator? Yes, that was it—something about the generator that he must think of.

"That's it!" he whispered aloud and jumped up into the cab. "Sam, the generator—"

He started the motor and put the truck into a roaring turn. The engine-room was at the back of the hill, part of the central complex protected by sandbags and by the fortifications on the high ground above it. Craig parked the truck close to the steps that led down into the powerhouse, and he ran down and burst into it.

The generator was a twenty-five-kilowatt Lister, a big squat green machine, and its fuel tank was bolted on steel brackets to the wall above it. Craig tapped the side of the tank and it gave back a reassuring dull tone.

"Full!" Craig breathed. "Forty glorious gallons, at least!"

•   •   •

The road twisted like a dying python and the truck, her fuel-tank brimming was unwieldy and stiff on the turns. Craig had to wrench the wheel into them with both arms. The uphills were steep and the speed bled away to a walking pace as Craig changed down through the gears. Then they roared down the far side, too fast for safety, the empty truck bouncing them about unmercifully as they hit the deep ruts.

Craig almost missed the causeway at the bridge, and they lurched out over the drop with the edge crumbling away under the big double backwheels before he swerved back and they went lumbering over the narrow timber bridge.

"Time?" he asked, and Sarah checked her watch in the dash-board lights.

"Four fifty-three."

Craig glanced away from the bright tunnel of the headlights and for the first time he could see the silhouette of the tree-tops against the lightening sky. At the top of the slope he pulled into the verge and switched on the radio set. He searched the channels slowly, listening for military traffic, but there was only the buzz of static.

"If they are in range, they are keeping mum." He switched off the set and pulled out into the track again marvelling at the swiftness of the African dawn. Below them in the valley, the landscape was emerging out of the fleeing night, the great forested plain leading from the foot of the hills down to the mission station stretched below them.

"Ten miles," said Tungata.

"Another half-hour," Craig replied and sent the Toyota bellowing down the last hills. Before they reached the bottom, it was light enough for him to switch off the headlights. "No point in drawing attention to ourselves."

Suddenly he sat up straighter, alarmed by the change in the engine note of the truck; it was harsher and louder.

"Oh God, not that, not now," he whispered and then realized that he was hearing the sound not of the Toyota, but of another motor outside the cab. It was growing louder, closer, and more compelling. He rolled down the side-window and stuck his head out into the cool rush of the wind.

Sally-Anne's Cessna was roaring down from behind them, only fifty feet above the road, sparkling blue and silver in the first rays of the sun.

Craig let out a whoop of joy and waved wildly.

Swiftly the Cessna overhauled them and drew level. Sally-Anne's beloved face looked down at him from the cockpit. She had a pink scarf around her head, and those thick eyebrows framed her eyes. She was laughing, as she recognized Craig, and she waved and mouthed at him, "Go for it!" Then she was roaring past, climbing, waggling the wings of the Cessna from side to side, heading for the airstrip.

They burst out of the forest, racing through the maize fields that surrounded the tiny mission village. The tin roofs of the church and the schoolhouse glittered in the sunrise. From the huts beside the road, a few sleepy villagers, yawning and scratching, came out to watch them pass through.

Craig slowed the truck, and Sarah shouted through the window, "Soldiers coming! Big trouble! Warn everybody! Go into the bush! Hide!"

Craig had not thought that far ahead. The retaliation of the Third Brigade on the local population would be horrific. He accelerated through the village and the airstrip was a kilometer ahead, the tattered wind-sock undulating on its pole at the far end. The Cessna was circling low overhead. Craig saw Sally-Anne lower her undercarriage and start her turn onto final approach for the landing.

"Look!" said Tungata harshly, and another aircraft came roaring in, from their left-hand side, low and fast, another much larger, twin-engined machine. Craig recognized it immediately.

It was an old Dakota transport, a veteran of the desert war in North Africa, and the bush war in Rhodesia. It was sprayed with non-reflective anti-missile grey paint and it was now decorated with the Zimbabwe air force roundels. The main hatch just abaft the wing-root was open, and there were men poised in the opening. They were dressed in camouflage jump jackets and helmets. The bulky bundle of their parachutes dangled below their buttocks. Two of them were in the hatchway, but others crowded up close behind them.

"Paras!" shouted Craig, and the Dakota banked steeply towards them and passed so low that the blast from the propellers churned the tops of the standing maize in the field beside them. As the aircraft flashed past, Craig and Tungata simultaneously recognized one of the men in the hatchway.

"Fungabera!" Tungata snapped. "It's him!"

As he said it, Tungata threw open the door at his side and clambered up the outside of the cab to reach the ring-mounted machine-gun. Despite his size and weakness, he was so quick that he reached the gun and swung it and got off a long burst before the Dakota was out of range. Tracers flew under the Dakota's port wing, close enough to alarm the pilot and make him throw the aircraft into a tight climbing turn.

"They are climbing up to drop altitude!" Craig shouted.

Surely Fungabera had seen and recognized the blue and silver Cessna. He would have realized that it was the escape plane and that the truck was heading for a rendezvous at the airstrip. His paratroopers could be more swiftly deployed by dropping, than by landing the Dakota. He was going to drop in and seize the airstrip with his paras before the Cessna could take off again. A thousand feet was safe drop altitude, but these were crack troopers. The Dakota levelled out on its drop run, five hundred feet, Craig estimated, and they were going to make the drop down the length of the airstrip.

The Cessna was just coming in over the fence at the far end of the strip. As Craig glanced back at her, Sally-Anne touched down and then taxied at speed down the strip towards the racing Toyota.

Above the airstrip the tiny figure of a man fell clear of the lumbering Dakota and the green silk parachute flared open almost instantly. He was followed in rapid succession by a string of other paras, and the sky was filled with a forest of sinister mushrooms, poisonous green and swaying gently in the light morning breeze, but sinking towards the parched brown turf of the airstrip.

The Cessna reached the end of the strip and swung around sharply in a 180-degree turn. Only then did Craig realize that Sally-Anne had been far-seeing enough to assess the danger and urgency, and that she had landed with the wind behind her, accepting the hazard of the higher approach speed and the longer roll-out in order to be able immediately to turn back into the wind for her take-off, which would be with a full load and under attack from the paras.

On the cab, Tungata was firing up into the sky, measured controlled bursts, hoping more to intimidate the descending paras than to inflict casualities. A man dangling on swinging parachute-shrouds makes an almost impossible target.

Sally-Anne was leaning out of the open cockpit door, shouting and waving them on. Already she was running up her engine to full power, holding the Cessna on the wheel-brakes. They bumped over the verge of the runway and Craig swung the Toyota into a brake-squealing skid, parking so as to screen and protect the aircraft and themselves while they made the transfer.

"Get out," he yelled at Sarah, and she jumped down and ran to the aircraft. Sally-Anne grabbed her arm and helped her swing up and tumble into the back seat.

On the cab, Tungata fired a last burst with the heavy-machine gun. The first three paras were down, their green parachutes rolling softly in front of the light breeze, and Tungata's bullets kicked dust among them. Craig saw one of the paras fall and be dragged away loose and lifeless on his shrouds. Craig grabbed the AK 47 and the bag of spare ammunition and shouted, "Let's go, Sam, Let's go!"

They ran to the Cessna, and Tungata, weak and sick, fell at the steps. Craig had to drag him to his feet and shove him up.

Sally-Anne let go the brakes before Tungata was aboard, and Craig ran beside the Cessna as it gathered speed. Tungata fell into the back seat beside Sarah, and Craig jumped up and got a hold. Though he was hampered by the AK rifle and bag, he dragged himself into the front seat beside Sally-Anne.

"Get the door closed!" Sally-Anne screamed, without looking at him, all her attention on the strip ahead. The dangling seat-belt was jammed in the door and Craig wrestled with it as they built up to rotation speed. Craig managed to extricate the strap and slam the door closed. When he looked up, he saw papatroopers sprinting forward from the edge of the strip to intercept the Cessna.

It did not need the shiny general's star on the front of his helmet to identify Peter Fungabera. The set of his shoulders, the way he carried his head, and the fluid catlike grace of his run were all distinctive. His men were spread out behind him. They were almost directly ahead of the Cessna, only four or five hundred paces.

Sally-Anne rotated and the Cessna lifted its nose, bounced lightly and became airborne. Peter Fungabera and his line of paratroopers disappeared from view under the nose and engine section as the Cessna climbed away, but the aircraft would have to pass directly over the top of their heads at little more than a few hundred feet.

"Oh mother!" Sally-Anne spoke in almost conversational tones, "this is it!" And as she said it, the instrumental panel in front of Craig exploded, covering him with fine chips of glass like sugar crystals. Hydraulic fluid sprayed over the front of his shirt.

Machine-gun fire came in through the floor of the cabin and tore out through the thin metal roof so that the interior was filled with a gale of swirling winds as the slipstream found the holes.

In the back seat, Sarah cried, and the body of the machine was racked and jarred by the storm of AK 47 bullets. Craig felt the seat under him hump as bullets smacked into the metal frame. Jagged punctures appeared miraculously in the wing-roots just outside his window.

Sally-Anne shoved the control wheel forward and the Cessna dived back towards the airstrip again with a gut-swooping rush, ducking under the maelstrom of machine-gun fire and giving them a moment's respite. The brown earth came up at them, and Sally-Anne caught the Cessna's suicidal dive and held it off, but the wheels hit the surface and they bounced wildly thirty feet back into the air. Craig saw two paratroopers dive to the side as the plane raced towards them.

That wild dive towards the earth had pushed their speed way up, so that Sally-Anne could instantly throw the Cessna into a maximum-rate turn, the port wing-tip brushing the earth. Her face was contorted and the muscle stood proud in her forearms with the effort of holding the Cessna's nose up in the turn and preventing her from going in. Ahead of them on the left-hand side of the airstrip, only a hundred yards or so from the verge, stood a single tree with dense, widespread branches. It was a marula, ninety feet tall.

Sally-Anne leveled out for an instant and flew for the marula. Her wing-tip almost touched its outmost branches, and immediately she threw the Cessna into an opposite turn, neatly placing the tree between them and the line of paratroopers on the airstrip behind.

She kept at ground level, her undercarriage brushing the tops of the maize plants in the open fields, glancing up in the rear-view mirror above her head to keep the marula tree exactly behind the Cessna's tail, blanketing the paratroopers' field of fire.

"Where is the Dakota?" Craig asked, raising his voice above the rush of wind through the cabin.

"It's going in to land," Tungata called, and twisting in his seat, Craig had a glimpse of the big grey machine going in low over the treetops behind them, lined up for the airstrip.

"I can't get the undercarriage up." Sally-Anne was thumbing the rocker switch but the three green eyes of the undercarriage warning light glared at her from the console. "We have damage there. It's stuck."

The forest beyond the open fields rushed towards them and as she eased back on the control wheel to lift the Cessna over the tree-tops, a hydraulic lead burst under the shot-ruptured engine housing and hydraulic fluid sprayed in viscous sheets over the windscreen.

"Can't see!" Sally-Anne cried, and pulled open her side-window, flying by reference to the horizon under her wing-tip.

Craig checked the shattered panel. "We've got no instruments.

338

Airspeed's gone, rate of climb, artificial horizon, altimeter, gyro compass—"

"The undercarriage—" Sally-Anne interrupted him. "Too much drag, it will cut down our range—we'll never make it back!"

She was still climbing but gradually starting to come around onto her course, using the compass in its glass oil-bath above her head, when the engine stuttered, almost cut—and then surged again in full power.

Quickly Sally-Anne adjusted pitch and power-settings.

"That sounded like fuel starvation," she whispered. "They must have hit a fuel line." She switched the fuel-tank selector cock from "starboard" to "both" and then glanced up at Craig and grinned. "Hi there! I missed you something awful."

"Me too." He reached across and squeezed her thigh.

"Time check." Businesslike again.

"0517 hours," Craig told her and looked overside. The brown snake of the Tuti road was angling away towards the north, and they were crossing the first line of hills. Vusamanzi village would be out there a few miles beyond the road.

The engine missed again, and Sally-Anne's expression was taut with apprehension.

"Time?" she demanded again.

"0527," Craig told her.

"We will be out of sight of the airstrip by now. Out of earshot, too."

"Fungabera won't know where we are, where we are heading."

Tungata leaned forward over the seats. "They've got a helicopter gunship at Victoria Falls. If they guess that we are heading for Botswana, they will send it down to intercept."

"We can outrun a helicopter," Craig guessed.

"Not with our undercarriage down," Sally-Anne contradicted him, and without another warning the engine cut out completely.

It was suddenly eerily quiet, just the whistle of the wind through the bullet-holes in the fuselage, the propeller windmilling softly for a few seconds longer, and then with a jerk stopping dead and pointing skywards like a headman's blade.

"Well," Sally-Anne said softly, "it's all immaterial now. Engine out. We are going in." And then briskly she began her preparations for a forced landing as the Cessna started to sink gently away towards the broken hilly and forested land beneath them. She pulled on full flap to slow their airspeed.

339

"Seat-belts, everybody," she said. "Shoulder-straps also."

She was switching off the fuel-tanks, the master switches, shutting down to prevent fire on impact.

"Can you see an opening?" she asked Craig, peering hopelessly through the smeared windscreen.

"Nothing." The forest was a dark-green mattress below them.

"I will try to pick two big trees and knock our wings off between them—that will take the speed off us. But it's still going to be a daddy of a hit," she said, as she struggled with the panel of her side-window.

"I can knock it out for you," Tungata offered.

"Good," Sally-Anne accepted.

Tungata leaned over and with three blows of his bunched fist smashed the Perspex sheet out of its frame. Sally-Anne thrust her head out, slitting her eyes against the wind.

The earth came up towards them, faster and faster, the hills seemed to grow in size, beginning to tower above them, as Sally-Anne made a gentle gliding turn into a narrow valley. She had no airspeed indicator, so she was flying by the seat of her pants, holding up the nose to bleed off speed. Through the hazy smear of the windshield Craig saw the loom of trees.

"Doors unlocked and open!" Sally-Anne ordered. "Keep your straps fastened until we stop rolling, then get out as fast as you can and run like a pack of long thin dogs!"

She pulled up the nose. The Cessna stalled and the nose dropped, again like a stone, but she had judged it to a microsecond, for before it could drop through the horizontal, she hit the trees. The wings were plucked out of the Cessna, and the passengers were hurled against their shoulder-straps with a force that grazed away the skin and bruised their flesh. But even though the impact took most of their speed off, the dismembered carcass of the aircraft went slithering and banging into the forest. They were slammed from side to side and shaken in their seats, the fuselage slewing violently and wrapping sideways around the base of another tree and coming, at last, to rest.

"Out!" yelled Sally-Anne. "I can smell gas! Get out and run!"

The open doors had been ripped away from their hinges, and they flung off their seat-belts and tumbled out onto the rocky ground, and they ran.

Craig caught up with Sally-Anne. The scarf had come off her

head and her long dark tresses streamed behind her. He reached out and put an arm around her shoulders, guided her towards the lips of a dry ravine and they leaped into it and crouched panting on the sandy bottom, clinging to each other.

"Is she going to flame out?" Sally-Anne gasped.

"Wait for it." He held her, and they tensed themselves for the whooshing detonation of leaking gasoline and the explosion of the main tanks.

Nothing happened. The silence of the bush settled over them, so they spoke in awed whispers.

"You fly like an angel," he said.

"An angel with broken wings."

They waited another minute.

"By the way," he whispered, "what the hell is a long thin dog?"

"A greyhound," she said, giggling with reaction from fear. "A dashhound is a long short dog." And he found he was giggling with her as they hugged each other.

"Take a look." She was still laughing nervously. They stood up cautiously and peered over the rim of the ravine. The fuselage was crushed and the metal skin of the Cessna had crumpled like aluminum foil, but there was no fire. They climbed out of the ravine.

"Sam!" Craig called. "Sarah!"

The two of them stood up from where they had taken cover at the foot of the rocky side of the valley.

"Are you all right?"

All four of them were shaken and bruised. Sarah had a bloodied nose and a scratch on her cheek, but none of them had been seriously hurt.

"What the hell do we do now?" Craig asked, and they stood in a huddle and looked at each other helplessly.

● ● ●

They ransacked the shattered carcass of the Cessna—the toolbox, the first-aid kit, the survival kit with the flashlight, a five-litre aluminum water-bottle, thermal blankets and malt tablets, the pistol, the AK 47 rifle and ammunition, the map-case—and Craig unscrewed the compass from the roof of the cabin. Then they worked for an hour trying to hide all traces of the crash from a searching aircraft. Between them Tungata and Craig dragged the

341

severed wing sections into the ravine and covered them with dried brush. They could not move the fuselage and engine section, but they heaped more branches and brush over it.

Twice while they worked, they heard the sound of an aircraft in the distance. The resonant throb of twin engines was unmistakable.

"The Dakota," Sally-Anne said.

"They are searching for us."

"They can't know that we are down," Sally-Anne protested.

"No, not for certain, but they must know that we took a real beating," Craig pointed out. "They must realize that there is a good chance that we are down. They will probably send in foot patrols to scout the area and question the villagers."

"The sooner we get out of here—"

"Which way?"

"May I suggest something?" Sarah joined the discussion deferentially. "We need food and a guide. I think I can lead us from here to my father's village. He will hide us until we have decided what we are going to do, until we are ready to go."

Craig looked at Tungata.

"Makes sense—any objections, Sam? Okay, let's do it."

Before they left the site of the crash, Craig took Sally-Anne aside.

"Do you feel sad? It was a beautiful aircraft."

She shook her head. "I don't get sentimental over machinery. Once it was a great little kite, but it's buggered and bent now. I save my sentiments for things that are more cuddly," and she squeezed his hand. "Time to move on, darling."

Craig carried the rifle and pointed for them, keeping half a mile ahead and marking the trail. Tungata, lacking stamina, took the drag, with the two girls in the centre.

That evening they dug for water in a dry river-bed and sucked a malt tablet before they rolled into the thermal foil survival blanket. The girls took the first two sentry goes, while Tungata and Craig spun a coin for the more arduous later watches.

Early the next morning, Craig cut a well-used footpath, and when Sarah came up she recognized it immediately. Two hours later they were in the cultivated valley below Vusamanzi's hilltop village, and while the rest of the party took cover in the standing maize, Sarah climbed up to find her father. When she returned an hour later the old witch-doctor was with her.

He came directly to Tungata and went down on his arthritically swollen knees before him, and he took one of Tungata's feet and placed it upon his silver pate. "Son of kings, I see you," he greeted him. "Sprig of great Mzilikazi, branch of mighty Kumalo, I am your slave."

"Stand up, old man," Tungata lifted him up, and used the respectful term *kehla*, honoured elder.

"Forgive me that I do not offer refreshment," Vusamanzi apologized, "but it is not safe here. The Shona soldiers are everywhere. I must lead you to a safe place, and then you can rest and refresh yourselves. Follow me."

He set off at a remarkable pace on his skinny old legs, and they had to lengthen their stride to hold him in view. They walked for two hours by Craig's wrist-watch, the last hour through dense thorn thicket and broken rocky ground. There was no defined footpath, and the heated hush of the bush and the claustrophobic crowding in of the hills was enervating and oppressive.

"I do not like this place," Tungata told Craig softly. "There are no birds, no animals, there is a feeling here of evil—no, not evil, but of mystery and menace."

Craig looked about him. The rocks had the blasted look of slag from an iron furnace and the trees were deformed and crooked, black as charcoal against the sun and leprous silver when the sun's rays struck them full on. Their branches were bearded with trailing lichens, the sickly green of chlorine gas. And Tungata was correct, there were no bird sounds, no rustles of small animals in the undergrowth. Suddenly Craig felt chilled, and he shivered in the sunlight.

"You feel it also," said Tungata, and as he spoke the old man disappeared abruptly, as though he had been swallowed by the black and blasted rock. Craig hurried forward, suppressing a shudder of superstitious dread. He reached the spot where Vusamanzi had disappeared and looked around, but there was no sign of the old man.

"This way," Vusamanzi's voice was a sepulchral echo. "Beyond the turn of the rock."

The cliff was folded back upon itself, a narrow concealed cleft, just wide enough for a man to squeeze through. Craig stepped round the corner and paused to let his eyes adjust to the poor light.

Vusamanzi had taken a cheap storm lantern from a shelf in the rock above his head and was filling the base with paraffin from

343

the bottle he had carried in his pouch. He struck a match and held it to the wick.

"Come," he invited, and led them into the passageway.

"These hills are riddled with caves and secret passages," Sarah explained. "They are all dolomite formations."

A hundred and fifty yards farther on, the passage opened into a large chamber. Soft natural light filtered in through an opening in the domed roof high above their heads. Vusamanzi extinguished the lantern and set it down on a ledge to one side of a hearth, man-made from blocks of limestone. The rock above the hearth was blackened with soot, and there was a pile of old ash upon the floor. Beside it was a neat stack of firewood.

"This is a sacred place," Vusamanzi told them. "It is here that the apprentice magicians live during the training period. It was here, as a young man, that I served under my own father and learned the ancient prophecies and the magical arts." He gestured to them to sit down, and all of them slumped thankfully to the rocky floor. "You will be safe here. The soldiers will not find you. In a week or a month, when they grow weary of searching for you, it will be safe for you to leave. Then we will find a man to guide you."

"It's spooky," Sally-Anne whispered, when Craig translated this for her.

"Some of my women are following us with food. They will come every second day while you are here, with food and news."

Two of Sarah's half-sisters arrived at the cavern before darkness fell. They carried heavy bundles balanced upon their heads, and they set about preparing a meal immediately. Their laughter and merry chatter, the flicker of the flames on the hearth, the smell of wood-smoke and food cooking, partially dispelled the oppressive atmosphere of the cavern.

"You must eat with the women," Craig explained to Sally-Anne. "It's the custom. The old man will be very unhappy—"

"He looks such an old dear, but underneath he turns out to be just another male chaunvist pig," she protested.

The three men passed the beer-pot around their circle and ate from the communal bowl in the centre, and the old man spoke to Tungata between mouthfuls.

"The spirits prevented our first meeting, Nkosi. We waited for you to come that night, but the Shona had taken you. It was a time of sorrow for all of us, but now the spirits have relented, they have delivered you from the Shona and brought us together at last." Vusamanzi looked at Craig. "There are things of great portent that you and I must discuss—tribal matters."

"You say that the spirits have arranged my escape from the Shona," Tungata replied. "It may be so—but if it is, then this white man is their agent. He and his woman have risked their very lives to free me."

"Still, he is a white man," said the old man delicately.

"His family has lived in this land for a hundred years—and he is my brother," said Tungata simply.

"You vouch for him, Nkosi?" the old man persisted.

"Speak, old man," Tungata assured him. "We are all friends here."

The magician sighed and shuffled and took another handful of food. "As my lord wishes," he agreed at last, and then abruptly, "You are the guardian of the old king's tomb, are you not?"

Tungata's dark eyes hooded in the firelight.

"What do you know of these things, old man?" he countered.

"I know that the sons of the house of Kumalo, when they reach manhood, are taken to the tomb of the king and made to swear the oath of guardianship."

Tungata nodded reluctantly. "This may be so."

"Do you know the prophecy?" the old man demanded.

And Tungata nodded and said, "That when the tribe is sorely in need, the spirit of the old king will come forth to give them succour."

"The spirit of Lobengula will come forth as a fire," the old man corrected him.

"Yes," Tungata agreed. "Lobengula's fire."

"And there is much, much more. Do you know the rest of it, son of Kumalo?"

"Tell it to me, old father."

"The prophecy goes on thus: *The leopard cub will first break an oath, then break his chains. The leopard cub will first fly like an eagle, then swim like a fish. When these things have come to pass, the fire of Lobengula will be freed from the dark places and come forth to succour and save his people.*"

They were all silent, considering this conundrum.

"The leopard-skin is the prerogative of the house of Kumalo," Vusamanzi reminded them. "Thus the leopard cub of the prophecy would be a descendant of the royal house."

Tungata grunted non-committally.

"I do not know that you have broken an oath," the old man went on, "but you have broken the chains with which the Shona bound you."

"Eh-eh!" Tungata nodded, his face closed and impassive.

"You escaped from Tuti in an *indeki*, flying like an eagle indeed," the old man pointed out, and again Tungata nodded, but in English he murmured to Craig: "The beauty of these ancient prophecies is that they can be moulded to fit nearly any circumstance. They gain a little or lose a little with each repetition, depending on the mood and the motives of the seer at the time." Then he reverted smoothly to Sindebele. "You are wise, old man, and well versed in magic, but tell us what of the swimming of the fish? I must warn you that I am not able to swim, and that the only one thing I truly fear is death by drowning. You must seek another fish."

Vusamanzi wiped the grease off his chin and looked smug.

"There is something else I must tell you," Tungata went on. "I have entered Lobengula's tomb. It is empty. The body of Lobengula has gone. The prophecy has been voided long, long ago."

The old magician showed no distress at Tungata's words. Instead he sat back on his heels and unscrewed the stopper of the snuff-horn that hung around his neck.

"If you have entered the king's tomb, then you have broken your oath to defend it intact," he pointed out, with a wicked twinkle of his eyes. "The oath-breaking of the prophecy—could that be it?" He did not wait for a reply but poured red snuff into the palm of his hand and drew it up each nostril. He sneezed ecstatically, with tears running down his withered old cheeks.

"If you broke your oath, Nkosi, it was beyond your power to prevent it. The spirits of your ancestors drove you to it and you are without blame. But, now let me explain the empty tomb." He paused and then seemed to take off at a tangent. "Have either of you heard of a man who lived long ago, a man they called Taka-Taka?" They both nodded.

"On the maternal side Taka-Taka was the great-grandfather of Pupho here." Tungata nodded at Craig. "Taka-Taka was a famous white soldier in the old days of Lobengula. He fought against the king's impis. Taka-Taka is the sound that his machine-guns made when the warriors of the Matabele went against him."

"Old Sir Ralph Ballantyne," Craig agreed. One of Rhodes'

right-hand men, and the first prime minister of Rhodesia." He changed back into Sindebele. "Taka-Taka lies buried in the Matopos Hills close by the grave of Lodzi, of Cecil Rhodes himself."

"That is the one." Vusamanzi wiped the snuff from his upper lip, and the tears from his cheeks with his thumb. "Taka-Taka, the soldier and the robber of the sacred places of the tribe. It was he who stole the stone birds from the ruined city of Great Zimbabwe. It was he also who came into these very hills to desecrate the tomb of Lobengula and to steal the fire-stones that hold the spirit of the king."

Now both Craig and Tungata leaned forward attentively. Craig said, "I have read the book that Taka-Taka wrote describing life—" Old Sir Ralph's handwritten diaries were part of Craig's personal treasure that he had left at King's Lynn when Peter Fungabera had driven him out. "I have read the very words of Taka-Taka, and he does not tell of reaching Lobengula's tomb. And what are these fire-stones you speak of?"

The old man held up a restraining hand. "You go too swiftly, Pupho," he admonished Craig. "Let the son of Kumalo explain these mysteries to us. Have you heard of the fire-stones, Tungata Zebiwe, who was once Samson Kumalo?"

"I have heard something of them," Tungata agreed cautiously. "I have heard that there was a huge treasure of diamonds, diamonds collected by Lobengula's *amadoda* from the white man Lodzi's mines in the south—"

Craig started to interrupt but Tungata silenced him. "I will explain later," he promised, and turned back to the old magician.

"What you heard is the truth," Vusamanzi assured him. "There are five beer-pots filled with the fire-stones."

"And they were stolen by Sir Ralph, by Taka-Taka?" Craig anticipated.

Vusamanzi looked severe. "You should go to the women's fire, Pupho, for you chatter like one of them."

Craig smothered a smile and sat back suitably chastened while Vusamanzi rearranged his skin cloak before going on.

"When Lobengula was put to earth and his tomb sealed by his half-brother and loyal induna, a man named Gandang—"

"Who was my great-great-grandfather," Tungata murmured.

"Who was your great-great-grandfather," the old man agreed. "Gandang placed all the king's treasures with him in the tomb and then led the vanquished tribe of Matabele back. He went back to

347

treat with Lodzi and this man Taka-Taka, and the tribe went into the white man's bondage. But one man stayed in these hills. He was a famous magician named Insutsha, the Arrow. He stayed to guard the king's tomb, and he built a village near the tomb, and took wives and bred sons. Insutsha, the Arrow, was my grandfather—" They made small movements of surprise, and Vusamanzi looked complacent. "Yes, do you see how the spirits work? It is all planned and predestined—the three of us are bound by our history and our blood-lines, Gandang and Taka-Taka and Insutsha. The spirits have brought us, their descendants, together in their marvellous fashion."

"Sally-Anne is right—it's bloody spooky," said Craig, and Vusamanzi frowned at his gauche use of a foreign language.

"This Taka-Taka, as I have hinted already, was a famous rogue, with a nose like a hyena and an appetite like a vulture." Vusamanzi gave this summation with relish and glanced significantly at Craig.

"Got it!" Craig smiled inwardly but kept a solemn expression.

"He learned of the legend of the five pots of fire-stones, and he went among the survivors of Gandang's impi, the men who had been present at the time of the king's death, and he spoke sweet and gentle words and offered gifts of cattle and gold coins— and he found a traitor, a dog of a dog who was not fit to be called Matabele. I will not speak the name of this piece of offal, but I spit on his unmarked and dishonoured grave." Vusamanzi's spittle hit the embers of the fire with a hiss.

"This dog agreed to lead Taka-Taka to the king's burial place. But before he could do so, there was a great war between the white men, and Taka-Taka went north and fought against the German induna called Hamba-Hamba, 'the one-who-marches-here-and-there-and-is-never-caught.'"

"Von Lettow-Vorbeck," Craig translated, "the German commander in East Africa during the 1914–18 war." And Tungata nodded agreement.

"When the war was over Taka-Taka returned and he called the Matabele traitor, and they came into these hills with the dog of a dog leading them—four white men with Taka-Taka as their chief— and they searched for the tomb. They searched for twenty-eight days, for the traitor did not remember the exact location and the tomb was cunningly concealed. However, with his hyena nose Taka-Taka smelled it out at last, and he opened the royal tomb, and he found wagons and guns, but the king's body and the five

348

beer-pots for which he hungered so violently were gone!"

"This I have already seen and told you," Tungata said. It was an anticlimax and Tungata turned one palm up in a gesture of resignation, and Craig shrugged, but Vusamanzi went on resolutely.

"They say that Taka-Taka's rage was like the first great storms of the rains. They say he roared like a man-eating lion and that his face went red and then purple and finally black." Vusamanzi chortled with glee. "They say he took his hat from his own head and threw it on the ground, then he took his gun and wanted to shoot the Matabele guide, but his white companions restrained him. So he tied the dog to a tree and beat him with a kiboko until he could see his ribs sticking out of the meat of his back. Then he took back the gold coins and cattle with which he had bribed him. Then he beat him again and finally, still squealing like a bull elephant in musk, Taka-Taka went away and never came back to these hills."

"It is a good tale," Tungata agreed, "and I will tell it to my children." He stretched and yawned. "Now it grows late."

"The tale is not yet told," said Vusamanzi primly and placed a hand on Tungata's shoulders to prevent his rising.

"There is more?"

"There is indeed. We must go back a little, for when Taka-Taka and his companions and the traitor dog first arrived in these hills to begin the search, my grandfather Insutsha grew immediately suspicious. Everybody knew of Taka-Taka. They knew he did nothing without purpose. So Insutsha sent three of his prettiest young wives to where Taka-Taka was camped, bearing small gifts of eggs and sour milk, and Taka-Taka answered the girls' questions and said that he had come into these hills to hunt rhinoceros." Vusamanzi paused, glanced at Craig, and elaborated: "Taka-Taka was also a renowned liar. However, the prettiest of the wives waited for the traitor dog of a Matabele at the bathing-pool of the river. Under the water she touched that thing of which it is said, the harder it becomes, the softer becomes the brain of the man who wields it, and the faster it waggles, that fast waggles his tongue. With the girl's hand on his man-spear, the Matabele traitor spilled out boasts and promises of cattle and gold coins, and the pretty wife ran back to my grandfather's village."

Vusamanzi had all their attention again, and he clearly relished it.

"My grandfather was thrown into terrible consternation. Taka-Taka had come to desecrate and rob the king's tomb. Insutsha fasted and sat vigil, he threw the bones and stared into the water-divining vessel, and finally he called his four apprentice witch-doctors to him. One of the apprentices was my own father. They went in the full moon and opened the king's tomb and made sacrifice to placate the king's ghost, and then, with reverence, they bore him away, and they resealed the empty tomb. They took the king's body to a safe place and deposited it there, with the beer-pots of bright stones—although my father told me that in their haste one of the beer-pots was overturned and broken, and that they gathered up the fallen stones and placed them in a zebra-skin bag, leaving the broken shards in the tomb."

"Both the apprentices and Taka-Taka overlooked one of the diamonds," Tungata said softly. "We found the clay shards and a single diamond where they had left it."

"Now you may go to sleep—if you are still weary, Nkosi." Vusamanzi gave his permission, with a gleam in his rheumy old eyes. "What? You want to hear more? There is nothing else to tell. The tale is finished."

"Where did they take the king's body?" Tungata asked. "Do you know the place, my wise and revered old father?"

Vusamanzi grinned. "It is indeed an unexpected pleasure to find respect and honour for age in the young people of this new age, but to answer your question, son of Kumalo, I do know where the king's body is. The secret was passed to me by my father."

"Can you lead me to the place?"

"Did I not tell you that this place in which we now sit is sacred? It is sacred for good reason."

"My God!"

"Here!" both Craig and Tungata exclaimed together, and Vusamanzi cackled happily and hugged his bony old knees, well pleased with their reaction.

"In the morning I will take you to view the site of the king's grave," he promised, "but now my throat is dry with too much talking. Pass the beer-pot to an old man."

•   •   •

When Craig woke, the first morning light was diffusing through the hole in the roof of the cavern, milky and blued by the smoke

350

from the cooking-fire where the girls were busy preparing the morning meal.

While they breakfasted, and with Vusamanzi's reluctant permission, Craig related in English the outlines of the tale of Lobengula's reburial to Sarah and Sally-Anne. They were both enthralled and immediately on fire to join the expedition.

"It is a difficult place to reach," the old man huffed, "and it is not for the eyes of mere women-folk." But Sarah smiled her sweetest, stroked the old man's head and whispered in his ear, and finally, after a further show of gruff severity, he relented.

Under Vusamanzi's direction, the men made a few simple preparations for the expedition. In one of the ancillary branches of the cavern beneath a flat stone was a hidey-hole containing another kerosene lantern, two native axes and three large coils of good-quality nylon rope—which the old man clearly prized highly.

"We liberated this fine rope from the army of Smithy during the bush war," he boasted.

"One great blow for freedom," Craig murmured, and Sally-Anne frowned him to silence.

They set off down one of the branches of the cavern, Vusamanzi leading, carrying one of the lanterns, followed by Tungata with one of the rope coils, the girls next, and Craig with a second coil of rope and the other lantern in the rear.

Vusamanzi strode along the passage as it narrowed and twisted. When the passage forked, he did not hesitate. Craig opened his claspknife and marked the wall of the right-hand fork, then hurried to catch up with the rest of the party.

The system of tunnels and caves was a three-dimensional maze. Water and seepage had mined the limestone of the hills until it was as perforated as Gruyère cheese. In some places they scrambled down rock scree, and at one point they climbed a rough, natural staircase of limestone. Craig blazed every twist and turn of the way. The air was cold and dank and musky with the smell of guano. Occasionally there was a flurry of shadowy wings around their heads, and the shrill squeal of disturbed bats echoed down the passageways.

After twenty minutes they came to an almost vertical drop of glossy smooth limestone, so deep that the lantern glow did not reach the depths. Under Vusamanzi's direction, they secured the end of one coil of nylon rope to a pillar of limestone and, one at a time, slid down fifty feet to the next stage. This was a vertical fault in the rock formation, where two geological bodies had shifted slightly and formed an open crack in the depths of the earth. It was so narrow that he could touch either wall, and in the lantern light Craig could just make out the bright eyes of bats hanging inverted from the rocky roof above them.

Uncoiling the second rope behind him as he went, Vusamanzi cautiously climbed down the treacherous floor of the crack. The crack widened as it descended, and the roof receded into the gloom above their heads. It reminded Craig of the great gallery in the heart of Cheops pyramid, a fearsome cleft through living rock, dangerously steep, so they had to steady themselves with the rope at every pace. They had almost reached the limit of the rope, when Vusamanzi halted and stood tall on a tilted slab, lit by his own lantern, looking like a black Moses descended from the mountain.

"What is it?" Craig called.

"Come on down!" Tungata ordered, and Craig scrambled down the last slope and found Vusamanzi and the others perched on the rockslab, peering over the edge into the still surface of a subterranean lake.

"Now what?" Sally-Anne asked, her voice muted with awe of this deep and secret place.

The lake had filled the limestone shaft. Across the surface, a hundred and fifty feet away, the roof of the shaft dipped into it at the same angle as the floor on which they stood.

Craig used the flashlight that they had salvaged from the wrecked Cessna for the first time. He shone it into the water that had stood undisturbed through the ages so that all sediment had settled out of it, leaving it clear as a trout stream. They could see the inclined floor of the gallery sinking away at the same angle into the depths. Craig switched off the flashlight, conserving the batteries.

"Well, Sam"—Craig put one hand on his shoulder—"Here's your big chance to swim like a fish." Tungata's chuckle was brief and insincere, and they both looked at Vusamanzi.

"Where now, revered father?"

"When Taka-Taka came to these hills and my grandfather and my father saved the king's body from defilement, there had been seven long, terrible years of drought scorching the land. The level of the water in this shaft was much lower than it is now. Down there"—Vusamanzi pointed into the limpid depths—"there is another branch of the rock. In that place they laid Lobengula's

352

body. In the many years since then, good and plentiful rains have blessed the land, and each year the level of these waters has risen. The first time I visited this place, brought here by my father, the waters were below that pointed rock—"

Briefly Craig switched on the flashlight and in its beam the splintered limestone lay thirty feet or more below the surface.

"But even then the king's grave was far below the surface."

"So you have never seen the grave with your own eyes?" Craig demanded.

"Never," Vusamanzi agreed. "But my father described it to me."

Craig knelt at the edge of the lake and put his hand into the water. It was so cold that he shivered and jerked his hand out. He dried it on his shirt and, when he looked up, Tungata was watching him with a quizzical expression.

"Now you just hold on there, my beloved Matabele brother," Craig said vehemently. "I know exactly what that look means— and you can forget all about it."

"I cannot swim, Pupho my friend."

"Forget it," Craig advised him.

"We will tie one of the ropes around you. You can come to no harm."

"You know where you can put your ropes."

"The torch is waterproof—it will shine underwater," Tungata went on with equanimity.

"Christ!" Craig said bitterly. "African rule number one: when all else fails, look around for the nearest white face."

"Do you remember how you swam across the Limpopo River for a ridiculous wager, a case of beer?" Tungata asked sweetly.

"That day I was drunk, now I'm sober." Craig looked at Sally-Anne for support and was disappointed.

"Not you too!"

"There are crocs in the Limpopo. No crocs here," she pointed out.

Slowly Craig began to unbutton his shirt, and Tungata smiled and began readying the rope. They all watched with interest while Craig unstrapped his leg and laid it carefully aside. He stood one-legged in his underpants at the edge of the pool while Tungata fastened the end of the rope around his waist.

"Pupho," Tungata said quietly, "you will need dry clothes after-wards. Why do you wish to wet these?"

"Sarah," Craig explained and glanced at her.

"She is Matabele. Nudity does not offend us."

Sarah smiled. "Leave him his secrets, though I have none from him." And Craig remembered her naked in the water below the bridge. He sat on the edge of the rock-slab and pulled off his underpants, tossing them on top of the heap of his other clothing. Neither of the girls averted their eyes, and he slid into the water, gasping at the cold. He padded out gently into the centre of the pool and trod water.

"Time me," he called back to them. "Give me a double tug on the rope every sixty seconds. At three minutes, pull me up regardless, okay?"

"Okay." Tungata had the coils of rope between his feet, ready to feed out.

Craig hung in the water and began to hyperventilate, pumping his lungs like a bellows, purging them of carbon dioxide. It was a dangerous trick. An inexperienced diver could black out from oxygen starvation before the buildup of CO_2 triggered the urge to breath again. He drew in a lungful and flipped his leg and lower body above the surface in a duck dive, and went down cleanly into the cold clear water.

Without a glass face-plate, his vision was grossly distorted, but he held the flashlight beam on the sharp pinnacle of limestone thirty feet below and went down swiftly, the pressure popping and squeaking in his ears.

He reached it and gave himself a push-off from the rock. He was going down more readily now as the water pressure compressed the air in his lungs and reduced his buoyancy. The steep rocky floor of the pool flew in a myopic blur past his face, and he rolled on his side and scanned the walls of gleaming limestone on each side for an opening.

There was a double tug on the rope around his waist—one minute gone—and he saw the entrance to the tomb below him. It was an almost circular opening in the left-hand wall of the main gallery, and it reminded Craig of the empty eye-socket in a human skull.

He sank down towards it and put out a hand to brace himself on the limestone sill above the opening. The mouth of the tomb was wide enough for a man to stoop through. He ran his hand over the walls and they were polished by running water and silky

354

with a coating of slime. Craig guessed that this was a drain-hole from the earth's surface carved out of limestone by the filtering of rain-waters over the millennia.

He was suddenly afraid. There was something forbidding and threatening about this dark entrance. He glanced back towards the surface. He could see the faint reflected glow of old Vusamanzi's lantern forty feet above him, and the icy water sapped his vitality and courage. He wanted to thrash wildly back towards the surface, and he felt the first involuntary pumping of his lungs.

Something tugged at his waist, and for an instant he teetered on the edge of wild panic before he realized it was the signal. Two minutes—almost his limit.

He forced himself forward into the entrance of the tomb. It angled gently upwards again, round as a sewer pipe. Craig swam for twenty feet flashing the torch beam ahead of him, but the water was running murky as he stirred up the sediment from the floor.

Abruptly the passage ended and he ran his hand over rough rock. His lungs were beginning to pump in earnest and there was a singing in his ears. His vision was clouded with swirling sediment and the beginnings of vertigo, but he forced himself to stay on and examine the end of the tunnel from side to side and top to bottom, running his free hand over it.

Quickly he realized that he was feeling a wall of limestone masonry, packed carefully into place to block off the tunnel, and his spirits plunged. The old witch-doctors had once again sealed Lobengula's tomb and, in the brief seconds he had left, he realized that they had made a thorough job of it.

His searching fingers touched something with a smooth metallic feel lying at the foot of the wall. He took it up and turned away from the wall, shoving himself down the passage, with panic and the need for air rising in him. He reached the main gallery again, still carrying the metallic object in one hand.

High above him, the lantern glowed and he swam upwards, with his senses beginning to flutter like a candle flame in the wind. Darkness and stars of light played before his eyes as his brain starved and he felt the first deadly lethargy turning his hands and his foot to lead.

With a jerk, the rope around his waist came tight, and he felt himself being drawn swiftly upwards. Three minutes, and Tungata was pulling him out. The lantern light spun dizzily overhead as

355

he windmilled on the end of the rope. He could not prevent himself, he tried to breathe, and freezing water shot down his throat and went into his lungs, stinging like the cut of a razor.

He exploded out through the surface. Tungata was waist-deep, hauling double-handed on the life-line. The instant he broke through, Tungata seized him, a thick muscled arm around his chest, and he dragged Craig to the edge.

The two girls were ready to grab his wrists and help him up onto the slab. Craig collapsed on his side, doubled up like a foetus, coughing and heaving the water from his lungs and shaking violently with cold.

Sally-Anne rolled him onto his stomach and bore down on his back with both hands. Water and vomit shot up his throat, but his breathing gradually eased and at last he sat up wiping his mouth. Sally-Anne had stripped off her own shirt and was chafing him vigorously with it. In the lantern light his body was dappled blue with cold and he was still shivering uncontrollably.

"How do feel?" Sally asked.

"Bloody marvellous," he gasped. "Nothing like a bracing dip."

"He's all right," Tungata assured them. "As soon as he starts snarling, he's all right."

Craig cupped his hands over the chimney of the lantern for warmth. Gradually his shivering eased.

Sarah leaned across to Tungata and, with a wicked smile directed at Craig's naked lower body, whispered something.

"Right on!" Tungata chuckled and imitated a black American accent: "And what's more, these honkies ain't got no rhythm neither."

As Craig reached quickly for his underpants, Sally-Anne rushed loyally to his defense. "You're not seeing him at his best. That water is freezing."

Craig's hands were stained red-brown with rust. They marked his underpants, and he remembered the metal object he had found at the wall of the tomb. It lay where he had dropped it at the edge of the slab.

"Part of a trek chain," he said, as he picked it up. "From an ox wagon."

Vusamanzi had been squatting silently on one side, at the edge of the lantern light. Now he spoke: "That chain was from the king's wagon. My grandfather used it to lower the king's body down the shaft."

"So you have found the king's grave?" Tungata asked. This mundane little scrap of metal was for all of them the proof that changed fantasy to fact.

"I think so"—Craig began strapping on his leg—"but we will never know for certain." They all watched his face and waited. Craig suffered another paroxysm of coughing, then his breathing settled and he went on: "There is a passage, just as Vusamanzi described. It is about another fifteen feet below that pinnacle and it goes off to the left, a round opening with a shaft that rises sharply. About twenty feet from the entrance, the shaft has been blocked with masonry, big blocks and lumps of limestone, packed closely together. There is no way of telling how thick the wall is, but one thing is certain, it is going to take a lot of work to get through it. I had about twenty seconds' endurance at the face, not long enough to prise out even a single block. Without diving apparatus, nobody is going to get past that seal."

Sally-Anne was shrugging on her damp shirt over her white bra, but she stopped and stared at him challengingly. "We can't just give up, Craig darling, we can't just walk away and never know. It would eat me up not knowing—a mystery like that! I'd never be happy, never again as long as I lived."

"I'm open to suggestions," Craig agreed sarcastically. "Anybody got a scuba tucked in their back pocket? How about paying Vusamanzi a goat and he can make the water jump aside, shades of Moses and the Red Sea."

"Don't be flippant," said Sally-Anne.

"Come on, somebody, be intelligent and inventive. What? No takers? Okay, then let's get back to where there is a fire and a little sunlight."

Craig dropped the rusted piece of chain back into the pool.

"Sleep well, Lobengula, 'the one who dives like the wind.' Keep your fire-stones beside you, and *shala gashle*, stay in peace!"

      •   •   •

The climb back up through the maze of passages and interleading caverns was a dismal and silent procession, although Craig checked and re-marked each turn and juncture as he passed it.

When they reached the main cavern again, it took only a few minutes to blow the embers on the hearth and boil a canteen of water.

The strong, oversweetened tea warmed away the last of Craig's chills and heartened them all.

"I must return to the village," Vusamanzi told them. "If the Shona soldiers come and do not find me, they will become suspicious. They will begin to bully and torture my women. I must be there to protect them, for even the Shona fear my magic." He gathered up his pouch and cloak and his ornately carved staff. "You must remain in the cavern at all times. To leave it is to risk discovery by the soldiers. You have food and water and firewood and blankets and paraffin for the lanterns. There is no need for you to go out. My women will come to you the day after tomorrow with food and news of the Shona." He went to kneel before Tungata. "Stay in peace, great prince of Kumalo. My heart tells me that you are the leopard cub of the prophecy and that you will find a way to free the spirit of Lobengula."

"Perhaps I will return here one day with the special machines that are necessary to reach the king's resting-place."

"Perhaps," Vusamanzi agreed. "I will make sacrifice and consult the spirits. They might condescend to show me the way." At the entrance of the cave he paused and saluted them. "When it is safe, I shall return. Stay in peace, my children." And then he was gone.

"Something tells me it's going to be a long, hard time," said Craig, "and not the most attractive place to pass it."

They were all active and restlessly intelligent people, and the confinement began to irk almost immediately. Tacitly they divided the cavern, a communal area around the hearth and a private area at either end for each couple. The seepage of water down the rockface, when collected in a clay pot, was sufficient for all their needs, including ablutions, and there was a vertical pot-hole shaft in one of the passages which served as a natural latrine. But there was nothing to read and—a lack that Craig felt keenly—no writing material. To alleviate the boredom Sarah began teaching Sally-Anne Sindebele, and her progress was so rapid that she could soon follow ordinary conversation and respond to it fairly fluently.

Tungata recovered rapidly during those days of enforced inactivity. His gaunt frame filled out, the scabs on his face and body healed rapidly, and he regained his vitality. It was often Tungata who led the long, rambling discussions at the fireside, and that irrepressible sense of humour that Craig remembered so well from the old days began to break through the sombre moods that had at first overwhelmed him.

When Sally-Anne made a disparaging remark about neighbouring South Africa and its apartheid policies, Tungata contradicted her with mock severity.

"No, no, Pendula—" Tungata had given her the Matabele name of "the one who always answers back." "No, Pendula, rather than condemning them, we black Africans should give thanks for them every time we pray! For they can bring a hundred tribes together with a single rallying cry. It is only necessary for one of us to stand up and shout, 'Racist apartheid Boers!' and all the others stop beating each other over the head and for a moment we become a band of brothers."

Sally-Anne clapped her hands. "I'd love to hear you make that speech at the next meeting of the Organization for African Unity!"

Tungata chuckled at her. They were becoming good friends. "Another thing we have to be grateful for—" he went on.

"Tell me more," she incited him.

"Those tribes down there are some of the fightingest niggers in Africa—Zulus and Xhosas and Tswanas. We have got our hands full with the Shona. Imagine if that lot were turned loose on us also. No, from now on my motto is going to be 'Kiss an Afrikaner every day'!"

"Don't encourage him," Sarah pleaded with Sally-Anne. "One day he is going to talk like this in front of people who will take him seriously."

At other times Tungata lapsed back into those intense and somber moods. "It is like Northern Ireland or Palestine, only a hundred times bigger and more complex. This conflict between ourselves and the Shona is a microcosm of the entire problem of Africa."

"Do you see a solution?" Sally-Anne demanded.

"Only a radical and difficult one," he told her. "You see, the European powers in their nineteenth-century scramble for Africa divided the continent among themselves with no thought for tribal boundaries, and it is an entrenched article of the Organization for African Unity that these boundaries are sacrosanct. One possible solution would be to overturn this article and repartition the continent along tribal boundaries, but after the terrible experience of partitioning India and Pakistan, no rational person would support that view. The only other solution seems to me to be a form of federal government, based loosely on the American system, with the state divided into tribal provinces possessing autonomy in their own affairs."

Their talk ranged across time, and for the entertainment and instruction of the two girls, both Craig and Tungata related the history of this land between the Limpopo and Zambezi rivers, with each of them concentrating on the role played by their own nations and families in its discovery and occupation and the strife that had torn it.

Twice on successive days their talk at the hearth was interrupted by sounds from the world outside the cavern—the unmistakable whistling, clattering roar of a helicopter rotor hammering through the air in coarse-pitch setting, and they fell silent and looked up at the roof of stone above them until the sound faded. Then the talk would turn to their chances of escape from the forces that pursued and hunted them so relentlessly.

Every second day the women came from Vusamanzi's village, travelling in the darkness of pre-dawn to elude the eyes in the sky above them. They brought, as promised, food and news.

The Third Brigade troopers had come to the village, surrounding it first and then storming in and ransacking the huts. They had cuffed one of the young girls and they had shouted threats and badgered the old man, but Vusamanzi had faced them down with dignity and in the end his formidable reputation for magic had protected them. The soldiers had left without stealing much of value, without burning a single hut or killing more than a few chickens—but they had promised to return.

However, a massive man-hunt was still in progress over the entire area. On foot and from the helicopters the Shona scoured the forest and hills during the hours of daylight, and hundreds of escapees from the camp had already been recaptured. The girls had seen them being transported in heavy trucks, naked and chained together.

As far as Vusamanzi knew, the Shona had not yet discovered the wrecked Cessna, but it was still extremely dangerous, and Vusamanzi had ordered the girls to impress upon them they must remain in the cavern. He would come to them in person when he judged it safe to do so.

This news depressed them all and it took all Craig's best story-telling and clowning to lighten the mood in the cavern. He turned their attention back to their perennially favourite topic, the tomb of Lobengula and the vast fortune they liked to believe it contained. They had already discussed in detail the equipment that would be needed to enable the team of divers to open the tomb and reach the burial area, and now Sally-Anne asked Tungata, "Tell us, Sam, *if* there were a treasure, and *if* you could reach it, and *if* it were as rich as we hope, how would you use it?"

"I think it would have to be treated as belonging to the Matabele people. It would have to be placed in trust and used for their benefit, firstly to procure for them a better political dispensation. To be pragmatic, a negotiator with that sort of financial clout behind him would find it easier to get the attention of the British Foreign Office and the American State Department. He could prevail upon them to intervene. The government in Harare would have to take them seriously. Options which are at present closed to us would become accessible."

"After that, it would finance all sorts of social programmes— education, health, the forwarding of women's rights," Sarah said, for the moment her timidity put aside.

"You would use it to make land-purchases to add the existing tribal trustlands," Craig added, "financial assistance to the peasant farmers, aid for tractors and machinery, blood-stock improvement programmes—"

"Craig"—Sally-Anne laid her hand on his good leg—"isn't there *any* way at all to reach the burial chamber? Couldn't you try another dive?"

"My precious girl, for the hundredth time, let me explain that I could probably move a single rock with each dive, and twenty dives would kill me."

"Oh God, it's so frustrating!" Sally-Anne jumped up and began pacing between them and the fire. "I feel so helpless. If we don't do something, I'm going to go mad. I feel as though I am suf-focating—I need a good breath of oxygen. Can't we just go outside for a few minutes?" And then immediately she answered herself: "That just isn't on, I know. Forgive me. I'm being silly." She looked at her wrist-watch. "My God, I've lost all track of time, do you realize it's after midnight already?"

Craig and Sally-Anne lay on their mattress of cut grass and tanned skins, holding each other close and whispering with their lips touching each other's ears so as not to disturb the other pair at their end of the cavern.

361

"I am ashamed of my part in having him imprisoned. He is such a marvellous man, darling, sometimes I feel so humble when I listen to him."

"He might just make it to greatness," Craig agreed.

"Coming back here to free him may be the most important thing that you and I ever do in our lives."

"If we get away with it," Craig qualified.

"There must be some justice in this naughty world."

"It's a nice thought."

"Kiss me good night, Craig."

Craig loved to listen to her sleeping, the gentle sound of her breathing, and to feel the total relaxation of her body against his, with only the occasional little snuggling movement in his arms, but tonight he could not follow her into sleep.

Something was snagged in his subconscious like a burr in his sock, and the longer he lay, the fiercer became its irritation. Something somebody had said that evening—he figured it that far—but every time it started to rise to the surface of his mind, he tried too hard and it sank away again. At last he resorted to the old trick of emptying his mind, imagining a waste-paper basket and as each unbidden thought came, he tore it in half, crumpled it, and dropped it into the imaginery basket.

"Christ!" he said loudly, and sat bolt upright. Sally-Anne was jolted awake and came up beside him, pushing the hair out of her eyes and mumbling drowsily.

"What is it?" Tungata called across the cavern.

"Oxygen!" cried Craig. Sally-Anne had said, "I am suffocating—I need a good breath of oxygen."

"I don't understand," Sally-Anne mumbled, still more asleep than awake.

"Darling, wake up! Come on!" He shook her gently. "Oxygen! The Cessna is equipped for high-altitude flight, isn't it?"

She stared at him. "Oh sweet heavens, why didn't we think of it before?"

"Life-jackets—do you have them?"

"Yes. When I was doing the flamingo survey over Lake Tanganyika, I had to have them installed. They are under the seat cushions."

"And the oxygen system, is it a recycling circuit?"

" Yes."

"Pupho!" Tungata had lit the lantern and carried it across to them, with Sarah naked and unsteady on her feet trailing behind him like a sleepy puppy. "Tell us, Pupho, what is happening?"

Craig grinned at him, as he reached for his pants. "Sam, you beauty, you and I are going for a little walk."

"Now?"

"Now, while it is still dark."

•   •   •

There was enough moon to light their way as far as Vusamanzi's village. They bypassed the hilltop, not wanting to alarm the old man. A village dog yapped at them, but they found the footpath and hurried along it.

Morning found them still on the footpath.

Twice they were forced to take cover. The first time, they almost ran head-on into a patrol of camouflage-clad Shona troopers. Tungata, who was on point, warned Craig with the hand-signal for dire danger. They lay in a thick yellow stand of elephant grass beside the path and watched them go padding silently past. Afterwards, Craig found that his heart was racing and his hands shaking.

"I'm getting too old for this," he whispered.

"Me too," Tungata agreed.

The second time they were warned by the whacking beat of helicopter rotors, and they dived into the ravine beside the path. The ungainly machine dragon-flyed down the far crest of the valley, with a machine-gunner in the fuselage port and the helmeted heads of an assault squad popping up behind him like those poisonous green toadstools. The helicopter passed swiftly and did not return.

They overran the spot where they had originally intersected the footpath and had to backtrack for almost a mile, so it was late afternoon when they approached the wreck site.

They closed in with elaborate caution, circling the area and casting for ingoing spoor, checking with infinite patience that the wreck had not been discovered and staked-out. Finally, when they walked up, they discovered that it was undisturbed and exactly as they had left it.

Tungata climbed back up the side of the valley and stood guard with the AK 47 while Craig began stripping the equipment they had come for. The four inflatable life-jackets were under the seats, as Sally-Anne had told him. They were of excellent quality, impregnated nylon, each with a carbon dioxide cartridge for inflation and a non-return valve on the mouthpiece for topping up. Attached to the bosom cushions were a whistle and—blessings upon the manufacturer—a light globe powered by a long-life battery. Under the pilot seat was—a thousand more blessings—a repair kit for the jackets, with scissors and scraper and two tubes of epoxy cement.

The steel oxygen bottles were bolted into a rack behind the rear bulkhead of the passenger compartment. There were three of them, each of two-litre capacity. From them flexible plastic tubing carried along behind the panelling to each seat and terminated in a face-mask with two built-in valves. The user inhaled pure oxygen and exhaled a mixture of unused oxygen, water vapour and carbon dioxide. This was passed through the exit valve and ran through the two metal canisters under the floorboards. The first canister contained silica gel which removed the water vapour, the second canister was packed with soda lime which removed the carbon dioxide, and the purified oxygen was cycled back to the face-masks. When the pressure of pure oxygen in the system fell to that of ambient atmosphere, it was automatically supplemented from the three steel bottles. The flexible tubing was fitted with top-quality aluminum couplings, T-pieces and bends, all of the bayonet-fitting type.

Working as carefully as time would permit, Craig stripped out the system and then converted the heavy-duty canvas seat-covers into carry bags. He packed the salvaged equipment into them, making up two heavy bundles.

It was dark by the time that he whistled Tungata down from the hillside. Each of them shouldered a bundle and they started back.

When they intersected the footpath, they spent nearly half an hour sweeping their tracks and hiding any sign of their detour from the path.

"You think it will hold good in daylight?" Craig asked doubtfully. "We don't want to signpost the wreck."

"It's the best we can do."

They stepped out on the path, pushing hard, and despite their heavy, uncomfortable packs, they shaved an hour off their return time and reached the cavern just after dawn.

Sally-Anne said nothing when Craig stepped into the cavern.

She merely stood up from the fire, came to him and pressed her face against his chest. Sarah bobbed the traditional curtsey to Tungata and brought him the beer-pot, letting him refresh himself before bothering him with greetings. Only after he had drunk did she kneel beside him, clap her hands softly and whisper in Sindebele, "I see you, my lord, but dimly, for my eyes are filled with tears of joy!"

·   ·   ·

The Shona sergeant had been on foot patrol for thirty-three hours without rest. The previous morning they had made a brief and indecisive contact with a small band of the escapees they were hunting, an exchange of fire that had lasted less than three minutes, then the Matabele guerrillas had pulled out and split up into four groups. The sergeant had gone after one group with five men, followed them until nightfall and then lost them on the rocky rim of the Zambezi valley. He was bringing in his patrol now for re-supply and new orders.

Despite the long patrol and the trauma of a good contact and hot pursuit, the sergeant was still vigilant and alert. There was an elastic spring in his stride, his head turned restlessly from side to side as he moved down the footpath, and the whites of his eyes under the brim of his jungle hat showed clear and sharp.

Suddenly he gave the urgent hand-signal for deployment, and as he changed the AK 47 from one hip to the other to cover his left flank and dropped into cover, he heard his men spread and go down behind, covering him and backing him. They lay in the elephant grass beside the track, searching and waiting while the sergeant examined the small sign that had alerted him. It was a bunch of long grass on the opposite side of the path. The stems had been broken and then lifted carefully to try to disguise the break, but they had sagged slightly again. It was the type of sign a man might make when leaving the path to set up an ambush beside it.

The sergeant lay for two minutes, and when there was no hostile fire, he doubled forward ten paces and then went flat again, rolling twice to throw off an enemy's aim. He waited two minutes longer.

Still no fire—and he came up cautiously, and went forward to the damaged clump of grass. It was man sign. A small band of men had left the path here or joined it, and they had swept their spoor. A man only took this much trouble if he was anticipating pursuit. The sergeant whistled up his tracker and put him to the spoor.

The tracker worked out from the path, casting ahead, and within minutes he reported, "Two men, wearing boots. One of them walks with a slight favour to his left leg. They were headed down the valley." He touched one of the footprints in a sandy patch. An ant-lion had built its tiny cone-shaped trap in the toe of the spoor, giving the tracker an accurate timing.

"Six to eight hours," said the tracker, "during the night. They went on the path, but we cannot follow them. Their spoor has been covered by others."

"If we cannot find where they are going, then we will see where they came from," said the sergeant. "Backtrack them!"

Three hours later the sergeant walked up to the wreck of the Cessna.

•   •   •

Craig slept for a few hours and then by the light of the paraffin lantern began modifying the oxygen equipment for use underwater. The central part of his primitive oxygen rebreathing set was the bag. For this he used one of the inflatable life-jackets. Oxygen from the steel bottle was introduced into the bag through the one-way valve of the mouthpiece, the connection made with a length of flexible tubing.

As he worked, Craig explained, "At a depth of forty feet underwater, the pressure will be greater than two atmospheres. You remember your high school physics: thirty-three feet of water equals one atmosphere, plus the pressure of the air above it—two atmospheres, right?"

His interested audience of three made affirmative sounds.

"Right! So for me to be able to breathe freely, the oxygen has to be fed into my lungs at the same pressure as the surrounding water. The oxygen in the bag is under the same ambient pressure as I am, *et voilà*!"

Sally-Anne applauded him. "My old daddy always used to say, it's brains what counts!"

"The chemicals in these two canisters remove the water vapour and carbon dioxide from the air that I exhale, and the purified oxygen goes back into the bag via this tube, and I breathe it again."

He was sealing the new connections to the bag with epoxy cement from the repair kit.

"As I use up the oxygen in the bag, I keep topping it up with fresh oxygen from the steel bottle strapped on my back. Like this—" He cracked the tap of the black and white-coded bottle and there was an adder hiss of escaping gas.

"There are a few problems, of course—" Craig began work on altering the shape of the face-mask to give him a watertight fit.

"Such as?" Sally-Anne asked.

"Buoyancy," Craig answered. "As I use up the oxygen in the bag I will become less buoyant, and the steel bottle will pull me down like a stone. When I top up the bag I'll tend to shoot up like a balloon."

"How will you beat that?"

"I will weight myself with rocks to get down to the tomb entrance and once I'm there, I'll rope myself down to stay there."

Craig was making up a backpack on which were suspended the two canisters and the oxygen bottle. Carefully he positioned the steel bottle so that he could reach the tap over his shoulder.

"However, buoyancy isn't the big problem," he said.

"You've got more?" Sally-Anne demanded.

Craig grinned "As many as you ask for. But did you know that pure oxygen breathed for an extended period at more than two atmospheres absolute, that is at any depth below thirty-three feet, becomes a deadly gas, as lethal as the carbon monoxide in the exhaust fumes of an automobile?"

"What can you do about that?"

"Not much," Craig admitted. "Except limit the duration of each dive, and monitor my own reactions very carefully while I am working at the wall of the tomb."

"Can't you work out how much safe time you will have before it starts to poison—"

Craig interrupted, "No, the formula would be too complicated and there are too many variables to calculate, from my body mass to the exact water-depth. Then there is a cumulative effect of the poisoning. Each successive dive will become more risky."

Sally-Anne stared at him. "Oh my God, darling."

"We will keep the dives short, and we will work out a series of signals," Craig reassured her. "You will give me a rope-signal

367

from the surface every minute, and if I don't reply or if my reply is not immediate and decisive, you will haul me out. The poisoning is insidious but gradual. It will affect my reactions to the signal before I go out completely. It gives us a little leeway."

He set the bulky equipment carefully aside, close to the fire, so that the warmth would hasten the setting of the epoxy cement.

"As soon as the joints are sealed we can test it, and then go for the bank."

"How long?"

"It's twenty-four-hour epoxy."

"So long?"

"Rest will increase my resistance to the effects of oxygen poisoning."

*   *   *

The forest was too dense to allow the helicopter to alight. It hovered above the tree-tops, and the flight engineer on the winch lowered General Peter Fungabera into a hole in the mat of dark-green vegetation below them.

Fungabera turned slowly on the thin steel cable, and the down-draught from the rotors fluttered his camouflage battle-jacket about his torso. Six feet above the earth, he slipped out of the padded sling and dropped clear, landing neatly as a cat. He returned the salute of the Shona sergeant who was waiting for him, cleared the drop area quickly and looked up as the next man was lowered from the hovering helicopter.

Colonel Bukharin was also dressed in camouflage and jump helmet. His scarred face seemed impervious to the tropical sun— it was bloodless and almost as pale as those cold arctic eyes. He shrugged off the helping hands of the Shona sergeant and strode on up the valley. Peter Fungabera fell in beside him and neither man spoke until they reached the crumpled and shattered fuselage of the Cessna.

"There is no doubt?" Bukharin asked.

"The registration, ZS-KYA. You must remember I have flown in this aircraft," Peter Fungabera replied, as he went down on one knee to examine the belly of the fuselage. "If further proof is needed," he touched the neat puncture in the metal skin, "machine-gun fire from directly below."

"No corpses."

"No." Peter Fungabera straightened up and leaned into the

368

cockpit. "No blood, no indication that any of the occupants was injured. And the wreck has been stripped."

"It could easily have been looted by the local tribesmen."

"Perhaps," Peter agreed. "But I don't think so. The trackers have examined the signs and this is their reconstruction. After the crash twelve days ago, four people left the site, two of them women, and one of the men with an unbalanced gait. Then within the last thirty-six hours, two men returned to the wreck. They are certain it was the same two—the boot prints match, and one of them has the same favour to his left leg."

Bukharin nodded.

"On the second visit the wreck was stripped of much loose equipment. The two men left the area carrying heavy packs and joined the footpath that crossed the head of the valley about six miles from here. There the tracks have been confused and covered by other traffic."

"I see." Bukharin was watching him. "Now tell me your other conclusions."

"There are two black and two white persons. With my own eyes I saw them at Tuti airstrip. The one black is undoubtedly Tungata Zebiwe—I recognized him."

"Wishful thinking? He is your one last hope of making good our bargain."

"I would know that man anywhere."

"Even from an aircraft?"

"Even then."

"Go on," Bukharin invited.

"The other black person I did not recognize. Nor did I get a good enough view to positively identify either of the whites but the pilot is almost certainly an American woman named Jay. Although the aircraft belongs to the World Wildlife Trust, she had the use of it. The other white is probably her lover, a British writer of sensational fiction, who has an artificial leg, accounting for the unbalanced tracks. These three are unimportant and expendable. The only one of importance is Zebiwe. And now we know that he is still alive."

"We also know that he has eluded you, my dear General," Bukharin pointed out.

"I do not think he will continue to do so much longer." Peter Fungabera turned to the sergeant who was standing attentively behind him. "You have done well. Very well, so far."

"Mambo!"

"I believe that this Matabele dog and his white friends are being hidden and fed by the local people."

"Mambo!"

"We will question them."

"Mambo!"

"We will start with the nearest village. Which is it?"

"The village of Vusamanzi lies beyond this valley and the next."

"You will move in and surround it. Nobody must leave or escape, not a goat, not a child."

"Mambo!"

"When you have secured the village, I will come to supervise the interrogation."

•   •   •

Craig and Tungata made three climbs down to Lobengula's pool at the foot of the grand gallery, carrying the makeshift diving gear, the spare oxygen bottles, the underwater lamps that Craig had made up with the batteries and globes scavenged from the life-jacket, firewood and fur blankets to warm Craig after each dive, and provisions to avoid the necessity of climbing back to the upper cavern for meals.

After discussion it was agreed that the two girls would take turns at remaining in the upper cavern, to meet the messengers from Vusamanzi's village and to carry down a warning to the others in the event of a Shona patrol stumbling on the entrance.

Before testing the diving equipment, Craig and Tungata made a careful survey of the route down to the pool, choosing the positions on which they would fall back if they were ever forced to defend the inner recesses of the cave system against a Shona attack. Although neither of them mentioned it, they were both acutely aware that there was no final position, no ultimate escape-hole from the mountain depths, and that any defence must end at the icy waters of the pool.

Tungata made the only open acknowledgement of this when, in plain sight of the other three, he took four 7.62 mm bullets for the Tokarev pistol, wrapped in a scrap of goat-skin, and wedged them in a crack in the limestone wall beside the pool. The two girls watched him with sickly fascination, and though Craig made a show of checking his breathing equipment, they all understood.

This was the final assurance against torture and slow mutilation, one bullet for each of them.

"Okay!" Craig's voice was overloud for the silence of the gallery. "I'm going to see how efficiently this contraption is going to drown me."

Tungata lifted the set and Craig knelt and slipped his head through the yoke of the life-jacket. Sally-Anne and Sarah settled the bottle and canisters on his back, and then strapped them in place with strips of canvas cut from the seat covers. Craig checked the knots. If the set ever failed, he must be able to jettison it in a hurry.

At last he hopped into the pool, shuddered at the cold as he fitted the mask over his mouth and nose, secured the strap behind his head and half-filled his chest bag with oxygen. He gave the three on the bank a thumbs-up sign and lowered himself below the surface.

As he had anticipated, buoyancy was his first problem. The pull of the bag on his chest rolled him onto his back like a dead fish, and with the thrust of his one leg, he was unable to right himself. He paddled back to the slab and began the irksome business of experimenting with rock weights to adjust his attitude in the water. In the end he found that the only way to do it was to hold an excessively heavy stone and let it draw him down head-first. However, as soon as he released the stone, he was borne irresistibly upwards.

"At least the joints are watertight," he told them when he surfaced again, "and I'm getting oxygen. There is a lot of water leaking in around the edges of the mask, but I can purge that in the usual way." He demonstrated the trick of holding the mask at the top and forcing the accumulated water out of the bottom with a sharp exhalation of breath.

"When are you going to go for the wall?"

"I guess I'm as ready now as I'll ever be," Craig admitted reluctantly.

•   •   •

Peter Fungabera smiled gently. "You must understand that I wish to be as a father to you. I look upon you as my children."

"I can understand this Shona chattering as little as I can the barking of baboons from the hilltops," Vusamanzi replied courteously, and Fungabera made a gesture of irritation as he turned to his sergeant.

"Where is that translator?"

"He will be here very soon, mambo."

Tapping his swagger-stick against his thigh, Peter Fungabera walked slowly down the ragged rank of villagers that his troopers had gathered in from their hoeing on the maize fields and had flushed from the huts. Apart from the old man, they were all women or children. Some of the women were as ancient as the witch-doctor, with white woolly pates and wizened dugs hanging to their waists. Others were still capable of child-bearing. They had fat infants strapped to their backs or standing naked at their knees. Snot had dried white around the toddlers' nostrils and flies crawled unnoticed on their lips and at the corners of their eyes, and they stared up at Peter as he passed with fathomless eyes. There were still younger women, with firm full breasts and glossy skin, prepubescent girls as well as uncircumcised boys. Peter Fungabera smiled kindly at them, but they stared back at him without expression.

"My Matabele puppies, we will hear you yap a little before this day is done," he promised softly and turned at the end of the line. He walked back slowly to where the Russian waited in the shade of one of the huts.

"You will get nothing out of the old one." Bukharin took the ebony cigarette-holder from between his teeth and coughed softly, covering his mouth with his hand. "He is dried up, beyond pain, beyond suffering. Look at his eyes. Fanatic."

"I agree. These *sangoma* are capable of self-hypnosis. He will be impervious to pain." Peter Fungabera shot back the cuff of his battle-jacket and glanced impatiently at his watch. "Where is that translator?"

It was another hour before the Matabele trustee from the rehabilitation centre was hustled up the path from the valley. He fell on his knees before Fungabera, blubbering and holding up his manacled hands.

"Get up!" Then, to the sergeant "Remove his manacles. Bring the old man here."

Vusamanzi was led into the centre of the village square.

"Tell him I am his father," Fungabera ordered.

"Mambo, he replies that his father was a man, not a hyena."

372

"Tell him that although I cherish him and all his people, I am displeased with him."

"Mambo, he replies that if he has made Your Honour unhappy, then he is well content."

"Tell him he has lied to my men."

"Mambo, he hopes for the opportunity to do so again."

"Tell him that I know he is hiding and protecting and feeding four enemies of the state."

"Mambo, he suggests that Your Honour is demented. There are no hidden enemies of the state."

"Very well. Now address all these people. Repeat that I wish to know where the traitors are hidden. Tell them that if they lead me to them, then nobody in this village will come to any harm."

The translator stood before the silent rank of women and children and made a long and passionate plea, but when he ended, they stared back at him stolidly. One of the infants began to scream petulantly, and its mother swung it under her arm and pressed her swollen nipple into its tiny mouth. There was silence again.

"Sergeant!" Peter Fungabera gave terse orders, and Vusamanzi's hands were snatched behind his back and bound at the wrists. One of the troopers fashioned a hangman's noose in a length of nylon rope and tossed the free end of the rope over one of the main supports of an elevated maize bin at the edge of the square. They stood Vusamanzi under the maize bin and dropped the noose over his head.

"Now tell his people that when any one of them agrees to lead us to the traitors, this punishment will end immediately."

The translator raised his voice, but he had not finished before Vusamanzi called over him in a firm voice, "My curse upon any of you who speak to this Shona pig. I command silence upon you, no matter what is done. He who breaks it will be visited by me from beyond the grave. I, Vusamanzi, master of the waters, command this thing!"

"Do it!" Peter Fungabera ordered, and the sergeant inched in the slack in the rope. The noose closed around the old man's neck, and gradually he was forced up onto his tiptoes.

"Enough!" Peter Fungabera ordered and they secured the free end of the rope.

"Now, let them come forward and speak."

The translator moved down the rank of women, urging them and finally pleading unashamedly, but Vusamanzi glared at his women fiercely, unable to speak but still commanding them with all his will.

"Break one of his feet," ordered Fungabera, and the sergeant faced the old man and, with a dozen blows, using the butt of his rifle like a maize stamp, he crushed Vusamanzi's left foot. As the women heard the brittle old bones snap like kindling for the hearth, they began to wail and ululate.

"Speak!" Peter Fungabera commanded.

Vusamanzi stood on one leg, his neck twisted to one side at the pull of the rope. His damaged foot began to swell, like a balloon being inflated, to three times its natural size, the skin stretched black and shiny as an overripe fruit on the point of splitting open.

"Speak!" Peter Fungabera ordered the second time, and the mourning cries of the women drowned him out.

He nodded to the sergeant. "Break his other foot!"

As the rifle-butt shattered the complex of small bones in Vusamanzi's right foot, he fell sideways against the rope, and the sergeant stepped back grinning at the contortions of the old man as he tried frantically to relieve the pressure of the rope by taking his weight on his mutilated feet.

All the women were screaming now, and the children's cries swelled the anguished chorus. One of the old women, the senior wife, broke the line and ran forward with both thin arms outstretched towards her husband of fifty years.

"Leave her!" Peter Fungabera ordered the guards who would have restrained her. They stepped aside.

The frail old women reached her husband and tried to lift him, crying out her love and her compassion, but she did not have the strength even for Vusamanzi's emaciated body. She succeeded only in relieving the pressure on his larynx enough to prolong the agonies of his strangulation. The old man's mouth was open, hunting for air, and white froth coated his lips. He was making a harsh, cawing sound, and the old wife's antics were ludicrous.

"Listen to the Matabele rooster crow and his ancient hen cackle!" Fungabera smiled, and his troopers guffawed delightedly.

It took a long time, but when at last Vusamanzi hung still and silent with his face twisted up to the sky. His wife sank to the earth at his feet and rocked her body rhythmically as she began the keen of mourning.

Peter Fungabera walked back to the Russian, and Bukharin lit another cigarette and murmured, "Crude—and ineffective."

"There was never any chance with the old fool. We had to get him out of the way and set the mood." Peter dabbed at his chin and forehead with the tail of his scarf. "It was effective, General, just look at the faces of the women."

He tucked the scarf back into the neck of his smock and strolled back to the women.

"Ask them where the enemies of the state are hidden." But as the translator began to speak, the old woman sprang to her feet and rushed back to face them.

"You saw your lord die without speaking," she screeched. "You heard his command. You know that he will return!"

Peter Fungabera altered the grip on his swagger-stick and with little apparent effort drove the point of it up under the old woman's ribs. She screamed and collapsed. Her spleen, enlarged by endemic malarial infection, had ruptured at the blow.

"Get rid of her," Fungabera ordered, and one of the troopers seized her ankles and dragged her away behind the huts.

"Ask them where the enemies of the state are hidden."

Fungabera walked slowly along the rank, looking into their faces, evaluating the degree of terror that he saw in each pair of black Matabele eyes. He took his time over the selection, coming back at last to the youngest mother, barely more than a child herself, her infant strapped upon her back with a strip of patterned blue cloth.

He stood in front of her and stared her down. Then, when he judged the moment, he reached out and took her wrist. He led her gently to the centre of the open square, where the remains of the watch-fire still burned.

He kicked the smouldering ends of the logs together, and, still holding the girl, waited until they burst into flame again. Then he twisted the girl's arm, forcing her to her knees. Slowly silence fell over the other women, and they watched with deadly fascination.

Peter Fungabera loosened the blue cloth and lifted the infant off the girl's back. It was a boy, a chubby infant, with skin the colour of wild honey. His little pot-belly was gorged with his mother's milk, and there were creases of fat like bracelets at his wrists and ankles. The general tossed him up lightly and as he fell seized one ankle. The child shrieked with shocked outrage, dangling upside down from the man's fist.

"Where are the enemies of the state hidden?"

The child's face was swelling and darkening with blood.

"She says she does not know."

Peter Fungabera lifted the child high above the flames.

"Where are the enemies of the state?"

Each time he repeated the question he lowered the infant a few inches.

"She says she does not know."

Suddenly he lowered the little wriggling body into the very heart of the flames, and the child squealed with a totally new sound. Fungabera lifted it clear of the flames after a second and dangled it in front of the mother's face. The flames had frizzled away the child's eyelashes and the tight little criss-curls from its scalp.

"Tell her that I will roast this little piglet slowly and then I will force her to eat it."

The girl tried to snatch her child back, but he kept it just beyond her reach. The girl started screaming a single phrase, repeating it over and over again, and the other women sighed and covered their faces.

"She says she will lead you to them."

Peter Fungabera dropped the infant into her arms and strolled back to the Russian. Colonel Bukharin inclined his head slightly in grudging admiration.

*   *   *

Forty feet down Craig hung suspended before the wall of the tomb. He had anchored his waist-strap to a lump of limestone and, by the feeble yellow light of the lamp from one of the life-jackets, was carefully examining the masonry for a weak point of entry. Using his hands to supplement his water-distorted vision, he found that there was no break or aperture, but that the foot of the wall was composed of much larger lumps of limestone than the top. Probably the availability of large rocks within easy portability of the tomb had been exhausted as the work progressed and the old witch-doctor and his apprentices had fallen back on smaller material, and yet the smallest was larger than a man's head.

Craig seized one of these and struggled to dislodge it. His hands had been softened by the water, and a tiny puff of blood clouded the water as his skin split on the sharp edge of the stone, but there was no pain, for the cold had numbed him.

Almost immediately the blood-stain in the water was obscured by a shadow as the dirt and debris that had lain so long undisturbed swirled into suspension at his efforts. Within seconds he was totally blinded while the water was filthied, and he switched off the lamp to conserve the battery. Small particles of dirt irritated his eyes, and he closed them tightly, working only by sense of touch.

There are degrees of darkness, but this was total. It was a darkness that seemed to have physical weight and it crushed down upon him, emphasizing the hundreds of feet of solid rock and water above him. The oxygen he drew into his mouth had a flat chemical taste, and every few breaths a spurt of water would find its way around the ill-fitting seal of his mask and he choked upon it, forcing himself not to cough, for a coughing fit might dislodge the mask entirely.

The cold was like a terminal disease, sapping and destroying him, affecting his judgement and reactions, making it more and more difficult to guard against the onset of oxygen poisoning, and each signal on the rope from the surface seemed to be an eternity after the last. But he worked at the wall with a grim determination, beginning to hate the long-dead ancestors of Vusamanzi for their thoroughness in building it.

By the time his half-hour shift finally ended, he had pulled down a pile of rock from the head of the wall and had tunnelled a hole three or four feet into the masonry just wide enough to accommodate his upper body with its bulky oxygen equipment strapped to it, but there was still no indication as to just how much thicker the wall was.

He cleared the rock he had dislodged, kicking it down the incline of the chute and letting it fall away into the depths of the grand gallery. Then, with soaring relief, he untied the anchor-rope and slid down after it and began the long ascent to the surface of the pool.

Tungata helped him clamber out of the water onto the slab, for he was weak as a child and the equipment on his back weighed him down. Tungata pulled the set off over his head, while Sarah poured a mug of black tea and ladled sticky brown sugar into it.

"Sally-Anne?" he asked.

"Pendula is standing guard in the upper cavern," Tungata answered.

Craig cupped his hands around the mug and edged closer to the smoky little fire, shaking with the cold.

"I have started a small hole in the top of the wall and gone into it about three feet, but there is no way of guessing how thick it is or how many more dives it will need to get through it." He sipped the tea. "One thing we have overlooked: I will need something to carry the goodies, if we find them." Craig crossed his fingers and Sarah made her own sign to ward off misfortune. "The beer-pots are obviously brittle—old Insutsha broke one—and they will be awkward to carry. We will have to use the bag I made from the canvas seat-covers. When Sarah goes up to relieve Pendula, she must send them down."

As the numbness of cold was dispelled by the fire and hot tea, so the pain in his head began. Craig knew that it was the effect of breathing high-pressure oxygen, the first symptom of poisoning. It was like a high-grade migraine, crushing in on his brain so that he wanted to moan aloud. He fumbled three pain-killers from the first-aid kit and washed them down with hot tea.

Then he sat in a dejected huddle and waited for them to take effect. He was dreading his return to the wall so strongly that it sickened his stomach and corroded his will. He found that he was looking for an excuse to postpone the next dive, anything to avoid that terrible cold and the suffocating press of dark waters upon him.

Tungata was watching him silently across the fire, and Craig slipped the fur cape off his shoulders and handed the empty mug back to Sarah. He stood up. The headache had degraded to a dull throb behind his eyes.

"Let's go." he said, and Tungata laid a hand on his upper arm and squeezed it before he stooped to lift the oxygen set over Craig's head.

Craig quailed at this new contact with the icy water, but he forced himself into it, and the stone he held weighted him swiftly into the depths. In his imagination the entrance to the tomb no longer resembled an eyeless socket, but rather the toothless maw of some horrible creature from African mythology, gaping open to ingest him.

He entered it and swam up the inclined shaft, and anchored himself before the untidy hole he had burrowed into the wall. The sediment had settled. In the glow of his lamp the shadows and shapes of rock crowded in upon him, and he wrestled with another

378

attack of claustrophobia, anticipating the clouds of filth which would soon render him blind. He reached out. The rock was brutally rough on his torn hands. He prised a lump of limestone free, and a small slide of the surrounding stones sent sediment billowing around his head. He switched off his lamp and began the cold blind work again.

The rope-signals at his waist were his only contact with reality and finite time. Somehow they helped him to control his mounting terror of cold and darkness. Twenty minutes, and his headache was breaking through the drugs with which he had subdued it. It felt as though a blunt nail was being driven with hammer-blows into his temple, and as though the iron point was cutting in behind his eyes.

"I can't last another ten minutes," he thought. "I'm going up now." He began to turn away from the wall and then just managed to prevent himself.

"Five minutes," he promised himself. "Just five minutes more."

He forced his upper body into the opening, and the steel oxygen cylinder struck a rock and rang like a bell. He groped around the edges of a triangular-shaped rock that had been frustrating his efforts for the past few minutes. Once again he wished for a short jimmy bar to get into that crack and break it open. His fingers ached as he used them instead, getting them in under the rock, and then he wedged himself against the sides of the hole and began to jerk at it, slowly exerting more strength with each heave, until his back was bunched with muscle and his belly ached with the effort.

Something moved and he heard rock grate on rock. He heaved again. The crack closed on his fingers and he screamed with pain into his mask. But the pain of his crushed fingertips unlocked reserves of strength he had not yet tapped. He flung all of this against the rock and it rolled, his fingers came free and there was a rumbling, clanking roar of falling, sliding stone blocks.

He lay in the hole and hugged his injured fingers to his chest, whimpering into his mask, half-drowning in the water that had flooded in when he screamed.

"I'm going up now," he decided. "That's it. I've had enough." He began to wriggle out of the aperture, gingerly putting out one hand to push himself backwards. He felt nothing. In front of him, his hand was waving around in the open. He lay still, the water sloshing in his mask, trying to make a decision. Somehow he

379

knew that if he pulled out now and surfaced, he would not be able to force himself to enter the pool again.

Once more he groped ahead, and when he touched nothing, he inched forward and reached out again. His anchor-line held him and he slipped the knot, crept forward a little farther and the pack on his back jammed up under the stone roof. He rolled half onto his side and was able to free it. Still he could touch nothing ahead of him. He was through the wall, and a sudden superstitious dread seized him.

He pulled back and the pack hit the roof again, and this time it jammed solidly. He was stuck fast. Immediately he began to fight to be free. His breathing increased, overcoming the mechanical efficiency of the valves in his mask so that he could get no more oxygen. As he starved, his heart began to race and the pulse in his ears deafened him.

He could not go backwards. He kicked with his one good leg and, with his stump, got a purchase against smooth rock. He pushed forward with both legs. In a sudden rush similar to the moment of childbirth, he slid forward through the hole in the wall of the tomb into the space beyond.

He groped wildly about him and one hand hit the smooth wall of the shaft at his side, but now he was free of his anchor and the buoyancy of the bag on his chest bore him helplessly upwards. He threw up both hands to prevent his head striking the roof of the shaft and to grab a handhold. Under his numbed fingertips the rock was as slippery as soaped glass. As he ascended, so the oxygen in the bag expanded with the release of pressure and he went up more swiftly, only the signal-rope at his waist slowing his headlong upward rush. As he struggled to stabilize himself, the excess oxygen poured out of the sides of the mask, and panic at last rode him completely. He was swirled aloft in total, terrifying blackness.

Suddenly he burst out through the surface and lay on his back bobbing around like a cork. He tore the mask off his face and took a lungful of air. It was clean, but faintly tainted with the smell of bat guano. He lay on the surface and sucked it down gratefully.

The rope tugged rapidly at his waist. Six tugs repeated. It was the code question from Tungata. "Are you all right?" His uncontrolled ascent must have ripped rope off the coil that lay between

Tungata's feet and thoroughly alarmed him. Craig signalled back to reassure him and fumbled with the switch of his lamp.

The dim glow of light was dazzling to his eyes, which had been blinded so long, and they smarted from the irritation of the muddied waters. He blinked.

The passage had come up at a sharply increased angle from the masonry wall until it was now a vertical shaft. The old witch-doctors had been forced to chip niches in the walls and build in a ladder of rough-hewn timber to enable them to make the ascent. The poles of the ladder were secure with bark rope and were latticed up the open shaft above Craig's head, but the light of his lantern was too feeble to illuminate the top of the steep shaft. The ladder disappeared into the gloom.

Craig paddled to the side and steadied himself with a handhold on the primitive wooden ladder while he assembled his thoughts and figured out the lay of the shaft and its probable shape. He realized that by returning to water-level, he must have ascended forty feet after his access through the wall. He must have travelled an approximately U-shaped journey—the first leg down the grand gallery, the bottom of the U along the shaft to the wall, and the last leg up the steeper branch of the shaft to return to water-level again.

He tested the timber ladderwork, and though it creaked and sagged a little, it bore his weight. He would have to jettison the diving-gear and leave it floating in the shaft while he climbed up the rickety ladder, but first he must rest and regain full control of himself. He put both hands to his head and squeezed his temples. The pain was scarcely bearable.

At that moment, the rope at his waist jerked taut—three tugs, repeated. The urgent recall—the signal for mortal danger—something was desperately wrong, and Tungata was sending a warning and a plea for help.

Craig crammed the mask back onto his face and signalled, "Pull me up!"

The rope came taut and he was drawn swiftly below the surface.

•   •   •

The young Matabele mother was allowed to keep her infant strapped to her back, but she was manacled by her wrist to the wrist of the Third Brigade sergeant.

Peter Fungabera was tempted to use the helicopter to speed the pursuit and recapture of the fugitives, but finally he made the decision to go in on foot, silently. He knew the quality of the men he was hunting. The beat of a helicopter would alert them and give them a chance to slip away into the bush once again. For the same reason of stealth, he kept the advance party small and manageable—twenty picked men—and he briefed each of them individually.

"We must take this Matabele alive. Even if your own life is the exchange, I want him alive!"

The helicopter would be called in by radio as soon as they had good contact, and another three hundred men could be rushed up to seal off the area.

The small force moved swiftly. The girl was dragged along by the big Shona sergeant, and, weeping with shame at her own treachery, she pointed out the twists and forks of the barely distinguishable path.

"The villagers have been feeding and supplying them," Fungabera murmured to the Russian. "This path has been used regularly."

Bukharin glanced up at the slopes of the valley that overlooked the path. "Bad place for an ambush. They may have elements of the escapees with them."

"An ambush will mean a contact—I pray for it." And once again the Russian felt satisfaction at his choice of man. This one had the heart for the task. Now it needed only a small change in the fortunes of war, and his masters in Moscow would have their foothold in central Africa.

Once they had it, of course, this man Fungabera would need careful watching. He was not just another gorilla to be manipulated with a heavy pressure on the puppet strings. This one had depths that had not yet been fathomed, and it would be Bukharin's task to undertake this exploration. It would require subtlety and finesse. He looked forward to the work. He would enjoy it just as he was enjoying the present chase.

He swung easily along the track behind Fungabera, pacing him without having to exert himself fully, and there was that delicious tightness in his guts and the stretching of the nerves, the heightening of all the senses—that special rapture of the man-hunt.

Only he knew that the hunt would not end with the taking of

the Matabele. After that there would be other quarry, as elusive and as prized. He studied the back of the man who strode ahead of him, delighting in the way he moved, in the long elastic strides, in the way he held his head upon the corded neck, in the staining of sweat through the camouflage cloth—yes, even the odour of him, the feral smell of Africa.

Bukharin smiled. What a set of trophies to crown his long and distinguished career—the Matabele, the Shona and the land.

These mental preoccupations had in no way distracted Bukharin's physical senses. He was fully aware that the valley was narrowing, of the increased steepness of the slopes above and the peculiar stunted and deformed nature of the forest. He reached forward to touch Peter's shoulder, to draw his attention to the change in the geological formation of the cliff beside them, the contact of dolomite on country rock, when abruptly the Matabele woman began to shriek. Her voice echoed shrilly off the cliffs and repeated through the surrounding forest, shattering the hot and brooding silences of this strangely haunted valley. Her screams were unintelligible, but the warning they carried was unmistakable.

Fungabera took two swift strides up behind her, reached over her shoulder and cupped his hand under her chin. He placed his other forearm at the base of her neck and with a clean jerk pulled her head back against it. The girl's neck broke with an audible snap. Her screams were cut off as abruptly as they had begun.

As her lifeless body dropped, he spun and urgently signalled to his troopers. They reacted instantly, diving off the path and circling swiftly out ahead in the hooking movement of encirclement.

When they were in position, Fungabera glanced back at the Russian and nodded. Bukharin moved up silently beside him, and they went forward together, weapons held ready, quickly and warily.

The faint track led them to the base of the cliff and then disappeared into a narrow vertical cleft in the rock. Fungabera and Bukharin darted forward and flattened themselves against the cliff on each side of the opening.

"The burrow of the Matabele fox," Fungabera gloated quietly. "I have him now!"

• • •

"The Shona are here!" A woman's scream came from outside the cavern, muted by the fold of the rock and the screening brush. "The Shona have come for you! Run! The Shona—" Her voice was cut off suddenly.

Sarah sprang up from the fire, overturning the three-legged iron cooking-pot, and she fled across the cavern, snatching up the lantern as she went, racing into the maze of passages.

From the head of the steep natural staircase into the grand gallery she screamed her warning down towards the pool, "The Shona are here, my lord! They have discovered us!" And the echoes magnified the terror and urgency of her voice.

"I am coming to you!" Tungata boomed back up the gallery, and he came bounding up the shaft into the light of her lantern. He climbed the stone staircase, swinging himself up on the rope, and placed an arm around her shoulders.

"Where are they?"

"At the entrance. There was a voice, one of our women calling a warning—I could hear the fear in her—and then it was cut off. I think she has been killed."

"Go down to the pool. Help Pendula to bring up Pupho."

"My lord, there is no escape for us, is there?"

"We will fight," he said, "and in fighting we may find a way. Go now. Pupho will tell you what to do."

Carrying the AK 47 at the trail, Tungata disappeared into the passage leading upwards towards the main cavern. Sarah scrambled down the rock rampway, in her haste falling the last few feet, barking her knees.

"Pendula!" she called, desperate for the comfort of human contact.

"Here, Sarah. Help me."

When she reached the slab at the bottom of the gallery, Sally-Anne was waist-deep at the edge of the pool, straining on the rope.

"Help me, it's stuck!"

Sarah jumped down beside her and grabbed the tail of the rope. "The Shona have found us." She heaved on the rope.

"Yes. We heard you."

"What shall we do, Pendula?"

"Let's get Craig out of here first. He will think of something."

Suddenly the rope gave, as forty feet below Craig managed to

384

force himself through the narrow opening in the wall, and the two girls hauled him upwards hand over hand.

Oxygen bubbles burst in a seething rash on the surface of the pool, and they saw Craig coming up through the gin-clear water, the masking transforming him into some grotesque sea-monster. He reached the surface and ripped the mask off his head, snorting and coughing in the fresh air.

"What is it?" he choked out as he splashed to the edge of the rock-slab.

"The Shona are here." Both girls together, in English and Sindebele.

"Oh God!" Craig collapsed weakly onto the slab. "Oh God!"

"What shall we do, Craig?" They were both staring at him piteously, and the cold and the pain in his head seemed to paralyse him.

Abruptly the air around their heads reverberated as though they were within the sounding body of a kettledrum beaten at a furious tempo.

"Gunfire!" Craig whispered, covering his ears to protect them. "Sam has made contact."

"How long can he hold them?"

"Depends on whether they use grenades or gas—" He left it hanging and straightened up, shivering violently. He stared back at them. They seemed to sense his despair and looked away.

"Where is the pistol?" Sarah asked fearfully, glancing up at the twist of goat-skin in the crack of the rock wall.

"No," Craig snapped. "Not that." He reached out and caught her arm. He pulled himself together, shaking off despair as he shook the water from his hair.

"Have you ever used an aqualung?" he demanded of Sally-Anne. She shook her head.

"Well, now is as good a time—"

Fearfully Sally-Anne stared into the pool. "I couldn't go in there!"

"You can do anything you have to do," he snarled at her. "Listen, I have found another branch of the shaft that comes up above the surface. It will take three or four minutes—"

"No." Sally-Anne cringed away from him.

"I'll take you through first," he said, "then I will come back for Sarah."

"I would rather die here, Pupho," the black girl whispered.

"Then you'll get your wish."

Craig was already changing the oxygen bottle, screwing on one of the fresh cylinders, and he turned his attention back to Sally-Anne.

"You put your arms around me and breathe slowly and easily. Hold each breath as long as you can, then let it out carefully. The hole in the wall is narrow, but you are smaller than I am. You'll make it easily."

He lifted the oxygen set over her head and lowered it onto her shoulders. "I will go through first and pull you behind me. Once we are through it is straight up. As we go up just remember to exhale as the oxygen in your lungs expands again or you will pop like a paper bag. Come on."

"Craig, I'm afraid."

"Never thought I'd hear you say that."

Waist-deep in the pool he fitted the mask over the lower half of her face.

"Don't fight it," he told her. "Keep your eyes closed and relax. I will tow you. Don't struggle. For God's sake, don't struggle."

She nodded at him, gagged by the mask, and again the gallery echoed to the deafening roar of automatic-rifle-fire from above.

"Closer," Craig muttered. "Sam is being driven back." Then he called to Sarah on the slab above them.

"Give me my leg!" Sarah handed it down to him. He strapped it to his belt. "While I'm away, pack all the food you can find into the canvas bags. The spare lamps and batteries also. I'll be back for you inside ten minutes."

He began to hyperventilate, holding to his chest the boulder that would weight them down. He gestured to Sally-Anne and she waded up behind him and put her arms around him under his armpits.

"Take a good breath and play dead," he ordered, and filled his own lungs for the last time. He fell forward with Sally-Anne clinging to his back and they dropped together down towards the tomb entrance.

Halfway down Craig heard the click of the valves in her mask and felt Sally-Anane's chest subside and swell as she breathed. He tensed for her coughing fit. There wasn't one.

They reached the entrance and he dropped the stone and drew

her up to the wall. Gently he disentangled her hands, trying to make his movements calm and unhurried. He backed into the aperture, holding both her hands, and pulled her in after him. Unencumbered by the oxygen gear, he slid through easily.

He heard her breathe again. "Good girl!" he applauded silently. "Good brave girl!"

For a moment her gear jammed in the aperture, but he reached forward and freed it, then eased her towards him. She was through. Thank you, God, she was through.

Now up! They were accelerating, pressure squeaking in his ears. He prodded her sharply in the ribs, and heard the rush of bubbles as she released the expanding oxygen from her lungs.

"Clever girl." He squeezed her hand, and she squeezed back.

The ascent took so long that he began to fear he had lost his way and taken a false branch of the tunnel, and then suddenly they broke out through the surface and he pumped for air.

Gasping, he reached across and switched on her lamp.

"You're not good," he panted. "You are simply bloody marvellous!"

He towed her to the foot of the ladder and began stripping off her oxygen gear.

"Get up the ladder, out of the water," he grunted. "Here, strap my leg to the rung. I'll be back soonest."

He did not waste time on the difficult task of donning the gear while treading water, instead he tucked the canisters under his arm.

He had no stone to weight himself down, so he depressed the valve and emptied the oxygen bag. The set was now negatively buoyant, starting to pull him under. He could not use oxygen so he would have to free-dive again. He hung onto a rung of the ladderwork while he pumped his lungs with air, and then duck-dived.

At the wall he slid backwards through the opening, pulling the empty set after him. With the bag deflated, it came through readily enough. At the entrance to the grand gallery, he opened the tap of the oxygen cylinder. Gas hissed into the bag, swelling it, and immediately it was buoyant again. It drew Craig rapidly up to the surface of the pool.

Sarah was perched on the edge of the slab, but she had the canvas bags packed and ready.

"Come on!" Craig gasped.

"Pupho, I cannot."

"Get your little black arse down here!" he rasped hoarsely.

"Here, take the bags, I will stay."

Craig reached up and caught her ankle. He yanked her off the slab, and she splashed into the water and clung to him.

"Do you know what the Shona will do to you?" Roughly he pulled the yoke of the set over her head, and there was another burst of machine-gun fire above them, the ricochets wailing off the upper walls of the gallery.

Craig pressed the mask over her face.

"Breathe!" he ordered. She sucked air through the mask.

"Do you see how easy it is?"

She nodded.

"Here, hold the mask on your face with both hands. Breathe slowly and easily. I will carry you—lie still. Do not move!" She nodded again. He strapped the canvas bags to his waist and picked up the weight stone. He began hyperventilating.

From above them came the pocking report of a grenade-launcher. Something clattered down the gallery and the entire cavern was lit by the fierce blue glare of a phosphorus flare.

With a rock tucked under one arm and Sarah under the other, Craig ducked below the surface. Halfway down he felt Sarah try to breathe and immediately he knew they were in trouble. She took water, and began choking and wheezing into her mask. Her body convulsed against him, and she began writhing and struggling. He held her with difficulty. She was surprisingly strong, and her hard slim body twisted in his arms.

They reached the entrance to the shaft. As Craig let the weight fall, their buoyancy altered drastically. Sarah whirled on top of him and drove an elbow into his face. The blow stunned him and for a moment he relaxed his grip. She broke away from him, starting to rise rapidly, kicking and windmilling.

He reached up and just managed to grip her ankle. Anchoring himself on the sill of the entrance, he hauled her down again and in the lamp-glow saw that she had torn the mask off her face. It was snaking wildly about her head on its hose.

He dragged her bodily towards the wall, and she clawed at him and kicked him in the lower belly, but he raised his knees to protect his groin and swung her bodily around. Holding her from behind, he dragged her to the hole, and she fought him with the maniacal strength of terror and panic. He got her halfway through the wall before the hose caught in a crack in the rock, anchoring them.

While he struggled to free it, Sarah began to weaken. Her movements became spasmodic and uncoordinated. She was drowning.

Craig got both his hands on the hose and a foothold on the rock of the wall. He pulled with all the strength of his arms and his body—and the hose ripped out of the oxygen bag. The gas escaped through the rent in a roar of silver bubbles, but Sarah was free.

He pulled her out of the hole and started pedalling upwards, his one leg only just pushing them against the weight of the purged oxygen set and the drag of the canvas food-bags at his waist.

Craig's struggles to subdue Sarah had burned up his own oxygen reserves. His lungs were on fire, and his chest spasmed violently. He kept on pedalling. Sarah was quiescent in his arms, and he felt that despite all his efforts they were no longer moving, that they were hanging in the black depths, both of them slowly drowning. Gradually the urge to breathe passed, and it all ceased to be worth further effort. It was much easier just to relax and let it happen. Slowly he became aware of a mild pain. Through his indifference he wondered vaguely about that, but it was only when his head broke surface that he realized that someone had him by the hair.

Even in his half-drowned state, he realized that Sally-Anne must have seen the lamp-glow below the surface and recognized their predicament. She had dived down to them, seized Craig by the hair and dragged him up to the surface.

As he struggled for breath, he realized also that he still had his grip on Sarah's arm. The girl was floating face-down on the surface beside him.

"Help me"—he choked on his own breath—"get her out!"

Between them, they stripped the damaged oxygen set off her and lifted the unconscious girl onto the first rung of the ladderwork above the water, where Sally-Anne cradled her face-down over her lap. Sarah hung there like a drowned kitten.

Craig put his finger into her mouth, making sure that her tongue was clear, and then pressed the finger down into her throat to trigger the retching reflex. Sarah spewed up a mixture of water and vomit, and began to make small uncoordinated twitching movements.

Hanging in the water beside her, Craig splashed the vomit off her lips and then covered her mouth with his own, forcing his breath down into her lungs while Sally-Anne cradled the limp body as best she could on the awkward perch.

"She's breathing again."

Craig lifted his mouth off Sarah's. He felt sick and dizzy and weak from his own near-drowning.

"The diving set is buggered," he whispered. "The hose is torn out." He groped around for it, but it had sunk into the shaft.

"Sam," he whispered, "I've got to go back for Sam."

"Darling, you can't—you've done enough. You'll kill yourself."

"Sam," he repeated, "got to get Sam."

Clumsily he untied the straps of the canvas food-bags and hung them beside his leg on the ladder. He clung to the ladder, breathing as deeply as his aching lungs would allow. Sarah was coughing and wheezing, but she was trying to sit up. Sally-Anne lifted and held her on her lap like a child.

"Craig, darling, come back safely," she pleaded.

"Sure thing," he agreed, allowing himself the indulgence of another half-dozen breaths of air, before he pushed himself off the ladder and the cold waters closed around his head again.

The underwater section of the grand gallery, even down as deep as the mouth of the shaft, was lit by the phosphorus flares, and as Craig ascended, so the intensity of the light increased to a crackling electric blue like the glare of brute arc lamps.

As he broke through the surface of the pool, he found that the upper gallery was filled with the swirling smoke of the burning flares. He gasped for air and immediately pain shot down his throat into his chest and his eyes burned and smarted so that he could barely see.

"Tear-gas," he realized. The Shona were gassing the cavern.

Craig saw Tungata was in the water, crouched waist-deep behind the slab of rock. He had torn a strip from his shirt, wet it and bound it over his mouth and nose, but his eyes were red and running with tears.

"The whole cavern is swarming with troopers," he told Craig, his voice muffled by the wet cloth, and he stopped as a stentorian disembodied voice echoed down the gallery, its English distorted by an electronic megaphone.

"If you surrender immediately, you will not be harmed."

As if to punctuate this announcement, there was the "pock" of a grenade-launcher and another tear-gas canister came flying down the gallery, bouncing off the limestone floor like a football belching out white clouds of the irritant gas.

"They are down the staircase already. I couldn't stop them." Tungata bobbed up from behind the edge of the slab and fired a short burst up the gallery. His bullets cracked and whined from the rock, and then the AK went silent and he ducked down.

"The last magazine," he grunted and dropped the empty rifle into the water. He groped for the pistol on his belt.

"Come on, Sam," Craig gasped. "There is a way through beyond this pool."

"I can't swim." Tungata was checking the pistol, slapping the magazine into the butt and jerking back the slide to load.

"I got Sarah through"—Craig was trying to breathe through the searing clouds of gas—"I'll get you through."

Tungata looked up at him.

"Trust me, Sam."

"Sarah is safe?"

"I promise you, she is."

Tungata hesitated, fighting his fear of the water.

"You can't let them take you," Craig told him. "You owe it to Sarah and to your people."

Perhaps Craig had discovered the only appeal that would move him. Tungata pushed the pistol back into his belt.

"Tell me what to do," he said.

It was impossible to hyperventilate in the gas-laden atmosphere.

"Get what air you can and hold it. Hold it, force yourself not to breathe again." Craig wheezed. The tear-gas was ripping his lungs and he could feel the cold and deadly spread of lethargy like liquid lead in his veins. It was going to be a long, hard road home.

"Here!" Tungata pulled him down. "Fresh air!" There was still a pocket of clean air trapped below the angle of the slab. Craig drank it in greedily.

He took Tungata's hands and placed them on the canvas belt. "Hold on!" he ordered, and when Tungata nodded, he pulled one last long breath, and they ducked under together. They went down fast.

When they reached the wall there was no bulky oxygen set to encumber them, and Craig pulled Tungata through with what remained of his strength. But he was slowing and weakening drastically, once again losing the urge to breathe, a symptom of anoxia, of oxygen starvation.

They were through the wall, but he could not think what to do next. He was confused and disoriented, his brain playing tricks with him. He found he was giggling weakly, precious air bubbling out between his lips. The glow of the lamp turned a marvellous emerald green and then split into prisms of rainbow light. It was beautiful, and he examined it drunkenly, starting to roll onto his back. It was so peaceful and beautiful, just like that fall into oblivion after an injection of pentathol. The air trickled out of his mouth and the bubbles were bright as precious stones. He watched them rise upwards.

"Upwards," he thought groggily, "got to go up!" and he kicked lazily, pushing weakly upwards.

Immediately there was a powerful heave on his waist-belt, and he saw Tungata's legs driving like the pistons of a steam locomotive in the lamplight. He watched them with the weighty concentration of a drunkard, but slowly they faded out into blackness. His last thought was, "If this is dying, then it's better than its publicity," and he let himself go into it with a weary fatalism.

He woke to pain, and he tried to force himself back into that comforting womb-darkness of death, but there were hands bullying and pummelling him and the rough-barked timber rungs of the ladder cutting into his flesh. Then he was aware that his lungs burned and his eyes felt as though they were swimming in concentrated acid. His nerve ends flared up, so that he could feel every aching muscle and the sting of every scratch and abrasion on his skin.

Then he heard the voice. He tried to shut it out.

"Craig! Craig darling, wake up!" And the painful slap of a wet hand against his cheek. He rolled his head away from it.

"He's coming round!"

•　　•　　•

They were like drowning rats at the bottom of a well, clinging half-submerged to the rickety ladderwork, all of them shivering with the cold.

The two girls were perched on the lower rung, Craig was strapped to the main upright with a loop of canvas under his armpits, and Tungata, in the water beside him, was holding his head, preventing it from flopping forward.

With an effort Craig peered around at their anxious faces and then he grinned weakly at Tungata. "Sam, you said you couldn't swim—well, you could have fooled me!"

"We can't stay here." Sally-Anne's teeth chattered in her head.

"There is only one way—" They all looked up the gloomy shaft above them.

Craig's head still felt wobbly on his neck, but he pushed Tungata's hand away and forced himself to begin examining the condition of the timberwork.

It had been built sixty years ago. The bark rope that had been used by the old witch-doctors to bind the joints together had rotted and now hung in brittle strings like the shavings from the floor of a carpentry shop. The entire structure seemed to have sagged to one side unless the original builder's eye had not been accurate enough to erect a plumb-line.

"Do you think it will hold us all?" Sarah voiced the question.

Craig found it difficult to think. He saw it all through a fine mesh of nausea and bone-weariness.

"One at a time," he mumbled, "lightest ones first. You, Sally-Anne, then Sarah—" He reached up and untied his leg from the rung. "Take the rope up with you. When you get to the top, pull up the bags and the lamps."

Obediently Sally-Anne coiled the rope over her shoulder and began to climb.

She went swiftly, lightly, but the ladderwork creaked and swayed under her. As she went upwards, her lamp chased the shadows ahead of her up the shaft. She drew away until only the lamp-glow marked her position, then even that disappeared abruptly.

"Sally-Anne!"

"All right!" Her voice came echoing down the shaft. "There is a platform here."

"How big?"

"Big enough—I'm sending down the rope."

It came snaking down to them, and Tungata secured the bags to the end.

"Haul away!"

The bundle went jerkily up the shaft, swinging on the rope.

"Okay, send Sarah."

Sarah climbed out of sight, and they heard the whisper of the girls' voices high above. Then, "Okay—next!"

"Go, Sam!"

"You are lighter than I am."

"Oh, for Chrissake, just do it!"

Tungata climbed powerfully. The timberwork shook under his weight. One of the rungs broke free and fell away beneath his feet.

"Look out below!"

Craig ducked under the surface, and the pole hit the water above him with a heavy splash.

Tungata clambered out of sight, and his voice came back, "Carefully, Pupho! The ladder is breaking up!"

Craig pulled himself out of the water and, sitting on the bottom rung, strapped on his leg.

"God, that feels good." He patted it affectionately and gave a few trial kicks.

"I'm coming up," he called.

He had not reached the halfway point when he felt the structure move under him and he flung himself upwards too violently.

One of the poles broke with a report like a musket-shot, and the entire structure lurched sideways. Craig grabbed the side-frame just as three or four cross-rungs broke away under him and fell, hitting the water below with a resounding series of splashes. His legs were dangling in space, and every time he kicked for a foothold he felt the timberwork sag dangerously.

"Pupho!"

"I'm stuck. I can't move or the whole bloody thing will come down."

"Wait!"

A few seconds of silence and then Tungata's voice again: "Here's the rope. There is a loop in the end."

It dropped six feet from him.

"Swing it left a little, Sam."

The loop swung towards him.

"A little more! Lower, a little lower!" It dangled within reach.

"Hold hard!"

Craig made a lunge at it and got his arm through the loop.

"I'm coming on!"

He released his hold on the side-frame and swung free. He was too weak to climb.

"Pull me up!"

Slowly he was drawn upwards and, even in that dangerously exposed position, Craig appreciated the strength that it needed to lift a full-grown man this way. Without Tungata, he would never have made it.

He saw the glow of the lamp reflected off the walls of the shaft and getting closer, and then Sally-Anne's head peering over the edge of the platform at him.

"Not far now. Hold on!"

He came level with the edge of the rock platform, and there was Tungata braced against the far wall, a loop of the rope over his back and shoulder, hauling double-handed on the rope with the cords standing out in his throat and his mouth open, grunting with the effort. Craig hooked his elbow over the edge and then as Tungata heaved again he kicked wildly and wriggled over the edge on his belly.

It was many minutes before he could sit up and take an interest in his surroundings again. The four of them were huddled, shivering and sodden, on a canted platform of water-worn limestone, just large enough to accommodate them.

Above them, the vertical shaft continued upwards, disappearing into darkness, the walls smooth and unscalable. The ladderwork built by the old witch-doctors reached only as high as this platform. In the silence, Craig could hear the drip of water somewhere up there and the squeak of bats disturbed by their voices and movements. Sally-Anne held the lamp high, but they could not make out the top of the shaft.

Craig looked about the ledge—it was about eight feet wide—and then in the far wall he saw the entrance to a subsidiary branch of the tunnel, much lower and narrower than the main shaft, cutting into the rock on the horizontal.

"That looks like the only way to go," Sally-Anne whispered. "That's where the old witch-doctors were headed."

Nobody replied. They were all exhausted by the climb and chilled to the bone.

"We should keep going!" Sally-Anne insisted, and Craig roused himself.

"Leave the bags and rope here." His voice was still hoarse and scratchy from the tear-gas and he coughed painfully. "We can come back for them when we need them."

He did not trust himself to stand. He felt weak and unsteady and the black drop of the shaft was close at his side. He crawled on hands and knees to the opening in the far wall.

"Give me the lamp." Sally-Anne handed it to him and he crawled into the low entrance.

There was a passage beyond. After fifty feet the roof lifted so that he could rise into a crouch and, steadying himself against the wall with his free hand, go on a little faster. The others were following him. Another hundred feet, and he stooped through a last low natural doorway of stone and then stood to his full height. He looked about him with swiftly rising wonder. The others coming out of the opening behind him jostled him, but he hardly noticed it. He was soon enraptured by his new surroundings.

They stood in a group, close together, as if to draw comfort and courage from each other, and they stared. Their heads moved slowly, craning upwards and from side to side.

"My God, it beautiful," whispered Sally-Anne. She took the lamp from Craig's hand and lifted it high.

They had entered a cavern of lights, a cavern of crystal. Over countless ages the sugary crystalline calcium had been deposited by water seepage over the tall vaulted ceiling and down the walls. It had dripped onto the floor and solidified.

It had crafted marvellous sculptures in glittering iridescent light. On the walls there were traceries, like ancient Venetian lace, so delicate that the lamplight shone through them as though through precious porcelain. There were cornices and pillars of monolithic splendour joining the high roof to the floor, there were suspended marvels of rainbow colours shaped like the wings of angels in flight. Huge spiked stalactites hung as menacingly as the burnished sword of Damocles, or as the white teeth in the upper jaw of a man-eating shark. Others suggested gigantic chandeliers, or the pipes of a celestial organ, while from the floor the stalagmites rose in serried ranks, platoons and squadrons of fantastic shapes, hooded monks dressed in cassocks of mother-of-pearl, wolves and hunchbacks, heroes in gleaming armour, ballerinas and hobgoblins, graceful and grotesque, but all burning with a million tiny crystalline sparks in the lamplight.

Still in a small group, hesitantly, a step at a time, they moved forward down the length of the cavern, picking their way through the gallery of tall stalagmitic statues and stumbling over the daggerlike points of limestone that had broken off the ceiling and littered the floor like ancient arrowheads.

Craig stopped again, and the others pressed up so closely to him that they were all touching.

The centre of the cavern was open. The floor had been swept of fallen debris and, in the open space, human hands had built from gleaming limestone a square platform, a stage—or a pagan altar. On the altar, with legs drawn up against his chest, clad in the golden and dappled skin of a leopard, sat the body of a man.

"Lobengula." Tungata sank down on one knee. "The one who drives like the wind."

Lobengula's hands were clasped over his knees, and they were mummified, black and shrunken. His fingernails had continued growing after death. They were long and curved, like the claws of a predatory beast. Lobengula must once have worn a tall head-gear of feathers and fur, but it had fallen from his head and now lay on the altar beside him. The heron feathers were still blue and crisp, as though plucked that very day.

Perhaps by design, but more likely by chance, the sitting corpse had been placed directly beneath one of the seepages from the roof. Even as they stood before the altar, another droplet fell from high above and, with a soft tap, burst upon the old king's forehead, and then snaked down over his face like slow tears. Millions upon millions of drops must have fallen upon him, and each drop had laid down its deposit of shining calcium on the mummified head.

Lobengula was being transformed into stone. Already his scalp was covered with a translucent helmet, like the tallow from a guttering candle. It had run down and filled his eye-cavities with the pearly deposit; it had lined his withered lips and built up the line of his jaw. Lobengula's perfect white teeth grinned out of his stone mask at them.

The effect was unearthly and terrifying. Sarah whimpered with superstitious dread and clutched at Sally-Anne, who returned her grip as fervently. Craig played the lamp beam over that dreadful head and then slowly lowered it.

On the rock altar in front of Lobengula had been placed five dark objects. There were four beer-pots, hand-moulded from clay with a stylized diamond pattern inscribed around each wide throat, and the mouth of each pot had been sealed with the membrane from the bladder of a goat. The fifth object was a bag, made from the skin of an unborn zebra foetus, the seams stitched with animal sinew.

"Sam, you—" Craig started, and his voice cracked. He cleared

397

his throat and started again. "You are his descendant. You are the only one who should touch anything here."

Tungata was still down on one knee, and he did not reply. He was staring at the old king's transformed head, and his lips moved as he prayed silently. Was he addressing the Christian God, Craig wondered, or the spirits of his ancestors?

Sally-Anne's teeth chattered spasmodically, the only sound in the cavern, and Craig placed his arms around the two girls. They pressed against him gratefully, both of them shivering with the cold and with awe.

Slowly Tungata rose to his feet and stepped forward to the stone altar. "I see you, great Lobengula," he spoke aloud. "I, Samson Kumalo, of your totem and of your blood, greet you across the years!" He was using his tribal name again, claiming his lineage as he went on in a low but steady voice. "If I am the leopard cub of your prophecy, then I ask your blessing, oh king. But if I am not that cub, then strike my desecrating hand and wither it as it touches the treasures of the house of Mashobane."

He reached out slowly and placed his right hand on one of the black clay pots.

Craig found that he was holding his breath, waiting for he was not sure what, perhaps for a voice to speak from the king's long-dead throat, or for one of the great stalactites to crash down from the roof, or for a bolt of lightning to blast them all.

The silence drew out, and then Tungata placed his other hand on the beer-pot. Slowly he lifted it in a salute to the corpse of the king.

There was a sharp crack and the brittle baked clay split. The bottom fell out of the pot, and from it gushed a torrent of glittering light that paled and rendered insipid the crystalline coating of the great cavern. Diamonds rattled and bounced on the altar stone, tumbling and slithering over each other, piled in a pyramid, and lay smouldering like live coals in the lamplight.

• • •

"I cannot believe these are diamonds," Sally-Anne whispered. "They look like pebbles, pretty, shiny pebbles, but pebbles."

They had poured the contents of all four pots and of the zebra-skin bag into the canvas food-bag, and, leaving the empty clay pots at the feet of the old king's corpse, they retreated from Lobengula's presence to the end of the crystal cavern nearest the entrance passage.

"Well, first thing," Craig observed, "legend was wrong. Those pots weren't a gallon each, more like a pint."

"Still, five pints of diamonds is better than a poke in the eye with a rhino horn," Tungata countered.

They had salvaged a dozen poles from the top section of the ladderwork in the shaft and built a small fire on the cavern floor. As they squatted in a circle around the pile of stones, their damp clothing steamed in the warmth from the flames.

"If they are diamonds," Sally-Anne was still skeptical.

"They *are* diamonds," Craig declared flatly, "every single one of them. Watch this!"

Craig selected one of the stones, a crystal with a knife edge to one of its facets. He drew the edge across the lens of the lamp. It made a shrill squeal that set their teeth on edge, but it gouged a deep white scratch in the glass.

"That's proof! That's a diamond!"

"So big!" Sarah picked out the smallest she could find. "Even the smallest is bigger than the top joint of my finger." She compared them.

"The old Matabele labourers picked only those large enough to show up in the first wash of gravel," Craig explained. "And remember that they will lose sixty per cent or more of their mass in the cutting and polishing. That one will probably end up no bigger than a green pea."

"The colours," Tungata murmured, "so many different colours."

Some were translucent lemon, others dark amber or cognac, with all shades in between, while again there were those that were untinted, clear as snow-melt in a mountain stream, with frosted facets that reflected the flames of the smoky little fire.

"Just look at this one."

The stone Sally-Anne held up was the deep purplish blue of the Mozambique current when the tropic midday sun probes its depths.

"And this." Another as bright as the blood from a spurting artery.

"And this." Limpid green, impossibly beautiful, changing with each flicker of the light.

Sally-Anne laid out a row of the coloured stones on the cavern floor in front of her.

"So pretty," she said. She was grading them, the yellows and golds and ambers in one row, the pinks and reds in another.

"The diamond can take any of the primary colours. It seems to take pleasure in imitating the colours proper to other gems. John Mandeville, the fourteenth-century traveller, wrote that." Craig spread his hands to the blaze. "And it can crystallize to any shape from a perfect square to octahedron or dodecahedron."

"Blimey, mate," Sally-Anne mocked him, "what's an octahedron, pray?"

"Two pyramids with triangular sides and a common base."

"Wow! And a dodecahedron?" she challenged.

"Two rhombs of lozenge shape with common facets."

"How come you know so much?"

Craig smiled. "I wrote a book—remember? Half the book was about Rhodes and Kimberley and diamonds."

"Enough already," she capitulated.

Craig shook his head. "Not nearly enough. I can go on. The diamond is the most perfect reflector of light. Only chromate of lead refracts more light, only chrysolite disperses it more, but the diamond's combined powers of reflection, refraction and dispersion are unmatched."

"Stop!" ordered Sally-Anne, but her expression was still interested, and he went on.

"It's brilliance is undecaying, though the ancients did not have the trick of cutting it to reveal its true splendour. For that reason, the Romans treasured pearls more highly and even the first Hindu artisans only rubbed up the natural facets of the Kohinoor. They would have been appalled to know that modern cutters reduced the bulk of that stone from over seven hundred carats to a hundred and six."

"How big is seven hundred carats?" Sarah wanted to know.

Craig selected a stone from the ranks that Sally-Anne had set out. It was the size of a golf ball.

"That is probably three hundred carats. It might cut to a paragon, that is, a first-water diamond over a hundred carats. Then men will give it a name, like the Great Mogul or the Orloff or the Shah, and legends will be woven around it."

"Lobengula's Fire," Sarah hazarded.

Craig nodded. "Good! A good name for it. Lobengula's Fire!"

400

"How much?" Tungata wanted to know. "What is the value of this pile of pretty stones?"

Craig shrugged. "God knows. Some of them are rubbish—" He picked out a huge amorphous lump of dark grey colour in which the black specks and fleckings of its imperfections were obvious to the naked eye and the flaws and fracture lines cut through its interior like soft silver leaves. "This is industrial quality. It will be used for machine tools and the cutting edges in the head of an oil drill, but some of the others—the only answer is that they are worth as much as a rich man will pay. It would be impossible to sell them all at one time. The market could not absorb them. Each stone would require a special buyer and involve a major financial transaction."

"How much, Pupho?" Tungata insisted. "What is the least or the most?"

"I truly don't know. I could not even hazard." Craig picked out another large stone, its imperfect facets frosted and stippled to hide the true fire in its depths. "Highly skilled technicians will work on this for weeks, perhaps months, charting its grain and discovering its flaws. They will polish a window on it, so they can microscopically examine its interior. Then, when they have decided how to 'make' the stone, a master cutter with nerves of steel will cleave it along the flaw line with a tool like a butcher's cleaver. A false hammer-stroke and the stone could explode into worthless chips. They say the master cutter who cleaved the Cullinan diamond fainted with relief when he hit a clean stroke and the diamond split perfectly." Craig juggled the big diamond thoughtfully. "If this stone 'makes' perfectly, and if its colour is graded 'D', it could be worth, say, a million dollars."

"A million dollars! For one stone!" Sarah exclaimed.

Craig nodded. "Perhaps more. Perhaps much more."

"If one stone is worth that"—Sally-Anne lifted a cupped double-handful of diamonds and let them trickle slowly through her fingers—"how much will this hoard be worth?"

"As little as a hundred million, as much as five hundred million," Craig guessed quietly, and those impossible sums seemed to depress them all, rather than render them delirious with joy.

Sally-Anne dropped the last few stones, as though they had burned her fingers, and she hugged her own arms and shivered. Her damp hair hung in lank strands down her face. In the firelight all of them looked exhausted and bedraggled.

"Then as we sit here," said Tungata, "we are probably as rich as any man living—and I would give it all for one glimpse of sunlight and one taste of freedom."

"Pupho, talk to us," Sarah pleaded. "Tell us stories."

"Yes," Sally-Anne joined in. "That's your business. Tell us about diamonds, help us forget the rest. Tell us a story."

"All right," Craig agreed, and while Tungata fed the fire with splinters of wood, he thought for a moment. "Did you know that Kohinoor means 'Mountain of Light' and that Baber, the Conqueror, set its value at half the daily expense of the entire known world? You would think there could be no other gem like it, but it was only one of the great jewels assembled in Delhi. That city outstripped imperial Rome and vainglorious Babylon in its treasures. The other great jewels of Delhi had marvellous names also. Listen to these: the Sea of Light, the Crown of the Moon, the Great Mogul—"

Craig ransacked his memory for stories to keep them from dwelling on the hopelessness of their position, from the despair of truly realizing that they were entombed alive deep in the earth.

He told them of the faithful servant whom de Sancy entrusted with the great Sancy diamond, when he sent it to Henry of Navarre to add to the crown jewels of France. "Thieves learned of his journey, and they waylaid the poor man in the forest. They cut him down and searched his clothing and his corpse. When they could not find the diamond, they buried him hastily and fled. Years afterwards, Monsieur de Sancy found the grave in the forest and ordered the servant's decomposed body to be gutted. The legendary diamond was found in his stomach."

Sally-Anne shuddered. "Ghastly."

"Perhaps," Craig agreed with her. "But every noble diamond has a sanguine history. Emperors and rajahs and sultans have intrigued and mounted campaigns for them, others have used starvation or boiling oil or hot irons to prick out eyes, women have used poison or prostituted themselves, palaces have been looted and temples have been profaned. Each stone seems to have left a comet's train of blood and savagery behind it. And yet none of these terrible deeds and misfortunes ever seemed to discourage those who lusted for them. Indeed, when Shah Shuja stood before Ranjit Singh, 'the Lion of the Punjab,' starved to a skeleton and with his wives and family broken and mutilated by the tortures that had at last forced him to give up the Great Mogul, the man

402

who had once been his dearest friend, gloating over the huge stone in his fist, asked, 'Tell me, Shah Shuja, what price do you put upon it?'

"Even then Shah Shuja, broken and vanquished, knowing himself at the very threshold of ignoble death could still answer, 'It is the price of fortune. For the Great Mogul has always been the bosom talisman of those who have triumphed mightily.'"

Tungata grunted as the tale ended and prodded the pile of treasure in the firelight before him with a finger. "I wish one of these could bring us just a little of that good fortune."

And Craig had run out of stories. His throat had closed painfully from cold and talking and the searing tear-gas and none of the others could think of anything to say to cheer them. They ate the unappetizing scorched maize cakes in silence and then lay down as close to the fire as they could get. Craig lay and listened to the others sleeping, but despite his fatigue, his brain spun in circles, chasing its tail, and keeping him awake.

The only way out of the cavern was back through the subterranean lake and up the grand gallery, but how long would the Shona guard that exit? How long could they last out here? There was food for a day or two. Water seepage from the cavern roof would give them drink. But the batteries of the two lamps were failing—the light they gave was turning yellow and dull. The timber from the ladder might feed the fire for a few days more, and then—the cold and the darkness. How long before it drove them crazy? How long before they were forced to attempt that terrible swim back through the shaft into the arms of the waiting troopers at the—

Craig's broodings were violently interrupted. The rock on which he lay shuddered and jumped under him, and he scrambled to his hands and knees.

From the shadows of the cavern roof one of the great stalactites, twenty tons of gleaming limestone, snapped off like a ripe fruit in a high wind and crashed to the floor barely ten paces from where they lay. It filled the cavern with billows of limestone dust. Sarah awoke screaming with terror, and Tungata was thrashing around him and shouting as he came up from deep sleep.

The earth tremor lasted for seconds only, and then the stillness, the utter silence of the earth's depths, fell over them again and each looked into the others' frightened faces across the smouldering fire.

"What the hell was that?" Sally-Anne asked, and Craig was reluctant to answer. He looked to Tungata.

"The Shona—" Tungata said softly. "I think they have dynamited the grand gallery. They have sealed us off."

"Oh my God." Slowly Sally-Anne covered her mouth with both hands.

"Buried alive." Sarah said it for them.

• • •

The shaft was just over 160 feet deep from the edge of the platform to water level. Tungata plumbed it with the nylon rope before Craig began the descent. It was deep enough to kill or maim anybody who slipped and fell into the chasm.

They secured the end of the rope to one of the poles wedged like an anchor in the opening of the tunnel that led to the crystal cavern, and Craig abseiled down the rope to the water at the bottom of the shaft once more. Gingerly he committed his weight to the rickety remains of the ladderwork as he neared the surface of the water and then lowered himself into it.

Craig made one dive. It was enough to confirm their worst fears. The tunnel leading into the grand gallery was blocked by a heavy fall of rock. He could not even penetrate as far as the remains of the wall built by the witch-doctors. It was sealed off with loose rock that had fallen from the roof, and it was dangerously unstable. His groping hands brought down another avalanche of rumbling, rolling rock all around him.

He backed out of the tunnel and fled thankfully to the surface. He clung to the timber ladderwork, panting wildly from the terror of almost being pinned in the tunnel.

"Pupho, are you all right?"

"Okay!" Craig yelled back up the shaft. "But you were right. The tunnel has been dynamited. There is no way out!"

When he climbed back to the platform, they were waiting for him, their expressions grim and taut in the firelight.

"What are we going to do?" Sally-Anne asked.

"The first thing to do is to explore the cavern." Craig was still gasping from the swim and the climb. "Every corner and nook, every opening and branch of every tunnel. We will work in pairs. Sam and Sarah, start working from the left—use the lamps with care, save the batteries."

Three hours later, by Craig's Rolex, they met back at the fire.

The lanterns were giving out only a feeble yellow glow by now, the batteries almost drained and on the point of failing.

"We found one tunnel at the back of the altar," Craig reported. "It looked good for quite a way, but then it pinched out completely. And you? Anything?" Craig was cleaning a scrape on Sally-Anne's knee where she had fallen on the treacherous footing. "Nothing," Tungata admitted. Craig bound the knee with a strip torn from the tail of Sally-Anne's shirt. "We found a couple of likely leads, but they all petered out."

"What do we do now?"

"We will eat a little and then rest. We have got to try and sleep. We will need to keep our strength up." Craig realized it was an evasion even as he said it, but, surprisingly, he did sleep.

When he awoke, Sally-Anne was cuddled against his chest, and she coughed in her sleep. It was a rough phlegmy sound. The cold and damp was affecting them all, but the sleep had refreshed Craig and given him strength. Although his own throat and chest were still painful from the gas, they seemed to have eased a little and he felt more cheerful. He lay back against the rock wall, careful not to disturb Sally-Anne. Tungata was snoring across the fire, but then he grunted and rolled over and was silent.

The only sound in the cavern now was the drip of water from the seepages in the roof, and then, very faintly, another sound, a whispering, so low that it might have been merely the echoes of silence in his own ear. Craig lay and concentrated his hearing. The sound annoyed him, niggled at his mind as he tried to place it.

"Of course"—he recognized it—"bats!"

He remembered hearing it more clearly when he had first reached the platform. He lay and thought about it for a while and then gently eased Sally-Anne's head off his shoulder. She made a soft gurgling in her throat, rolled over and subsided again.

Craig took one of the lanterns and went back into the tunnel that led to the platform and the shaft. He flashed the lantern only once or twice, conserving what was left in the batteries, and in the dark he stood on the platform with his back against the rock wall and listened with all his being.

There were long periods of silence, broken only by the musical pinging of water drips on rock, and then suddenly a soft chorus of squeaks that echoed down the chimney of the shaft, then silence again.

Craig flicked on the lantern. The time was five o'clock. He was not certain if it was morning or evening, but if the bats were roosting up there, then it must still be daylight in the outside world. He squatted down and waited an hour, at intervals checking the slow passage of time, and then there was a new outburst of far-off bat sounds, no longer the occasional sleepy squeaks, but an excited chorus, many thousands of the tiny rodents coming awake for the nocturnal hunt.

The chorus dwindled swiftly into silence, and Craig checked his watch again. Six thirty-five. He could imagine, somewhere up above, the airborne horde pouring out of the mouth of a cave into the darkening evening sky, like smoke from a chimney-pot.

He moved carefully to the edge of the platform, steadied himself on the side-wall and leaned out over the drop very cautiously, keeping a handhold. He twisted his head to look up the shaft, holding the lantern out to the full stretch of his arm. The feeble yellow light seemed only to emphasize the blackness above him.

The shaft was semicircular in plan, about ten feet across to the far wall. He gave up on trying to penetrate the upper darkness and concentrated on studying the rock of the shaft wall opposite him, prodigally using up the battery of the lamp.

It was smooth as glass, honed by the water that had bored it open. No hold or niche, nothing, except—He strained out over the drop for an extra inch. There was a darker mark on the rock just at the very edge of his vision, directly opposite him, and well above the level of his head. Was it a stratum of colour, or was it a crack? He could not be sure, and the light was fading. It could even be a trick of shadow and light.

"Pupho"—Tungata's voice spoke behind him and he pulled back—"what is it?"

"I think this is the only way open to the surface." Craig switched off the lantern to save it.

"Up that chimney?" Tungata's voice was incredulous. "Nobody could get up there."

"The bats—they are roosting up there somewhere."

"Bats have wings," Tungata reminded him, and then, after a while, "How high up there?"

"I don't know, but I think there may be a crack or a ledge on the other side. Shine the other lamp, its battery is stronger."

They both leaned out and stared across.

"What do you think?"

"There is something there, I think."

"If I could get across to it!" Craig switched off again.

"How?"

"I don't know. Let me think."

They sat with their backs against the wall, their shoulders just touching.

After a while Tungata murmured, "Craig, if we ever get out of here—the diamonds. You will be entitled to a share—"

"Do shut up, Sam. I'm thinking." Then, after many minutes, "Sam, the poles, the longest pole in the ladder—do you think it would reach across to the other side?"

They built a second fire on the ledge, and it lit the shaft with an uncertain wavering light. Once again Craig went down the rope, onto the remains of the timber ladder, and this time he examined each pole in the structure. Most of them had been axed to shorter lengths, probably to make it easier to carry them down through the tunnels and passages from the surface, but the side-frames were in longer pieces. The longest of these was not much thicker than Craig's wrist, but the bark was the peculiar pale colour that gave it the African name of "the elephant-tusk tree." Its common English name was "leadwood," and it was one of the toughest most resilient woods of the veld.

Moving along it, measuring it with the span of his arms, Craig reckoned this pole was almost sixteen feet long. He secured the end of the rope to the upper end of the pole, shouting up to the platform to explain what he was doing, and then he used his clasp-knife from the kit to cut the bark rope holding the pole into the ladderwork. There was the terrifying moment when the pole finally broke free and hung on the rope, swinging like a pendulum, and the entire structure, deprived of its kingpin, began to break up and slide down the shaft.

Craig hauled himself up the rope and flung himself thankfully onto the platform, and when he had recovered his breath, the pole was still dangling down the shaft on the end of the rope, although the rest of the ladderwork had collapsed into the water at the bottom.

"That was the easy part," Craig warned them grimly.

With Tungata and himself providing the brute strength, and the two girls coiling and guiding the rope, they worked the pole up an inch at a time until the tip of it appeared above the level of the platform. They anchored it, and Craig lay on his belly and used

407

the free end of the rope to lasso the bottom end of the pole. Now they had it secured at both ends and could begin working it up and across.

After an hour of grunting and heaving, and coaxing, they had one end of the pole resting against the wall of the shaft opposite them, and the other end thrust back into the tunnel behind them.

"We have got to lift the far end," Craig explained while they rested, "and try and get it into that crack on the far wall—if it is a crack."

Twice they nearly lost the pole as it rolled out of their grip and almost fell into the well below, but each time they just held it on the rope and then began the heart-breaking task all over again.

It was after midnight by Craig's watch before they at last had the tip of the pole worked up the far wall to the height of the dark mark, only just visible in the beam of the lamp.

"Just an inch to the right," Craig grunted, and they rolled it gently, felt the pole slide in their hands, and then with a small bump the tip of it lodged in the crack in the wall opposite them and both Craig and Tungata sagged onto their knees and hugged each other in weary congratulations.

Sarah fed the fire with fresh wood and in the flare of light they reviewed their work. They now had a bridge across the shaft, rising from the platform on which they stood at a fairly steep angle, the rear end jammed solidly against the wall behind them, and the far end wedged in the narrow crack in the opposite wall.

"Somebody has to cross that." Sally-Anne's voice was small and unsteady.

"And what happens on the other side?" Sarah asked.

"We'll find out when we get there," Craig promised them.

"Let me go," Tungata said quietly to Craig.

"Have you ever done any rock-climbing?" Tungata shook his head. "Well, that answers that," Craig told him with finality. "Now we'll take two hours' rest—try and sleep."

However, none of them could sleep, and Craig roused them before the two hours were up. He explained to Tungata how to set himself up firmly as anchorman, sitting flat with both feet braced, the rope around his waist and up over his back and shoulder.

"Don't give me too much slack, but don't cramp me," Craig explained. "If I fall I'll shout 'I'm off!' Then jam the rope like this and hold with everything you've got, okay?"

He hung one of the lanterns over his shoulder with a strip of canvas as a sling and then, with both the girls sitting on the end of the pole to hold it firmly, Craig straddled it and began working out along it with both feet dangling into the void. The loop of rope hung behind him as Tungata fed it out.

Within a few feet Craig found that the upward angle was too steep, and he had to lie flat along the pole with his ankles hooked over it and push himself upwards with his legs. He moved quickly out of the firelight, and the black emptiness below him was mesmeric and compelling. He did not look down. The pole flexed under the weight of each of his movements. He heard the far tip of it grating against the rock above him. But at last his fingertips touched the cold limestone of the shaft wall.

He groped anxiously for the crack and felt a little lift of his spirits as his fingers made out the shape of it. It ran vertically up the shaft, the outside lips about three inches wide, just enough to accommodate the end of the pole, then it narrowed quickly as it went deeper.

"It's a crack all right!" he called back. "And I'm going to have a shot at it."

"Be careful, Craig."

"Christ!" he thought. "What a stupid bloody thing to say."

He reached up to a comfortable stretch of his left arm and thrust his hand, with the fingers folded into a loose fist, as deeply as it would go into the crack. Then he bunched his fist, and as it changed shape it swelled and jammed firmly in the crack and he could put his weight on it.

He pulled himself into a sitting position on the pole bridge, drew one knee up to his chest and with his free hand reached down and locked the clip on his artificial ankle. The ankle was now rigid.

He took a full breath and said softly, "Okay, here we go."

He reached up with his free hand, pushed it into the crack and made another "jam-hold" with his right fist. He used the strength of both arms to pull himself up onto his knees, balancing on the pole.

He relaxed the lower hand and it slipped easily out of the crack. He reached up as high as he could and thrust it into the crack and expanded his fist again. He pulled himself upright, and he was standing on the pole facing the wall.

He stepped up with his artificial foot, turning it so the toe went into the crack as deeply as the instep and then when he straightened his leg the toe twisted and bit into both sides of the rock crack. He stepped up, leaving the pole below him.

"Good old tin toes," he grunted. His good leg and foot could not have borne the weight, not without specialized climbing boots to protect and strengthen them.

He reached up and took a jam-hold with each hand and lifted himself by the strength of his arms alone. As soon as the weight came off his leg, he twisted the foot, slipped it out of the crack and pulled up his knee to make another toe-hold eighteen inches higher. Suspended alternately on his arms and then on his one leg, he pushed upwards, and the rope slithered up after him.

Now that he was out of the firelight and into darkness, he had only his sense of touch to guide him, and the black drop seemed to suck at his heels as he hung out backwards from the sheer wall. He was counting each step upwards, reckoning each at eighteen inches, and he had gone up forty feet when the crack started to widen. He had to reach deeper into it each time to make a jam, and in consequence each of his steps became shorter and placed more strain on his arms and leg.

Forced contact with the stone had abraded the skin off his knuckles, making every successive hold more agonizing, and the unaccustomed exercise was cramping the muscle on the inside of his thigh and groin into knots of fire.

He couldn't go on much longer. He had to rest. He found himself pulling in against the wall, pressing himself to it, touching the cold limestone with his forehead like a worshipper. *To lie against the wall is to die*, that is the first law of the rock-climber. It is the attitude of defeat and despair. Craig knew it, and yet he could do nothing to prevent it.

He found he was sobbing. He took one fist out of the crack and flapped it, loosening the fingers, forcing blood back into them, and then he held them to his mouth and licked the broken skin. He changed hands, whimpering as fresh blood flowed back into the cramped hand.

"Pupho, why have you stopped?" Tungata was no longer paying out the rope and he was anxious.

"Craig, don't give up, darling. Don't give up." Sally-Anne had sensed his despair, and there was something in her voice that gave him new strength.

Gradually he pushed himself outwards, hanging back from the

wall, coming into balance again, his weight on the leg. He reached up, one hand at a time, left and right, hold hard, pull up the leg, step up—and again, and then the whole hellish tortuous thing again, and yet again. Another ten feet, twenty feet—he was counting in the darkness.

Reach up with the right hand and—and—nothing. Open space. Frantically he groped for the crack—nothing. Then his hand struck rock out to one side. The crack had opened wide into a deep V-shaped niche, wide enough for a man to force his whole body into it.

"Thank you, God, oh thank you, thank you—" Craig dragged himself up into it, wedging his hips and shoulders, and hugging his damaged hands to his chest.

"Craig!" Tungata's shout rang up the shaft.

"I'm all right," Craig called back. "I've found a niche. I'm resting. Give me five."

He knew he couldn't wait too long, or his hands would stiffen and become useless. He kept flexing them as he rested.

"Okay!" he called down. "Going up again."

He pushed himself upwards with the palms of his hands on each side of the cleft, facing outwards into the total darkness of the shaft.

Swiftly the cleft opened and became a wide, deep chimney, so that he could no longer reach across it with his arms. He had to turn sideways, wedge his shoulders on one side of it, and walk up the other side with his feet, wriggling his shoulders and pushing up with his palms on the stone under him a few inches at a time. It went quickly, until abruptly the chimney ended. It closed to a crack so narrow that reaching upwards he could not even fit his finger into it.

He reached around the top of the chimney out onto the wall of the shaft. He groped as high as he could reach and there was no hold or irregularity in the smooth limestone above him.

"End of the road!" he whispered, and suddenly every muscle in his body began to shriek in silent spasms of pain, and he felt crushed under a load of weariness. He did not have the energy for that long dangerous retreat back down the chimney, and he did not have the strength to keep himself wedged awkwardly in the rocky cleft.

Then abruptly a bat squeaked shrilly above him. It was so close and clear that he almost relaxed his grip with shock. He caught

411

himself, and though his legs juddered under the strain, he worked his way sideways to the outermost edge of the chimney. The bat squeaked again, and was answered by a hundred others. It must be dawn already—the bats were returning to their roosts somewhere up there.

Craig balanced himself so that he had his outside hand free. He groped for the lantern on its strip of canvas around his neck and held it out into the open shaft. Then he twisted his head, and wriggled even farther outwards until he was holding with only the point of one shoulder, and his head was protruding around the sharp corner of the chimney into the open shaft.

He switched on the lantern. Instantly there was a hubbub of alarmed bats—their terrified shrills and the flutter of their wings—and three feet above Craig's head, impossibly out of reach, there was a window in the rock wall, from which the sounds reverberated as though from the brass throat of a trumpet. He stretched for it, but his fingers were twelve inches short of the sill.

As he yearned upwards, the yellow glow of the lantern faded away. For some seconds the filaments still burned redly in their tiny glass ampoule and then they too died, and the darkness rushed back to engulf Craig, and he retreated into the chimney.

In frustration he hurled the useless lantern from him, and it clattered against the rock as it fell, each rattle becoming fainter until seconds later there was a distant splash as it hit the water far below.

"Craig!"

"Okay. I dropped the light."

He heard the bitterness and despondency in his own voice, but he tried once more to reach the window above him. His fingernails scratched futilely on the stone, and he gave up and began slipping back down the chimney. In the V-shaped niche where the crack and chimney met, he wedged himself again.

"What is happening, Craig?"

"It doesn't go," he called down. "There is no way out. We are finished, unless—" He broke off.

"What is it? Unless what?"

"Unless one of the girls will come up and help me."

There was silence below him.

"I'll come," Tungata broke the silence.

"No good. You are too heavy. I couldn't hold you."

Silence again, and then Sally-Anne said, "Tell me what to do."

"Tie on to the end of the rope. Use a bowline knot."

"Okay."

"All right, come out across the pole. I'll be holding you."

Peering down he could see her silhouetted against the soft glow of the fire as she worked her way across. He took up the slack in the rope carefully, ready to jam it if she fell.

"I'm across."

"Can you find the crack?"

"Yes."

"I'm going to pull you up. You must help me by pushing with your toes in the crack."

"Okay."

"Go!"

He felt her full weight come on the rope, and it bit into his shoulder.

"Push up!" he ordered, and as he felt the load lighten, he grabbed the slack.

"Push!" She came up another four inches.

"Push!" It seemed to go on and on, and then she screamed and the rope burned out in a hard, heavy run across his shoulder. He was almost jerked out of his niche.

He fought it, jamming hard, feeling the skin smear off his palms on the harsh nylon until he stopped it. Sally-Anne was still screaming, and the rope pendulumed back and forth as she swung sideways along the wall.

"Shut up!" he roared at her. "Get hold of yourself."

She stopped screaming, and gradually her swings became shorter.

"I lost my footing." Her voice was almost a sob.

"Can you find the crack again?"

"Yes."

"All right, tell me when you are ready."

"Ready!"

"Push up!"

He thought it would never end, and then he felt her hand touch his leg.

"You made it," he whispered. "You wonderful bloody female."

He made a space for her in the chimney below him and he helped her into it. He showed her how to wedge herself securely, and then he held her shoulder, squeezing hard.

"I can't go any further." Her first words after she recovered.

"That was the worst, the rest is easy."

He wouldn't tell her about the window—not yet. He cheered her instead.

"Listen to the bats. The surface must be close, very close. Think of that first glimpse of sunlight, that first breath of sweet dry air."

"I'm ready to go on," she said at last, and he led her up the chimney.

As soon as it was wide enough to cross over, he made her climb ahead of him, so that he could place her feet with his hands, and help her to push upwards when the chimney became too wide for her to be able to exert her full strength.

"Craig. Craig! It's closed. It has pinched in. It's a dead end."

Her panic was just below the surface and he could feel she was shaking as she choked down her sobs.

"Stop it," he snapped. "Just one more effort. Just one, I promise you."

He waited for her to quieten, then he went on: "There is a window in the wall just above your head, just around the corner of the chimney. Only a foot or two—"

"I won't be able to reach it."

"Yes! Yes, you will. I'm going to make a bridge for you with my body. You will stand on my stomach. You'll reach it easily. Do you hear me? Sally-Anne, answer me."

"No." Very small and faint. "I can't do it."

"Then none of us is going anywhere," he said sharply. "It's the only way out. You do it or we rot here. Do you hear me?"

He worked up close beneath her, so that her sagging buttocks were pressed into his belly. Then he braced with all his strength, pressing with both legs into one side of the chimney and with his shoulders into the other, forming a human bridge beneath her.

"Slowly let go," he whispered. "Sit on my stomach."

"Craig, I'm too heavy."

"Do it, damn you. Do it!"

Her weight came onto him, and the pain was too much to bear. His sinews and muscles were tearing, his vision filled with flashing lights.

"Now straighten up," he blurted.

She came up onto her knees. Her kneecaps bit into his flesh like crucifixion nails.

"Stand!" he groaned. "Quickly!"

414

She tottered on the unsteady platform of his body as she came upright.

"Reach up! High as you can!"

"Craig, there is a hole up here!"

"Can you get into it?"

No reply. She shifted her stand on him, and he cried aloud with the effort of holding her.

She bounced, and then her weight was gone. He heard her feet scrabbling against the shaft and the brush of the rope as she dragged herself upwards. The rope followed her like a monkey's tail.

"Craig, it's a shelf—a cave!"

"Find somewhere to tie your end of the rope."

A minute, and another—he couldn't hold out, his limbs were numb, his shoulders were—

"I've tied it! It's safe."

He tugged on the rope and it came up firm and secure. He took a loop around his wrist and let his feet go. He swung out of the chimney and dangled into the open shaft.

He pulled himself up the rope, hand over hand, and then he tumbled over the sill into the stone window, and Sally-Anne hugged him to her bosom. Too far gone to speak, he clung to her like a child to its mother.

"What is happening up there?" Tungata could not contain his impatience.

"We have found another lead," Craig called back. "It must be open to the surface somewhere. There are bats."

"What must we do?"

"I am going to drop the rope. There will be a loop in it. Sarah first. She will have to cross the pole and get into the loop. The two of us will be able to pull her up." It was a long message to shout. "Do you understand?"

"Yes. I'll make her do it."

Craig tied a loop in the end of the rope, and then, still without light crawled back to the anchor-point that Sally-Anne had chosen. He ran his hands over it. It was a pinnacle of rock, twelve feet back from the ledge and her knot was good. He went back and dropped the looped end down into the shaft. He lay on his stomach and peered into the echoing darkness. The first glow was far below, a dull furnace redness. He could hear the whisper of their voices.

"What's keeping you?" he demanded.

Then he saw the shape, only just visible in the firelight, moving

415

out across the pole bridge. It was too big to be one person, and then he realized that both Tungata and Sarah were on the pole together. Tungata was coaxing her across, riding out backwards and drawing her after him.

They moved out of sight, directly below the window.

"Pupho, swing the rope to the left."

Craig obeyed, and felt the tug on it as Tungata grabbed the swinging loop.

"All right, Sarah is in the loop."

"Explain to her that she must walk up the rock as we pull her."

Sally-Anne sat directly behind Craig, the rope running over his shoulder to her. Craig had his feet braced against the side-wall.

"Pull!" he ordered, and quickly she picked up the rhythm of it. Sarah was small and slim, but it was a long haul and Craig's hands were raw. It was five minutes of hard work before they dragged her over the sill and the three of them rested together.

"All right, Sam. We are ready for you now." He dropped the loop into the shaft.

There were three of them on the rope, sitting one behind the other, but Tungata was a big, heavy man. Craig could hear the girls whimpering and sobbing with the effort.

"Sam, can you jam yourself into the chimney?" Craig gasped. "Give us a rest?"

He felt the weight go off the rope, and the three of them lay in a heap and rested.

"All right, let's go again."

Tungata seemed even heavier now, but finally he came tumbling into the window, and none of them could talk for a while.

Craig was the first to find his voice. "Oh, shit, we forgot the diamonds! We left the bloody diamonds."

There was a click and a yellow glow of light as Tungata switched on the second lantern that he had brought up with him. They all blinked owlishly at each other, and Tungata chuckled hoarsely.

"Why do you think I was so heavy?"

He held the canvas bag in his lap, and as he patted it, the diamonds crunched together with a sound like a squirrel chewing nuts.

"Hero!" Craig grunted with relief. "But switch off, there are only a few minutes' life left in that battery."

They used the lantern in flashes. The first flash showed them that the rock window opened into a low-roofed cave, so wide that they could not make out the side-walls. The roof was coated with a furry mass of bats. Their eyes were myriad pinpricks of reflected light and their naked faces were pink and hideous as they stared down at them, hanging upside-down.

The floor of the cave was carpeted with their droppings. The reeking guano had filled every irregularity, and the floor was level and soft underfoot, deadening their footfalls as they went forward in a group, holding hands to keep contact.

Tungata led them, flashing the lantern every few minutes to check the floor ahead and to reorientate himself. Craig was in the rear with the coiled rope looped over his shoulder. Gradually the floor started to slope upwards under them and the roof hung lower.

"Wait," said Sally-Anne. "Don't switch on the light again."

"What is it?"

"Ahead—up the slope. Is it my imagination?"

Craig stared into the blackness ahead, and slowly out of it emerged a faint nimbus, a lessening of the utter blackness.

"Light," he whispered. "There is light up there."

They started forward, bumping into each other in their haste, running and pushing, laughing as the light strengthened and they could make out each other's shapes, the laughter becoming wild hysteria. The light turned to a golden glory ahead and they fought their way up the soft, yielding slope of guano towards it.

Gradually the roof pressed down onto them, forcing them to their knees, and then onto their bellies, and the light was a thin horizontal blade that blinded them with its brilliance. They clawed their way towards the light, stirring the guano dust so that it coated their faces and choked them, but they whooped and shouted hysterically through it.

Craig saw that Sarah was weeping unashamedly, tears shining on her face. Tungata was bellowing with wild laughter, and Craig flung himself forward and grabbed his ankles just as he reached the low slitted entrance of the cave.

"Wait, Sam. Be careful."

Tungata tried to kick his hands away and crawl on, but Craig held him.

"Shona! There are Shona out there."

That name halted and silenced them. They lay just within the threshold of the cavern, and their euphoria evaporated.

"Craig and I will go ahead to scout the lie of the land." Tungata groped in the guano and passed a rock the size of a baseball back to Craig. "It's the best weapon I have. You two women will stay here until we call you, okay?"

Craig took a double handful of the guano and blackened his face and limbs with it. Then he slipped the coil of rope off his shoulder and crawled up beside Tungata. He was content to let Tungata take control now. In the cavern, Craig had been the leader, but out there was Tungata's world. In the bush Tungata was a leopard man.

They crawled up the last few feet to the entrance. It was a low horizontal slit in the rock, less than eighteen inches high and screened by golden elephant grass growing just beyond the threshold. It was facing east, for the early morning sunshine was blazing into their faces. They lay for a while, letting their eyes adjust to its glare after those days of dark.

Then Tungata slid forward like a black mamba, barely moving the tall grass as he went through it.

Craig gave him a count of fifty and followed him. He came out on a hillside with the stratum of limestone forming buttresses across it, over which grew the stunted, desiccated brush and wiry elephant grass. They were just below the summit, and the slope dropped away steeply below them into the heavily forested valley. Already the morning sun was hot and Craig revelled in it.

Tungata was lying below him, and he gave Craig the hand-signal, "Cover my left side."

Craig moved carefully into position, walking on his elbows and dragging his legs.

"Search!" Tungata gave him the peremptory signal, and they lay for fully ten minutes scrutinizing the ground below, above and on both sides, covering every inch, every bush and rock and field.

"All clear," Craig signalled, and Tungata began to move along the contour of the slope towards the shoulder of the hill. Craig kept behind and above him, covering him.

A bird came towards them, a black and white bird with a disproportionally large yellow beak, a huge, semitically curved yellow bill that gave it its common name of hornbill. Its flight was characteristically erratic and swooping, and it settled on a low bush jut ahead and below Tungata—but almost immediately it let out a harsh squawk of alarm and hurled itself into the air again, swooping away down the hillside.

"Danger!" Tungata made the urgent hand-signal, and they froze.

Craig stared at the clump of rock and grass and bush from

which the hornbill had fled, trying to discover what had alarmed it.

Something moved, a tiny stirring, and it was so close that Craig clearly heard the flare of a match being struck and lit. A feather of ethereal smoke drifted from the clump of brush and prickled his nostrils with the stink of tobacco burning. Then he made out the shape of a steel battle-helmet, covered with camouflage net. It moved away as the man wearing it drew again on his cigarette.

Now Craig saw the whole picture. In his camouflage jacket, the man was lying behind a light machine-gun on a tripod. The barrel of the weapon was bound with streamers of hessian to disguise its stark outline.

"How many?" Tungata signalled the question, and then Craig saw the second man. He was sitting with his back to the base of the low thorn-tree. The shadow of the branches over his head blended perfectly with the tiger stripes of his camouflage. He was a big man, bare-headed, with a sergeant's chevrons on his arm, and a Uzi machine-gun laid beside him.

Craig was about to signal, "Two," when the man slipped a soft pack of cigarettes out of his breast-pocket and held it out. A third man, who had been lying flat on his back in the shade, sat up and accepted the pack. He tapped out a cigarette and then tossed the pack to a fourth man, who rolled onto his elbow to catch it, revealing himself for the first time.

"Four!" Craig signalled.

It was a machine-gun post, perfectly sited on the shoulder of the hill to cover the slopes below. Peter Fungabera had obviously anticipated the existence of bolt-holes from the main cavern. The hills must all be staked out with nests of machine-guns. It was mere fortune that had brought them out above this post. The gunner was facing downhill; his mates were stretched out relaxed and bored from days of unrewarded vigil.

"Move into attack position," Tungata signalled.

"Query?" Craig flicked his thumb. "Four! Query?" Craig questioned the odds.

"Go right!" Tungata signalled, and then enforced the order with the clenched fist. "Imperative!"

Craig felt his blood charging with adrenalin, the heat of it spreading down his limbs, his mouth drying out. He clutched the round stone in his right hand.

They were so close that he could see the wet spit on the tip of the cigarette as the machine-gunner took it from his lips. The nest was littered with their rubbish: paper wrappers and empty food-cans and cigarette butts. Their weapons were laid carelessly aside. The man lying on his back had covered his eyes with his arm and the burning cigarette stuck up like a candle from his lips. The sergeant against the tree was whittling a piece of wood with his trench-knife. The third had unbuttoned his jacket and was minutely searching his own chest hair for body vermin. Only the man behind the gun was alert.

Tungata was sliding into position beside Craig.

"Ready?" He raised his hand and glanced at Craig.

"Affirmative."

Tungata's hand came down, the order to execute.

Craig went in, rolling over the edge of the nest, and he hit the man with the trench-knife. He hit him in the temple with the stone, and he knew instantly that it was too hard. He felt bone break in the man's head.

The sergeant sagged forward without a sound, and at the same instant Craig heard a soft scuffle and grunt behind him as Tungata took on the machine-gunner. Craig did not even glance around. He snatched up the Uzi machine-gun and cocked it.

The searcher after body vermin looked up and his jaw sagged open as Craig thrust the muzzle into his face, pressing the circle of steel against his cheek and glaring into his eyes, dominating him, compelling silence.

Tungata had picked up the sergeant's fallen trench-knife and now he dropped onto the reclining trooper, driving one knee into his diaphragm, forcing all the air from his lungs in a single explosive sigh, and then pressing the point of the knife into the soft flesh below his ear. Still on his back, the man struggled to refill his lungs as his face swelled and contorted.

"If any man cries out," Tungata whispered, "I will cut off his testicles and stick them in his mouth."

It had all taken less than five seconds.

Tungata knelt beside the sergeant whom Craig had stoned, and felt for the pulse in his throat. After a few seconds he shook his head, and began stripping the corpse of its battle-jacket. He shrugged into it. It was too small for him, binding across the chest.

"Take the gunner's uniform," he ordered, while he took the Uzi from Craig and covered the two prisoners with it.

420

The machine-gunner's neck was broken. Tungata had jerked back his helmet and the strap had caught under his chin. The dead man's camouflage jacket stank of rancid stale sweat and tobacco smoke, but it fitted Craig well enough. The steel helmet was too big—it came down to his eyes—but it covered his long straight hair.

Tungata thrust his face close to those of the prisoners.

"Drag the bodies of these Shona dogs with you."

Craig and Tungata covered them while they pulled the two naked dead men, feet first, through the grass to the cave entrance and then rolled them down the slope into the dark interior.

The two women were shocked and silenced.

"Strip!" Tungata ordered the prisoners. When they were in their army-issue shorts, Tungata ordered Craig, "Tie them!"

Craig gestured them to lie on their stomachs, and using the nylon rope bound their wrists at the small of the back, then pulled up their legs and bound wrists to ankles. It was a hog-tying that left them helpless. Then he pulled the stockings off their feet and stuffed them into their mouths and tied the gags in place.

While he was working, Tungata was dressing Sarah and Sally-Anne in the discarded battle-dress. The clothes were many sizes too large, but the women folded back the cuffs at wrists and ankles and belted the trousers in a bunch around their waists.

"Black your face, Pendula," Tungata ordered, and Sally-Anne smeared herself. "Hands also. Now cover your hair." He pulled a beret out of a pocket of his purloined jacket and tossed it to her.

"Come on." Tungata picked up the canvas bag of diamonds and started back up the slope. He led them back to the abandoned machine-gun nest.

Tungata tipped up a field pack, emptying it out onto the ground, and then shoved the bag of diamonds into the pack and rebuckled it. He slung the pack onto his back.

Craig had been ransacking the other equipment. He passed two grenades to Tungata and stuffed two more into his own pockets. He found a Tokarev pistol for Sarah, and gave another Uzi to Sally-Anne. There was an AK 47 for himself, with five spare magazines. Tungata kept the second Uzi. Craig added a water-bottle to his load. He broke open an emergency pack of chocolate and they all stuffed their mouths as they prepared to leave. It tasted so good that Craig's eyes watered.

"I'll take the point," Tungata spoke through a sticky mouthful of chocolate. "We'll try and get down into the valley, under cover of the trees."

They kept just under the shoulder of the hill, going directly down the slope, taking the chance that the open slope to their right was clear.

They were just above the tree-line when they heard the helicopter. It was coming up the valley. It was still behind the shoulder of the hill, but coming on fast.

"Hit the ground!" Craig ordered, and slammed Sally-Anne between the shoulder-blades with the flat of his hand. They went down and pushed their faces to the earth, but the beat of the rotor changed, altering to coarse pitch, and now the sound was stationary, just out of their line of sight behind the fold of rocky hillside.

"It's landing," Sally-Anne said, and the engine noise died away. Sally-Anne cocked her head. "She's down, she's landed. There! He has cut the motor."

In the silence they could hear, very faintly, orders being shouted.

"Pupho, come up here," Tungata ordered. "You two, wait."

Craig and Tungata crawled up the shoulder of the hill and very slowly raised their heads to look over the crest.

Below them, a quarter of a mile down the valley, there was a small level clearing at the edge of the forest. The grass had been flattened and there was an open-sided canvas sun shelter at the edge of the trees on the far side of the clearing. The helicopter stood in the centre of the clearing, and the pilot was climbing down from the fuselage port. There were uniformed troopers of the Third Brigade under the trees near the tent, and in the tent they could make out three or four men sitting at a table.

"Advance headquarters," Craig murmured.

"This is the valley that we entered. The main cave is just below us."

"You are right." Craig had not recognized the ground from this direction and height.

Tungata pointed into the trees. "Looks as though they are pulling out." A platoon of camouflaged troopers was moving back down the valley in Indian file.

"They probably waited for forty-eight hours or so after dynamiting the grand gallery. Now they must have given us up for dead and burried."

"How many?" Tungata asked.

"I can see"—Craig screwed up his eyes—"twenty at least, not counting those in the tent. There will be others staking out the hills, of course."

Tungata drew back from the skyline and beckoned to Sally-Anne. She crawled up beside him.

"What do you make of that machine?" he pointed at the helicopter.

"It's a Super Frelon," she replied without hesitation.

"Can you fly it?"

"I can fly anything."

"Damn it, Sally-Anne, don't be clever," Craig whispered irritably. "Have you ever flown one of those?"

"Not a Super Frelon, but I have five hundred hours in helicopters."

"How long would it take you to start up and get moving, once you're in the cockpit?"

Now she hesitated. "Two or three minutes."

Craig shook his head. "Too long."

"What if we can pull the guards away from the clearing while Pendula starts up?" Tungata asked.

"That might work," Craig agreed.

"This is it then." Tungata set it out quickly. "I will track up to the head of the valley. You take the women down to the edge of the clearing. Got it?"

Craig nodded.

"Forty-five minutes from now"—he checked his wrist-watch—"nine-thirty exactly, I will start throwing grenades and firing with the AK. That should pull most of the Shona away from the clearing. As soon as the shooting starts, you head for the helicopter. When I hear the helicopter lift off, I'll run out on the open slope, there!" He pointed up the valley. "Just below that rock sheet. The Shona will not have reached me by that time. You can make the pick-up from there."

"Let's do it." Craig passed Tungata the AK 47 and the spare magazines. "I'll keep the Uzi and one grenade." He took the submachine-gun from Tungata.

"Take the diamonds also." Tungata shrugged out of the straps of the backpack and pushed it across to Craig.

"See you later." Craig slapped his shoulder, and Tungata slid away down the slope.

Craig led the women straight down along the spine of the hill,

423

keeping in the scrub and broken rock. It was a relief to reach the tree-line and discover a ravine that angled back along the edge of the clearing. They crept down it, Craig cautiously lifting his head above the bank to check their progress every few hundred feet.

"This is as close as we can get to the helicopter," he whispered and they sank down, resting below the lip of the bank. Craig slipped out of the heavy pack and had another look over the bank.

The helicopter stood out in the open, a hundred and fifty paces away. The pilot was squatting beside the landing-gear in the shade cast by the fuselage. The Super Frelon was a bulky, blunt-nosed machine, painted dull sage-green. Craig sank down again beside Sally-Anne.

"What range does it have?" Craig asked in a whisper.

"Not certain," Sally-Anne whispered back. "With full tanks about six hundred miles, I'd guess."

"Pray for full tanks." Craig glanced at his Rolex. "Ten minutes." From his pocket he handed them each another slab of chocolate.

Sally-Anne's sweat had streaked the blackening on her cheeks. Craig mixed dirt and water from the bottle into a muddy paste and repaired her make-up. Then she did the same to him.

"Two minutes." Craig checked the time and glanced over the bank.

The helicopter pilot stood up and stretched, then he climbed back into the Super Frelon.

"Something is happening," Craig murmured.

The helicopter partially obscured his view of the tent across the clearing, but he could see that there was activity over there as well.

A small group was leaving the tent. The guards were saluting and strutting about importantly, and then suddenly the rotor of the helicopter turned and the starter motor whirred noisily. Blue smoke fired from the exhaust vents and with a roar the main engine of the Super Frelon came to life.

A pair of officers left the group in front of the tent and started across the clearing, heading for the helicopter.

"We have got trouble," Craig muttered grimly, "they are pulling out." And then he started, "That's Fungabera!"

Fungabera was wearing the burgundy beret with silver leopard's-head cap-badge, the bright rows of decoration ribbons on his chest, and the scarf in the opening of his battle-jacket. Under one arm was tucked his swagger-stick. While he walked, he was in deep discussion with a tall, elderly white man whom Craig had never seen before.

The white man wore a plain khaki safari jacket. His head was bare. His hair was cropped to the scalp and his skin had a peculiarly repulsive pasty-white texture. He carried a black leather attaché case which was locked to his wrist with a steel chain. He cocked his head to listen to Peter Fungabera's impassioned discourse as they walked towards the waiting helicopter.

Halfway between the tent and the helicopter, the two of them came to a stop and argued animatedly. The white man was gesticulating vehemently with his free hand. He was close enough now for Craig to notice that his eyes were so pale that they gave him the sightless stare of a marble bust. His skin was pocked with ancient scars, yet he was very much the dominating figure of the pair. His manner was brusque, almost contemptuous, as though he now regarded Peter Fungabera as superfluous, unworthy of his serious attention. Fungabera, on the other hand, had the shattered look of a survivor of an aircrash. He appeared confused. His voice was raised so that Craig could hear its pleading tone, if not the actual words. This was hardly the man that Craig had known.

The white man made a gesture of dismissal and, turning away, started once more towards the helicopter.

At that moment there was the crumping detonation of an exploding grenade and the two men in the clearing turned quickly to look up the valley in the direction from which the explosion had sounded. Now there was a burst of automatic AK 47 fire from the same direction and immediately the urgent shout of orders around the tent. Troopers began doubling along the edge of the clearing, heading up the valley.

Another burst of automatic fire, and the attention of every man was focused in that direction. Hastily, Craig pulled the pack on his back.

"Come on!" he snapped. "You know what to do!" The three of them scrambled out of the ravine and moved out into the clearing.

"Don't hurry," Craig cautioned them softly. They kept in a compact group, moving quickly but purposefully over the open ground towards Fungabera and his companion.

Craig took the grenade from his pocket and with his teeth drew the pin. He held the grenade in his left hand. In his right he carried the Uzi, loaded and cocked and with rapid-fire selected. They were within five paces before Peter Fungabera glanced around and his astonishment was almost comical as he recognized Craig, even under his mud mask.

"At this range I can cut you in half," Craig warned him, lifting the Uzi to the level of Peter's belly. "This grenade is armed. If I drop it, it will blow us all to hell." He had to shout above the sound of the helicopter's engine.

The white man spun to face him, and his pale arctic eyes were savage.

"Go for the pilot," Craig ordered, and the two women ran to the fuselage port of the helicopter.

"Now, both of you," Craig told the two men, "walk to the helicopter. Don't hurry, don't shout."

Craig followed three paces behind them. Before they reached the helicopter, the pilot appeared in the open port, both his hands high above his head, and Sarah behind him with the Tokarev pistol in his back.

"Get out!" Craig ordered, and with obvious relief the pilot jumped down to the ground.

"Tell them that General Fungabera is a hostage," Craig said. "Any attack will endanger him. Do you understand?"

"Yes," the pilot nodded.

"Now walk back to that tent. Walk slowly. Don't run. Don't shout."

The pilot set off gratefully, but as soon as he was clear, he broke into a trot.

"Get in!" Craig gestured to the port with the Uzi, but Peter Fungabera glared at him and his head sank down menacingly on his wide shoulders.

"Don't do it." Craig backed off a pace, for there was an air of desperation about Fungabera, the reckless quality of a man with nothing more to lose.

"Move!" Craig ordered. "Get up that ladder!" And Fungabera charged at him. Almost as though he were courting death, he ran straight into the muzzle of the Uzi. However, Craig was poised to meet him. He brought up the weapon and crashed the barrel across the side of Fungabera's head with a force that dropped him onto his knees.

As he went down, Craig swung the Uzi back onto the white man, anticipating any move he might make.

"Help him up the ladder," he ordered, and although the white man was encumbered by the black attaché case chained to his wrist, the menace of the Uzi was persuasive and he stooped over Peter Fungabera and lifted him to his feet. Still stunned by the blow, Peter reeled in the man's grasp. He was mumbling, dazed.

"It doesn't matter now, it's all over anyway."

"Shut up, you fool," the white man hissed at him.

"Get him into the helicopter." Craig prodded the Uzi into the white man's back, and the pair started towards the ladder.

"Keep the gun on them, Sarah," Craig called and glanced over his shoulder. The helicopter pilot had almost reached the edge of the clearing. "Hurry it up," Craig snarled at them, and the white man shoved Peter Fungabera through the port and clambered up after him, with the black case dangling on its chain from his wrist.

Craig jumped up into the body of the helicopter.

"Over there!" he ordered his two prisoners to the bench seat. "Strap yourselves in!" Then to Sarah, "Tell Pendula to get going!"

The helicopter lifted off and rose swiftly out of the clearing, and Craig tossed the grenade out of the open port. It dropped away and exploded in the forest far below. Craig hoped the explosion would heighten the confusion down there.

Craig stood behind Peter Fungabera with the Uzi pressed to the nape of his neck, while with his free hand he reached over and pulled the Tokarev pistol from the holster on Peter's hip. He thrust it into his own pocket, then he backed off and buckled on the engineer's safety straps at the doorway. As Sarah clambered down from the cockpit, he ordered, "Cover them both!" and he leaned out of the port and peered ahead.

Almost immediately, he saw Tungata. He was already out of the trees, just below the rock slope, waving both hands over his head, brandishing the AK 47.

"Hold on! I'm going down for the pick-up," Sally-Anne's voice squealed from the two-way speaker above Craig's head.

The big helicopter dropped swiftly down towards where Tungata was waiting, and Sally-Anne steadied the machine and hovered above his head.

All around Tungata the grass was blown flat by the down-draught and Tungata's stolen battle-jacket rippled and whipped about his body. He threw the AK 47 aside and looked up at Craig. The helicopter sank down the last few feet, and Craig leaned out of the hatch and made an arm for him. Tungata jumped and they

427

locked arms at the elbows and Craig swung him aboard.

"Okay!" he yelled up at the speaker. "Go for it!" And they went bounding up into the sky so swiftly that Craig's knees buckled.

At a little over a thousand feet, Sally-Anne went straight and level and turned onto a westerly heading.

Tungata turned to the figures on the bench seat and checked. He stared at Fungabera ferociously, but the man slumped, still dazed and beaten, on the bench seat.

"Where did you find them, Pupho?" Tungata asked huskily.

"They are a little present for you, Sam." Craig handed him the Uzi submachine-gun. "It's loaded and cocked. Can I leave you to look after this pair of beauties?"

"It will afford me the greatest of pleasure." Tungata turned the gun on the two men sitting side by side on the bench seat.

"I'm going to see how Pendula is making out." Craig began to turn away, but something in the way the captive white man was holding himself alerted him, and he turned back quickly. The white prisoner had used the confusion to unlock the steel cuff from his wrist, and now he hurled the black attaché case across the hold towards the open port.

In a reflex action, Craig threw himself to one side, like a basketball player intercepting a pass, and he got a hand on the flying case, deflecting it aside so that it missed the open doorway and clattered against the bulkhead. He dived for it and hugged it to his chest.

"This must be a very interesting piece of goods," he observed mildly, as he stood up. "I'd watch that one, Sam, he is as tricky as he is beautiful."

Lugging the case, Craig made his way forward and clambered up into the raised cockpit. He dropped into the co-pilot's seat next to Sally-Anne and shrugged out of the pack that contained the diamonds. He wedged it securely beside the seat.

"So you *can* fly this damned thing after all, bird lady!"

She grinned at him, her teeth very white in her blackened face.

"I'm heading back towards the pan where we left the Land-Rover."

"Good thinking—how's the fuel?"

"One tank full, the other three-quarters—we should have plenty."

Craig placed the attaché case in his lap and checked the locks. They were combinations.

"How long to the border?" he asked.

"We are making 170 knots, less than two hours—better than walking home, isn't it?"

"My oath!" Craig grinned back at her.

With his clasp-knife he ripped out the combination locks and opened the lid of the attaché case. On top there were two spare shirts and a ball of socks, a bottle of Russian vodka half full, a cheap wallet containing four passports, Finnish, Swedish, East German and Russian and airline tickets for Aeroflot.

"Well-travelled gentleman!" Craig unscrewed the top of the vodka bottle and took a swig. "Brrr!" he said. "That's the real stuff!" He passed the bottle to Sally-Anne and lifted the shirts. Under them were three green-covered folders, stamped with Cyrillic lettering and black hammer and sickle crests.

"Russian, by God! The man is a Bolshie!"

He opened the top folder and his interest quickened. "It's typed in English!" He read the top page and became gradually immersed in the contents. He did not even look up when Sally-Anne asked, "What's it say?"

He skimmed through the first file and then the other two. Twenty-five minutes later he looked up with a stunned, bemused expression and stared unseeingly through the windshield.

He shook his head. "I can hardly believe it. They were so damned sure of themselves. They even typed it out in clear English for Peter Fungabera's benefit. No attempt at concealing it. They didn't even bother to use code names."

"What is it?" Sally-Anne glanced sideways at him.

"Boggles the mind." He took another mouthful of vodka. "Sam has got to read these!"

He stood up and, balancing against the lurch and surge of the helicopter, dropped down into the hold and hurried back to Tungata.

Tungata and Sarah sat opposite the two hostages. Tungata had used the spare seat-belts to truss them securely at wrist and ankles. Peter Fungabera seemed to have recovered a little, and he and Tungata were glaring at each other, arguing with the acrimony and deadly concentration of mortal enemies.

"Cool that!" Craig dropped onto the bench beside Tungata.

"Give me the Uzi." Craig took it from him. "Now read what is in here!" He placed the attaché case on Tungata's lap.

"Delighted to meet you, Colonel Bukharin," Craig said pleasantly. "You must be happy to be missing the Moscow winter?" He pointed the Uzi at his belly.

"I am a senior member of the diplomatic corps of the United Soviet—"

"Yes, Colonel, I have read your visiting card." Craig indicated the files. "On the other hand I, Colonel, am a desperate fugitive quite capable of doing you a serious injury if you don't shut up."

Then he turned to Fungabera. "I do hope you are looking after King's Lynn properly, remembering to wipe your feet and all that?"

"You escaped once, Mr. Mellow," Peter Fungabera said softly. "I don't make the same mistake twice."

And despite the gun in his hands and the fact that Fungabera was trussed up like a sacrificial goat, Craig felt a chilly little breeze of fear down his spine and he could not go on holding the smouldering gaze of hatred with which Fungabera fixed him. He glanced sideways at Tungata.

He was skimming quickly through the green files, and as he read his expression changed from disbelief to outrage.

"Do you know what this is, Pupho?"

Craig nodded, "It's a blueprint for bloody revolution, written out in plain English, obviously for the benefit of Peter Fungabera."

"Everything—they cover everything. Look at this. The lists of those to be executed—they spell out the names—and those who can be relied on to collaborate. They have even prepared the radio and television announcements for the day of the coup!"

"Page twenty-five," Craig suggested. "Check that."

Tungata turned to it. "Me—" He read on. "Sent to a clinic in Europe, mind-bending treatment, the mindless traitor, to lead the Matabele peoples into perpetual slavery—"

"Yes, Sam, you were the pivot on which the whole operation turned. When Fungabera lost you in the cavern—when he dynamited the grand gallery—he admitted defeat. Just look at him now."

However, Tungata was no longer listening. He dumped the attaché case and its contents back on Craig's lap and leaned forward until his face was a foot from Fungabera's. He thrust forward that craggy lantern jaw and slowly his eyeballs glazed over with the reddish sheen of rage.

"You would sell this land and all its peoples into a new slavery, into an imperialism that would make the rule of Smith's regime appear benign and altruistic by comparison? You would condemn your own tribe, and mine and all the others—Madness—" In his rage, Tungata was becoming incoherent. "A rabid dog, crazy with the lust for power."

Suddenly he roared, involuntarily giving vent to his anguish and hatred and outrage. He hurled himself at Peter Fungabera and seized the wide nylon strap that bound him. With the other hand he unclipped the Shona's seat-belt and jerked him off the bench. With the strength of a wounded buffalo bull, he swung him bodily across the hold towards the square open port of the fuselage.

"Mad dog!" he roared, and before Craig could move he had thrust Peter Fungabera backwards through the opening.

Craig tossed the Uzi to Sarah and sprang to Tungata's side. Tungata had been dragged to his knees by the weight of Fungabera's body and he was clinging with one arm to the jamb of the doorway. With the other hand he still had a grip on the strap around Fungabera's chest.

Peter Fungabera dangled outboard. His hands were strapped helpless, his neck twisted back so that he stared up into Tungata's face above him. The fierce brown hills of Africa lay two thousand feet below him, the black stone crests bared like the teeth of a man-eating shark.

"Sam, wait!" Craig screamed above the wind-roar and the deafening beat of the engine.

"Die, you treacherous, murderous—" Tungata roared down into Peter Fungabera's upturned face.

Craig had never seen such naked terror as that in Peter Fungabera's eyes. His mouth was wide open and the wind blew his spittle over his lips in silver strings, but no sound came from his throat.

"Wait, Sam," Craig screamed, "don't kill him. He is the only one who can clear you, can clear all of us. If you kill him you'll never be able to live in Zimbabwe again—"

Tungata rolled his head sideways and stared at Craig.

"Our only chance to clear ourselves!"

The glaze of rage began to fade from Tungata's eyes, but the muscles stood out in his arms from the effort of holding Peter Fungabera's body against the whip and buffet of the wind.

"Help me!" he grated, and in one movement Craig snatched

431

the safety-belt, pulling it off the inertia reel, and buckled it around his own waist. He dropped belly-down on the deck, hooked his ankles around the base of the bench and reached down and out to get a double grip on the nylon strap. Between them they lifted Fungabera back into the port, and his legs were so rubbery with terror that they could not bear his weight when he tried to stand.

Tungata hurled him backwards across the cabin, where he hit the rear bulkhead. He slid down it and rolled onto his side, pulling up his knees into the foetal position, and under the rushing weight of defeat and capitulation he moaned quietly and covered his head with both arms.

Craig climbed unsteadily up into the cockpit and sank into the co-pilot's seat.

"What the hell is happening?" Sally-Anne demanded.

"Nothing serious. I only just managed to stop Sam killing Peter Fungabera."

"Why did you bother?" Sally-Anne raised her voice above the clatter of the rotor overhead. "I'd love a shot at that swine myself."

"Darling, can you get a radio connection to the United States Embassy in Harare?"

She thought about it. "Not from this aircraft."

"Give them the registration of the Cessna. I'll lay odds it hasn't been reported missing yet."

"I'll have to go through Johannesburg approach. They're the only station with sufficient range."

"I don't care how—just get Morgan Oxford on the blower."

Johannesburg approach radio responded promptly to Sally-Anne's call and accepted her call-sign with equanimity.

"Report your position, Kilo Yankee Alpha."

"Northern Botswana"—Sally-Anne anticipated by an hour's flying time—"*en route* Francistown to Maun."

"What is the number you wish to connect in Harare?"

"Person-to-person with the cultural attaché, Morgan Oxford, at the United States Embassy. I'm sorry, I don't know the number."

"Hold on." And in less than a minute Morgan Oxford spoke through the static.

"Oxford here. Who is this?"

Sally-Anne passed the microphone to Craig, and he held it to his lips and depressed the transmit button.

"Morgan, it's Craig, Craig Mellow."

"Holy shit!" Morgan's voice became strident. "Where the hell

432

are you? All hell is breaking out. Where is Sally-Anne?"

"Morgan, listen. This is deadly serious. How would you like to interrogate a full colonel of Russian intelligence, complete with his files of planned Russian aggression in and destabilization of the southern half of the African continent?"

There was nothing but the hum of static for many seconds and then Morgan said, "Wait ten!"

The wait seemed much longer than ten seconds, and then Morgan came back.

"Don't say anything else. Just give me a rendezvous point."

"These are map references—"

Craig read off the map coordinates that Sally-Anne had scribbled down for him. "There is an emergency landing-strip there. I will light a signal-fire. How long for you to get there?"

"Wait ten!" This time it was shorter. "Dawn tomorrow."

"Understood," Craig acknowledged. "We will be waiting."

"Over and out." He handed the microphone back to Sally-Anne.

"Border crossing in forty-three minutes," she told him. "By the way, that mud pack suits you. I'm beginning to think it's an improvement."

"And you, beautiful, are a racing certainly for the cover of *Vogue*!"

She blew the hair off her nose and stuck her tongue out at him.

• • •

They crossed the border between Zimbabwe and Northern Botswana and seventeen minutes later they saw the hired Land-Rover standing exactly where they had left it on the edge of the wide white salt-pan.

"My God, Sarah's buddies are still there—that's constancy for you." Craig made out the two tiny figures standing beside the vehicle. "We'd better warn them, or when they see the government markings they are going to start shooting."

Sarah called down to the waiting Matabele through the "sky-shout" loud hailer as they approached, reassuring them, and Craig saw them lower their rifles as the Super Frelon sank lower. He could make out the beatific grins on the upturned faces of the two young Matabele.

Jonas had shot a springbok that morning, so there was a feast of broiled venison steaks and salted maize cakes that evening, and afterwards they drew lots for guard duty over the two prisoners.

They first heard the drone of an approaching aircraft when it was still pearly half-light the next morning, and Craig drove out onto the pan in the Land-Rover to light the smudge-fires. It came from the South, an enormous Lockheed cargo plane with U.S. air-force markings. Sally-Anne recognized it. "That is the N.A.S.A. machine based at Johannesburg to monitor the shuttle program."

"They are really taking us seriously," Craig murmured, as the Lockheed lowered itself to earth.

"It has amazingly short take-off and landing capability," Sally-Anne told him. "Just watch."

The gigantic aircraft pulled up in the same distance that the Cessna had used. The nose section opened like the bill of a pelican and five men came down the ramp, led by Morgan Oxford.

"Like five sardines from a can," Craig observed, as they went forward to greet them. The visitors all wore tropical suits, white shirts with button-down collars and neckties and they all moved with athletes' balance and awareness.

"Sally-Anne. Craig." Oxford shook hands briefly and then acknowledged Tungata. "Of course, I know you, Mr. Minister. These are my colleagues." He did not introduce them, but went straight on, "Are these the subjects?"

The two young Matabele brought the prisoners forward at gun-point.

"Son of a gun!" Morgan Oxford exclaimed. "That's General Fungabera. Craig, are you out of your mind?"

"Read what is in here"—Craig proffered the attaché case— "and then you tell me."

Morgan accepted the case. "Wait here, please."

Jonas and Aaron led the two captives towards the aircraft and the Americans came forward to receive them.

Peter Fungabera was still bound at the wrists with the nylon straps from the helicopter. He seemed to have shrunk in physical stature; he was no longer an impressive, debonair figure. The cloak of defeat weighed him down. His skin had a grey tone and he did not lift his eyes as he came level with Tungata Zebiwe.

It was Tungata who reached out and seized his jaw in one hand, pressing his fingers into his cheeks, forcing his mouth open and twisting his head up so he could look into his face. For long seconds he stared into Peter Fungabera's eyes, and then contempt-uously he pushed him away, so that Peter staggered and might

434

have fallen had not one of the Americans steadied him.

"At the bottom of nearly every bully and tyrant lurks a coward," Tungata said in that deep rumbling voice. "You did right when you stopped me killing him, Pupho. A clean drop from the sky is too good for the likes of him. He goes now to a juster fate. Take him out of my sight, for he sickens me to the gut."

Fungabera and the Russian were led into the interior of the Lockheed, and Craig and his party settled down to wait. It was a long wait. They sat in the shade thrown by the Land-Rover and chatted in a desultory, distracted fashion, breaking off every now and then as the squawk and warble from the radio in the Lockheed carried to where they sat.

"They're talking to Washington," Craig guessed, "via satellite."

It was after ten o'clock before Morgan came down the ramp again, accompanied by one of his colleagues.

"This is Colonel Smith," he told them, and the way he said it, he didn't mean to be taken literally. "We have appraised the items you have delivered to us, and we conclude, at this stage, anyway, that they are genuine."

"That's very generous of you," Craig dead-panned.

"Minister Tungata Zebiwe, we would be very grateful if you could spare us a deal of your valuable time. There are persons in Washington very anxious to talk to you. It will be to our mutual benefit, I assure you."

"I would like this young lady to accompany me," Tungata indicated Sarah.

"Yes, of course." Morgan turned to Craig and Sally-Anne. "In your case it's not an invitation, it's an order—you're coming with us."

"What about the helicopter, and the Land-Rover?" Craig asked.

"Don't worry about them. Arrangements will be made to have them returned to their rightful owners."

•   •   •

Three weeks later, at the United Nations building in New York, a file was handed to the head of the Zimbabwe delegation. It contained excerpts from the three green files, and transcripts of the debriefing of General Peter Fungabera by persons unnamed. The file was rushed to Harare, and as a direct result an urgent request was made by the Zimbabwe government for the repatriation of General Fungabera. Two senior inspectors of the Zimbabwe police Special Branch flew to New York to escort the general home.

When the Pan Am flight landed at Harare, General Fungabera descended the boarding staircase from the first-class section of the Boeing handcuffed to one of the police inspectors. There was a closed van waiting on the tarmac.

There was no media coverage of his return.

He was driven directly to Harare central prison, where sixteen days later he died in one of the interrogation cells. His face, when his corpse was spirited out of the rear entrance to the main prison block, was so altered as to be unrecognizable.

A little after midnight that same night, a ministerial black Mercedes went off the road at speed on a lonely stretch of country road outside the city and burst into flames. There was one occupant. By his dental bridgework, the charred body was identified as that of General Peter Fungabera, and five days later he was buried with full military honours in "Heroes' Acre," the cemetery for the patriots of the *chimurenga* on the hills overlooking Harare.

●　　●　　●

On Christmas Day at ten o'clock in the morning, Colonel Bukharin left his escort of American military police at the allied guardhouse at Check-point Charlie and set out across the few hundred yards to the East Berlin side of the frontier.

Bukharin wore an American military-issue greatcoat over his safari clothes, and a knitted fisherman's cap on his bald head.

Halfway across, he passed a middle-aged man in a cheap suit coming in the opposite direction. The man might once have been plump, for his skin seemed too large for his skull and it had the grey, lifeless tone of long captivity.

They glanced at each other incuriously as they passed.

"A life for a life," thought Bukharin, and suddenly he felt very tired. He walked at last with an old man's short hobbled gait over the icy tarmac.

There was a black sedan waiting for him beyond the frontier buildings. Two men were in the back seat and one of them climbed out as Bukharin approached. He wore a long civilian raincoat and a wide-brimmed hat in the style much favoured by the K.G.B.

"Bukharin?" he asked. His tone was neutral but his eyes were cold and relentless.

When Bukharin nodded, he jerked his head curtly. Bukharin slid into the rear seat and the man followed him in and slammed the door. The interior was overheated and smelled of garlic and last night's vodka sweated through unwashed pores.

The sedan pulled away and Bukharin lay back and closed his eyes. It was going to be bad, he thought; it might even be worse then he had anticipated.

* * *

Henry Pickering hosted the luncheon in the private dining-suite of the World Bank overlooking Central Park.

Sarah and Sally-Anne had not seen each other for almost five months, and they embraced like sisters and then went into a huddle in a corner of the private lounge, trying to catch up with each other's news in the first thirty seconds, ignoring everybody else.

Tungata and Craig were more restrained.

"I feel so guilty, Pupho—five months. It was too long."

Craig forgave him. "I know how they have kept you busy, and I have been jumping about myself. Last time I saw you was in Washington—"

Tungata nodded. "Nearly a month of talks with the American State Department, and then here in New York with the Zimbabwe ambassador and the World Bank. There is so much to tell, that I don't know where to begin."

"All right, as a start," Henry Pickering suggested, "tell him about the dispensation that you prised out of the Zimbabwe government."

"That's a good start," Tungata agreed. "First of all, my conviction and sentence under the poaching charge have been set aside—"

"Sam, that's the very least they could do—"

Tungata smiled and clasped his arm. "That's for starters. That confession that you signed for Fungabera has been declared void, as it was obtained under duress. The order declaring you an enemy of the state and people has been rescinded, the sale of Rholands' shares to Fungabera has been declared null and void. King's Lynn and Zambezi Waters revert to you."

Craig stared at him wordlessly as he went on. "The prime minister has accepted that all the acts of violence committed by either of us were acts of self-defence, everything from your killing of the Third Brigade troopers who were pursuing you on the

437

Botswana border to the theft of the Super Frelon helicopter, and he has issued a full pardon—"

Craig merely shook his head.

"Then the Third Brigade has been withdrawn from Matabeleland. It has been disbanded and integrated into the regular army, the pogrom against my people has been called off, and independent observers have been allowed into the Matabele tribal areas to 'monitor the peace.'"

"That's the best news yet, Sam."

"Still more—still more," Tungata assured him. "My Zimbabwe citizenship and passport have been returned to me. I am allowed to return home, with the assurance that there will be no check placed on my political activities. The government is to consider a referendum on instituting a form of federal autonomy for the Matabele people, and, in return, I am to use all my influence to convince the armed dissidents to come in from the bush and surrender their weapons under general amnesty."

"It's all that you have been working towards—congratulations, Sam, I really mean that."

"Only with your help." Tungata turned to Henry Pickering. "Can I tell him about Lobengula's Fire!"

"Wait," Henry Pickering took both their arms and turned them towards the dining-room. "Let's start lunch first."

The dining-room was panelled in light oak, a perfect frame for the set of five Remington paintings of the Old West that decorated three walls. The fourth wall was an enormous picture window that looked out across the city and Central Park. The curtains were open.

From the head of the table Henry smiled down at Craig. "I thought we had better pull out all the stops," and he showed Craig the wine label.

"Wow! The '61."

"Well, it's not every day that I entertain the current number one best-selling author—"

"Yes, isn't it wonderful!" Sally-Anne cut in. "Craig was number one in the New York *Times* the very first week of publication!"

"What about the TV deal?" Tungata asked.

"It's not signed yet," Craig demurred.

"But my information is that it soon will be," said Henry, as he filled the wineglasses. "Ladies and gentlemen, I give you the toast:

Craig Mellow's latest opus, and its long ride at the top."

They drank, laughing and festive, and Craig protested with his glass untouched. "Come on! Give me a toast that I can drink as well."

"Here it is!" Henry Pickering held up his glass again. "Lobengula's Fire! Now you can tell him."

"If those two women will stop chattering for ten seconds—"

"Not fair!" Sally-Anne protested. "We never chatter, we seriously debate."

Tungata smiled at her as he went on, "As you know, Henry arranged for Lobengula's diamonds to be placed in safe-keeping and for them to be appraised. Harry Winston's top men have vetted them and come up with an estimate—"

"Tell us!" Sally-Anne called. "How much?"

"As you know, the diamond market is in a very serious depression at the moment—stones selling for seventy thousand dollars two years ago are fetching only twenty thousand—"

"Come on, Sam, don't tease us!"

"All right, Winston's have valued the collection at six hundred million dollars—"

Everybody spoke at once and it took a while for Tungata to regain the floor.

"As we all agreed from the beginning, the diamonds are to be placed in a trust fund, and I am going to ask Craig to be one of the trustees."

"I accept."

"However, fourteen of the stones have already been sold. I authorized the deal, and the proceeds from it were five million dollars. The entire amount has been handed over to the World Bank in complete discharge of capital and interest on the loan made to Craig." Tungata drew an envelope from his inside pocket. "Here is the receipt, Pupho, your share of Lobengula's Fire. You are free and clear of all debt now. King's Lynn and Zambezi Waters are yours."

Craig turned the envelope between his fingers, staring at Tungata, struck dumb, and Tungata's smile faded as he leaned towards him and spoke seriously. "In return, there is one thing I would ask from you, Pupho."

"Ask it," said Craig. "Anything."

"Your promise that you will return to Africa. We need men

like you to help stave off these new dark ages that threaten to overwhelm the land we both love."

Craig reached across the table and took Sally-Anne's hand.

"You tell him," he said.

"Yes, Sam, we are coming home with you," she said softly. "That's a promise."

*　　*　　*

Sally-Anne and Craig drove up the hills of King's Lynn in the old Land-Rover. The late afternoon had turned the grasslands to cloth-of-gold, and the trees on the crest of the hills wove delicate lacework against the high serene blue of the African summer sky.

They were waiting for them on the lawns under the jacaranda trees—all the house servants and herders from King's Lynn. When Craig embraced Shadrach, the old man's empty sleeve flapped against his skinny chest.

"Do not worry, Nkosi, I can work better with one arm than any of these puppies can with two."

"I will make you a bargain," Craig suggested, so that all could hear. "I will lend you an arm, if you will lend me a leg." And Shadrach laughed until the tears dripped onto his shirt and his newest and youngest wife had to lead him away.

Joseph waited on the wide veranda, aloof from the common throng, resplendent in snowy white *kanza* and with the tall chef's cap on his head.

"I see you, Nkosikazi," he greeted Sally-Anne gravely, as she reached the top of the stairs, but he could not disguise the sparkle of pleasure in his eyes.

"I see you also, Joseph. And I have decided we will have two hundred guests at the wedding," she answered in fluent Sindebele, and Joseph covered his mouth with both hands in astonishment, the first time she had ever seen him off balance.

"Hau!" he said, and then turned to his underlings.

"Now we have a truly great lady at Kingi-Lingi who understands all your monkey chatter," he told them sternly. "So woe unto any of you who lie or cheat or steal!"

Craig and Sally-Anne stood at the top of the stairs, holding hands while the people of King's Lynn sang the song that welcomes the traveller home after a long and dangerous journey, and when it was ended, Craig looked down at her.

"Welcome home, my darling," he said.

440

And while the women ululated and danced so that the heads of the infants strapped to their backs jerked like little black puppets and the men roared approval, Craig kissed her on the mouth.

ABOUT THE AUTHOR

Wilbur Smith was born in Zambia and was educated in Michaelhouse and Rhodes University. He has lived all his life in Africa, and his commitment to that continent is deep.

A full-time writer since 1964, he is the author of fifteen novels. He also finds time to travel out of Africa and enjoy his other interests—such as numismatics, wild-life photography and big game fishing. He and his wife make an annual safari into the dwindling wilderness of Central Africa, and at other seasons he fishes by boat in the Indian Ocean for tuna and other game fish.

Mr. Smith lives with his wife in Constantia, South Africa.